When Hearts Unravel

Victoria Lum

When Hearts Unravel

By Victoria Lum

Published by Eternal Hearts Publishing

Cover Design Copyright © 2025 Y'All That Graphic

Editing by Theresa Leigh and Amy Briggs

Proofreading by Virginia Tesi Carey

ISBN (Paperback): 979-8-9900169-9-6

ISBN (E-Book): 979-8-9900169-8-9

Author's Note

DEDICATION

To all the girls who think "I can fix him," this one's for you. I hope you love our devastating bad boy, Rex Anderson.

RELATIONSHIP TREE
LA HEARTS SERIES

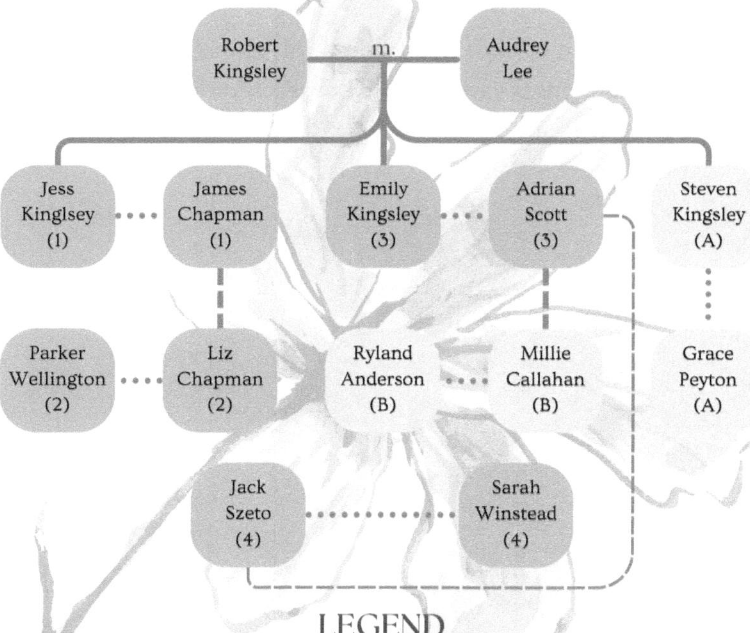

LEGEND

— Best friends   •••• In a relationship   ▬ ▬ Siblings   m. Married

BOOKS

1	The Sweetest Agony	A	When Hearts Ignite
2	The Coldest Passion	B	When Hearts Collide
3	The Harshest Hope	C	When Hearts Surrender
4	The Brightest Spark	D	When Hearts Awaken
	LA Hearts Series	E	When Hearts Remember
	The Orchid Series	F	When Hearts Unravel

THE ORCHID SERIES

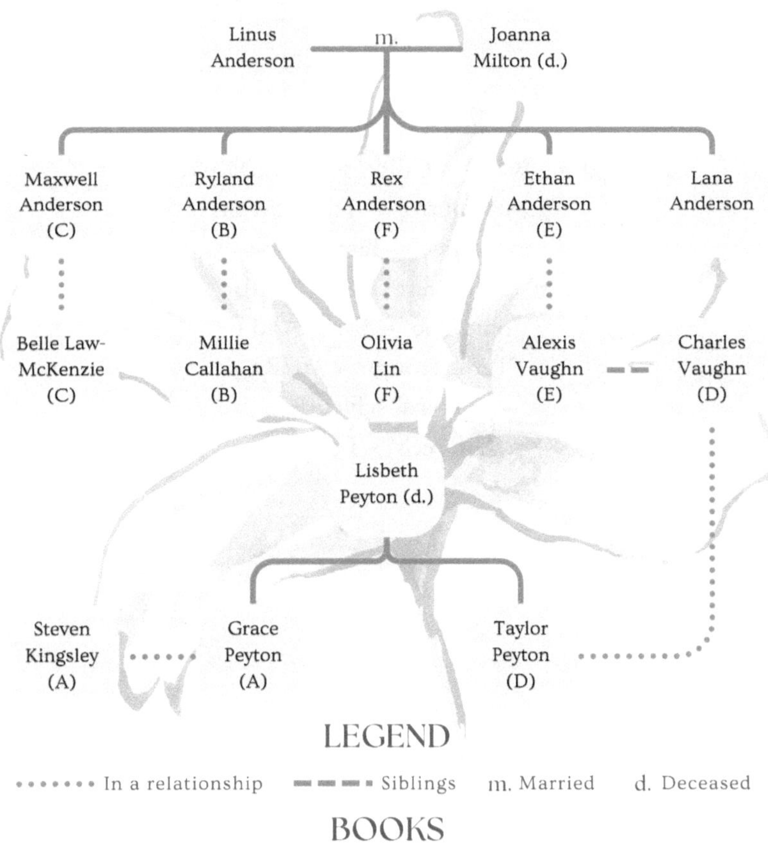

LEGEND

•••••••• In a relationship   ▬ ▬ ▬ ▬ Siblings   m. Married   d. Deceased

BOOKS

1	The Sweetest Agony	A	When Hearts Ignite
2	The Coldest Passion	B	When Hearts Collide
3	The Harshest Hope	C	When Hearts Surrender
4	The Brightest Spark	D	When Hearts Awaken
	The Orchid Series	E	When Hearts Remember
		F	When Hearts Unravel

Playlist

"Everything Black" – Unlike Pluto and Mike Taylor
"Lose Control" – Teddy Swims
"Messier" – Tate McRae
"Fire on Fire" – Sam Smith
"John Doe" – Tones And I
"Panic Room" – Au/Ra
"Sirens" – Fleurie
"The Feels" – Labrinth

Cast of Characters

The Andersons are a large family, but their stories are all standalones and can be read in any order. If you're new to their world or diving back in, here's a list of the main characters you'll encounter:

<u>The Anderson Family:</u>

- Linus Anderson – The patriarch of the family and retired from Fleur Entertainment.

- Maxwell Anderson – The eldest son and CEO of Fleur Entertainment; fraternal twin to Ryland. Broody and burdened, he carries the weight of the world on his shoulders.

- Ryland Anderson – The second son and former COO of Fleur Entertainment; fraternal twin to Maxwell. Now a full-time professor.

- Rex Anderson – The third son and CMO of Fleur Entertainment. A self-proclaimed playboy extraordinaire.

- Ethan Anderson – The fourth son and CFO of Fleur Entertainment. Quiet and introspective; an old soul with secrets.

- Lana Anderson – The youngest sister in the main Anderson family line and the Chief of Public Relations at Fleur Entertainment. Sophisticated and fiercely loyal.

- Grace Peyton-Anderson – The older half-sister of the Anderson siblings and a finance guru.

- Taylor Peyton-Anderson – The younger half-sister of the Anderson siblings. A gothic, take-no-prisoners ballerina.

<u>Other Important People:</u>
- Steven Kingsley – Grace's significant other, set to join Fleur Entertainment as COO after Ryland vacates the role.

- Charles Vaughn – Best friend of the Anderson brothers and Steven, CEO of the Bank of Columbia, and currently being driven insane by Taylor.

- Millie Callahan – Ryland's significant other, a PhD student with dreams of changing the world.

- Belle Law-McKenzie – Maxwell's significant other, the belle of the ball who loves rescuing animals and is a fashion designer.

- Olivia Lin – Taylor's friend, a psychiatrist specializing in anxiety and addiction disorders. Observant, smart, and fiercely loyal.

CHAPTER ONE

WHEN A KID TURNS six, he's probably waking up in the morning with his heart pounding, wondering if he'll get that Lego superhero set with the villain included or the monster truck Transformer he begged his parents for. He'll try to temper his excitement because he's a big boy now, or so his mom said the night before.

But when I turned six, I didn't get toys. I didn't get a smile.

Instead, I became a murderer.

Dark hair spreads like a fan on the hardwood floor. Vacant eyes staring at the ceiling, a dried tear streak marring her cheek. Her key-shaped necklace stained in red.

The image shifts—I'm taller, a full-grown man now, but no less afraid.

Crimson rivers seep out of a bullet wound, the blood quickly staining the pristine blouse. Helpless, frightened eyes snare onto mine, icy fingers gripping my hand as life bleeds out of her.

The two women I've failed, and the price was their lives.

Unfortunately for me and my diagnosed HSAM, or highly superior autobiographical memory, I can *never* forget.

"No, no, no." I thump my fist against the one-sided window in Mystique's back office, which overlooks the writhing bodies partying on the dance floor below.

It's one of the more popular clubs inside The Orchid, the crème de la crème, exclusive establishment for the rich and famous within my family's company, Fleur Entertainment Holdings.

The pulsing bass shakes the windowpane, and if this were two years ago, before what happened to Raya, I'd be down there in the crowd, beautiful women draped over my arms, basking in the attention from the loving masses.

But this isn't two years ago.

My phone rings and I toss four Velowake pills into my mouth before chasing them down with whiskey.

"Anderson. How can I do you for?"

Orgasm on demand? A nice spanking because you've been a bad girl? Or maybe some good breath play because you want me to take control away from you?

I swallow a chuckle. Fuck, I'm going out of my mind.

Of course you are. Sane people don't wake up naked on the balcony, not knowing how they got there.

"It's me," a familiar soft voice answers.

I straighten, the smile slipping off my face.

Ava, Raya's daughter. My mistakes have living victims, and she's one of them.

"I...I just want to wish you a happy birthday and to tell you it's not your fault, so don't blame yourself."

Her words are a right hook to my liver, and I want to throw up.

Hands trembling, I snatch the bottle of Velowake and toss three more pills into my mouth.

Four won't cut it today.

"You there?" Ava asks.

"Yeah. I'm here." My voice is hoarse. "I'll never forgive myself and neither should you."

"It's been two years. It's those bastards' fault. They should pay for this, not you." Her voice rises, then a shaky exhale comes across the line. "Just don't—"

I end the call. I can't do this.

"Fuck!" Why does everyone want to forgive me? *"It's not your fault, Rex." "It's shitty luck." "Don't borrow guilt that isn't yours."* Why can't they let me take responsibility for once?

Because it *is* my fault.

All of it.

My phone buzzes from an incoming text and I know it's Ava again. She and her younger sister, Cora, rarely contact me. They aren't supposed to after they escaped to Monaco two years ago, a journey which cost Raya her life.

It wasn't supposed to end that way.

Ava

> Those bastards will get what they deserve, mark my words.

Ava

> Mom would've been fifty today. If she were here, she'd wish you a happy birthday. And she'd be grateful because if it weren't for you, Cora and I wouldn't be alive.

Guilt twists my insides. I shouldn't have hung up on her. Ava meant well. *She's twenty-three, and she handles her emotions better than you. Instead of grieving her mom's death, she called you because she knew you'd feel like shit.*

Blowing out a breath, I send her a reply.

Rex

> Thanks for the birthday wishes. Take care of your sister. Don't do anything stupid. And don't text me again. It's too dangerous.

My phone clatters to the table, and a dull pain radiates inside my skull. *Sleep,* my mind screams at me. *You need sleep. Maybe that's why you have blackouts.*

But if I sleep, the nightmares...memories come.

"You should listen to her, you know," a sardonic voice murmurs from the doorway.

I close my eyes. *Of course,* he's here to witness me at my rock bottom. Always getting a front-row seat to my dark moments. "What are you doing here, Casey? Eavesdropping?"

He chuckles. "You asked me to come. Here I am."

"I must've been drunk. You can go now."

"Nah. You look like shit. Aren't you supposed to celebrate today? Your birthday on top of kicking off the cruise line? The imminent success of your genius brainchild, as you like to remind me?"

The Orchid's inaugural cruise, a one month luxurious journey in the Mediterranean, and a three-billion-dollar venture, is the first large-scale enterprise my oldest brother and CEO, Maxwell, asked me to take on. Definitely not the run-of-the-mill campaign I usually lead in my chief marketing officer role. I'm supposed to be part of its maiden journey to make sure everything goes well.

My siblings have never trusted me with important tasks before. Like I'm worthy and dependable. Like I'm not just a jokester and the prince of pleasure.

Maybe if I pulled this off, this emptiness inside me would disappear and I wouldn't feel so guilty about Mom and Raya's deaths.

The thought is hollow. How can a cruise for rich pansies make up for two lost lives?

But I can't disappoint Maxwell and the others.

Dejected, I slide my hand into my pocket and clench the red marble I always carry around. It reminds me of everything I've lost and my role in the family.

"Rex? Did you hear me?" Casey asks.

"What do you think I'm doing? Getting ready for the party, you dipshit."

"The dipshit you invited." He smirks.

Rolling my eyes, I ignore him. Casey would never know because I'd die before telling him, but he's right. He keeps me afloat. He's been by my side through thick and thin for most of my life. Whenever I'm drowning, he'd hoist me, slap my face, then tell me to start swimming.

Casey sighs. "You need me. Who else would put up with you for all these years?"

I feel his pitying gaze boring into me as he tsks under his breath. "Thirty-seven doesn't become you. You're crashing out from all the partying, drinking, and not sleeping."

"It's called chronic insomnia. And if I look like shit, then you do too. There isn't a party you say no to either."

"That's because I'm your best friend and someone needs to save your ass. Rex, stop punishing yourself. Stop playing Russian Roulette with your life. What are you trying to prove? That you're no longer the scaredy cat from when we were kids?"

I recoil from his words, thinking back to the little boy who had the world but didn't know better, who let fear rule his life until it cost him and his family everything.

I'm not that kid anymore.

A ball of fire bolts up my esophagus. Before I know it, I'm in Casey's face and yanking him up by his collar. "Get out of my business. Fuck off."

He doesn't flinch. Instead, he shoves me off him. "I won't watch you destroy your life. That's what you're doing. If I can't save you, no one can. And fuck, I care about you. Your family cares about you too. Let us in."

I'm a murderer.

I shove him out of the room and slam the door shut, hoping he'll take the hint and leave.

And you think a cruise will make you feel better. Good luck with that. I shove the thoughts away. Beggars can't be choosers. At least it's a target, something to do.

Don't disappoint your family, Rex.

"If you won't let me in," Casey pounds on the door, "find a therapist, a doctor, a fucking professional. Get help! Don't be a coward. It doesn't have to be like this."

I stride back to the overlook window, eager to get away from Casey's voice, because I don't know how to unravel my emotions or thoughts.

Then, as if fate wants to rub salt in my wounds, I spot *her* down below.

An innocent, lost lamb surrounded by hyenas.

Sleek black hair fastened into her usual no-nonsense bun, an unassuming white dress covering her petite figure, Olivia hugs her large handbag in front of her like a shield.

Dr. Olivia Lin, to be exact—gifted, perfectly put-together psychiatrist and my younger sisters' best friend.

The fucking order to my chaos.

The woman I avoid.

I don't need anyone else poking inside my fucked-up mind. God knows the last brain doctor did a number on me.

But Olivia—the woman with eyes who see too much—I remember how she looked at me, her eyes narrowed with suspicion, a few months ago at my brother, Ethan's wedding. She caught me fake smiling at the happy couple, not because I wasn't thrilled for them. I was. But I was also spiraling because I realized I could never have that happiness for myself.

After all, how do I atone for Mom and Raya's deaths?

"Rex?" Casey hollers. "Fine. Go brood in silence. I'm out of here. But make no mistake, this doesn't mean I'm giving up on you. I'll see you on the damn cruise."

My earlier guilt eats away at me.

I shouldn't blow up at him. This isn't me. I'm the charmer, the Anderson everyone loves. People come to me for a good time. They come to me to get away from my brooding brothers.

The neon strobe lights bathe the dance floor, highlighting the swaths of skin revealed by short skirts and barely there tops. Bodies writhe sinuously against each other, the promise of sin and chaos to follow, most likely in the adult-entertainment kink clubs and specialty rooms on our Rose floors, five levels within this building I'm intimately familiar with.

But somehow, I can't look away from the fully clothed woman in white.

What are you doing there, little lamb?

The innocent good girl.

In the rare moments when we'd be in the same room, I'd spot her rolling her eyes, her skin flushed, when I cracked lewd jokes with my siblings. Because I'm good at that—saying inappropriate things to make people laugh.

Olivia never bought it though. There were always disdain and pity when she looked at me. And the occasional, "You need help," she'd mutter when she brushed past me.

My fingers press against the cool glass and I'm hit with an irrational urge to race down there and drag her kicking and screaming out of my den of sin. Then I'll throw her back into her small, organized office, where she can treat her precious broken toys and ticking time bombs within the safety of four walls.

Or perhaps I'll tug that hair out of her neat little bun and mess it up.

As if she heard my thoughts, she whips her head up and stares at me.

Those bottomless dark eyes. The flawless ivory skin. The unblemished white dress.

If she wants ticking time bombs, I'll show her one.

The dark desire rocks my mind. I've felt it before whenever I see her from a distance, all prim and proper with my sisters. But it's never been this intense, this visceral.

My pulse riots and lungs constrict, and even though I know she can't see me, I can *feel* her seeing right through me.

It makes no fucking sense. I think back to the blackouts happening more frequently now.

I'm definitely going out of my mind.

"Shit. Shit. Shit."

Sweat beads on my skin and I yank my tie loose and unbutton my collar. I run my fingers through my hair, disheveling it because that's what the public expects from me.

I blink, and Olivia disappears from view. Did I imagine it all? Is this another symptom?

When is the damn Velowake going to kick in and put me out of my misery?

A minute later, my heart skips a telltale beat. Then another. It scatters to the thumps of the music—a car careening down a steep hill at a hundred miles per hour.

My lungs rake in a ragged inhale, the sudden oxygen waking my senses.

I smile.

There it is...the rush from Velowake—a brutal cocktail of synthetic caffeine analogs, adrenal regulators, and REMorphin, a compound designed to short-circuit dreams before they started.

No more nightmares. No more thoughts. No more feelings.

I'm Rex Anderson, the man who doesn't take life seriously. *I don't feel. I only have fun.*

I'm the party prince—peak confidence, alpha energy, sex god.

I don't feel. I only have fun.

Slowly, I straighten, wipe the sweat from my forehead, and check my appearance in the mirror. I watch in detached fascination as my lips twist into the usual charming grin, my toothpaste commercial worthy smile bright.

Ignoring the chaotic clattering of my heart, I grab my phone and leave the office.

I have a party to attend and a crowd to win over.

CHAPTER TWO

"Do you have enough refills?" I glance up from my laptop after typing session notes as my quarterly appointment with Maxwell ends.

"I'm good." He nods, his lips hitched in a barely there smile. The oldest of the seven Anderson siblings is a hard nut to crack.

"You sure? You were low on your Ativan last time." I cock my brow and level my stare at him.

Patients against therapy and medication like to feed me nonsense. Men, powerful men especially, think they're stronger by not taking medicine.

But the opposite is true. Admitting you need help is the strongest step you can take.

A muscle pulses in his jaw. Then, his dark eyes—the Anderson eyes, since all of them, save Grace, have the same striking slate-gray eyes—soften in clear resignation.

"Fine. You got me. I have five pills left. Damn it, you'd think I could control my social anxiety after three years of therapy. I run a multi-billion-dollar corporation, for God's sake."

My lips twitch. "Mr. Anderson, I've told you my spiel before. This is body chemistry. It isn't you. It isn't personal. You wouldn't tell a diabetic not to take insulin. Why wouldn't you take meds for your anxiety?"

He protests, and I know what he's going to say. *I'm the head of an old-money dynasty and responsible for the livelihoods of thousands of people. People rather throw themselves into the fire than piss me off. Yadda, yadda, yadda.*

I hold my hand up. "Nope. Not hearing it. You, mister, are a patient in this room. I'm the boss. I'm the queen of this hallowed space."

Twirling my finger in the air, I motion at the luxurious private room inside the gentlemen's club at The Orchid, which is a city in and of itself—Michelin starred restaurants, nightclubs, luxury apartments, a place where, if you were lucky enough to be a member, all your wishes could come true.

"Lucky me. Technically, I own this building," he mutters.

"And technically, I'm good friends with your wife." I send the refill to the pharmacy and shut my laptop. "I only do house calls this late for your family. So, lucky you."

Maxwell smirks and stands before buttoning his navy three-piece suit. He, like his siblings, must have some Viking blood, because he towers over me. Then again, that's not too difficult since I'm only five-foot-four.

After donning a wool coat, which is wise since the February chill in New York City is brutal, he turns to me.

"You know there's a thing called HIPAA, right? You aren't supposed to tell Belle what we discuss in our sessions."

"I don't need to tell Belle anything. I just need to mention her husband and baby daddy isn't behaving and she'll get it out of you."

Maxwell chuckles. "Ball-buster."

Someone knocks on the door as I gather my things. I curse myself for leaving my coat in the rideshare earlier when I was running late. This is what I get for ignoring my schedule and squeezing in a few last-minute patients this morning.

Seconds later, another tall man with the same striking good looks as Maxwell—thick dark hair, the same sharp jawline and piercing eyes—pops his head in.

He doles out a sly grin. "Olivia. What's the verdict? Is the asshole healed?"

"Ryland," I shake my head at Maxwell's fraternal twin and hide my smile, "you know that's not how it works. I'm a psychiatrist, not a magician. I can only help patients keep their symptoms at bay and teach them better ways of managing their conditions."

Ryland chuckles. "Yes, ma'am."

"If anything changes before our next appointment, Mr. Anderson," I turn back to Maxwell, "let me know. I can be flexible."

I'm always flexible for my patients because they need me. When dealing with mental health issues, one misstep can mean life or death.

He nods. "Why do you call me Mr. Anderson and Ryland by his name?"

My jaw tightens and a lump forms in my throat.

Because it's safer. It's a reminder for me to maintain professional distance. That way, I don't miss the red flags.

And I won't lose anyone else.

"Slow down, Mia!"

"Olive, live a little. The street's empty." She guns the gas and the car lurches forward.

I cling onto the handle for dear life while she laughs and cranks open the windows.

"We're flying and free!" she hollers over the loud roar of the wind. To my horror, she then yanks open the passenger seat compartment and pulls out a box. "Open it!"

"What? You crazy? Slow down, Mia!"

She giggles and flashes her high beams over the Pacific Coast Highway. "Open the present."

With my heart lodged firmly in my throat, I pry open the box. Swallowing my gasp, I pull out a pristine camera.

My dream camera.

"Happy eighteenth! Take a picture of me. It's loaded with film."

A car honks and reality rushes in. I scream when she swerves to avoid a collision.

"Wooohoo! Lighten up. Don't be the boring one for once. Embrace your fears!" Mia pumps her fist into the air. "Capture this moment, Olive. Carpe diem!"

Seize the day, my ass. Survive this night is more apt.

"You're nuts." But I aim my brand new Leica M6 camera at her and take a shot. The crisp snap of the shutter is the most beautiful sound to my ears, even with the wind blowing in my face.

Time stood still then, and I'll forever remember Mia that way—raven hair covering her face, a devious glint in her eyes, her sharp laughter slicing through the dark night.

Wild and brave. Happy and alive.

I clear my throat and force out a smile before glancing at my phone. Nine p.m. sharp.

"Session's over. Now I can call you Maxwell."

I brush past Ryland and step into the hallway.

"May I call you a car, Olivia?" Ryland asks.

"No, I'm fine. I'm heading to the Ladies' Lounge to meet with a friend."

Liar. I barely have time for my close friends, who happen to be his younger sisters Lana, Grace, and Taylor, and by extension, their best friends, Belle, Millie, and Alexis. I could probably even call the Anderson brothers—Maxwell, Ryland, Ethan—my friends.

There's one more brother—Rex—but I won't think about him. We're definitely not friends.

Either way, I'm married to my work, and patient case files and medical research papers are my confidants.

And in precisely forty-five minutes, I'll be in my usual spot, curled up safely under the covers in my Upper West Side studio apartment, wearing a face mask, a glass of Petit Syrah and a plate of Mom's almond cookies that taste like cardboard on the nightstand. I'll reread the session notes from my appointments today and prepare a new pitch for investors to fund the Anxiety and Depression Awareness Society, otherwise known as ADAS, for the next year.

The organization does important work—education, outreach, providing mental health help to people without access. My lungs constrict when I think about the email I got earlier today. Our biggest investor pulled out, citing financial difficulties. But it doesn't matter, I'll just work harder to get the money somewhere else.

I'll heal them all, one patient at a time.

It doesn't have to be this way. It's not your responsibility to save everyone, and are you really living? My chest hardens and I shake the thought away. Sure, it's lonely and tiring, but someone's got to do the work.

Yes. Working is more meaningful than going out and wasting life. It's what's expected of me—the good doctor, the perfect daughter. I'm happy. I should be happy. I nod to myself. *That's right.*

But the tightness doesn't go away.

"If you need a car later, just tell the concierge," Maxwell says as he walks to my side.

He levels his unnerving gaze at me. "You sure everything's okay, Olivia?"

"Playing doctor on the doctor, Maxwell?" I strain my smile wider, knowing I'm failing. Mia could lie without batting an eyelash. Not me.

Maxwell frowns, and soon Ryland's brows form a concerned pinch.

They look so similar now, even though they aren't identical twins.

Not like me and Mia. A dull ache throbs to life behind my rib cage.

I glance away. "Say hi to Belle and Millie for me. Too bad they aren't coming to the girls' meetup next week."

A misdirection. Maxwell loves his wife, Belle, and Ryland, likewise, is utterly devoted to his fiancée, Millie.

Without waiting for their response, I hurry to the elevator bay, my heart squeezing, a faint echo of the sensation I felt whenever Mia was in trouble—the time Dan Larkin, Pasadena High's resident bad boy and heartthrob cheated on her and she keyed his car, or when she got her rejection letter from Harvard, her dream school.

What's the use of having a twin-sense when your twin is gone?

My breathing is thready when I press the elevator call button. I reach into my tote and pull out my phone, finding a voicemail notification.

"Olivia, it's Ma. When are you coming to visit? Your birthday is in a few months. Your ba says he hasn't heard from you in a while. Are you taking care of yourself? Have you eaten yet? You young people think you're invincible, but before you know it, life will catch up and those health issues will start…"

The hollow ache in my chest recedes as I listen to Mom's rambling message and Dad clearing his throat in the background.

Have you eaten yet? It's her way of saying she loves me without *telling* me she loves me—the classic love language of Chinese immigrants.

"I saw a quality cut of pork belly at the market this morning. Come visit, and I'll make your favorite *hong shao rou*. We can go to a new restaurant together. You like to try different places out. You and your sis—" She falls silent. She still can't say Mia's name. "Anyway, make sure you eat on time. Call me."

Tears suddenly well in my eyes and I press my hand to my chest, trying to soothe the ache.

I want to call her back and tell her to say Mia's name. I want to scream into the receiver that *hong shao rou*, braised pork belly, has never been my favorite dish, that *pappardelle al cinghiale*, handmade pasta with wild boar ragu is. I want to remind her it was Mia who enjoyed trying out new places, not me. I want to ask her to stop sending me tins of almond cookies—cookies I force myself to eat because I was raised not to waste food—even though I never liked them. Mia did. Not me.

But does any of it matter now?

I can't bring myself to visit Los Angeles or to call her back. Especially not for this birthday. *Our* thirtieth—the year of *the* promise.

But then I remind myself my parents lost a daughter. That's devastating. No child should leave this earth before her parents.

Guilt seizes me as I remember I'm the only one they have left. I should be better than this.

I'm the good, obedient daughter. The oldest. The one they never had to worry about.

"Mystique is so lit tonight. The music and the deejay. It's the party of the month." The elevator door opens, and two bejeweled women in short skirts and slinky dresses chatter inside.

Not looking at them, I step in, my heart rate kicking up the way it usually does when I'm in tight spaces. But I can do it, not let my claustrophobia, among other fears, rule my life.

Focusing on my breathing, I think about my upcoming birthday, Maxwell and Ryland's concern, my parents, and the pile of work I have waiting for me at home.

And Mia.

"Carpe diem! That's the saying, right? I can't wait to get plastered."

My head snaps up, pulse rickety inside my ears. The promise I made to Mia floats to the surface. The one I haven't fulfilled yet because she wanted me to complete it when I turn thirty.

"Live for me. Promise me, Olive. When you're thirty, do it for me. Go to Valencia. Experience Las Fallas for me. Burn our regrets. Don't stop living because of me."

Carpe diem.

My chest seizes. The hairs on my forearms stand, and I brace myself for the chaos inside the club.

The elevator doors open, and loud, pulsing music and jovial laughter filter inside the small compartment. The women exit, clearly excited about their night ahead.

Carpe diem.

The twin-sense, which has been absent or faint in the past twelve years, flares to life for the very first time since Mia's death.

My to-do list vaporizes. I stick my hand out to keep the doors from shutting.

My lungs constrict and I step into the raucous environment of Mystique.

I'm needed inside.

CHAPTER THREE

"Here he is, the playboy prince and birthday boy, the Anderson *everybody* loves, the man behind the most expensive marketing campaign in history! Let's scream for Rex-a-Million!"

My nickname. Short for a million orgasms. Dealer of pleasure.

Piercing screeches and catcalls erupt in the club, and I fight the urge to cover my ears. Instead, I make an exaggerated bow to the crowd as I climb the steps of the small stage by the central dance floor at Mystique.

Beautiful women in barely there dresses shake their assets and blow me kisses, no doubt trying to catch the attention of the last Anderson bachelor—for love, money, or a fuck, I don't know.

Too bad. Love isn't for me and my cock has been malfunctioning for months now. It's like my body is saying goodbye by turning off my pleasures one by one.

You don't deserve love or pleasure.

Mom's dead because of me. Ava and Cora don't have a mother because of me. My family suffered because of me.

How will you ever redeem yourself?

Ignoring the pressure pressing on my lungs, I wink at a buxom redhead, and she nearly swoons.

The Wall Street bros near the front whistle and point, and a few of them mouth, *"Rex the Man."*

"Are we ready to party tonight?" I holler into the microphone.

The crowd roars.

"Are we getting plastered? Indulging in The Rose floors? Living tonight like it's our last?"

More cheers and the finance bros high five each other. They're definitely taking advantage of the five special floors, which house clubs and rooms designed for sex and kinks, from Noire, the primal play heaven, to Trésor, the fancy strip club. I've experienced and loved them all.

"Am I seeing *you* on the biggest, flashiest, most exclusive, first inaugural international cruise from Fleur Entertainment next month?"

I need the cruise to be a success. For my family.

To atone for my sins. To be worthy of the impeccable Anderson name. To find purpose and fix myself.

Give it up. How is a silly cruise going to fix anything?

I grab a classic old fashioned with a Luxardo cherry from the deejay, who no doubt got it from the bartender earlier—they all know my tastes—and chug it down before tossing the tumbler behind me, the sound of glass shattering inflaming the crowd.

"Yes! Rex. Rex. Rex. Rex. Rex."

Their chanting grows in volume, drowning out the voices screaming in my head. Thick fog bathes the club in spectral white mist as the pulsing lights add to the ambiance.

Murderer. Blood. Hollow eyes. The fear in them.

The damn memories won't leave me alone. I should ignore them. I shouldn't be afraid of them because the past is in the past.

I *should*. Fucking shoulds.

No. The pills and the drinks were supposed to drown out everything.

The crowd screams when I swivel my hips and moonwalk across the platform, my fingers moving to the top button of my shirt.

They're looking for a show—the Rex Anderson show. I'm good at this—bringing on the party, giving people what they need.

I'm the flirt, the jokester, the fun Anderson in a family of stiff-upper-lip old-money aristocrats, courtesy of our English ancestors.

But I'm different. I'm sex on a stick.

Murderer.

Chugging down another drink, I relish the burn singeing my throat, and finally, the sharp edges dull in my mind. I close my eyes and let the audience's roar of approval fan the wild flames licking my chest.

No more thoughts.

Just sensations.

Give people what they want.

The deejay turns up the music, a sexy club number, and a few blinding flashes light up the floor. A faint warning crosses my mind. *Paparazzi are here. Get a grip. Everyone's watching.* Lana, my younger sister and chief of public relations, allowed them on site today to generate hype for the cruise.

You're a fraud. No, stop it. I want the voices to stop.

I'm too far gone, too desperate for relief to care. Instead of climbing down the stage and finding a hole to crawl into, I shrug out of my jacket and toss it behind me.

The heat from the spotlight chars my skin, a surface-level burn that's nothing compared to the inferno incinerating my insides. The heavy bass, a chaotic *thump, thump, thump,* deafens my ears.

Slowly, I unbutton my dress shirt, needing to feel the AC because I'm being burned alive.

The crowd goes wild, the women screaming at my striptease. I slide my hand down my chest and abs, gyrating my hips, thrusting to the sensual beats of the music.

Sensations. Just sensations.

Suddenly, two girls appear next to me, security fast at their heels.

"It's okay," I mouth to the guards.

Women. Maybe they'll make me forget.

"Gorgeous ladies, are you enjoying yourselves tonight?" I direct my classic panty-melting grin at the voluptuous brunette, and she giggles.

"The party is awesome." The redhead from earlier clings to me. "Do you remember me from last time, Rexy?" She bats her fake eyelashes.

If only I could forget.

"You're Jenny with the best lips from Trésor six months ago." I pull her closer and whisper in her ear, "You were wearing the red minidress with sky-high heels."

She also had a penchant for moaning like a porn star when she gave head. Her technique? More teeth than tongue, more slobbering than suction.

I had to concentrate really hard to come that night. My malfunctioning dick didn't help, but I couldn't disappoint the ladies.

"You remembered!" She rubs herself all over me, her barely covered tits grazing my abs.

But my dick doesn't stir.

The brunette, clearly not wanting to miss out, turns my face toward her, and gives me her best come-hither look. "We can get out of here and celebrate your birthday privately. I don't mind sharing, Rex."

The three of us are now writhing on stage in a sexy dance.

I should be turned on. I should haul them into a kink room and bury my guilt into their warmth.

But my cock doesn't twitch. My nerves might as well be dead. The alcohol, the Velowake, the abundance of tits and ass around me—nothing works.

Only darkness pulls me in.

Frustrated, I tear my eyes away, noticing the club goers finally turning their attention away from us.

"Rexy, what do you say? I'll let you come inside me bare," Jenny whispers.

I swallow a snort. That'll never happen. I *never* have sex without protection. Too many gold diggers want child support from one of the richest families in the country.

But before I respond, I spot a flash of innocent, angelic white among the sea of glitter and black.

Olivia.

She hasn't left yet. I didn't imagine her earlier.

The crowd jostles her, and she tumbles. I'm hit with an irrational urge to jump off the stage and cage her in, to snarl at the bastards who weren't paying attention because they got too close to her.

Because they almost hurt her.

I want to feel her trembling in my grasp. I want her to hold on to me for dear life as the room devolves into madness.

I want to tell her she doesn't belong here in the den of sin, dressed like a little nun, not with her elfin face, her hair the color of midnight, her whiskey-colored eyes that see too much.

I want to mark up her white dress, shred it with my teeth, and mess up her hair before I fist those luscious strands in my hand and pull.

Then I want to demolish the control and poise she wears like a second skin, the very qualities I desperately crave but don't have.

Will she see the brokenness, the ticking time bomb within me?

How do you deal with fucked-up bombs outside your safe little office, Olivia?

CHAPTER FOUR

Clutching my oversized tote bag to my chest, I look around as cold sweat beads on my back. There are too many people and I don't have enough space.

I can't breathe.

I want to crawl out of my skin.

This is a mistake.

I'm reminded of the Halloween party Mia dragged me to when we were seventeen—twins dressed in sexy bunny outfits—only to realize no one else was in costume. Mia laughed and wiggled her fluffy bunny tail at the gaping crowd. I wanted to melt into the ground and disappear.

The sense of déjà vu is strong as I come to a stop several feet from the makeshift stage. Everyone around me is halfway to drunk. *What am I doing here?* This isn't me. I'm the responsible, boring, and safe twin who should be at home munching almond cookies and working right now.

Responsible. Safe. Boring. *Is that what you really want for the rest of your life, Olive?* Mia's imaginary voice ghosts in my mind.

Shut up. You don't get a say. You aren't here anymore.

Suddenly, a sultry heat slithers over my body, and thoughts of escape flee my mind.

Because I make the mistake of looking up and I see *him*, the man who's everything I'm not, and someone I should stay far away from.

With two beautiful women in his arms, Rex Anderson looks like a debauched fallen angel, his thick, almost-black hair disheveled in that sexy, just got out of the shower way. His dark eyes are glazed, the perfect amount of scruff on his chiseled jaw that makes you wonder how it'll feel against your skin.

He's wearing his usual lazy smile I know melts the panties off most women, if the gossip rags could be trusted. His crisp white shirt is fully unbuttoned, toned abs and rippling muscles lovingly caressed by the strobe lights sweeping over the club. And the way he swivels his hips, it looks like he's having sex on stage.

I swallow, my breaths quickening.

Despite being friends with his siblings, I don't know him well. It's not that he's unapproachable, because he obviously is. I've seen the jokes he lobs at his serious brothers, dragging reluctant smiles from them like it's his life's purpose. Then, there are the loving pranks he pulls on Lana, whom I've heard he was closest to growing up. Grace and Taylor, the Andersons' youngest half-siblings, once told me Rex immediately welcomed them into the fold when they discovered they shared the same dad a few years ago.

But the party prince makes it his purpose to avoid me on the rare occasions when we're in the same room, as if I'm contagious with an incurable illness. At first, it was the little things—him not looking me in the eye when I said hello. I had tried small talk. I had tried soft insults to rile him up.

But nothing. He'd always look through me as if I were invisible.

It's disconcerting—the warmth he shows others and the frigidness he directs toward me.

I can't help but think something's off about him. But no one in his family seems to notice.

So maybe I'm wrong.

Maybe the sharp gaze that occasionally snags on mine, but then will quickly swivel away when he catches me looking, is just dislike.

Or maybe it's contempt.

And I'm trying, but failing, not to be offended.

I'm used to rejection and unease whenever people find out I'm a psychiatrist. They think I'll see through their defenses and secretly judge them.

But those people usually need help the most. They have something to hide.

And secrets fester from the inside out. I should know that better than anyone.

The brunette with curves for days is now pawing his chest, and an uncomfortable tug prickles my gut. Indigestion probably. I *should* eat on time.

Rex laughs, the sound I can't hear because of the booming music, but that wide, charming smile sends my heart into a fritz.

Normal physiological reactions from seeing a beautiful man. I'd be blind not to react.

Gritting my teeth, I watch him yank the two women closer, the three of them entangled in a half-naked, sultry dance under the spotlight. I can't help but wonder how it feels not to care what the rest of the world thinks of you. To do whatever you want whenever it strikes you.

To be free.

One woman is now dropping kisses all over his abs.

The indigestion flares again.

I tear my gaze away. I should leave. *Why the hell am I here? Just because someone said carpe diem?*

Mia isn't coming back. She'll never come back.

It's too late.

No matter what I do, how many lives I save, I'll never bring her back.

My ribs tighten, strangling my lungs, and my stomach churns.

I clutch my tote tighter against my chest, trying to stave off the sudden wave of nausea when someone plows into me from the side.

Momentarily disoriented, I'm thankful for the sensible flats I have on or I'd have gone down like a bowling ball in the gutter. The blond, clearly drunk culprit barely spares me a glance before mouthing an apology.

Determined to end this temporary lapse of sanity, I take a step toward the exit when the same searing heat burns the back of my neck again.

My hackles rise and I swivel toward the stage, finding an intense pair of slate-gray eyes boring into me.

Rex, still arms full of women, isn't smiling, even as his body sways to the music. He swirls an amber drink in his hand, the casualness of the gesture completely at odds with the blistering fire in his gaze.

My ears ring and my breath catches. Time distills into staccato fragments.

His gaze trails down my body, the sensation like a physical caress. His eyes darken, a pulse battering against his jawline as he stares at the tote in my arms before snapping his gaze to mine again.

The sexy duo rubs themselves on him, two feral cats gyrating their hips low toward the floor, using his body as a pole. But Rex doesn't appear to notice when they hump him. I, however, can't stop my lips from curling in disdain.

Ugh. Get a room.

His intense stare is riveted on me, and his lips part, like the beginnings of arousal have finally found him.

This split second change in his eyes—it's like a switch flipping off the disdain in my mind.

Suddenly, I forget how to breathe. And all I can think of is how those lips will feel against mine.

Every cell in my body stands at attention. My skin sensitizes—feeling my linen dress brushing against my legs, the tightness of my no-frills bra against my suddenly swelling breasts, the desperate craving I have to be touched, caressed, and kissed. This raw magnetism is palpable.

I don't remember ever feeling this way with anyone before, least of all him.

Air rushes out of my lungs. I should leave. He's a mess, a hedonistic flirt who probably goes through women like toilet paper. I shouldn't be attracted to him. It makes no sense.

His nostrils flare, like he can read my mind. His chest moves rapidly—up and down, up and down—each breath drawing attention to his perfectly sculpted body, glistening with a sheen of sweat.

My fingers twitch. The brunette says something and that fake smile of his reappears, but he doesn't look away from me.

Then, his tongue dips out, and he slowly wets those perfectly carved lips. He reaches into his drink and pulls out a cherry, his fingers playing with the stem before he brings the fruit to his lips. Keeping his eyes on me, he slowly swirls his tongue around the base of the cherry, then flicks it hard before feathering light lashes on it.

Sharp pleasure zings between my legs, my clit answering his suggestive motions with a telltale pulse. *Is this what he looks like when he goes down on you?* My nipples harden, the abrasion from my bra is the most torturous foreplay. Rex sucks the cherry into his mouth, the motion slow and sensual, his gray eyes now nearly obsidian.

Heat gathers in my core and I fight the urge to clench my thighs because I know he'll see it. But something must have given me away because after he finishes eating the fruit, he licks his lips like he's still famished.

Like he wants me.

Unbidden, I touch my tingling bottom lip, feeling his sexy swipe on my skin.

Those piercing eyes flash with darkness. *Danger, Olivia. Run.* He steps forward, only to be held back by his companions.

What am I doing? I'm better than this. I don't make bad decisions like flirting with my best friends' older brother, who clearly has problems. The man doesn't even like me, right?

The thought slaps me awake from this strange trance. Why do I want to shake him and climb him at the same time?

And why does it look like he'll let me?

It's Rex. He'll let anyone with a vagina use him. He's a playboy. I know his type. He prefers to ignore his problems and bury his head in the proverbial sand by surrounding himself with pleasure.

He's the definition of someone who doesn't want to do the work.

This is ridiculous. *I'm* being ridiculous.

I shake my head and straighten.

Whatever he sees on my face has him standing taller as well, the fire in his eyes replaced with ice.

The redhead grabs his face and plants her lips on his.

Acid roils in my gut, and I want to throw up. *You're disgusted, Olivia. That's why you're feeling this way.*

Still staring at me, Rex hauls the redhead close, then kisses her back. But just as abruptly, he pulls away. A small smirk tips his lips, like he's taunting me.

But then, the strangest thing happens.

His gaze softens, and he frowns.

Like something flashed through his mind, and now he's in pain.

I stumble back and press a hand to my chest, an answering ache flaring there. It has to be a trick of the flashing lights.

Because I recognize this expression. Twisted anguish hidden behind fake charm and smiles. Cries for help in the form of boisterous laughter.

Carpe diem.

I didn't notice the signs until it was too late.

Like a mirage, the hurt in his eyes disappears. Rex twists his lips into a cruel smirk and curls his arms around the women's waists again. *See what I have, Olivia? People fawning over me. I'm not alone like you.*

I narrow my eyes, then cock my brow. I'm delusional. This is Rex Anderson, the man who takes nothing seriously. Stop conflating Mia with him.

Before I can stop myself, I flick him the middle finger.

Not today, bastard.

He grins, the devious smile sending my pulse racing again.

Then, out of nowhere, searing flashes blind the stage in white. Chaos. Yelling. Reporters hurling questions at the devil.

"Rex! Don't you think your partying is getting out of hand?" someone shouts.

"Does your family know you're stripping on stage?"

"Are you high? On drugs? Aren't you worried about your upcoming cruise?"

I shrink back from the commotion, desperate to leave this hellhole. But when I take one last look at the perplexing man, I find him ignoring the press, his attention firmly on me.

Before I can analyze why butterflies are beating their wings in my stomach, I turn around and flee.

And I feel his stare the entire way out.

CHAPTER FIVE

"Hey! Before you go in there, I want to ask you for a favor." Lana hurries over, stopping me before I enter the double doors to the Ladies' Lounge inside The Orchid for brunch with the girls.

I stifle a yawn. My miles-long to-do list waves behind my eyes, mocking me. I fell asleep in front of my laptop last night.

"Come again?"

"Actually, scratch that. Two favors." She bats her eyelashes. "I need two favors, and it has to be you."

"I must be dreaming because what can I possibly do for *the* Lana Anderson?" I bite back a grin.

Before Grace and Taylor found out their dad was Linus Anderson, Lana was the youngest Anderson sibling and the only girl. And like all the other Andersons, sans one particular brother, she's easygoing.

She's now one of my best friends.

"Ah, shut up." She rolls her eyes. "You might have seen the headlines, but Rex got himself in a mess at Mystique. Striptease and dry humping on stage. Folks are literally jumping ship, including a few doctors scheduled to work on the cruise."

Rex. My pulse stutters.

The night a week ago won't leave me. The images appear at night as I lay on my bed—the searing intensity in his eyes, the palpable tension between us.

How my body heated and throbbed when he tongued the cherry like it was my clit.

Then, the gut feeling the man was hiding something. That the play-boy persona was an act.

I'd twist and turn, telling myself I had no business thinking about the asshole, but it was hopeless. Desperate, I'd convince myself fantasies weren't reality as my fingers slid down my stomach until they reached the tender spot between my legs, only to find it wet. It'd take a few seconds before I got myself off, but I'd still be unsated. Needy. Craving something.

The guilt would flood in, my inner voice telling me I should be disappointed in myself. How it was improper to fantasize about someone so obviously wrong for me.

"Why are you all red in the face?" Lana asks, drawing my attention back to her.

I clear my throat. I'm ridiculous. "The inaugural cruise all over the news?"

"Yes, it's a mess." She sighs. "We've backfilled most of the openings, but I still need a psychiatrist. I need *you*."

"Me? On a cruise? Why do you need a psychiatrist?" I deflect. "No way. I have patients to see."

"The cruise will be The Orchid on water, which means we'll have our version of the Rose floors aboard. You know how it is...sex, kinks, consensual dubious situations. Feelings getting involved. Plus, our patrons expect top medical care at all our facilities. So, it makes sense to have a psychiatrist who specializes in talk therapy. You know how rare that is."

I do know. Most psychiatrists focus on the medicine aspect of treatment, referring the talk therapy to therapists. But I prefer to be a one-stop shop. This way, I have all the facts.

I control all parts of the treatment plan.

Lana directs her doe-like eyes at me. "Please, Olivia. We'll make it worth your while. We'll set up state-of-the-art videoconferencing so you can still do your thing. We need someone we trust, and with you being Maxwell's doctor, well...that carries weight."

She leans down and clasps my shoulders. "*We need you.*"

"You look like that Uncle Sam poster right now." I imagine her in a top hat, pointing a finger at me. I snicker. I really should sleep more—I'm getting delirious.

"Imagine this. Crystal blue waters, swimming in Mykonos, white buildings and blue roofs dotting the horizon, exploring gothic castles and forts in Dubrovnik, burning sculptures in Valencia, stuffing your face with the best spaghetti in Tuscany—"

Burning sculptures in Valencia.

My heart palpitates, and I grip her wrist. "Hold on, rewind. Burning sculptures? Are you talking about Las Fallas Festival?"

Her slate-gray eyes light up. "Yes! Sanctioned, controlled destruction. Once-in-a-lifetime opportunity, right? It's amazing..."

I don't hear her anymore. All I can hear are the words Las Fallas Festival.

"Live for me. Promise me, Olive. When you're thirty, do it for me. Go to Valencia. Experience Las Fallas for me. Burn our regrets. Don't stop living because of me."

"Olivia, do me a solid?" Lana shakes me.

The promise I made to Mia echoes in my mind.

No. I can't drop everything and go. It'd be irresponsible. I have patients. I need to figure out the ADAS funding. I'm so busy, I can't even eat on time. No way. There's no way I can do this—

"We'll talk later. You don't need to decide right now." Lana peers at me. "Just think about it, okay?"

She pats my shoulder, and we enter Ladies' Lounge.

Our feet come to an abrupt halt.

The lounge is turned upside down as The Orchid staff pushes furniture against the walls. I clock the lighting, cameras, and equipment with more knobs and buttons than I can count.

"I have to be dreaming because this definitely isn't brunch." Yes, dreaming would make more sense than the idea of me going on a cruise.

"Go back to sleep, Olivia. Then you can finish your six patient files, insurance peer reviews, ADAS emails—"

"She's talking to herself. The shrink needs to be shrunk," someone whispers.

Redhead. Sly grin. Alexis Vaughn—no—Alexis Anderson, now that she married Ethan.

"Psst. That's old slang and derogatory. Doctor. Psychiatrist. Use the right title." Lana snickers.

A handyman hammers a nail into the faux-stage. *Definitely not sleep-walking.* "Okay, I give up. What's going on? This is one of Alexis's items, isn't it? She lured us in with drinks and gossip and now we're pawns for her bucket list."

"Ding, ding, ding!" Alexis exclaims. "Aren't unexpected surprises the best?"

No. Definitely not. I like to-do lists and plans. Preferably months in advance.

"Surprises, by definition, are unexpected, Lexy," I reply.

She beams at me, then explains the surprise for the day—to record a version of Shakespeare's *Twelfth Night.* It's one of her bucket list items, and Taylor has an upcoming ballet performance based on the play. It's random, but that's expected of her. Alexis flies by the seat of her pants and we love her for it.

Usually.

But something about this one makes me uneasy.

"I'm more of a behind-the-scenes type—fetching water, giving high fives, handing out tissues." I eye the makeshift stage dubiously. "So, I'll be standing over here cheering you guys on."

Mia would've loved this. If she were here, she'd volunteer to go first. She'd create costumes out of tablecloths and use wine for blood or water for tears. I'd follow her with tissues, blotting her faux-blood and tears, righting props she'd chuck in a moment of passion.

"Hell no." Taylor shakes her head as she ambles over. "If I'm suffering through this, you're going down with me."

As luck would have it, after a competitive session of rock, paper, scissors, I have to go first.

Huffing a breath, I grab a stack of scene cards containing the modern English translations of the original play from Alexis and hand one to Taylor.

"Act Two, Scene Four. Viola is traveling with her twin brother, Sebastian, and after a shipwreck, she thought he died. To protect herself, she pretends to be a man named Cesario and begins working for Duke Orsino," Taylor intones with the enthusiasm of a man about to meet the guillotine.

"Gee, you're inspiring my creative juices, Tay." I snort.

"Fuck you. In ballet, I don't have to talk, okay? I just dance." She sticks her tongue out. Taylor is a principal ballerina in the top ballet company in the country. Not that you can tell with her incessant cursing, dark makeup, and nose piercings she calls her mood rings.

"Is there a Razzie award for the worst theatrical performance? We can definitely win one." Heat crawls up my face. I hate being in the center of attention.

"Suddenly, she's all jokes and smiles."

"Enough chitchat. Read!" Alexis shouts in a...megaphone?

I take over reading. "Viola falls in love with Orsino, who thinks she's a guy. Cue shenanigans."

We get into our positions, and I wince as the spotlight hits my face. I want to flee, to go back to the safety of my office and analyze other people's problems, to help others. Save lives.

But I sneak a glance at Alexis, finding her bright eyed and excited. I don't want to be a buzzkill and disappoint her by not participating.

It's just a play, damn it. Recite a few lines and it'll be done before I know it.

The cameraman makes a hand motion, and Alexis tells us to begin.

"My dad had a daughter once, and she fell in love with someone. Desperately. If I were a woman, maybe I'd fall in love with someone like you," I murmur, gripping the scene card tightly.

Love isn't for me. Frankly, I'm afraid of it—of being blinded by an emotion that drives people to do stupid things. I don't think my heart has skipped a beat for any man.

An image of Rex at the club flashes through my mind. The raw sexuality in his gaze, the way his fingers grazed down his rippling torso, all the while looking like he was pissed at me or wanted to devour me alive.

The unwanted pulsing between my legs.

No. That's just the environment. Lust maybe. Nothing more.

I can't afford to be blind again, especially in my profession. Lives are at stake.

But I know what it's like to pretend, like Viola is doing in this scene—masquerading as a man to the person she loves.

"What happened to your sister?" Taylor asks, pitching her voice low, clearly getting into her role as the duke.

"I...never found out." Dizziness swamps me. The old ache flares in my chest.

I never got my answers either. Mia didn't leave them for me. There were only riddles, questions, clues.

No closure.

Only bottomless grief.

Silence falls in the room and I hear my laborious breaths. I wet my lips and push through the next lines. "I-I never knew how she felt. Whatever it was, she'd let it eat her alive. She smiled through the pain, s-she..."

My eyes prickle. I can see it so clearly—Mia's face, identical to mine, her eyes shining with mischief, but underneath it all, there was a hollowness, wasn't there? She'd sleep too much, and I'd think it was because she partied too hard.

Deep down, I suspected something, right? I remember asking if something was wrong. That she could talk to me or, if she wanted to, she could go to the school counselor. After one Saturday where she slept for twenty hours straight, I dragged her out of bed, took her to the self-help section in the bookstore and pulled out books about sleep disorders and vitamin deficiencies.

She pushed them away and laughed at me. She distracted me with her plans for Sunday—the blockbuster film she wanted to see and she asked about my upcoming chemistry test, knowing I was worried because I hated formulas.

She didn't want to do the work to help herself.

Exhaling, I focus on the scene card in my hand.

I want to scurry away. I don't want to be Viola—or Mia's twin.

"She kept it all in, you see," I rasp, my heart splintering. "She acted like everything was fine, but inside? She was destroyed. But that's love, right?"

Everything has two sides to it. Love and hate. Happiness and grief.

I hate how Mia left me, how selfish she was. We were two sides of a whole—the light and the dark, chaos and calm.

I miss her so damn much.

Now, I'm a fraud—an impostor masquerading as a doctor, the broken trying to heal the broken.

A fake.

"End scene." Alexis snaps the clapper, and I flinch. "Olivia, for someone who's supposed to be in the background, you were born to be in the spotlight. That's no Razzie material... It's so damn good."

The girls nod and I force out a laugh.

"Don't expect a repeat performance." I look down at my shoes, afraid to catch their gazes because I'm *not* Mia. I'm not the brave and exuberant twin with the poker face.

I'm not supposed to be in the spotlight.

But you want to, don't you? Aren't you tired of playing it safe, of hiding in the shadows? Well, no one is blocking you anymore.

Horror sweeps through me, colliding with the spark of excitement flickering behind my rib cage.

It's evil, these thoughts. I'd give anything to have Mia here with me, blocking the sunlight and all.

"Ack, I need to use the restroom. Drank too much." Taylor dashes off and the rest of the room comes alive as the staff prepares for the next scene.

Resting my hand on my chest, I take a few deep breaths before looking up, finding Lana staring quizzically at me.

"You okay? You don't seem yourself."

"I'm fine. Just stressed."

"And *that's* why you need to be on the cruise! Work and play. You might even meet a hot European guy and have a nice fling with him. Seriously, I've known you for what...two years now? I've never seen you date anyone. Go to Europe! Work hard, get laid by someone who speaks a sexy language."

She waggles her brows, and I can't help but smile at her energy. It isn't a hard sell, but even if I want to go on the cruise, I don't know if I can swing it.

But something she said earlier gives me pause.

"Hold on. You said two favors. Going on the cruise is one... What's the other?"

She grimaces and takes a sudden interest in her nails.

"Lana?" My muscles tense. *I won't like this.*

"The whole thing with Rex...we're really worried about him. The partying. The chaos. He's losing his grip. We think it's time for him to see a professional."

She sighs, her face solemn. "We're meeting at Maxwell's later to talk to him. He won't get help unless we force it on him, and he's going to be an ass about it. But he wants to be on the cruise. He's worked hard on it for the past year." She looks imploringly at me. "We want *you* to help him on board."

"No way." The refusal slips out automatically. Being confined on a cruise with him? The man who unnerves me? And he's an unwilling patient?

Lana's eyes widen. "Is there something going on I should know? You love helping people."

My pulse riots and I twist the fabric of my dress. "W-What? Nothing." *Absolutely nothing.* Before last week, I barely interacted with him. *But you were aware of him, weren't you? Ah, shut up, Olivia.* "I just don't believe in forcing people into treatment."

They have to want to do the work.

"Come on, Olivia. You've helped Maxwell, and he's doing so well because of you. Just do a few sessions with Rex and if it doesn't work out, you've tried your best. Please, Olivia. Four therapy sessions in a month. That's it. I'll owe you. *Forever.* I'll be there too. I mean, I can't go until the Dubrovnik stop, but you won't be alone. *Please?*"

She bats her ridiculously long eyelashes at me again, and I struggle not to smile. The woman can charm a maximum security prison guard into letting her escape.

"Fire Festival in Valencia," she says, "I saw that spark in your eyes. You *know* you want to go. Win-win!"

My promise to Mia echoes in my mind. She wanted me to go to Las Fallas. That was the last thing she asked of me.

I didn't think much of it when Mia mentioned it the night before prom. We were talking about moving to Boston in a few months because I got into Harvard and she, Northeastern. I was excited about living away from home for the first time, and she hoped I'd meet a guy who could make me laugh because I was too serious.

I didn't notice how she asked me to go to Las Fallas *for* her, like she wouldn't be around to do it with me.

I didn't notice how she didn't talk about meeting a guy of her very own.

I just responded with, "You'll change your mind tomorrow. What's the point in planning twelve years ahead?"

But there was no tomorrow. Not for her.

I didn't notice until it was too late.

My heart twists and shrivels, the pain sharp in my chest. The air thins and a chilly breeze scrapes across my skin, even though I know the AC isn't on. It's winter after all.

Hiding my clammy hands behind my back, I swallow.

"I heard from a little bird you've been trying to secure funding for ADAS... What if Fleur throws in a five million dollar contribution and names ADAS as one of our key philanthropic partners?"

My eyes snap to hers, finding her trying her best not to look like the tortoise who just crossed the finish line, glancing back and finding the jaw-slacked hare staring at her in disbelief.

She knows she's making a good case for herself.

I bite my lip, and her gaze softens.

Lana says quietly, her voice serious, "You can totally say no. I know I can get overly excited about things, but don't feel like you need to say yes because of me. Only go if you can. I don't want to cause problems for you either. You and our friendship are more important to me."

She pats my hand. "And the funding...regardless of your answer, I'll petition the board for the donation. It'll be easy to get their approval if you're part of the cruise, but I'll try anyway."

I stare at her, and she smiles at me reassuringly. She means it. I can say no if I want to.

But do I want to?

If I go, not only can I keep the promise I made to Mia, but I can also secure the much-needed funding for ADAS. And the coveted spotlight from a company as big as Fleur will draw in more donations.

Many people can get the mental health treatments they desperately need.

It feels fated. Like it's the right thing to do.

"Fine." Pulse racing, I strain a smile at an expectant Lana. "I'll...I'll do it. Don't make me regret it."

I'll live for Mia—live enough for both of us, just like how Viola pretended to be Cesario in the play.

Even if I have to put up with the devil for a few weeks.

CHAPTER SIX

"WHAT *WERE* YOU THINKING, Rex? They say you're doing drugs. On your fucking birthday and the celebration of our inaugural cruise, no less."

Maxwell tosses a pile of newspapers and tabloid magazines onto the coffee table in the two-story library at the Anderson Estate, our family home, where he now lives with his wife Belle and their toddler son, Levi.

He's clearly pissed off, and I don't blame him. We Andersons pride ourselves on keeping our reputations clean. Our ancestors were dukes and marquesses, and those manners had been hammered into us since before we could talk.

My copy of the perfection gene must be defective.

"Look, I'm not speaking to you as the CEO who's worried about the cruise venture. I'm talking to you as your brother. You're spiraling, Rex. What's going on?" Maxwell leans forward and levels his penetrating gaze at me.

My head throbs. Casey and I may have hit the bar too hard last night. I barely slept because the damn nightmares kept me up again. And when I finally did, I had another blackout.

Woke up in my tub this time, water up to my chest. I could've drowned.

That would put me out of my misery. I snort.

But hey, it's not sleepwalking. I drift back to my appointment with Dr. Kingston, a somnologist, two weeks ago. He's the tenth doctor I've seen over the years for my random symptoms—intense insomnia, blackouts, random trembling and shakes, feeling my heart will give out at any moment.

This time, we did a sleep observation. According to my brain activity, I was apparently awake during my blackouts. Another diagnosis ruled out.

"See a neurologist and check out brain functions," was his recommendation. The mole at the corner of his right eye sneered at me. He had an incessantly annoying habit of clicking his pen five times between every sentence.

I'm losing my marbles, literally.

Damn HSAM and photographic memories.

Fuck, I'm tired.

"Come on, lighten up. Now that you old farts are all tied down and enjoying domestic bliss and shit, someone's gotta party it up on your behalf, right?" I chuckle. This usually works—deflecting, making jokes. "Save the death glare for the boardroom, bro. At least let me put on some armor first."

The room falls silent. My pulse kicks up.

They aren't falling for it.

"Rex? Talk to us. We're your family," Maxwell says.

They won't understand even if I explain. They'll just repeat what they told me all those years ago when Mom died—that it wasn't my fault.

"Fuck. You couldn't have done this at the gentlemen's club? Or my apartment? You had to drag me up at the crack of dawn and haul me over here as punishment?"

I close my eyes. Even the dim morning light streaming in from the stained-glass windows worsens my headache.

"Did you miss the press camped outside The Orchid? Or all the nosy patrons?" This voice belongs to Ryland. The twins—always siding with each other.

"We're worried about you," Steven Kingsley murmurs. He's a close friend and my brother-in-law now, since he married Grace two years ago.

"That's what Casey said," I mutter, my eyes flickering open.

Maxwell clears his throat, side-eyes Ryland, and the duo share one of those mysterious silent twin messages. I wonder what it's like to have someone understand you without saying a word.

Must be nice.

Ryland nods. "Casey...still talking to him? I thought you guys—"

"Who's Casey?" Steven asks.

I swallow and look at him. Steven has only been part of the inner circle for the past few years, so he doesn't know about Casey. "My best friend. You've never met him. He has social anxiety like Maxwell."

Steven scrunches his brows and shrugs. "Everyone's worried about you, then. And if Ethan and Alexis weren't doing another one of those bucket list items today, they'd be here too."

"Leave them alone. Let them enjoy their newlywed bliss." My brother, the yearner of the family, finally married the love of his life and our good friend, Charles Vaughn's younger sister, recently. "Fucking interventions—I can't believe you guys did it again. Completely overreacting."

I shudder, thinking about last month when Ethan rounded us inside The Menagerie, a specialty cocktail bar within The Orchid, and grilled me for an hour. Apparently, I resembled a walking zombie with dark circles under my eyes.

"Then how do you explain these photos?" Maxwell picks up a tabloid and practically breathes fire onto them. "Fucking Greg Masters. These headlines will sink our cruise before it leaves the dock. 'Party Prince's Desperate Striptease—Rex Anderson's Fall from Grace' and 'The Orchid Cruises—Front for Drugs and Debauchery?'"

I gnash my teeth together, which only makes the pounding in my head worse. Fuck Greg Masters and *Gossip Times*, the biggest tabloid in the country, which has taken an obsessive interest in our family.

Feeling like a bomb is about to go off inside my chest, I snatch the offending papers from him and scan the articles. The dates range from a week ago to as recent as yesterday. Normally, I don't read these things.

They just piss me off and goad me into making a scene, which has always been the paps' game all along.

"What the hell!" I hurl the papers onto the ground.

"Easy there. Just bad press. We've all been there." Charles picks them up. "Let's fix you first."

"There's *nothing* to fix!"

I stand and hiss as pain ricochets inside my skull. Perhaps Casey's right. I party too much and am throwing my life down the drain.

But what choice do I have? It's better than feeling empty all the time.

My phone buzzes in my pocket.

Gritting my teeth, I take it out, fully intending to power it off before chucking it across the room.

Then I see the text message.

Every molecule inside me freezes.

My feet move toward the door before my mind catches up.

"Where are you going?" Ryland hollers.

"Be right back. Need to take care of something important."

Something that may save me.

———◆———

Twenty minutes later, I'm pacing in the rose garden, my mind chaotic as I reread the text message for the thousandth time.

Elias

> You asked me to contact you if I ever needed your help again. I'm moving someone, a target of The Association, to safety, and The Orchid cruise is the perfect cover. Your shot at atonement, even though I think it's unnecessary. Don't make me regret asking you.

My chest tightens, a cocktail of fear and adrenaline swirling inside me. Elias Kent, a mobster who's helped my family out of a bind a few times, doesn't mince words or ask for favors lightly. If he needs my help, he's exhausted all other options.

Atonement.

The dark hole inside me. The constant guilt and hollowness nothing could snuff out—not Velowake, not parties, not women.

Not my work at Fleur, including heading up the massive cruise project for Maxwell.

But this. To save another woman.

A life saved for two lives lost.

I think about Raya—what she made me promise before she died—and Ava and Cora in Monaco, motherless and trying to make it on their own. They'll be on the run from The Association for the rest of their lives.

Anger surges up my spine at the thought of the criminal organization that tried to rope my family into its twisted web in the past because adding the old-money Andersons to the mix could only expand their power. I'll never forgive them for what they did to my siblings over the years.

Then I think about Mom, her body broken at the foot of the staircase, marbles scattered around her.

Will anything atone for those deaths?

Can I do it right this time, or will I just add another body count to my list of failures?

My stomach churns, and I fist my phone. Sweat drips off my forehead.

"Fuck!" I pace some more.

A sharp pressure forms at the base of my neck, my head throbbing now. I pop another Velowake into my mouth. My ribs constrict and I can't draw in a full breath.

Can I do this?

I don't know, but I'll die trying. I'll do anything rather than feel the way I do now—half alive.

The pressure suddenly lessens, and oxygen floods into my lungs.

Yes. This is the only way out.

With trembling hands, I unlock my phone and type a response.

Rex

I'm in. And…thank you.

Completely absorbed in my message, I barely notice the soft footsteps coming my way.

"I've been tasked with dragging you back inside. What's the emergency?"

I look up, finding Lana narrowing her eyes at me.

"Work stuff. You won't get it." Quickly, I hit send and stuff my phone into my pocket.

She scans my face and I hold still, hoping my sister doesn't pick up on anything. Lana is sharp, but you'll never hear me tell her that, because riling her up is a hobby of mine.

"Hm. Okay," she murmurs and waves me back toward the house. "What are you waiting for? Meet your executioner. Shoo. Go back in there. We aren't done with you yet."

Groaning, I follow her back into the house, but this time, I feel a little lighter.

Atonement. Elias's favor. The cruise.

Yes, this is what I need.

Chapter Seven

Moments later, Lana settles next to me with Grace and Taylor strolling into the library after us. Oh great, almost the entire gang. This torture will never end.

Taylor quips, "You look like shit. And you know I don't bullshit anyone. Shit is shit. And that's nothing to shit about." She looks pleased with herself as she plops onto the carpet.

"How can you say that to your *favorite* brother? And all those 'shits,' not exactly prima ballerina material now, isn't it?"

She gives me the middle finger. Charles chuckles and presses a kiss on his fiancée's hair.

"But seriously," Lana grabs my hand, "is there any truth to what they're saying? I can deal with the press, the PR, but are you do-ing...drugs?"

The room falls silent. I even hear the faint barking of Silas, Maxwell and Belle's one-eyed husky, running around the mansion somewhere.

The thudding of my heart intensifies.

Does Velowake count? No. Of course it doesn't. It's mainly made of caffeine. All legal substances. Borderline, maybe. Normally prescription required, which I definitely don't have. But still...not hard drugs. Not the ones she's referring to.

It's a line I've drawn for myself. Partying, alcohol, caffeine pills, and even the occasional joint or two, but no hard drugs.

Deep down, I'm afraid if I ever touch those substances, I'd become addicted and couldn't dig my way back out.

"Rex?"

I let out an incredulous scoff. "No, of course not. I was stupid, too excited about this cruise kicking off. Celebrated a little too hard, that's all. Sorry for making your life difficult."

Her eyes soften as she scans my face for tells. "Well, you've always made my life hard, so what's another day?"

"You little shit." I grin. "You love me."

"We won't force you to tell us what's wrong. But know you aren't alone. You have an army behind you." Maxwell clasps my shoulder. "But we think it's time for you to see a professional. A therapist or a psychiatrist."

"A *shrink*? No fucking way." I recoil, thinking about doctor number five, world-renowned Dr. Finneas Cambridge.

Silver-haired, wait list a year long, wore bow ties like an Olympic sport. Smelled like sardines and old newspapers. After two sessions, he blamed everything on "mommy issues," and my symptoms resulted from unresolved tension and abandonment fixation. How I was a textbook case of the Oedipus complex. What bullshit.

There's no way I'm seeing a shrink again.

Shaking my head, I say, "I just need to get away and clear my head. I'm sure being on the cruise will help—the ocean, the beaches, the exotic locations. I'll be fine."

And Elias's mission—I'm sure he'll tell me more eventually, but I assume this mystery woman is in a similar situation to Raya's. Ava and Cora's mom had been married to someone in The Association. She overheard something she wasn't meant to, and she'd paid for it with her life.

Whoever this new woman is, it *has* to end differently this time.

Maxwell grimaces. "About that..."

"What?" I stiffen. *Don't you dare. Don't you fucking dare.*

"I hate to do this to you, but you saw the passenger cancelations. The drug allegations are rattling the patrons. With the tabloids breathing down our necks, we think it's best if you sit this one out."

"But this is my project! I spent the last year crafting the itinerary, generating the campaigns, liaising with vendors, the travel teams, every fucking thing."

I *need* to be on the cruise to save that woman.

I need it more than I need food to survive.

Desperation and resentment flood my veins. I stalk to the windows. "No fucking way. You guys aren't pulling me off shit."

I jam my hand into my pocket and grip the red marble to the point of pain. This is what I get for being a fuck up—my family not trusting me.

I need atonement. I need to fix myself.

"It's the right choice, C. You work out whatever's been bothering you and we can distance your bad press from the launch," Ryland comments.

"You don't even work at Fleur anymore. Stay out of it, *B*. Go grade some papers or something," I grit out, pointedly reminding Ryland he vacated his COO role a few years ago to Steven when he pursued being a professor full time.

Our parents alphabetized our middle names by age. Maxwell's middle name is Angus, Ryland with Benedict, mine as Cassius, all the way down the alphabet to Taylor's middle name as Gianna. We use them as nicknames, and right now, as insults.

Maxwell glowers at me. "Well, *I* work at Fleur and I'm pulling the boss card. You have a right to keep your shit to yourself, but anything you do can and will reflect upon us. And if you won't find a therapist, we'll find one for you—"

"You're pulling some creative Miranda Rights now? Think this is a joke?"

"No, I don't think this is a joke. I want to kick your ass and knock some sense into you, but one of us has to be the adult here. Three billion dollars and hundreds of jobs are at stake. You're out, Rex. That's it. End of discussion. *Unless...*"

I whirl around, dread lining my gut.

I know that tone. The soft, raspy whisper laden with pretense. This was Maxwell's game all along. Everything before this was a fucking setup.

"What the hell are you planning?"

Maxwell's eyes shine with triumph. "If the cruise is that important to you, you can be on it under the condition you'll see the on-board psychiatrist."

"Come on, man. There's no big downward spiral here. Just a little scenic detour with bottle service. Let's not be dramatic. Save the drama for me, yeah?" I wiggle my eyebrows and force out a grin.

His face remains stony.

I sweep my gaze around the room, finding the same concerned expressions on everyone's faces.

They aren't laughing. They aren't falling for my jokes.

Nausea churns inside me as I narrow my eyes at Maxwell and murmur, "That's it? Go to a few sessions and you'll be okay?"

He shrugs. "Yep. Four sessions. Easy as that."

"Sur—" I can probably fool some balding old man who was arm-wrestled into babysitting a bunch of billionaires. I can feign contrition. People love me. I have everyone eating out of the palm of my hand.

But something in Maxwell's arrogant smirk gets my hackles up.

"Hold on, who's the doctor?"

Maxwell grins and clasps his hands over his lap. "Olivia. She's good and won't let you bullshit her."

I freeze, my voice suddenly leaving me. The image of her standing in the crowd at Mystique barrels into my mind. The way she stared at me, how she peeled back my layers and tossed them aside—all without moving a muscle.

And when her gaze roved over my body—a more potent caress than the two women rubbing themselves all over me—my cock stirred for the very first time in months.

Her eyes flared and those soft lips parted, like she could sense my body chemistry changing. Like she could read my secrets.

It was unnerving. It scrambled my mind. I felt naked to my soul.

And so I did what I do best—hide.

When the girls kissed me, I kissed them back, but I might as well have been kissing a wall, because I didn't feel a damn thing. The crowd roared because they expected the playboy act from me.

But the entire time, I couldn't tear my gaze away from the temptation in white.

There were desire and disdain in her whiskey-colored eyes, a darkness in them calling to my own.

I couldn't help but think... What if I was kissing her? How would those supple, unvarnished lips taste? Would her perfect face with her perfect mind making the perfect decisions—would that somehow rub off on me?

Would the psychiatrist heal the fuck up?

And this is why you stayed away all this time.

This is also why she couldn't be my doctor. She laid me bare with a simple gaze.

The door abruptly opens and in toddles Levi in his denim overalls, with Belle hot on his heels.

"Dada!" The two-year-old doles out a toothy smile and waddles toward Maxwell. "Pway... Pway pwetend."

The tension melts as my siblings laugh at the pair of chunky thighs bumbling across the Persian carpet. Levi trips and falls flat on his face, but instead of crying, he gets back up, giggles, and continues toward his dad.

Maxwell squats and opens his arms wide, his lips curving into a rare, bright smile that still shocks me whenever I see it. Growing up, he barely smiled and always walked around with the weight of the world on his shoulders. But since marrying Belle, he's thawed and is so much happier.

"Sorry for interrupting." Belle beams at us. "Levi's into the whole I'm a triceratops phase and Maxwell's been assigned as the T-Rex. Kids and their imaginations."

A rock lodges in my throat at the image she painted. "It's all good. We're done anyway."

I'm reminded of how Mom had comforted me when I was five, after Maxwell and Ryland had run off to the two-story treehouse in the backyard and refused to come down. Back then, they called me the scaredy cat—afraid of heights, loud noises, unfamiliar strangers, among other things.

I was too scared to climb up the tall ladder, and the twins said even if I could, they wouldn't let me in because I wasn't a twin. It didn't matter I was only a year younger.

I was excluded.

Upset, I ran back inside the kitchen, my muddy shoes making a mess on the white-tiled floors. Mora, our chef, looked angry, probably because I left my toys in the kitchen again, but Mom, wearing her favorite penguin apron, shooed her away and squatted to my level, a wooden spatula in her hand.

"Rex, do you know cooking is like pretending? You use your imagination. You see, when I make this *Ragu Toscano*, I think about the love I put in it. They're little fairies dancing on the tomatoes, sprinkling magical dust into the pot. I imagine how when you eat it, you'll feel all of my love."

"Pretend? Like making up stories?"

She nodded. "Exactly. When I'm sad, angry, or scared, I play pretend. I create stories when I cook. Or I'd imagine my stuffed bunny, Alice, was alive. She'd cook with me and I wouldn't be afraid anymore."

I clutched my new T-Rex stuffed animal in my hands and stared up at her. Her brown hair was twisted in the back, the ceiling lights creating a halo behind her. She looked like an angel. I wondered how anyone could be so beautiful.

Wiping my tears on my sleeve, I looked down at my T-Rex. He was brave. He wasn't afraid of climbing trees and wasn't sad about his brothers not wanting to play with him. He ruled the world and *everyone* was afraid of him.

"Why are Maxwell and Ryland so brave? Why am I scared of everything?"

Mom laughed. "Silly. They used to be scared too, but sometimes, you have to face your fears in order to get over them. And in the meantime, I'm here and so is your friend."

She motioned to my T-Rex, and I hugged him, gave him a name.

Mom had smiled then. "Go on. Pick up your toys on the table and put them away. We always clean up after ourselves. I'll grab us some chocolate chip cookies and we can have a Mommy and Rex adventure, okay?"

Levi fake roars, drawing my attention back to the present.

Moments like this, having HSAM is bittersweet. I get to relive all the beautiful moments—every precious nugget embedded deep in my psyche. I remember the softness of her voice, how she smelled of freshly baked apple pies that day, the warmth of her body. Not a day goes by that I don't miss Mom, and in some ways, it's a relentless grief.

How can you truly let go of the past when you remember it all?

Levi giggles. He's the cutest triceratops in the world. Maxwell and Belle blow raspberries on his cheeks.

My heart twists at the image of outpouring love from the trio. Then I glance around the room, finding the same sticky, sweet emotion everywhere.

Grace holding hands with Steven, who's looking at her like she's his sole reason for existence.

Ryland grinning—the bastard smiles more now that he has Millie, his fiancée who used to be his student.

Even our resident goth, Taylor, has hearts in her eyes, her face flushing when Charles whispers something in her ear.

Lana laughs at Levi's happy shrieking because Maxwell is tickling him.

They don't need you to make them happy anymore.

That's been my role since Mom died. Give them joy because I took it away. But I think back to my earlier jokes—how they don't land anymore. How I can't make my family laugh anymore.

They don't need me now.

The hole widens inside my heart.

"You little monster. Daddy wasn't done with his meeting yet. Your uncle is being naughty." Maxwell buries his face in Levi's round tummy, eliciting more screeching and giggles.

"Uncle Rex is never naughty, only fun." I strain a lazy grin and walk to my nephew, who's trying to wiggle out of Maxwell's clasp, his grubby little hands reaching for me.

"Wax. Uncle Wax."

"Rex. Like the dinosaur...*roar*!" I grab him, hoist him under my arm like a football, and make a break for it.

Levi squeals, his joy piercing the heaviness in my chest.

"Uncle Wax is on timeout today. Your daddy says I'm in trouble. Why don't we break out of jail, find Silas, and play catch with him?"

"Pway! Doggie!"

"Do you know Uncle Wax used to have a T-Rex stuffy as a friend? His name was Kazoo. I think I know just what to get you for Christmas."

"T-Wax! Ka-Ka S-See," he repeats himself, the cute little pumpkin trying to mimic me.

In another life, I'd love to have a mini-me. I'd be a fun dad. My heart twinges. Too bad I'm stuck in the current one.

"Rex! What's your choice?" Maxwell hollers after me. "And don't say I didn't warn you; Greg Masters and the press will be on the cruise. We need good PR."

There's definitely no way I'm off the cruise. It's the only thing keeping me sane now. The only thing resembling meaning in my life.

It's my last lifeline as I hang over a cliff, my palms sweaty, my arms fatigued.

Images of Mom and Raya's stiff bodies slam into my vision.

It's atonement.

My palms sweat when I think about not being on the cruise. Not getting a chance to save someone. Or save myself.

There *is* no other choice. It's a desperate need. I'd do anything to be on board.

"Fine. I'll see Olivia on the cruise. But no meds. That's my condition."

I'm already hopped up on Velowake. I don't want more meds in my system. I don't trust myself enough to take them without abusing them.

But Olivia? I'll charm her and get her to give me a clean bill of health. I don't have to tell her anything.

It'll be fine.

But I have a feeling I've signed up for much more than I bargained for.

Chapter Eight

I HEAR THE LIGHTER clicking before I see him.

Slowly, I release my breath. He's here. This mission is happening. Other than a text last week with the location and time, Elias has been silent.

For a moment there, I was afraid he didn't want to involve me anymore. That he'd take away my chance at atonement.

"For someone who's supposed to be invisible, you sure make yourself conspicuous," I say.

The side door closes behind me with a bang, cutting off the icy early March wind and faint drizzle outside.

Looming shadows cloak the dark hangar at Teterboro, the structure empty except for one lonely jet parked inside. My aircraft is in the Fleur hangar on the other side of the airport, and I know my staff is getting it ready for our evening flight to Greece.

Our. Because Olivia will be there for my first mandatory therapy session.

My pulse quickens at the thought of the woman I'm not supposed to be attracted to because she's my sisters' best friend. And definitely not now, because she's the doctor to my patient.

The first time I saw her was a quick glimpse at Steven and Grace's wedding. She was in a sparkly dress that clung to her perfect curves.

Then there was the smile she directed at Taylor, her close friend, who later introduced her to the rest of the family.

That smile was blinding. Genuine. She radiated joy. It was like walking into a sweets shop and ingesting its entire inventory in one sitting. My fingers twitched. My heart banged against my rib cage. I felt lightheaded and nauseous.

I wanted that smile directed *at* me.

Then I thought, how could someone seem so happy when I was struggling inside?

A selfish and dark craving slithered in. To snuff out the smile as much as I wanted to see it again. I wondered if she was hiding any shadows like me. If she'd still smile that way if someone dug up her secrets.

It was certifiable. The thought alone terrified me, and I've stayed away from her ever since.

But because my willpower is abysmal, I keep thinking about the night at Mystique a month ago. Her guileless eyes, the hint of pain in them, a rousing echo calling to my own.

And that pure, unblemished white dress.

The same dark craving from years ago resurrects—only amplified.

Another dark rumination begins—deviant thoughts of what I'd like to do to her. Or better yet, how I wanted to undo her poised, good-girl exterior.

Unspool. Despoil. Thread by thread.

The clicking stops. Then starts back up again.

"You assume I was trying to make myself invisible," a familiar raspy voice finally replies.

His words are cryptic, but that's par for the course for the man who's known as the dealer of secrets. The fucker talks in riddles too.

Elias Kent steps out from behind the jet, the dreary daylight cloaking his angular face in stark contrast. The weather gods must love him because the bluish lighting somehow highlights the singular long scar spanning one side of his face.

It looks good. Sexy even.

Maybe I should get a scar. That'll make my outsides match my insides.

"Do I even want to know what you're thinking?" he asks, cocking one dark eyebrow.

"I'm thinking you look fucking hot with a scar. I need one. The ladies will dig it. Where do you think it should be? On the cheek like yours?"

His lips twitch. Barely, but I see it. See? I can charm even the coldest of criminals.

"But then people might accuse me of copying you, and Rex-a-Million copies no one. Maybe the upper lip like a dashing pirate. But the damn lighting won't hit it the same way."

He snaps the lighter shut and rolls his eyes. "You love hearing your own voice, don't you?"

"No. It gets monotonous hearing the voice equivalent of mind-blowing sex 24/7, but I can't deprive the world of that, you know? There's enough bad sex as is."

Elias rubs his temples and mutters something unintelligible under his breath. Probably like *I don't have time for this shit,* or *why did I wake up this morning?*

Or perhaps *I should stab him with a knife, carve him up like a Thanksgiving turkey, and feed his entrails to my enemies.*

If only. That'll end my miserable existence. I shudder in horror or excitement. I can't tell the difference anymore. I guess my quest to transform myself from the scaredy cat of my younger years to the daredevil I am now has worked too well.

He levels his deep green eyes at me. "I'm fucking regretting this already."

"Lighten up. Even the mobster needs a break from brooding all day."

"Are you sure you're up for this? Because we can't blow it this time."

The smile slips off my face, and I straighten, because this is important. This is my chance to redo it.

Oh please, Rex. Nothing will bring them back. There *are* no re-dos in life.

I clench my hands into fists. "I got this, Elias. I won't let you or her down."

Raya's dying moments barge into my mind—the same images I relive night after night.

Her hand grips mine, but the pressure is softening. Damn it, I'm losing her.

"Stay with me, Raya. Fuck. Stay with me." I cradle her in my arms. It wasn't supposed to end this way. They weren't supposed to find her.

She coughs, and blood seeps out of her bullet wound.

Fuck. So much blood. Just like Mom all those years ago.

I press my handkerchief onto her wound.

It's useless. She grows paler by the second.

"M-Make sure Ava and Cora are safe," she rasps, her breaths sawing out of her. "Don't let him find them. Get them o-out, tell them I'm sorry I can't b-be with them."

"Don't you dare, Raya. You tell them yourself. You'll see them soon."

Blood bathes my fingers. Desperation convulses my insides as I press harder. Two hands now.

Raya's eyes roll backward, and her grip on me slowly loosens. No. It can't end this way. I can't have another death on my hands.

She whispers, "P-Promise me. Tell them I l-love them."

Raw, anguished sobs bellow inside the nondescript motel room.

"No, Raya. Don't give up on me. You need to see your girls grow up and get married. Kids need their moms. F-Fuck. Don't—"

"I don't blame you." Her lips barely move, but I hear her.

Then she's gone.

It's only then when I realize the racking sobs come from me.

I remember the wet metallic smell of damp earth mixed with blood, the sound of raindrops hitting against the small picture window, her faint vanilla perfume.

I failed another mom with kids that day. Just like I failed our mom and my siblings suffered because of it. Logic tells me the two events aren't related, but it doesn't feel this way. The guilt presses heavily on my lungs. The what-ifs. The what could bes.

My mind's a maximum security prison, and I'm serving a life sentence.

Will the guilt ever go away? If I do this, get this other woman to safety, will I be able to breathe again?

Will I finally be free?

With determination pulsing through me, I stride to Elias. "It'll be different this time. I promise you. I joke and fuck around, but not with this. *Never* with this."

The mobster holds my gaze, his sharp eyes assessing. His leather gloves creak when he clenches, then releases his fingers.

Finally, he nods. "I believe you. Against all common sense, I believe you. You know the plan, right?"

"Unlike last time, she'll travel with me and be Rex Anderson's newest plaything. I'll flirt and act like she's one of my flings."

Frankly, I was lucky The Association didn't connect me with Raya last time. We tried to be discreet. I used a fake name and only interacted with her a few times while wearing a disguise.

I continue, "They won't suspect her at all because they won't think you'll hide her in plain sight. No one will believe Rex-a-Million the playboy will be involved in something so dangerous. When we get to Monaco, I'll meet with your person and he'll shuttle her to a safe house for a fresh start. Simple."

My pulse quickens as I go over the encrypted details he sent me last week.

I know the woman's new identity. Bree Williams, thirty-five, a graduate from Vassar, interior designer relocating to Monaco to work with the rich and famous. Based on what I've pieced together, she was a hacker who penetrated The Association's firewalls. She's on the run because of something she's found, but I don't know what.

It's suspicious as fuck and I should think twice before jumping into this mess.

Elias redacted much of the information, but I'm not surprised. There's a reason he's dangerous and feared by the mafia, the Bratva, and other criminal organizations alike. It isn't because he's bloodthirsty or gory, but because he has something on everyone and no one knows when he'll use their secrets against them.

I don't know what beef he has with The Association or why he's repeatedly tried to thwart them.

It doesn't matter.

I think about the unspeakable assault they did to Taylor when she was sixteen in a member-initiation ceremony where people commit an atrocious crime to join their ranks. Then, there was Alexis's coma for eight years, which wasn't from an accident at all, and Ethan nearly drowning in the Hudson last year. All because they want our family to join them, to be part of their greed and power to take over the world.

The Association wants the Andersons to be involved with them? Well, they fucking got their wish.

Elias nods. "Good. I'll be on the cruise at some point. That won't be unusual since I usually man the personnel on the Rose floors anyway. Act normal and it should be smooth sailing."

"A pun. You realized you just made a cruise pun?"

He ignores me. "Any questions before I bring her out so you can chat before the flight?"

At my silence, he turns and walks toward a nondescript door tucked in the back.

"What's in it for you, Elias? What do you have against The Association?" I holler after him.

Curiosity killed the cat, and apparently, I have a death wish.

I know my reasons for risking my life.

But Elias? I'd think he'd want to join The Association, not go after them.

It makes no sense.

Elias stops, the next words coming out in a barely there whisper. "Well, we all have our skeletons, don't we?"

CHAPTER NINE

SHE'S BEAUTIFUL.

I watch them from the corner of my eye in my spot at a small dinette in the jet. Rex is with a gorgeous woman—tall, statuesque, generous curves in all the right places, dark-chocolate-colored hair in a blunt bob only women with her bone structure can pull off. He snakes his arm around her waist, all the while balancing an air of intimacy with respectful distance at the same time.

They're laughing. He doles out one of those infamous panty-melting grins as he whispers something in her ear. A faint flush creeps up her face, which seems to be the desired response, based on the satisfied glint in his eyes.

My stomach twists—damn, I've heard of seasick, not air sick. Is it because I forgot to grab dinner before coming aboard?

The woman giggles, and Rex kisses her cheek. I narrow my eyes and imagine him as a voodoo doll.

Womanizer. A pinprick. *Someone who probably hasn't worked hard for a day in his life.* Another pinprick. *Has had everything handed to him. Asshole. Hedonist. Makes selfish decisions without caring how they impact others.* I chuck all my pins at the doll.

Your patient.

Blowing out a breath, I attempt to rationalize away my ridiculous thoughts.

I shouldn't think this way. This is mean and I'm a goddamn professional. Our personalities just don't jibe with each other, that's all. It's not the first time I have to work with someone I don't like. I'm doing this for the greater good—helping my friends and securing a much-needed donation for ADAS.

Rex Anderson is a troubled man, and even if the man is resistant to medication, as Lana told me before the trip, I can help him.

I don't miss the signs.

My stomach grumbles now. I glance at my cell. Eight p.m. I should've planned better.

I pull out one of Mom's cookies from my purse and munch on it. Ugh. Almond-flavored cardboard. I quickly swallow the whole thing.

Mom's call from last night reverberates in my ears. "Eat on time, Olivia," followed by her disappointing sigh when she said, "You aren't coming back, are you?" She tried enticing me with mentions of braised pork belly and a new sushi restaurant she found, activities Mia would've enjoyed.

She asked me if I received her tin of almond cookies, and I told her I even brought it with me so I could finish them before they went bad. Then she reminisced about how I loved her cookies when I was little, and I huffed out a laugh and changed the subject. No need to hurt her feelings.

"Why would you go on a cruise, Olivia? You have patients at home. They'd want to see you in person. This isn't like you," she said.

It's something Mia would do.

While she didn't mention her by name, my sister's presence permeated our conversation and I couldn't help but be hurt again.

Even in death, she shines brighter than me. The world is dimmer without her spark, her effervescence—the brave, exciting Lin twin.

But you can shine too, Olivia. What's holding you back?

Not everything has to explode like fireworks. Stars glow at night and their brightness is beautiful too.

Instead of ruminating on the hurt, I focus on Mom's parting words, "Have you eaten yet?"

Because that's how she tells me she loves me.

It's hard not to miss the person who's gone forever, but it doesn't mean she loves me any less.

Low murmuring reaches my ears and I look up again, finding Rex saying something to Bree before she disappears inside one of the two bedrooms in the back.

My gut knots again.

Definitely asking an attendant for some real food later.

Turning away, I admire the most luxurious airplane I've ever been on. Buttery soft tan leather, dark woods and sleek chrome lining the walls, deep navy and amber carpet which looks imported from somewhere.

It's surreal how I'm even here. My family is staunchly from the middle class, my parents owning a Chinese fusion restaurant in the San Gabriel Valley, a stone's throw away from downtown LA. I had student loans up to my eyeballs by the time I graduated from Harvard for undergrad and medical school.

Before everything happened with Mia, I thought I'd move back home after graduation, work at a research hospital for a handful of years before opening a small private practice. Our parents would be proud of us. I'd make a comfortable living and settle down with a regular guy who didn't live at home, knew how to cook and run a dishwasher, and we'd have two point five kids and live happily ever after.

But none of that happened.

Everything changed after my sister died.

And now I'm here, unable to return to LA, single, using work as a shield from anything risky or fun because I'm the only Lin twin earth side.

I have to be perfect. I have to make the right choices. I'm the only one my parents have left. I'm spared whatever affliction Mia had, so I need to spend the rest of my life saving people like her.

I have to live *for* her because she isn't here anymore.

And deep down, perhaps I'm trying to heal the brokenhearted because it's too late for me.

"Olivia, have I ever told you how beautiful your eyes are?"

I startle, so deep in my thoughts I didn't see him walking over.

Rex sprawls into the seat across from me, his fingers idly toying with a button on his shirt collar. Swallowing, I try not to notice how he's the definition of a virile, hot man.

How his dark and messy hair begs me to run my fingers through it. How his strong nose and the enticing divot on his top lip look like they came out of an art textbook depicting ideal male beauty.

And those eyes...the pools of quicksilver.

He winks.

I snap out of it. *What on earth has gotten into me?*

I frown. "Come again?"

"I know most guys would say they like blue eyes, or green," he crosses one ankle over his knee, the perfect posture of nonchalance, "but I like brown. And yours aren't really brown, right?"

He smiles, the whites of his teeth blinding, but it doesn't reach his eyes. "No. Brown's not the right word. Yours are the color of rich, smooth whiskey—one taste and I'll be bewitched for life."

My heart skips against my wishes.

Bewitched.

No one has ever used that word to describe the no-nonsense, play-it-safe Olivia Lin. It calls to the flickering energy nestled deep inside me, the incessant whisper, *"Don't you want to shine now? Aren't you tired of living in the shadows?"*

But as I examine his brittle smile, clock the dullness in his eyes, my chest caves a little.

Lip service. His compliment isn't real.

And I know what game he's playing at.

I school my face into one of indifference and pull out a notebook and a pen from my tote. Then I set it neatly on the desk—notebook to the left, pen to the right.

"Thank you. And whatever you're doing, save it. It won't work on me. And plus, your friend," I eye the closed bedroom door where

Bree was, "probably wouldn't appreciate her man flirting with another woman."

The sleazy pig.

Rex freezes, clearly not used to women not responding to his charm. *Take that, sucker. Don't give out compliments you don't mean.* I inwardly smile. It's petty and unprofessional, but I'm only human.

"I don't know what you're talking about. Only speaking the truth. And I'm not her man."

I frown. He isn't? They seem awfully chummy.

He shrugs but doesn't offer more. Then he reaches over and nudges my notebook to one side and flicks my pen to the other.

Like he knows it'll drive me nuts.

He cocks his brow.

I narrow my eyes.

Not taking the bait, asshole.

"Ready to begin our first session?" I grab the pen and uncap it. There's no one else in the dinette, so this place is as good as any.

Silence falls between us, and I wait.

One second.

Two seconds.

Three seconds.

The air thickens.

A muscle jumps in his jaw.

He's going to snap.

"Let's cut the fucking crap."

And there it is.

CHAPTER TEN

HIS FAKE SMILE VANISHES like an apparition, and in its place are hardened eyes and a clenched jaw.

"I'm sure Maxwell already told you I got dragged into this. I don't believe in your mental psychobabble, and I don't need help." He slowly leans over the table between us, a clear ploy to intimidate me with his size.

His cologne—sandalwood and pine—hits my nose.

My mouth waters. Dammit, I really need food.

"And I know you don't want to do this either. Lana told me she begged you to take me on. So let's stop wasting each other's time. You make a few notes, scribble whatever it is you want on that little notepad of yours. We'll stay out of each other's hair and you can enjoy your trip—shopping, sightseeing, spa treatments—while I do mine." Rex sits back down.

"You're telling me to lie?" I press my lips into a thin line, remembering what I thought about him that night at Mystique.

He doesn't want to do the work and you can't help someone who refuses to help themselves.

You can't help someone who doesn't even *ask* for help.

These people will ultimately hurt everyone around them. Then who's left to pick up the pieces?

"Call it whatever you want. If you're a stickler to the rules, which, judging from that adorable frown on your face, you are, then fine. We can have a few chats. Talk about the weather. Then, you can mark down we've met. Either way, I'm not doing this."

"You seem to have forgotten your participation in therapy is the prerequisite for your being on this cruise, Mr. Anderson." I take a deep breath and level my stare at him.

Angling the notebook toward me, I jot down some preliminary notes.

Uncooperative. Uses charm to get what he wants. When that fails, turns to intimidation.

Rex's eyes sharpen at my motions, the soft sounds of pen scratching against paper adding to the tension quickly rising between us.

He'll break. Men like him hate people they can't control. They definitely don't like the idea of someone taking down their secrets and not letting them see.

"Are you threatening me?" he rasps.

I pause my writing and set the notebook and pen down. Neatly, as always. "No. I'm a psychiatrist. Why would I threaten you?" Then I dole out a saccharine smile.

He flinches.

"I'm just reminding you of the deal. So, let me tell you how it's going to go, Mr. Anderson." It's my turn to lean forward now. "I'm a doctor because I want to help people. Mental health issues might be invisible to the naked eye, but they are real problems and near and dear to my heart. If left untreated, they devastate not only the patient, but also others around them."

I pull out my phone and flip to a few screenshots I saved because I predicted this would happen.

Turning it around, I show them to him. His face pales. "These are headlines of articles Maxwell stopped in the nick of time before they were published. I have videos too."

"Drunk billionaire spiraling out—Is Rex Anderson the downfall of a dynasty?"

"'He keeps popping these pills. I don't know what they are and I don't want any part of it,' a model and influencer exclaims. Exclusive on the playboy prince inside."

"A ménage à trois is no longer de rigeur. Rex-a-Million rumored to be the only man in a twelve-person orgy."

"Marketing genius destined for premature death? Rumors swirl about the remaining Anderson bachelor."

"I can show you more."

He shoves my phone to the side and looks away. A vein pulses in his temple. "No, I've seen enough."

"I don't know you well, Mr. Anderson. But then again, I don't think anyone truly knows you well. But an average, well-adjusted man in his mid-to-late thirties doesn't behave this way. And we all know you're anything but average, right?"

I tap my fingers on the table, drawing his attention back to me. "I don't want to fight you on this. I have no skin in the game other than a doctor caring about her patient and wanting what's best for him."

All right, that might be pushing it, since I want the Anderson funds for ADAS, but he doesn't need to know that.

Shoving the thought away, I add, "But you? If rumors are correct, this cruise venture is your idea—the first and most expensive project in recent years spearheaded by you. I don't know the first thing about planning a cruise, but I bet it's hard work. You don't put in those hours unless you want it to succeed, unless you have something to prove."

Rex stiffens, his face darkening as storm clouds brew over his head.

Standing up, I grab my tote bag and slip the notebook back inside. Emotions are too high right now and this session won't go anywhere. It's better to let him stew over it and try again next time.

"You have a wonderful family," I murmur.

He falters, his eyes snapping to mine. His gloomy countenance softens. Clearly, he's thinking about them.

The Andersons are a tight bunch. Each sibling would go to bat for each other, and I've witnessed it firsthand. When Maxwell was spiraling from untreated PTSD and anxiety, Ryland contacted me immediately, desperate to help his brother. The siblings rallied around Taylor when the press tried to eat her alive after her past trauma came to light.

My chest squeezes, and I wish I had that for myself.

Despite Mia's faults, I miss her so much.

"Maxwell thought you might be reluctant, and he instructed me to tell him if you backed out of therapy. One call from me and he'd send security to escort you back to the city. I was told, 'bound and gagged if need be.'"

I don't believe in violence, but now, having had my first real conversation with the infuriating man, I can understand where Maxwell is coming from.

Rex's jaw works, a flush creeping up his face. His hand curls into a fist, his arm trembling from restraint.

I don't know what comes over me.

Maybe it's the faint sheen of moisture gathering in his eyes, which could be a trick of the dim cabin lighting or the way his breath throttles out of him like he's ashamed.

Unbidden, I place my hand over his.

He freezes, and I jolt from the barrage of sensations coursing over my skin from that tiny point of contact. It's like being hit by lightning and surviving to tell the tale.

Quickly, I let go, but he snags my fingers with his, those silver eyes riveted at our hands.

My pulse roars in my ears. *Why am I touching him? I shouldn't touch my patients.*

I try pulling away, but he tightens his grip, the seconds dragging, the pressure increasing until it's borderline painful.

"You're playing with fire, Olivia," he growls.

My breath catches, the raspy, sinewy undertones of his voice prickling my skin, coiling between my legs.

Lighting me up like fireworks bursting in the night sky.

"L-Let go of me."

He strangles my hand in his and I whimper from the sensations—still not quite pain, but not far away from it, either. Then, abruptly, he loosens his grip.

Blood rushes back into my fingers, a thousand pinpricks exploding in my nerves. He fans the flames by skating his thumb over my palm, then moving to my inner wrist.

"You don't want the bomb to explode, Olivia. Don't test me." The warning is barely above a whisper.

But I do. I want to face the bomb head-on. Pick at it. Disarm it. Or maybe I want it to incinerate me.

Is this a latent, masochistic, perverse need? An occupational hazard?

I swallow, my mind dizzy, my lungs seizing like they can't draw in enough oxygen.

He swipes his thumb across my pulse again, and I watch those beautiful eyes of his darken as he rests his finger on my wrist, like he can tell how fast my heart is beating for him.

How maddening he's making me feel.

What the hell are you doing? This is completely unprofessional, Olivia. You know better than to get rattled.

I snatch my hand away, my chest heaving even though I barely moved a muscle.

Slowly, he angles his head up, and I see his face under the direct light for the first time.

His pupils are dilated, gray irises nowhere to be seen. The dark circles are prominent under his eyes. His lips part, his skin flushed. A muscle twitches in his sharp jawline, begging me to trace it with my fingers.

His gaze drops to my lips. My lungs stop working.

I'm thrown back to that night at Mystique again, except this time, he's within touching distance.

Kissing distance.

What would it feel like to be kissed by the prince of pleasure? What would it be like to let go?

My nipples harden and I stumble, taking a step back.

Danger.

"It's *Doctor* Lin to you, Mr. Anderson. Not Olivia. *Never* Olivia during our sessions. I don't cheat or lie for my patients. Never have and never will." I draw a deep inhale, and the temporary dizziness fades. "And I've never resorted to blackmailing my patients before, but you know what they say. There's always a first time."

Pivoting, I step toward the other bedroom, but not before turning back. "So don't *you* test me."

I stride away, my heart thundering, mis-calibrating. I can almost believe we're flying into the eye of a storm. But I need to do better—control my irrational thoughts and turbulent emotions, and not let him get to me. My professional reputation is at stake. The millions in funding for ADAS are at stake. He could complain to Maxwell or his peers about my unprofessionalism.

Stick it out for Las Fallas, Olivia. For Mia. Stick it out for patients benefiting from ADAS.

Tension thickens with each step I take, the distance between us stretching.

I expect him to blow up, to throw a tantrum, to grab me by my wrist and give me a piece of his mind.

But he doesn't.

Instead, he laughs, the low, dark chuckles renewing the heat in my veins.

Then he claps. Harsh. Loud. Whiplashes against my skin.

He mocks me.

"Little Olivia has claws," he murmurs. "Or I mean, *Doctor* Lin. I'm looking forward to testing *every single limit* you have."

A bolt of heat shoots straight to my clit as unwanted images of limbs tangled in passion invade my mind. *Insanity.* Maybe Lana's right. I need to find a man on this trip and get laid. It's been too long, and it's messing with my head.

I quicken my pace, needing distance from this unnerving, unsuitable man.

The devil incarnate.

"Until the next match, *Doctor*."

His chuckles follow me all the way to the open bedroom door.

Chapter Eleven

Biting my lip, I press my face against the passenger window, barely containing my excitement as our SUV careens down the narrow, winding road from the airport to Tourlos Port in Mykonos, where our cruise ship, The Orchid Royale, is docked.

I've never been to Greece before. Heck, I've rarely traveled outside the summer trips with Mia and my parents to Taiwan in middle school to visit our ailing grandparents. Even then, we wouldn't have time to sightsee. We'd spend most of our days at the elderly care center. I'd listen to Grandma ramble about me being too skinny, how I needed to eat more to have the energy to study and earn good grades.

Have you eaten yet?

I smile inwardly. Maybe Mom got the phrase from Grandma.

After cracking open the window, I poke my head out to get a better view of this beautiful city.

Soft chuckles reach my ears, and I hear the faint sound of a camera shutter. Then I feel the distinct pressure of someone's attention on me from the backseat.

I whip my head around.

Rex, manspread on the plush leather seat, a lazy tiger stretching out his limbs, is staring at me as if planning his next move to take me down. Bree sits quietly next to him.

He twirls his phone in one hand, his gaze sharpening as he scrapes his long fingers over the sexy scruff decorating his jaw. His attention settles over me like a blanket, and I don't know if I want to kick it off or snuggle deeper into it. He cocks his brow and winks.

Unable to help myself, I mutter to Bree, "Watch out for this one. He flirts with anyone with a vagina."

Ah shit. Why did I say that? I bite my tongue, and heat rushes to my face. The damn bastard chuckles.

Bree snaps her gaze to me, her eyes widening. "Oh, we're not like that." She glances at Rex then back at me. "None of my business."

Huh? That's what Rex implied last night. But the casual hand-holding, the brief touches. I'm so damn confused.

None of your business, Olivia.

Rex arches his brow again. He taunts, *"See, what did I say?"*

Rolling my eyes, I look away, finding Bree frowning, obviously deep in thought. She's clenching her sundress like she's nervous.

I frown as I watch her twist the fabric, releasing it, then twisting it again.

When she catches me looking, clear panic flashes in her blue eyes before it disappears. Then she smiles and relaxes.

Straining a grin, I turn my attention back to the infuriating man next to her, who still has his unnerving attention on me. And in this strange game of chicken, I look away as the car comes to a stop.

Without waiting for the staff to open the door, I jump out, clutching my Leica M6 camera hung around my neck, eager to get my first full glimpse of the city where we'll be spending the next few days before setting off to Santorini.

Locals and tourists on their scooters zoom by, a line of luxury sedans and limos idling at the curb. Porters dressed in livery assist women clad in the latest cruise fashions out of their cars. Mono-grammed luggage is neatly stacked and shuttled to the massive cruise ship ahead.

I ignore the chaos—the loud conversations in Greek and English, the blaring car honks. Instead of heading to the ship, I beeline toward a small clearing, my lungs raking in the crisp air of brine and rosemary, my eyes absorbing the endless stretch of vibrant cobalt of the Aegean Sea glinting under the harsh sunlight peeking from behind the clouds.

Carefully, I adjust the dials, lift my camera, and take a photo.

I'm here, Mia. About to turn thirty, on my way to Las Fallas. You asked me to burn our regrets. I know what regrets I have, but you never told me yours.

Perhaps this is why I bury myself in work and avoid vacations. When the mind slows down, it wanders. It was easy to distract myself before—the heavy coursework in college and medical school, the grueling hours of residency, working at the hospital, and then later on, starting my practice.

I told myself this was me using my time wisely, making responsible choices for my patients, and not having my parents worry about me.

But now, at the cusp of thirty, away from everything I've numbed myself with, I finally realize the extent of my hollowness. The frustration. The discontent.

Will I finally get the answers? Will I be at peace, something that has eluded me since that morning when I found her still in her bed, a bottle of sleeping pills empty by her bedside?

Will I finally stop blaming myself?

Heart heavy, I make my way to the cruise ship entrance, knowing the porters will take care of my luggage.

"Welcome aboard The Orchid Royale, Dr. Lin." A stewardess dressed in a lavender sheath dress smiles as I cross the threshold.

My eyes widen at the instant recognition. I'm a nobody in these circles. But then again, this is The Orchid on water. I shouldn't expect anything less.

She hands me a brochure on thick card stock. "Your stateroom is specifically tailored to your tastes. The information is inside. Your room has a biometric lock, which can only be opened with the fingerprint you provided in your application to The Orchid."

I thank her and follow the passengers in front of me, my attention riveted on the brochure.

Name: *The Orchid Royale*

Class: White Orchid-Class Ultra-Luxury Vessel

Length: 750 ft

Decks: 10 guest-accessible (plus restricted floors for staff, logistics, and The Bridge)

Cruising Speed: 20 knots

Guest Capacity: 500 (max)—never over 60% booked for maximum exclusivity

Crew-to-Guest Ratio: 1.5:1

Flag: Private registry

Designed in collaboration with Swiss naval engineers,
Japanese spa architects, and Parisian interior designers,
The Orchid Royale is more than a ship, it's a sanctuary
that sails.

Whistling under my breath, I marvel at the over-the-top luxury
described, from the Twilight Cinema on the sky deck to the multiple
specialty spas, infinity pools, and exclusive restaurants featuring the
top chefs of the world. The staterooms are one of a kind as well. Unlike typical cruise ships, each suite comes with a full gourmet kitchen
with gas stoves—I honestly don't know how this is to safety code,
but where there's a will, there's a way—housekeeper and concierge
services, all the bells and whistles.

And of course, The Orchid, even on water, isn't complete without the Rose floors, which in this case, span decks nine and ten. Now
I understand why, despite us docking at each location for a few days,
the itinerary doesn't mention moving to hotels on land.

There are probably *no* hotels that can match the features and
luxury offered aboard.

Soft laughter reaches my ears and I look up, my breath stalling
when I see the towering entryway atrium—three stories of clear glass,
backlit with warm lighting, large crystal chandeliers dangling from
the ceiling, the lights reflecting off the pale marble floors.

Everything glitters and shines. I'd imagine Mount Olympus
from Greek mythology looked something like this.

My mind swims back to Rex's expression last night when I
hedged my barely veiled threats, banking on him wanting this cruise
to succeed because he had something to prove.

As I scan my surroundings, taking in the delicate florals—vibrant
hydrangeas, lavender, orchids, twisting vines—the modern and sleek
chaise lounges and sofas placed throughout the welcome lobby, I can
only imagine how much work he's put into it. If this venture flopped,

it'd be hard for any company to absorb the losses, even if the entity was Fleur Entertainment Holdings.

But why is he trying to prove himself?

He's the chief marketing officer and successful by any measure. Why does he look so troubled? *What is the playboy prince hiding?*

The questions propel me to deck five, where the wellness pavilion and medical bay are located.

The latter is abuzz with activity—two nurses in lavender scrubs bustling around the brightly lit space. The decor is modern hospital meets minimalistic spa—white walls, marble floors, LED screens, chrome accents throughout.

A redheaded nurse with a pixie cut glances my way, her lips curving into a bright smile before she hurries toward me.

"You're Dr. Lin, right? I'm Jessa, the day shift triage nurse. We've been waiting for you, since the other doctors here are men. It'll be nice to have another woman on the team. That's Fiona." She points to the Asian nurse, who waves at me. "There are six of us and we rotate shifts. Want me to show you around?"

"Lead the way." I grin, liking her bubbly personality already.

"I was so happy to be chosen for this trip. Can you imagine? A month in paradise? Sure, we'll probably have to deal with snobs, but I can put up with anyone when I'm stuffing myself with the best carbs Europe has to offer," she prattles on.

"To the right are private patient rooms," she says, rolling her eyes. "Fancier than my hotel room, but still too basic for someone recovering from a cliff dive gone wrong."

"Or a shellfish binge they're convinced is a heart attack," I add. "Although, let me know if anyone is cliff diving. I'd hate to miss a live Darwin Award in action." I grin, referencing the awards given to individuals who removed themselves from the gene pool, a.k.a. dying, by the stupid choices they made.

"Exactly! I knew I'd like you."

"I think I'll enjoy my time here too."

We move past the standard defibrillators, crash carts, oxygen tanks, and various equipment I expect to be on board.

"What's in there?" I point to a closed metal door.

"Surgical unit. They even built in floor stabilizers in the event emergency surgery was necessary. Let's hope we don't need it."

My eyebrow lifts. "Of course, they'd have a surgical unit. Why am I even surprised?"

"They'd probably fly surgeons over here if shit happens. There's no such thing as expenses with these guys."

Nodding, I follow as she pivots down a corridor matching the decor from the outside—marble floors, glass walls, some of which are opaque, others clear, revealing private rooms.

"These are your offices. There's another patient entrance on the other side, away from the clinic. There are two other doctors on board—Dr. John Mackintosh, cardiologist, because most of these geezers are walking heart attacks, and Dr. Rhys Fenton, our generalist and trauma surgeon."

As if on cue, a striking man in a white coat with raven hair almost as black as mine steps out, thin silver frames perched on his nose. "Jessa, can you get me—"

He looks up and spots us, his lips slowly curving into a charming smile. I don't miss the quick but thorough scan he does of me.

"You're Dr. Olivia Lin. I'm Rhys. I've been a big fan since I read your exciting analysis on SSRIs and addiction therapies." He strides over and gives my barely outstretched hand a hearty shake. Then he directs another megawatt smile at me.

I wait for my heart to skip a beat. The man is tall, dark, and handsome, looks like he doesn't live at home, has all his hair and teeth, and can most likely run a dishwasher. His cooking skills are to be determined, but I'm hopeful.

But my body doesn't seem to care.

No flutter in my gut. No quickening pulse.

Instead, my mind wanders to the brooding playboy, the man, *my patient*, who doesn't seem to like me that much.

How my nipples beaded into hard points when his low laughter followed me back into the bedroom on the jet, where I tossed and turned most of the night, hallucinating the deep, rumbly voice whispering sweet nothings into my ear.

Dammit.

Rhys cocks his head to the side, clearly waiting for me to respond, and I inwardly slap myself. "Nice to meet you. Call me Olivia."

"And just like that, my day has gotten brighter," he murmurs. Turning to Jessa, he asks, "Can you get me Mr. Reinhart's files? He wants to meet later today."

Before stepping back into his room, he motions to the empty office next to him. "Looks like we'll be office mates, Olivia. I'd love to take you out for coffee—get to know you better." A flirty wink later, he disappears inside and closes his door.

"Looks like you're going to have your hands full," Jessa quips, sneaking me a sly grin.

"No way. Whatever you're thinking, it's not happening."

After idle chitchat and booting up my computer only to realize my schedule, including the teleconferences with my existing patients back in New York, has been preloaded, I shoot a quick message to my parents, telling them I've safely boarded the ship and not to worry about me.

Then I make my way to the sky deck with my camera.

I want the sun on my face and to snap some photos. Mia would appreciate them.

The sky deck is quiet as I turn at the top of the steps. Most guests are no doubt settling in their staterooms and resting.

"What do you mean there's a problem?"

The unmistakable low rasp stops me in my tracks.

It's Rex Anderson, and he sounds angry.

CHAPTER TWELVE

"THE ENTIRE ORCHESTRA CAME down with norovirus. They can't perform until Dubrovnik," a stocky man in a black suit says while blotting his forehead with a tissue.

He looks seconds away from expiring in front of Rex.

The party prince himself is anything but carefree at the moment. He glances in my direction but I duck behind a column just in time, my heart pounding.

Why the hell am I hiding, anyway? This is public space. It's not like I'm breaking any rules.

"Carpe diem, Olive. Break some rules." Mia's imaginary laughter reaches my ears.

"Do we have backup? Symphony under the stars is tonight, Gregory."

Gregory pinches his nose. "No, not for this one. Vienna Orchestra was the first to confirm and reconfirm. We didn't think there'd be a need for a backup."

"Fuck!" Rex slams his hands on the railing, his dark hair ruffled by the wind.

"Sir, perhaps we should apol—"

"Give me a second. Let me think."

What happens next has my traitorous pulse clamoring, the very reaction I was hoping to get when I met Dr. Rhys Fenton earlier.

Rex, in his towering, navy-suit-wearing glory, straightens. He grips the railing and tilts his face toward the sky.

The stark bluish daylight—the sun having disappeared behind thick clouds while I was at the medical bay—collides against the sharp panes of his face like a violent painting, as if the artist couldn't decide if he loved or hated his subject.

Rex's corded throat works. His eyes are closed, his lips moving, but I don't hear any words spoken.

A ridiculous thought crosses my mind. It's like he's trying to absorb the elements, to distill energy from them.

I grab my camera, my fingers moving on autopilot, and snap photo after photo, the image of him burning into my retina.

This version of Rex Anderson—raw, rough, and complicated—feels like the real him.

What are you hiding? Why are you hiding?

His eyes snap open, and he stares at the cerulean seas. "Here's what we're going to do. Spin a story in our favor. Call Lana and reword as you see fit."

Gregory takes out his phone. "Ready when you are, sir."

"Imagine a once-in-a-lifetime, mythical experience. The Temple of Apollo, an immersive auditory adventure set inside a reconstructed Grecian temple on the open seas."

An electrifying energy pulses from him as he weaves invisible threads to form a bewitching tapestry. "The Oracle of Delphi has learned of the prestigious individuals aboard this vessel and will bless us with her presence a millennium after she appeared in ancient Greece. She offers us the rare opportunity—delivering prophecies to the guests."

"Prophecies, sir?" Gregory blanches. "H-How are we—"

"Honestly, I don't fucking care. Get fortune cookies if you need to and make them sound fancy. There's nothing old money likes more than learning they are destined for greatness. Feeds their ego."

I stifle a snort. He isn't wrong there.

"Got it."

"The prime minister knows about the cruise. I'll call him to invite his most talented cultural musicians. We'll say we're spotlighting their culture and thanking them for their wonderful Greek hospitality. Ninety percent of the world's wealth is on this cruise and a lot of money can funnel into the government here. He'll bend over backward to accommodate."

Gregory nods, his fingers flying over his phone, clearly taking copious notes.

"You got the details, right? I don't need to do that for you, do I?"

"No, sir. We'll have everything prepared for tonight." The man has his phone to his ear as he scurries away to do Rex's bidding.

A satisfied sigh escapes Rex's lips as he faces the ocean again. I can't help but smile at what I just saw—quick thinking, creative and meaningful, like all the Fleur marketing campaigns I've seen before.

I used to think these campaigns, like last year's Project Echo, a silent red carpet premiere for a biopic about a non-verbal neurodivergent artist, resulted from his stellar marketing team. After all, before today, I've only seen him joking with his family, taking nothing seriously, or flirting shamelessly with women.

A prickle of guilt pinches me. This is why I shouldn't be so quick to judge. Back on the jet, I thought he was one of those guys who had everything handed to him. But now, I'm not so sure. Maybe all those successful campaigns came from him, because he's good at what he does.

Then what are you trying to prove, Rex?

The earlier tension in his shoulders isn't visible anymore, but instead of looking happy or relieved from a crisis averted, he takes out something from his pocket—a small red ball? After staring at it for a few seconds, he puts it away and grips the railing again, eyes closed, obviously deep in thought.

And because my impulse control is low today, I steal a few more photos of him.

"I'd think doctors are well educated enough to know eavesdropping and secretly taking photos of people are rude," he murmurs, his back still facing me.

I startle, my camera slipping out of my hands. Thank God it's strapped around my neck.

"I didn't want to intrude."

He scoffs. "So, where's that magical little notepad of yours? What did you glean from learning about my cruise getting off to a rocky start? Waiting for me to fail spectacularly? For trying to be anything but the fun Anderson?"

My brows pinch, my feet carrying me toward him before I realize what I'm doing. "Why do you do this?"

"What?" He finally turns to face me.

"Hate yourself. Talk down to yourself. Think you have nothing to offer other than the Rex-a-Million the public knows."

"I don't know what you're talking about." *Bullshit.*

"I'm not in a hurry. I'll wait." A wisp of hair slips out of my bun and I tuck it behind my ear. "We have an entire month for me to get the truth out of you."

Jaw clenching, he narrows his stormy eyes. "You know what? I've been trying to figure out why you're here. It can't only be a favor for Lana."

He steps toward me. "Is it money? I heard we're making a donation to your research society. You know, I can just wire you the funds from my personal account."

"No. I don't take handouts."

His piercing eyes rove over my face, then my body, and, damn it, my skin heats from his perusal.

Rex's nostrils flare. "No. Of course you won't." He leans in, and I smell his intoxicating scent of bergamot and amber.

"I'm good at reading people, Olivia." His voice ghosts over my skin and I shiver. "You're hiding something."

"And you're deflecting."

"I'm right though, aren't I? You accuse me of hiding because you're the one with secrets you don't want to see the light of day. So now who's deflecting?"

My traitorous heart kicks into a turbulent rhythm, much like the wind suddenly gusting around us. My training should kick in now—defensive patient equals backing away, softening my tactics, and redirecting the conversation.

But it doesn't.

Instead, panic rattles me.

How does he know? Are my guilt and loneliness so obvious on my face? Is he wandering in a dark forest too, foliage covered by fog, not knowing what lies ahead but having no choice other than to walk forward?

I square my shoulders and maintain a straight face, even if it feels like a thousand ants are crawling over my body.

Rex suddenly smiles.

Damn it. He must've seen something.

His stormy irises darken, and he cocks an arrogant brow. "Unless you're here for what other women want..."

I narrow my eyes. "Don't even try reverse psychology on me. I spent years in medical school studying the mind. You can't out-doctor the doctor."

"But that's it, isn't it, little Olive?"

Olive. Only Mia called me that. She used to say her name means "my" in Italian, and since we're twins, she nicknamed me "Olive."

My olive. Her best friend. Two peas in a pod.

The sudden pain spears me and I rub the soreness over my heart.

Rex's eyes snag on the movement. He steps closer, his presence heavy and menacing. Not because I'm afraid of him, but because I suddenly feel naked, all my scars exposed.

I hiccup. "Don't call me that."

"You're like everyone else. You want a good time, don't you?" A sinful smile curves his lips, one I've seen him use on models, actresses alike.

He steps into my space and I back away. "Is that pussy of yours achy, Olive? You want me to clear out those cobwebs? You want the Rex-a-Million special and have me fuck you until you can't walk straight? Is that why you're here?"

I gasp, shock at his inappropriate words slamming into me. My voice deserts me.

The asshole. Inappropriate. Infuriating. I want to strangle him.

But then, his comment replays in my mind.

A slow, sultry heat moves up my spine, and my pulse batters my ears.

"That's it, huh? My straitlaced doctor isn't so innocent, is she? You're panting. Breathless for me, aren't you? You know, you don't need to pretend to care about me as my doctor to get me interested. I've never fucked a psychiatrist before and I'm a curious man. Got to try everything once."

His gaze, the smolder of a devil, dips to my mouth and he rasps, "I wonder how these pretty pink lips would look wrapped around my cock. Do you want to taste it? My dick? My cum? Be used for your three fuck holes, to submit to me and stop thinking, delirious with pleasure?"

His words swirl around my body, brushing against my chest and settling deep inside my pussy. Unwanted images of me kneeling before him—him fisting my hair and using me only for his pleasure—fill my mind. My core clenches and the telltale wetness dampens my underwear.

Why am I turned on by this degradation? What's wrong with me?

It's easy to be swept away by the devil in his seductive tempest.

Maybe he'll make me forget the guilt, the pain, the loneliness.

The hole in my chest.

Don't let him succeed, Olivia. He's goading you. These are normal physiological reactions to a virile man. Nothing more.

"Stop it, Mr. Anderson." My command comes out in a breathy whisper, but it's better than being silent around this...asshole.

Rex smirks and treads closer. The backs of my legs hit a lounge chair and the next thing I know, I'm gripping the armrests for dear life, my body curving backward.

"Is that why you're here, Olive?"

He bends toward me, closing our distance, until I can almost taste the sweetness of his cologne, pick apart the unique musk of his skin, see the gold striations in his irises, marvel at how his pupils slowly eat away at the quicksilver. Then there's the perfect curve of his upper lip, beckoning me to touch it.

A moan perches in my throat. We aren't touching, but I feel him everywhere, through my cotton dress and underwear.

He growls, the low sound rippling down my body, and I can't help but squeeze my thighs together. Rex's eyes flash, clearly cataloging my involuntary movements.

Sparking a fire, he traces his finger over the rioting pulse on my neck.

I swallow my whimper as the flames burn me alive.

"Do you know where your pulse will beat harder...where each throb will drive you slowly out of your mind?" he rasps, his eyes riveted on my neck, unhinged fascination reflecting in those dark irises. Then he drags his gaze to my lips before returning to my neck.

I don't answer him. I *can't* answer him.

Instead, I curl my fingers tightly around the armrests, begging my body not to betray me, not to launch itself onto this sex god who looks like he wants to make a feast out of me.

"Your pussy," he answers, and I gasp.

His lips twitch, then he bends down, skims the tip of his nose on my pulse point. He drags a sensual path to my ear before blowing on it—the lightness of his breath scraping my skin in the worst type of torture.

"I'll circle my tongue around your clit. Not directly, can't let you come too quickly. I'll tease that hard, swollen nub until it throbs from the slightest breath I blow on it. Then, and only then, I'll insert one finger into your dripping fuck hole...just the pinky to start with, because I bet that pussy of yours is so fucking tight, I'll have to break you in."

My body shakes, the lewd images appearing in my mind. Wetness trickles to my thighs and I know I've soaked through my underwear.

Let me make you forget everything. The devil appears in my mind.

"But don't worry, you'll be soaked when you let me in. All the while, I lick, suck, and taste your essence. You'll moan, cry, thrash, and beg me with your sweet little voice to let you come. But I'll ignore you, slowly fucking you with my pinky until your eyes roll back and your legs spasm."

The sky swirls in my vision, my eyes fluttering closed as his nose grazes my throat—once, twice—each soft motion mimicking how he'd tease me below.

Slowly driving me out of my mind.

"Then what?" I shudder, the words slipping out of me before I can think better of it.

He stills. "I'll stop. Right when you're at the edge."

Rex's voice is hoarse and I feel the restraint in his body as he hovers just inches above me. "And I'll do it again. And again. And again. Until you're delirious with want, like you'll *die* if I don't fuck you."

The world falls silent and all I can hear and feel is the thundering of my heart, the ache between my legs, my mind blissfully blank.

Then a seagull squawks overhead, a knife piercing the veil.

The sound jolts me back into reality and horror crashes through me like a tsunami.

What the ever-loving fuck am I doing? I'm his doctor. I'm a professional. I'm better than this.

"That was interesting, Mr. Anderson," I force out the words, thankful my voice has taken on a clinical detachment again. Giving his chest a hard shove, I straighten myself into a standing position.

Rex steps back, his chest heaving, face flushed, a thin sheen of sweat dotting his forehead.

Is this how he'd look during sex?

I shove the ridiculous thought out of my mind and grit my teeth.

"When flirtation and intimidation fail, you resort to a well-used weapon in your arsenal—seduction. I'll have to jot that down in my 'magical little notepad' later on."

Finally, finding the rest of my strength, I stride to him, stand on my tiptoes, and get in his face. Well, as much as I can, given the almost one-foot height difference between us.

"Since this isn't an official session, I'll let the nickname slide. But call me Olive again and I'll cut your balls off and stuff them down your throat."

His eyes widen and a thrill trembles inside me. I've shocked him.

I smirk. "You do know psychiatrists go through medical school and residency, and I'm very, very good with a scalpel."

Without waiting for his response, I spin around and walk toward the stairs, head held high, even as frenetic energy pulses inside me.

Unprofessional. Pathetic. Ridiculous, Olivia. He's my best friends' older brother, my freakin' patient. He's fucking unhinged chaos. Everything about him screams no, stay away, approach in a hazmat suit.

My conscience hurls insults at me and the steady, rule-following Olivia is disappointed.

But deep inside, a latent part of my soul shakes with excitement, desperate to break free.

Carpe diem, break the rules. Be brave.

If Mia were here, she'd drag every little juicy detail out of me, a sly smile of approval on her face.

A sharp ray of heat hits my back and golden rays suddenly bathe the deck as the sun makes a reappearance from behind the clouds.

For the first time in a long time, I'm awake and alive.

As I turn into the winding staircase, I can't help but look back at the infuriating man.

But the spot he was standing at is empty, like the last ten minutes have been a figment of my fevered imagination.

My heart spasms, the strange excitement deflating like air leaking out of a punctured tire.

It's then I know.

If I'm not careful around Rex Anderson, not only is my professional reputation at stake.

But my body, and quite possibly...my heart.

CHAPTER THIRTEEN

"Smile, sweetheart," I murmur, curling Bree to my side as our luxury tender boat sweeps us toward Tragonisi Island Caves, located off the southeast coast of Mykonos.

Unfortunately, the damn Greg Masters, the sleazy bastard from *Gossip Times*, is also here, watching us like a vulture. Fuck Maxwell for insisting on Ron to tag along on this trip. It's the right PR move—staging controlled photo ops to show all is well with me and the cruise.

But it's so damn annoying.

Bree stiffens, her face flushed from the sun beating down on us. She's sitting ramrod straight, and I inwardly groan.

With me sleeping less than three hours a night, the random blackouts occurring more frequently, I'm not on my A-game and am most definitely going out of my mind.

But even I can smell the bullshit.

We can't sell a fake fling if I don't even believe it myself. But I need the press and public to buy the cover—that she's just my usual arm candy, like on every other vacation. Because everyone knows Rex Anderson doesn't do relationships.

And if she's just another pretty distraction, The Association won't look twice. The women I used to be seen with? Fame-chasing models and actresses, not someone who'd risk everything to hack and take down a criminal network. That's the game—hiding her in plain sight by giving her the ultimate spotlight. It's a calculated risk.

But damn it, we aren't selling it.

Grabbing the glass of cucumber water, I give Bree my toothpaste commercial worthy smile.

Her eyes widen when I press the water into her hands. "Drink up, sweetheart. As much as I love women swooning at my feet, I don't want you fainting inside the caves and falling into the water. Then I'd have to perform CPR. Not that I'm complaining. But you might not need CPR with me nearby. I restart hearts with my presence."

An incredulous snort reaches my ears and I freeze, recognizing the sound before I turn around.

Olivia, clad in a one-piece black swimsuit and a white cover up, looking as perfectly put together as ever, shakes her head and turns toward the turquoise waters, her camera in her hand. It's interesting. I see her carrying that thing everywhere and it looks like an older model. I wonder why she doesn't have something new and shiny or use her phone to take pictures like most tourists.

A conundrum, the infuriating woman.

I don't know how she does it—gets under my skin so easily. The surface-level grace and calm, lulling you into thinking she's a harmless kitten, then she unsheathes her claws and shows you she's a fucking tigress.

I almost lost control yesterday on the sun deck. That's never happened to me before. Thankfully, Casey wasn't there to witness it or else I'd get an earful from him. God knows where he's at these days. I thought he'd trail me everywhere on the cruise, but so far, I'd only seen him once—last night when I was nursing a drink at the bar.

The man's an unwanted fucking shadow. And if he were here, he'd psychoanalyze my obsession with Olivia.

Something about how she doesn't back down or take my bullshit has my cock resurrecting, my blood boiling. Her sweet scent of cotton and honey awakens my senses. She ignites a maddening craving to unnerve her the same way she carves up my insides.

God, when her lips parted as I described the lewd acts I thought would be too raunchy for her good-girl ears, I almost came in my pants.

Because if there's anything I know, it's women.

And this little innocent angel isn't so innocent, it turns out.

She was fucking turned on.

And I wanted to do every fucking thing I described to her, and more. And I think she'd take it, and take it well.

It's strange. This feeling toward her. Unnerving, even.

She makes me feel things other than emptiness.

My cock twitches and I swallow a groan because everything in my life—my mental state, my health, this cruise, this mission, all of it—is a mess.

I drag my gaze away from the good doctor to the woman next to me. *Focus, Rex. Flirt with Bree. Play the damn part.*

"Nervous about Monaco?" I skate my fingers on Bree's exposed thigh for the cameras. She's clad in an enticing red bikini, which *should* inflame my senses, but does absolutely nothing for me.

Because a certain no-nonsense doctor has bewitched me. *Shit.*

"Who wouldn't be? It's a big move, but I've made my choice."

The move. A.k.a. her hacking into The Association's servers and her present predicament of fleeing for safety and dropping off the face of the earth.

"What spawned the move then?" I roll the words around, careful of the phrasing. "What did you unearth at your previous home?"

Her eyes flare and snag on mine. She knows what I'm asking—what she found and why she's a high-level target for one of the most dangerous organizations in the world.

There's something bigger at play. When Elias first gave me the mission, I was so desperate for a chance at redemption, I didn't question anything.

But now I wonder. Things don't add up. Elias could disappear her without me helping. He could have a low-level lackey help her. Why is he personally overseeing the transport? With Raya, it made sense. Her husband was a high-level financier, and she discovered the identities of key people in the organization.

But what does a thirty-something-year-old hacker have that is so important?

What am I missing?

"I-I don't want to talk about it." She fidgets and I grab her hand to stop her from giving herself away. "Let's just say there was a landfill under where I was living. I needed to clean up the trash, or I'd get sick. Not only me, but also others around me. And even if I weren't successful, at least I'd have tried. My life would have meaning."

My throat constricts. We aren't talking about moving or garbage collection, but I know exactly what she means.

Two years ago, it was my search for meaning that landed me on a rescue mission with Elias. And when everything went sideways, not only did I not find clarity, I only dug my grave deeper, accumulating more debt than I could possibly repay.

It's why I'm on this little yacht tender right now, sailing the deep seas under the guise of relaxation, knowing I may lose my life and Bree's if I make one wrong move.

Because there's no way The Association isn't hot on our tails. They have resources. If Bree's on the run, it means they're onto her, or at least, her hacker identity.

They don't like loose ends.

A quiet shutter sound reaches my ears and I give Bree a perfunctory peck on her shoulder because Greg Masters is eyeing us from the back corner.

More camera clicks follow in rapid succession, but this time, it's from Olivia snapping away at everything—the clear skies today, no clouds to be seen, the vibrant turquoise waters we'd never see in New York, the dramatic rock formations and partially submerged caves jutting out in the distance.

When she sets down her camera, she lets out a heavy sigh, her lips tilting in a bittersweet smile. Her throat ripples as she blinks rapidly.

Is she fighting back tears?

I start to get up before I can stop myself. But then I freeze, remembering the eyes on me.

The thought of her being upset is unbearable. I want to haul her into my arms and tell her to let it out.

To cry, to hit me, or to scream.

Then to tell me what's wrong, so I can hunt down the bastards who hurt her and unleash my pent-up violence on them.

Why are you sad, little Olive?

I touched a raw nerve yesterday when I accused her of hiding because she was getting through my defenses.

But now, watching her whiskey eyes take on a faraway look, I'm surer than before.

She's haunted by something. Her perfectly collected exterior is as fake as my Rex-a-Million persona.

Unbidden, I whip out my phone and point it toward the ocean, pretending I'm taking a picture of the view.

But all I'm doing is capturing her, because something about her is captivating. Bewitching. Inflames my senses.

I know I can't have her, that I'm a fuckup and shouldn't drag anyone into hell with me, least of all the kindhearted Olivia, who's battling demons but still trying her damned best to heal others.

But I'm selfish. I want to steal a little piece of her for those lonely nights when I wake up bathed in sweat. I want to imagine a world where I was deserving of someone like her, gentle and beautiful from the inside out.

In this imaginary world, I'd have my own happy ending like Maxwell, a doting wife who loves me, a cheeky son with my smirk, or a cute daughter hugging me like I'm her hero.

But I won't get that. These dreams. Who'd want a man slowly going out of his mind?

And so I take photos of Olivia, the woman who's come closest to seeing my darkest parts. Stealing a sliver of light I've no right to touch.

I'll add thief to my titles after murderer.

A few minutes later, the guide stops our boats and sets the stage for the "Float and Forget" theme of this excursion, where we'll drift on saltwater in the semi-submerged caves, wearing waterproof headphones preloaded with custom sound therapy. An hour later, we'll be reborn, our troubles forgotten.

It's a load of shit, but it's luxe, and we've paid a hefty sum to rent out the entire area so no other visitors can intrude.

The patrons are gobbling it up.

"There are myths surrounding these caves. They say there once was a beautiful siren, Calliope. She, unlike her sisters, protected the ships sailing past these cliffs because Helios, a handsome sailor from Athens, would pass by this route monthly." Our guide, Helena, gestures toward the caves in front of us.

"But one day, her older sister, Daphne, fed up with her tactics, which would send the men far away, leaving the sisters hungry, decided to punish her. She told Calliope that Helios wanted to thank her for protecting him. That he was also secretly in love with her. Overjoyed when Helios passed by with his fleet this time, Calliope allowed her sisters to use their voices to lure the men in, so they could have a sweet moment before sending them back out to sea."

Olivia gasps, her hand flying to cover her mouth. My lips twitch. For someone who believes in science, she sure is paying rapt attention to a mythical story.

Helena says, "Daphne lied. As soon as the men were reeled in, the sisters tied Calliope up and feasted on the sailors in front of her, teaching her a lesson that sirens and humans could never be together. They were forbidden. Brokenhearted, Calliope refused to eat or drink, eventually wasting away and dying in these caves. It's said her soft cries can sometimes be heard inside, usually to people in danger of following in her footsteps."

Helena continues with her story and some instructions, and I don't really pay attention. I watch a staff member set circular, multicolored floats onto the water, each containing a bottle of water, a plate of fruit, and a headset. He's helping passengers into their individual floats.

"Perhaps the stories sound outlandish—but knowing what these caves have seen over the years, can anything truly be impossible? One thing is for sure—there's magic in these caves. People come out changed for the better. Rejuvenated, enlightened. Ladies and gentlemen, enjoy your excursion."

I shake my head. Ridiculous story, but she sold it. I make a note to give her a good tip later on.

Olivia gets on her bright yellow float, her camera left behind, no doubt for safety, and I watch her drift away, her eyes closed, a silver headset over her ears.

I help Bree into hers and murmur, "Enjoy yourself. We have everything under control. Soon, this will be in the past. You'll start a new life, safe and sound."

I assist the other passengers in disembarking. After all, we Andersons are known for our impeccable manners. A few women bat their eyelashes at me, and I automatically return winks of my own.

When the small boat is finally empty, I look at the caves, my gaze sweeping over the small rainbow-colored floats dotting the crystal waters like a modern art installation, when my attention snags on an anomaly.

A single yellow float out on its own, crashing against the jagged walls of the farthest cliff in the distance.

Empty.

Olivia's float, but where is she?

My chest seizes, and without thinking, I yank off my shirt and dive in.

CHAPTER FOURTEEN

My pulse riots and teeth chatter. It's too small. Too tight. Too suffocating.

I glance at the narrower alcove in front of me.

Are you sure you want to do this? This cave already prickles my claustrophobia. But it's manageable.

The one ahead, though—that's the real test.

A few minutes ago, when we floated out there, I closed my eyes and tried focusing on the meditative music. But instead of relaxation, Mia crept in. Then my parents. Then my loneliness. If I died right now, the world would lose an obedient daughter, a dutiful doctor, a decent friend.

But who the hell was Olivia Lin? Who would miss *her*?

The discontent and resentment I bottled up erupted inside me.

Why did I always have to be perfect?

Why couldn't I go where the wind blew me?

Why was I still stuck in the wreckage of the past, playing what I recognized was a role to make everyone around me feel better?

Why was I still afraid? Of small spaces. Of heights. Of failure.

I'm an adult. These fears shouldn't own me.

So I veered from the tour group and paddled to the cave farthest away from the others. No witnesses. No judgment. Just me tackling my fears.

I can do this. Do it for yourself.

Maybe I can come out of these caves rejuvenated, as the guide mentioned.

Emboldened, I take a deep breath.

Then dive.

I swim toward the soft glow ahead. Considering the underwater lights illuminating the tiny alcove clearly put there by the government, I know it's safe to enter.

My strokes are quick as I cut through the underwater entrance, the vibrant sea life—small silver fish, multicolored starfish and sea urchins dotting the rocks—keeping me company. I break the surface and rake in an inhale.

A sliver of sunlight cuts through a crevice in the cave's ceiling, illuminating the water.

Drawing attention to how dark and small this alcove is.

This space is much tighter than the previous one I was in.

Exposure therapy, Olivia. I run through the protocols in my mind. *You're safe. You're a skilled swimmer. There's nothing to be afraid of.*

Ground yourself. Name five things you see, smell, and hear. Starfish—pink. Sound of water lapping against the walls. Salt and—

My lungs seize and my stomach turns. I close my eyes and focus on breathing. *Salty water and—*

I'm safe. Pretend Mia were here. She'd laugh at me. She'd remind me not to let one elevator mishap in tenth grade freak me out for the rest of my life. After all, the technicians rescued me, didn't they?

They sure did.

Ten hours after I embarrassingly peed my pants.

It's all your fault, Mia. Putting these ideas in my head—Las Fallas, regrets, turning thirty. You should be here with me.

I tread water, my mind spinning, my heavy breathing bellowing against the jagged walls.

Too small. Too tight. Too suffocating.

I can't breathe.

"Shit. Shit. Shit." The world swirls, cold sweat breaking over my face.

I need to keep my wits about me and get out.

I need to escape.

Panic will kill me, not the waters or the cave.

Arms thrashing, I grapple at the rocks, desperate to find purchase and hang on until the terror subsides.

Suddenly, the gentle waves morph into violent crashes, further aggravating the storm thundering inside my ears. Dots blind my vision and I flail, desperate to escape.

Out of nowhere, two thick tendrils wrap around my waist, followed by a strong column of scorching heat plastered on my back.

Monster. I can't escape.

My screams echo in the chamber, deafening my ears as I fight off the intruder—Poseidon, Calliope, her evil sisters, my past—whoever's strangling me and pulling me down into the dark depths.

"Shit! Stop struggling!" Large hands grip my wrists before pinning them behind my back. Those tendrils, which I now realize are muscular arms, cinch me tightly against the massive body behind me.

"Let go of me!" I thrash harder, kicking my feet, throwing my head back against my would-be killer.

"Stop it, Olivia. Stop it! You're safe. It's me. You're safe."

My body stills, clearly recognizing the rumbly voice before my mind catches up.

Rex. The devil himself. What the hell?

"What the fuck are you doing out here, Olivia?" he rasps against my ear between rough, panting breaths.

I open my mouth to speak, but nothing comes out. Still petrified, I grip his arms, needing to hold on to something solid.

"Shhh, I got you. I got you."

Closing my eyes, I focus on his warmth. *Deep breaths in, longer exhales out.* These are strategies I give to patients suffering from anxiety and panic disorders.

Heck, I gave the same advice to Maxwell a few years ago when he was having a full-blown breakdown in my office.

Rex doesn't speak. He only holds me against him, murmuring *shhh* in my ears like he's soothing a spooked child.

"Focus on me. Look at the beauty around you. You don't get this in New York."

My mind spinning, I do as I'm told, cataloging the smoky rasp of his voice, the way he enunciates his words like a nighttime deejay would on the radio.

His caresses turn gentle and between his voice and his touch, something strange happens.

I'm able to breathe. I'm still afraid, my heart still threatening to stop at any moment, but I feel...safe.

It's disconcerting, like I've been pulled back from free falling into the abyss and am now hovering at the edge of panic. It's a monumental improvement.

Because he makes me feel safe.

I focus on the dim light glinting off the windswept walls carved by erosion. How the rocks glow golden under the singular sunbeam, but cool to a grayish-blue in the shadows, moss clinging to the honeycomb surfaces.

It's breathtaking.

Eventually, the rest of my senses flicker alive, and I notice what I missed before.

The hint of sandalwood drifting to my nose.

The broad, sculpted muscles plastered against my back.

His light breaths ghosting the sensitive spot under my ear.

I freeze, my nerves flickering on one by one, a backup generator kicking on after a blackout.

My body heats, and I notice the *now*.

In particular, the moment he realizes the intimate position we're in—our bodies meshed together, limbs intertwined, in a space no bigger than a coat closet.

My pulse riots again, this time not from fear, but from something twisted and heady.

I try spinning away, but he clamps me tighter against him.

Forbidden. Danger. Stay away.

Rex clearly senses my incoming panic, and he wordlessly takes my hand and motions toward the exit. He swims out to the larger cave, and I follow suit.

As soon as I break the surface of the water, my heart rate slows because I'm in a bigger space.

Rex pulls me flush against his body.

He presses his soft lips to my ear, the gentle graze sending sparks down my neck, straight to my breasts straining against my swimsuit, which does nothing to hide my hard nipples begging for his attention.

"What are you doing here, little Olive?" His words press into my skin. "Do you know how worried everyone was when they saw your float empty?"

No one came to find me, though. Only he did.

His fingers relax around my waist, but he doesn't let go. Instead, he slides them down to the sensitive gap where my thigh meets my suit before tracing the thin material inches away from my pussy. I'm thrown back to what he said that day on the sun deck—all the dirty, degrading words describing what he'd do to me if I let him.

And I want to let him do it all. Kiss me. Fuck me. Unravel me at the seams.

Bad decisions, Olivia.

And I want to make them.

I bite back a moan and claw at the rational side of my mind. Body chemistry, arousal, biological reactions of a man and a woman in a small, enclosed space.

Liar. Have you ever felt this way about another man before?

I refuse to answer. This can't be anything more.

He's my patient, even if we haven't had a successful therapy session yet. And emotions cloud the mind, making it impossible to be logical.

I need to be logical to catch the signs, to fix him.

And shit. He just found me during a panic attack. What a great doctor you are. Embarrassment heats my skin.

Using the remnants of my willpower, I tear myself away from him and plaster my back against the wall.

"Was everyone worried or were you worried, Mr. Anderson?"

A lonely sunbeam catches his eyes, rendering them prismatic. He swallows.

"The guide mentioned we could swim, or were you not paying attention? Why are you so worried about me not being in my float?"

Nostrils flaring, Rex stares mutely at me. His troubled gaze tells me stories his voice refuses to. As the seconds pass, a thought tickles my mind.

Goosebumps bead on my neck. *Yes. This has to be it.*

"Did you lose someone? Someone you could've saved?"

He draws a sharp inhale. His throat ripples. He looks away. *Bingo.*

I'm hit with an urge to comfort him, to place my hand on his chest and tell him I'm here and I understand.

Instead, I curl my fingers inward, my nails digging into my palms, and wait for him to respond.

"Who hasn't lost someone?" Deflection again. "All of us have—Mom, Grandma, the damn Anderson curse, which I'm sure Maxwell told you about."

Maxwell did. When he sought therapy a few years ago, he thought the curse plaguing the Anderson family since the mid-eighteen hundreds was real. As the eldest son, which this curse supposedly fell on, he couldn't fall in love with his wife, or she'd die an untimely death. Everyone in the family believed it. After all, the other Anderson wives to the eldest sons before him—his mom, grandma, grand aunt—all died young and in mysterious ways.

That fear, along with his anxiety, drove him away from Belle, but thankfully, the truth came to light later, and they uncovered a non-supernatural reason for all those deaths.

But losing a parent at a young age, no matter the reason, is a horrible trauma no kid should go through.

Is that really why Rex is spiraling...thirty years after his mom died?

It makes no sense. There has to be more to it.

"You know their deaths have nothing to do with you. The culprit was caught. The curse was dispelled."

Rex's nostrils flare and his lips twist in self-derision. "You know *nothing*, the truth of what happened. None of you do." His gaze finally meets mine, and he flinches at what he apparently sees on my face. "Don't you dare pity me."

He swims toward the exit, pausing before the threshold.

His voice is empty, completely devoid of the earlier warmth. "This is my cruise and I'm the only Anderson on board right now. It's my responsibility to make sure everyone is safe. Don't endanger yourself again, Olivia, or I won't be responsible for my actions."

Without waiting for my response, he swims out of the cave.

My mind reels from his cryptic riddles, the half-sensible nonanswers.

What on earth is he talking about?

CHAPTER FIFTEEN

THE GOOD DOCTOR STAYED away the past week, no doubt hiding in her office or dealing with other patients as we sailed to Santorini. It's for the best. I wouldn't be able to resist riling her up if she were close by. Plus, I was still reeling from my reaction that day when I thought she drowned.

The fear. The panic. The need to save her.

And when I found her struggling, scared, barely able to breathe?

I wanted to fight off her demons and protect her with my life.

What the fuck is going on?

I splash cold water on my face in the bathroom of my stateroom. They put me in the largest Rose signature suite on deck ten. Clearly, the event planner thought I should have the best accommodations on the ship, which, naturally, is on the Rose floor decks. She probably thought I'd appreciate being next to the kink rooms and sex clubs I frequented before.

My reputation precedes me.

I stare at my reflection after wiping my face. My skin is tanner than before, but can't hide the darkening shadows under my eyes. The hollows in my cheeks are more prominent. I doubt the scruff on my jaw can camouflage them for much longer.

Deep down, I hoped by leaving New York City and helping Bree escape, I'd somehow fix myself.

Maybe I'd be able to sleep without nightmares, or stop having these sporadic blackouts where I'd lose chunks of time.

But that didn't happen.

Instead, I jolted awake in the middle of the night without fail. Some nights I'd find myself in bed. Other nights I'd be elsewhere in my suite, with no recollection of how I got there or what I'd done. But the evidence was always there: beer bottles scattered across the floor one night, a half-cooked meal on the stove another night.

Some nights, I'd stare at nothingness, my heart racing, wondering if this was it for the rest of my life, and perhaps, if I should just let go.

What if nothing changes after this trip? What if I'm still trapped in this half-life?

My family doesn't need the jokester anymore. Everyone else has found peace. Dad's retired in the Hamptons, my siblings are in love, building lives that mean something.

What reason would I have to keep going then?

But lately, there's been a spark in the darkness, that singular star glowing, refusing to yield to the night sky.

Olivia.

When I couldn't sleep, I'd think of her.

How, in her presence, I'd get this electrifying energy pulsing through my veins, my calamitous emotions like live wires, sparking everywhere, threatening to electrocute everything in the vicinity.

It was nirvana—a new addiction. A defibrillator to the dying heart.

No one had ever impacted me this way before her.

My mind filled with scenarios of me kissing her, sucking out the venom of her sadness. I wanted to mark her fair skin with my teeth and unsheathe her claws so she could draw blood. Our demons would face each other and see who remained standing at the end.

Find her. Force her into my madness. You won't be alone anymore.

I'd fist my cock and fight the impulse to tug—once, twice, because that was all it'd take—to release the pent-up pressure building inside me.

But I wouldn't, because that's my punishment for being a depraved bastard.

Do I interrupt her dreams at night?

I chuckle and shake my head.

"You're losing it, Rex," I mutter. "Having an entire conversation with yourself in your head. That's a new low."

I can never give Olivia what she deserves—a good, mentally stable man with no demons, no blackouts, no overreliance on pills.

What am I even thinking? I don't do relationships. Shit, the lack of sleep is driving me out of my mind.

I swallow another Velowake pill for good measure and close my eyes.

"What the fuck did you get yourself into now?"

I jolt at Casey's voice. So typical of him to show up unannounced. Classic Casey. "Asshole, you finally decided to make an appearance."

"I'm not at your beck and call. We're on vacation. And I don't want to deal with your shitty attitude."

I smirk. "You love me, just like everyone else."

Casey sighs and raps his knuckles against the wall. "Because I've seen you in better days and I'm a stubborn fucker who's determined to get the old you back."

Which old me? The kid scared of loud noises who'd hide under the covers when it was thundering outside? The popular jock in college who could live it up like it was Armageddon?

Rolling up the sleeves of my white flannel shirt, I brush past Casey to grab my phone, wallet, and sunglasses from the fifteen-seater sofa in the living room.

Another full day of activities ahead. This time, there's a selection to choose from. A sunset ride along Caldera Rim, an archaeologist-led tour of the buried Minoan city of Akrotiri in Megalochori, capping off with an exclusive wine tasting, and exploring Pyrgos Village, the highest point of Santorini.

I have a feeling most people will follow the alcohol, the wine tasting in Megalochori.

My phone buzzes in my pocket and I take it out.

I take it no news is good news from you. Based on the pics posted by your paparazzi stalker, you guys are selling the playboy and arm candy image. I don't need to remind you of the stakes.

My fucking tail, a.k.a. Greg Masters, has been an annoying, relentless shadow.

Most days, I'd flash him a smile to tell him I know he's watching. He'd respond with a curl of his lips and a dare in his eyes, promising he'd be there when I screw up. Then he'd get his payday.

But the articles about the cruise have been decent. No alarming scandals. Maxwell should be happy.

I type a response.

If you're so worried, you should come aboard sooner.

Trust me, I've thought about it.

Well, doesn't that make you a dumb shit to rely on someone who's clearly untrustworthy.

I swear, Rex, there are days when I wonder.

Wonder what? Finish your damn sentence. I glower at my phone.

Strangle me? Toss me in shark-infested waters? Pull me into a dark alleyway and give me a hug because you don't want to get all mushy in public?

Three dots appear, then disappear.

I smirk, imagining the broody mobster flicking his lighter with one hand, rubbing his temple with the other. What a rare gift I have—the ability to inspire polarizing emotions in people.

"How's therapy going? Did I tell you I'm proud of you for doing it?" Casey says.

Sliding my phone into my pocket, I glance up, finding Casey idling in the foyer. He's smiling like I've impressed him. I haven't seen that in ages—the last time was when I was fifteen and confessed to Ryland I had driven his car into a ditch by accident.

I was scared shitless, but that wasn't anything new. The scaredy cat hadn't quite grown out of being spooked. I worked on it relentlessly, but my impulse was to hide in a hole and avoid terrifying things or people.

While Ryland was only sixteen then, he still had the same no-nonsense professor vibe he carries now. And the man could hold a grudge. But I told myself fear was good for me. Mom said I had to face my fears to get over them.

Casey was proud when I told Ryland. He said it was the right thing to do.

I survived my brother's wrath, but he'd never let me drive his cars again.

"You're silent. You fucked up, didn't you?" The warmth disappears from Casey's voice and his shoulder slumps. "What did you do?"

A slideshow of Olivia plays in my mind. Her observations of me are on point—my self-hatred, the anger I tamp down, how everything stems from secrets and loss.

If she was clinically detached, the way a doctor should be, I could've laughed it off and charmed her enough to distract her.

But she isn't. She acts like she cares. Like my pain somehow hurts her.

"You're not fucking the doctor, are you?"

"No, dipshit. Nothing happened between us."

"And it'll stay that way, you hear me? You're an Anderson with billions of dollars attached to your name. You can commit murder in broad daylight and get away with it."

Casey's voice becomes more urgent. "She can't, Rex. She's not a plaything. If you mess with her, you're messing with her career, her livelihood. Please, ruin your life, don't ruin anyone else's."

His words sink deep into my gut. He's right, as always.

Casey sighs. "She's good at what she does. Make an effort, won't you? Keep your dick inside your pants and *help* her help you."

Wetting my lips, I ignore him and the anvil compressing my lungs.

Before I walk out the door, I slide my hand into my pocket and grip my red marble, a reminder of my past, not that I'd ever forget. "Don't get your panties in a twist. Nothing's going to happen."

In another life, perhaps...

My chest aches, but I ignore it.

Nothing will happen.

I'll protect Olivia from myself.

I won't ruin her life if I can help it.

CHAPTER SIXTEEN

"This may be the best work trip I've ever been on," Rhys says, the sun dipping beneath the horizon in the distance, casting the whitewashed buildings and blue domes of Pyrgos Village in amber and violet. "Beautiful setting and..." he winks, "meeting new friends."

After spending a few days catching up on paperwork and conducting my first teleconferences with patients back in the city, I decided to venture off the cruise to see Santorini today. The girls were adamant I should have some fun outside of working and we're already a little over a week into the cruise.

On our group call last night, they grilled me. Relentlessly.

"Are European men hotter?" Alexis asks.

"Why do you care? You are married...to my brother." Taylor tsks, her snark coming off in waves.

"I have eyes too! And while Ethan fulfills all my needs—"

"Stopping you right there," Lana interrupts. "I don't need to know how our brother fulfills your needs. And since I'm the only single lady here, I'll ask. Olivia...are European men hotter?"

At my silence, Lana adds, "You better not tell me you haven't left the boat. I sent you there to get some R and R and get laid."

"I thought it was to do you a favor because your cruise was falling apart without me."

"Burn! Muahahaha." Taylor snorts.

"Oh my God, woman. You have needs too. A man can work out those kinks—"

Images of her infuriating brother barge into my mind, and I shake my head. Nope. Not going there. No kinks and no Rex. "Fine. You win. I'll go out so I don't rot in my office, okay?"

Lana narrows her eyes. "You're mocking me. And is that a blush I see? Something happened, huh? Did you meet a hot Greek god with a sexy accent who gave you orgasms all night long?"

Sexier than a mythological god.

I groan as Rex's handsome face flashes behind my eyelids. "There's no one. It's boring." Liar, liar, pants on fire. "And oh look, the reception is b-bad. G-Guess we w-will need to ch-chat when you get here, L-Lana."

"Don't you dare! Your image is crystal clear, and we have top of the line satellite reception on the ship. I'm not falling for it. Olivia, don't hang up—"

I hang up.

"Olivia?" Rhys stops. "Something on your mind?"

I falter and strain a smile. "Sorry. I haven't taken a vacation in years. I don't think I can turn my mind off. You travel a lot for work?"

Sneaking a glance at him, I take in his dark hair and chiseled bone structure. He really is good looking. I think back to Lana's suggestion for me to have a fling.

Rhys would be a good candidate—smart, charming, a doctor like me, so he understands the work hours and dedication I have for my job.

Mentally stable is a plus.

Olivia, we really need to work on your standards. Especially if being mentally stable is optional.

But still, I tick off the checkboxes on my invisible checklist. I *should* be attracted to Rhys. He's everything I could possibly want. Sure, my parents would be disappointed I wasn't bringing a Mandarin-speaking guy home who'd know our culture right off the bat—small things like bringing food when you first visit someone's home or taking off your shoes in the foyer before venturing inside—but I'm sure they'd get over it quickly if it was Rhys. He's a catch by all standards.

"Other than a few Doctors without Borders trips and a concierge doctor stint I did two years ago, who has time to travel? But this cruise is a good reminder. We can't save lives if we don't take care of ourselves. Mental health included. What the heck? Why am I talking out of my ass to a psychiatrist about mental health?" He grins, his brown eyes lighting up his face.

But I find myself thinking about a pair of quicksilver eyes, hollowed with pain. The man who's a walking definition of mentally unstable.

My heart skips several beats.

Dammit.

Needing to do something with my hands, I pull out a bag of Mom's almond cookies from my purse. I still have half a tin left in my stateroom.

I really don't want to eat them. *Well, why are you forcing yourself to eat them then? That's what you'd tell your patients.*

Ugh. Doctors make the worst patients.

Rhys looks at the cookies, his brows arching up.

I grin and hand them to him. "Have at it. Homemade cookies."

"Never say no to free food." He takes them and smiles.

He does have a nice smile.

But not as nice as someone you aren't supposed to think about.

As if I conjured the infuriating devil himself, I hear the teasing rasp of his laughter. I inwardly groan, unable to stop myself from searching for him.

It isn't hard to locate him. Rex stands out the way celebrities draw your attention when they walk down the red carpet. He's with Bree and idling in the distance, dressed in khaki shorts and a white linen shirt, sleeves rolled up, revealing muscular, tanned arms. His dark hair is windswept, with an errant lock falling over his forehead, begging me to brush it off his face.

He pops something into his mouth—a pill? I frown, thinking back to the headlines I showed him on the jet, the allegations of illicit drugs.

He crouches down, beaming at a robust older lady with graying hair who's shoving a loaf of bread at him. The woman flushes when he murmurs something to her. Bree throws her head back in laughter and clasps his shoulder like he's the most hilarious person on the planet.

My stomach sours. The regular heart-stealing comedian.

A stocky man snaps photos of them and my mind makes the connection. The paparazzi are here as well. This is a show.

"The playboy prince conquers the hearts of women—young and old." I can practically see the headlines.

It's all fake. Don't they see it? This lighthearted, devil-may-care attitude is as fake as the gorgeous Bree's tan.

Olivia, that isn't nice at all! I cringe, wanting to bang my head against the bright blue shutters affixed to the pebbly walls nearby. Bree is perfectly nice—shy even, but then, so am I. We haven't exchanged anything more than hellos, but she's nothing like the women I'd expect to capture Rex's attention—socialites and models giving off snobby airs.

Like they told me before, I don't sense romantic or intimate vibes between them when there's no one else around.

But then they act lovey-dovey in public.

It's strange.

"You know what this is, Olive," Mia taunts in my head. *"You're jealous."*

"Shut up. You only get to say that if you were here," I mutter under my breath.

"Sorry, were you talking to me?" Rhys asks as we close in on the bakery stand where Rex is still speaking with the owner in Greek, no less.

Why does he have to know a sexy foreign language too?

God isn't playing fair.

He's pointing at the various loaves, then the jars of olives and spices, his hands waving in the air. He's clearly interested in the topic. The old woman responds, motioning to her ingredients, like she's showing him how to cook. Then, he does something I don't expect. He takes out a small notebook and pen from his pocket and jots down notes.

His lips curve into a wide smile, his eyes crinkling at the corners.

He's happy. It's genuine. Whatever the topic is, it's something he's passionate about.

What is he writing down?

I'm only interested because he's my patient, that's all. Detached observation with zero emotions, all for the sake of treating him.

"Keep telling yourself that." Mia snickers.

I shove her imaginary comments away. Before this trip, I kept myself busy with work, filling my schedule with patients and conferences, so much I'd barely hear her voice in my head. And when she showed up occasionally, I knew it was because I missed her.

Being an identical twin was a unique bond few could understand.

Among the seven billion-plus people on earth, there was someone who looked and sounded exactly like me, someone who shared my DNA and sometimes, even my thoughts. The world may be a loud place favoring extroverts, and introverts like me slunk into the background. But I never had to *try* to be understood by my twin.

She just knew.

Sure, she was the sun to my shadow. No one noticed me when she was in the room.

But *she* saw me. Mom told me when we were born, we'd hold each other's hands in the bassinet, sleeping face-to-face like we couldn't bear to be separated.

And now she's gone.

"God, it's so beautiful out here, isn't it?" Rhys sighs happily and bumps my shoulder.

Smile. Flirt back. Here's a man who notices me and wants to know me better. I should be excited.

"Yeah, Olive. I'm so disappointed in you," Mia quips in my head again.

Shut. Up. You don't get to be disappointed in me.

Ever since I boarded the cruise, she's been in my head all the time.

I've spent years studying the brain and emotions. I know you never really get over the loss of a loved one.

This is grief.

It ebbs and flows like the currents rippling the ocean.

There's no time limit to grief. It can be a few months, a few years, or a few decades.

But this trip is putting it at the forefront.

Everything I'm doing now—talking to a handsome doctor, strolling through winding alleys, admiring the hanging flower baskets, iconic blue doors against white-walled homes—is things I was supposed to do with her.

Process the pain, push through to move through. That's what I'd tell my patients.

Why is it so hard? And why wasn't I brave enough to face it until now?

Releasing an exhale, I unhook the Leica around my neck to adjust the aperture and shutter speed before taking a few shots of vendors hawking their wares, two little boys chasing a Jack Russell Terrier, a priest in flowing black robes crossing the plaza.

Mia would've wanted to be in the center of these photos, grinning at the camera while stuffing her mouth full of olive-oil dipped bread, striking a pose in a spot she spent ten minutes choosing for the perfect lighting.

But I love these quiet moments. These regular vignettes of people living their lives, unassuming yet unflinchingly honest.

"You're a photographer, aren't you?" Rhys asks.

I smile as I click away. "It's a hobby. I like to—"

Screams suddenly erupt nearby.

I turn, the crowd shoving me.

Then I stumble. My heel catches on the cobblestones.

A loud roar quakes through the square, and I finally see them.

Two motorcyclists dressed in all black barrel toward us. The first one snatches my camera from my hands before I can react.

No! My Leica from Mia. "Stop! Give it back!"

Without thinking, I chase after the man. They can take anything—my purse, my money—but they can't take the only thing Mia left me.

The second motorcyclist brushes past me and beelines toward Bree. She stands alone, her face blanching, clearly petrified.

Horror sweeps through me when he grabs a fistful of her hair and drags her onto his bike.

"Let her go!" I hurry toward them, instinct driving me.

The motorcyclist stops in the middle of the road. He struggles with Bree, who's fighting back.

Pinning her to his lap, he fishes out something from inside his jacket. The metallic flash of the barrel stops me in my tracks.

A gun pointed straight at me.

I freeze as time stalls into fragments.

A booming sound ricochets. Followed by shrill screeches. The smell of gunpowder and the flash of fire.

I'm going to die.

Someone plows into me from the side, knocking me to the ground.

Pain explodes across my back, knocking the air out of my lungs. Dots appear in my vision.

"You okay?" A rough voice currently promises murder.

A dark silhouette appears above me. Thundering eyes glint with unholy light. Lips peeled back in a snarl.

Rex sweeps his hand down my body as if checking for wounds.

"Get B-Bree," I whisper. "I'm fine."

His eyes widen, like he's shocked at my mention of her.

A vein pulses in his temple. He nods.

Rex hauls himself off me and sprints toward the motorcyclist. The asshole has Bree immobile on his lap. He revs his engine, clearly seconds away from fleeing.

But he's not fast enough.

Rex reaches him before I can blink and tackles him to the ground. Bree scurries away, and Rhys and other locals form a protective circle around her.

I barely notice.

Because my attention is stolen by the vicious man pinning the motorcyclist under him. The men grapple for the gun, shots firing into the air. People scream and dive for cover.

"Who sent you?" Rex roars.

He twists the man's wrist. The gun clatters to the ground. Then he follows with a flurry of hits.

Jabs to the abdomen. Hooks to the face.

The heavy smacking sounds turning wet.

Then I notice the telltale crimson coating his hands.

"Did someone send you?"

Blood splatters onto his white shirt, soaking it in a matter of seconds. It streaks across his cheeks and eyebrows, which frame the most unhinged eyes.

His fists pummel the man, each strike harder than the last.

The man's barely moving as blood pools on the ground.

Rex is killing him. And he doesn't realize it.

This man—my friends' brother, my patient, the person disrupting my dreams—isn't fully here.

I scramble toward them, my legs finally working. The first motorcyclist swings back for his partner. He aims a gun at the duo on the ground.

"Rex! Watch out!" I scream.

The man cocks the trigger, fires off a round, then speeds away.

The two men are motionless when I reach their side.

My heart batters against my rib cage, my blood freezing in my veins. *No. Please. Please.* My ears ring as images flash into my mind—Mia, all those years ago, still and silent on her bed.

I can't lose anyone anymore.

A sob rips out of my throat, my hands trembling as I grab the shoulders of the infuriating man who has burrowed inside my heart without me noticing.

"Rex? Rex! Oh my God, please." I search his body for a bullet hole.

Where's the damn wound? Why isn't he moving?

Seconds or an eternity later, I hear him groan.

His eyes flicker open. Those beautiful slate-gray eyes.

Crushing, startling relief.

I collapse on top of him, tears pouring down my face. "You're okay. Oh my God, you're okay."

I barely notice the crowds. The sirens. The camera flashes. The voices—Rhys or Bree or someone else—asking if I'm all right.

I can only focus on the warmth of the man beneath me. The rapid movements of his chest. The hammering of his heart against my ear. The reassuring scent of amber and bergamot tinged with salt.

"Olive. What did I tell you in the cave? Don't you *dare* throw yourself in harm's way again."

His beautiful deep voice, as fine as the whiskey he likes to drink.

I'm not even mad he's calling me by Mia's nickname.

But then his words register in my mind. He's pissed at me when he almost got killed?

My vision still blurry, I fist his shirt and get in his face. "W-Why would you do that? Risk your life? Why would you do something so *stupid*? Do you know how scared I was?"

Those crystalline eyes snare mine. The bloodlust is gone, and in its place is an aching vulnerability.

With trembling fingers, I wipe off the blood splatter marring his handsome face. His lips part, the softest hiss escaping.

He heaves out a ragged exhale and swallows.

"He hurt you. I'll kill anyone who hurts you."

CHAPTER SEVENTEEN

"Was it The Association?" I ask Elias on the phone as I stride toward the sky deck three days later, needing some fresh air after I called him to see if he had updates about what happened in Pyrgos.

Two motorcyclists dressed head-to-toe in black, stopping only when they reached us.

I remember asking who sent them. Because deep down, I knew something was off.

The precision and speed with which they drew their guns. The single kill shot when it was obvious the man I beat up couldn't escape—eliminating loose ends.

"I'm confirming a few things, but I think you know my answer to that. If it was a robbery, they weren't really successful, were they? A lot of risk for a few purses and loose change," Elias answers.

And Olivia's camera.

I emailed a contact to see if they could locate it. The odds are slim to none, but it's important, judging by how she dashed after the motorcyclist when he snatched it from her hands.

And so I'll find it for her.

"So, Bree's in danger. Officially now." I swing open the door and step onto the deck, my eyes squinting from the cold sunlight.

"Yes. They obviously figured out her identity. I told her not to leave the ship for now."

My ribs tighten as guilt sweeps in. I didn't save Bree first. They almost took her. They would've taken her if she hadn't fought back.

It didn't even occur to me to go to her first, because all my attention was riveted on Olivia.

Fuck. I can't mess this up. I can't have another death happen on my watch.

"Do I need to fly out earlier?" Elias asks. "Because what the hell happened to you? I saw photos of the bastard—I can barely make out a face. You better hope forensics showed the bullet killed him and not you."

I groan, a fifty-pound cannonball sitting on top of my chest.

I don't know how to answer him.

The surge of violence three days ago obliterated all rational thought, and I can't bring myself to regret it.

My fingers tighten on my phone, and I hiss from the sharp pain. Raw knuckles requiring ten stitches will do that to you.

Shit. I was a savage.

"Rex? I can pull you out if you can't handle it. You had a shit ton of witnesses, you don't just—"

"He hurt her."

The confession pours out of me, and silence fills the line.

It's the only answer I have.

My mind still quakes from the red-hazed memories of the scariest moment in my adult life.

The asshole pointing a gun at Olivia.

Her eyes wide with fear.

The murderous craze surging in my veins when I pushed her out of the way, not caring about my safety.

Then I let my monster out.

My ears rung. Logic winked out. Only one thought percolated in my mind.

Kill him. Kill the bastard.

Turn him into ground meat so he could never hurt her again.

Then the strange split second when the man lying beneath me, taking my punches, became...*me.*

The same gray eyes rimmed with dark circles, a deranged smile twisting his lips.

That only spurred me on.

"I can't let him hurt her, Elias. Don't ask me more." A shaky exhale escapes me.

I'm a madman. If Olivia hadn't stopped me, I would've killed the man. Heck, I probably killed him.

I can't care about her. I should stay away.

But fuck, my willpower is disappearing.

"I see." I hear the familiar clicking of his lighter. "I understand more than you think," he murmurs cryptically.

"Aren't you going to ask me who I'm talking about?" My lips curl in self-derision. I'm a violent madman with no self-control. Add that to my list of unhinged traits. "Or do you know that too?"

"You threw yourself in front of a bullet for *her* while the woman you're supposed to protect is being kidnapped. I'd say it's pretty self-explanatory, wouldn't you? You Andersons lose your minds when your hearts are involved."

"Nothing's involved."

"Keep telling yourself that." He chuckles softly. "You still in this, or you want out?"

Determination pulses through me. I have to see this through. "Good luck in hell trying to pull me out."

"Thought you'd say that." The clicking stops and amusement leaves his voice. "Lie low. I'll let you know if I find anything. Lana and I'll meet you in Dubrovnik."

"Lana? Why are you traveling with my sister? And does she know?"

"Global warming, one flight versus two, saving on jet fuel. Take your pick. You Andersons have a target on your back now. It's better this way. And she doesn't need to know."

He hangs up before I can ask more questions.

Head dipped down, I barely notice the wide open seas and the other passengers walking by. I tug my hair, my head swirling with what I can do, and what I should do next.

Everything's unraveling. Spinning out of control.

Then I smell it.

The faint sweet scent of honey and cotton.

Olivia.

I spin around just in time to see her marching up to me, her lips pursed and eyes narrowed. She's wearing another simple dress—blue this time. Her hair is in the same tidy little bun.

God, she's so beautiful.

My heart skips a beat, and my lips twitch.

And just like that, the earlier heaviness vanishes.

Her magic.

"I've been looking for you everywhere. I don't care if you go all macho-man on me, because you'll meet me for your next session. No more delays." She crosses her arms over her chest.

I bite back my smile. Busted. I have been rescheduling our mandatory heart to hearts.

"Didn't you learn in your intro to psychology classes you're signaling a closed-off attitude when you do that?" I motion to her arms.

She lets out the smallest growl. "Don't change the subject. Mr. Anderson, we need to meet. What happened three days ago was traumatizing for everyone involved. You almost died. You need to talk to someone about it."

"We're back to Mr. Anderson now, huh? What happened to 'Rex'? I seem to recall someone bawling on top of me, crying out my name because she was terrified I'd gotten shot."

A faint blush creeps onto her cheeks, and a muscle twitches in her jaw.

She's so fucking sensitive. Unable to help myself, I lean in, my pulse galloping. I wonder what else I can do to make her blush harder. "Olive...I like it. My name on your lips. Say it again."

I waggle my brows.

Her nostrils flare and I swallow a chuckle.

But instead of blowing up, Olivia presses a hand to her chest and takes a deep breath. Then she rearranges her features into a mask of serenity.

"I hate to do this, but..." she slides out her phone from her pocket, "I think it's time to give big brother a call. After all, Maxwell has sent me a few messages and I've been busy all morning, so I haven't replied yet. We don't want him worried, do we?"

I freeze. She's pulling the Maxwell card on me again. "You threatening me again?"

She blinks her large, innocent eyes.

Nope. Not falling for that, you little devious, too smart for your own good doctor. Fuck, why does she get my blood pumping?

"What? When did I say that? I'm just giving my *employer* an update like any consummate professional would do."

The vixen taps on her cell, and the next thing I know, ringing sounds erupt from the speakers.

I reach for the phone, but she spins away, a sly grin on her face. Cold sweat beads my upper lip as panic surges inside me. *I can't let her call Maxwell; I need to stay on this cruise.*

"Fine. Name the time and place. I'll be there."

Olivia's eyes widen, like she isn't expecting me to agree. But when she opens her mouth, a voice travels from the speakers.

"Domino's Pizza, would you like to hear our meat lover's special today?"

An American accent. She called back home just to mess with me.

The flush deepens on her face, and she ends the call.

"You played me," I murmur, a tickle crawling up my chest. The panic earlier slowly shifts into something infinitely more enticing. "Pizza delivery. Fucking pizza."

"What can I say? I'm famished after talking to assholes and I love the meat lover's pizza."

Then, a thought occurs to me and I step up to her, watching the color leave her face, her smugness completely gone.

Bending down, I whisper, "Meat lover's special, huh? You like your meat? Long, thick, and juicy?"

Olivia hiccups, her sassy mouth clearly rendered speechless.

My gaze drops to her lips as they part. Her tongue dips out. This brazen, luscious mouth. I want to smother it with my hand or taste it.

A pulse flickers in her neck and a telltale throb pulses in my cock. Of all the women in the world, my cock now only reacts to the one woman I should stay away from.

She clears her throat and straightens—her David to my Goliath. I bite back a smile.

"I'm picky about my meat, Mr. Anderson. If it's overdone, I'll shred it with my teeth, then spit it out."

I recoil, imagining her chewing off my dick with a sick smile on her face.

She doles out a satisfied smirk. "Tomorrow. Two p.m. My office. See you there, Mr. Anderson. Show up or it won't be Domino's Pizza I'm calling."

Damn it, I forgot David *beat* Goliath.

CHAPTER EIGHTEEN

THE NEXT DAY, I find myself on a patient bed in the medical bay while I wait for the doctor to check the stitches in my hands. I look at the clock on the wall.

One forty. Twenty minutes before the good doctor picks apart my mind.

My phone vibrates *again*.

"Fuck," I mutter, noticing yet another incoming text message.

When my phone buzzes nonstop like operators hammering Morse code during World War I, I know I'm in deep shit.

Better to deal with it now before they fly out and check on me. Knowing my siblings, this is definitely something they would do.

I pull up the family group chat and groan at the barrage of texts waiting for me. They decided to re-name the chat to "Rex's Unending Intervention," which is par for the course in their antics to single out one of us each year.

Maxwell

> Before I lose it as a CEO, I'm asking as your brother to return my calls. I'm worried.

Ryland

> C, the headlines aren't flattering. *Gossip Times* said you could've stopped when the man was down? What happened? Are you okay? Let's hope the autopsy shows the bullet killed him, not you.

Oh look, the same worry as Elias. I wonder if the mobster has talked to him already. But at least he isn't calling me by my two full middle names, Cassius Wentworth. That's when I know he's pissed.

Ethan

> Bullshit. Greg Masters is out to get him. Why the hell would you stop when the perp had a gun? You disarm them. Permanently. Give him no chance to fight back.

Charles

> You sound like Elias.

Steven

> But wasn't the gun on the ground already? Elias sent us photos of the crime scene. It was a bloodbath. I have to say I'm impressed, Rex. Didn't know you had it in you.

That answers my question. Damn Elias. He probably looped in my siblings, hoping they could rein me in. Make me think before I act. I'm a ticking time bomb and I bet Elias senses it.

Taylor

> I'm proud. The assholes had it coming. And just to let you know, ladies love an unhinged, morally gray man.

Charles

> I can attest to that. *wink* And I got the girl.

Grace

> You guys! Charles had a good reason for avenging Tay. And we keep forgetting. This *isn't* Rex! He's the fun one! The cuddly teddy bear!

I grimace. God's gift to mankind, sure, but a teddy bear? Come on!

Lana

> C, I hate you for making me worry. I'm counting down the days until I get there. Because you apparently need babysitting.

I roll my eyes and text them a sign of life—a pic of me blowing a kiss, flashing my bandaged knuckles at the same time. Then I send another one of me giving them the middle finger.

Rex

> Teddy bear, really? You have so many better options. The fun Anderson, the life of the party, sex god, lady whisperer, dopamine king. I mean, I can go on, but if you don't use your creativity, you lose it.

Maxwell

> He lives. So what do you have to say for yourself?

Alexis

> Off to the girls' chat. We'll get it out of Olivia, since Rex is obviously dodging us.

My heart stutters. Olivia, my hard-ass, sweet Olivia.
Not your Olivia. She can't be yours, Rex.

Rex

> Ever heard of HIPAA?

More pings ensue and I groan, but then a new message comes through—one not from my family.

Unknown number

> This is my new number. Had to ditch the old one. I know you said I shouldn't text you because it's dangerous.

Ava. Raya's daughter.

I saw the news. Are you okay? Is it really a robbery? Or are they after you because you helped us? Are they a fucking shadow to you too?

I frown. Is something going on with them? We've disappeared them. They should be safe.

Are you guys okay? Do you need help?

We're fine. Sorry. I'm just pissed. But we're worried about you. Glad you're okay.

"Sorry for the delay, my last appointment went long." Dr. Rhys Fenton pulls up a chair next to me and I put my phone away. "Let's take a look and see how it's healing, shall we?"

"This really isn't necessary," I mutter, showing the man my hand.

He carefully unwraps the bandages and I scope him out. This man, who works closely with my Olive.

Fuck. Not your Olive!

Full head of hair, tall—but not as tall as me, of course—passable muscles. I'd give him an eight with me being an eleven on the scale of ten.

He must be popular with the ladies.

Then I remember how he was with her that day at Pyrgos. He made her smile. He nudged her shoulder, and she didn't recoil.

He shouldn't be touching her.

You basket case. You shouldn't touch her.

Lava rushes through my veins and my hand jerks in his grasp.

Dr. Fenton frowns, pauses his examination, and looks up. "Everything okay? Is the pain tolerable?"

I grunt.

He chuckles and shakes his head as he affixes fresh bandages over my wounds. "Looking good. No signs of infection."

"I could've told you that." Throwing the blankets off me, I swing my legs off the bed.

I have no time for this—to be coddled over a few stitches, or to be near someone I clearly don't like, judging by my impulse to tell him to fuck off.

As I approach the door, he says, "You know, that was brave. What you did—covering Dr. Lin with your body when the asshole shot at her."

I freeze, my pulse kicking up a notch.

"I can't help but wonder if there's something going on between the two of you. Not that it's any of my business, but everyone knows you're her patient and the rules are strict—"

"Well, it's a good thing it's *none of your business then,* huh?" Spinning around, I face him, finding his shrewd eyes narrowed, lips pursed.

The charming doctor is gone, and in his place is a suspicious man who's clearly jealous and is marking his territory.

She'll never be yours.

I gnash my teeth. "Dr. Lin is my physician and a family friend. I won't have anyone question her reputation by implying any wrongdoing."

There can't be any wrongdoing. Not by me or anyone else.

CHAPTER NINETEEN

"I'M SORRY. THERE ARE no leads yet, Dr. Lin. But rest assured, the local chief of police is coordinating the search," Laura, the personal concierge assigned to me, says apologetically through the phone. I called to her after my last patient appointment—a patron who had an anxiety attack on board—ended early.

A lump forms in my throat. The Leica is irreplaceable. I had plans for the pictures I took with the camera, plans I would carry out at Las Fallas. And now, those photos, along with my memento from Mia, are gone.

I've failed her and lost another piece of myself.

"Thanks for looking into it. Please keep me posted."

Laura murmurs more apologies before hanging up.

It's only a camera, Olivia. You could've lost your life.

When I was in elementary and middle school, my parents enrolled us in a Saturday Chinese school. Boy, did we complain. Other kids got to sleep in, watch TV and have fun, but we needed to be up at eight and go to class. We'd practice a language I didn't use except with my parents, and do homework.

Tons of homework.

But now, as an adult, I'm appreciative. There are things I've learned—the culture, the idioms. One of which is *qian cai nai shen wai zhi wu*, which roughly translates to "money and possessions are things outside of oneself." Possessions and wealth can come and go, but they don't matter in the grand scheme of things. Because what's most important is ourselves and our loved ones.

But what if those loved ones are gone? What if you're alone in the world?

You aren't alone, Olivia. I remind myself of my girls.

Lana called me right after the attack, worried about me. Taylor and Grace video chatted with me. Taylor waved her fists in the air, promising wrath and fury at whoever did this to us. Belle and Alexis called from the Anderson Estate, with Belle showing me Silas the husky, saying dogs make everything better.

I talk back to my negative thoughts, knowing I should be grateful I survived the attack when someone knocks on the door.

My head snaps up and I glance at my phone. Two thirty-five.

Of course he's late.

"Come in."

Raking in one more fortifying breath, because I know I'll need it, I pull out my notebook and pen, ready for another game of chess with the most infuriating Anderson of the bunch.

The devil strolls in, a lazy grin on his lips, his sky-blue shirt half-buttoned, revealing a swath of sun-kissed skin, his hair sticking out in multiple directions like he couldn't be bothered to comb it.

It all works on him somehow—the handsome, I don't take life seriously billionaire.

Too bad it's fake though.

"He hurt you. I'll kill anyone who hurts you."

His fervent vow from that day causes the swarm of butterflies taking residence in my gut to flap their wings.

He looked murderous then. Unhinged.

He was utterly glorious.

He threw himself on top of me to save my life.

I shouldn't be thinking like this. I shouldn't be attracted to this behavior.

He's your patient. He's mentally unwell. This is ridiculous.

"My little Olive. Were you waiting for me? Sorry. Popular man, lots of appointments." He winks and shrugs.

He reminds me of how pit bulls show you who they are with their menacing barks, but those fluff balls, Chow Chows? They may look like a stuffed animal but are among the most aggressive dog breeds in the world.

I press my lips together and tamp down my impulse to yell at him.

Calm. Professional. Poise. Don't let him rile you, Olivia.

"Thanks for coming," I say, making sure my voice is sweet. "Have a seat."

His eyes widen, like he's surprised I haven't called him out about his tardiness.

Nope. Everything he wants me to do, I'll do the opposite.

"You like your meat? Long, thick, and juicy?"

Argh! I bite my cheek as my face flames. The devil.

He arches his brow, and I take a deep breath, quashing down my inappropriate thoughts.

"So, I'm here. What's on the docket, Doc?" He chuckles. "Docket...Doc, nice rhyme to it. Would make a good marketing slogan."

Rex pulls up a chair across from my desk, sits down, and slides his hands behind his head. "It's exhausting to be a genius sometimes."

"I can imagine how tiring that can be, not being able to turn off your brain." I return his perusal with a small smile.

A muscle twitches in his forehead and his eyes narrow slightly before relaxing.

"You look ravishing today, Olive. Not everyone can pull off the serious doctor look with that bun of yours. But you just look like a sexy librarian to me. Do you dress like this to tempt your patients?"

My smile strains against my lips. *You asshole, you're on.*

I grip my pen tighter. "Are you tempted?"

"Definitely." Those startling gray eyes darken.

"To do what?" My pulse shoots off to a rickety start. *Don't goad him. Disengage, dammit.*

Rex leans in slowly, his hands flattening on the desk. "You don't want to know, little Olive. It might corrupt your innocent mind."

"My patients suffer from an array of mental illnesses. Trust me, I'm not easily scared. And sometimes, I find discussing someone's fantasies reveals a lot about the workings of his or her mind."

Angling the notepad toward me, I jot down a few sentiments.

Rex Anderson is the devil. He's infuriating, makes me want to throttle him, but I'm a goddamn professional!

I circle "goddamn professional" for good measure. I sigh. I feel better already.

He stares at my pen scraping against paper, the furrow between his brows deepening. I cock my head and purse my lips, pretending I'm uncovering earth-shattering secrets from him and jotting them down.

A low growl rumbles from his throat.

This works every time.

"And you're here, obviously not because you have a problem, as you've previously mentioned, but because your behavior back in New York City has caused concern for your family. So, let's unravel your heart and your mind. And together, we can identify the threads you previously missed but are showing through your actions."

After flipping to a new page to hide the evidence of my frustrations, I set the notepad down.

Then I smile at him again and wait.

His jaw works, his gaze skating over my face, my neck, to the simple white sheath dress I have on, then back up.

I force myself to remain still and let him look, or intimidate, his fill.

The seconds tick by and the stark silence only fans the invisible flames in the room.

The world can burn around us, but I'm willing to play a game of chicken with him again, and this time, I won't lose.

Finally, his nostrils flare and his lips twitch. "Stop it."

Checkmate.

"Stop what?"

"Playing my game against me. I've practiced my entire life, and trust me, you can't outplay me."

"I wasn't aware we were playing a game?" I tap one finger on my notepad—the *click, clack* sound akin to a leaky faucet dripping throughout the night.

Enough to drive you nuts.

"What do you want from me?" he rasps. "What the *hell* do you want with me?"

To save you from self-destruction. To save your family from bottomless sorrow and guilt when they find you dead somewhere. To save them from spending their lives seeking atonement, to search for answers, the same questions rattling inside their minds night after night.

Why didn't I see the signs? Why didn't I do something sooner?

I see your signs. I need to save you like you saved me.

"I want honesty, Mr. Anderson," I murmur.

My chest twinges when I see resignation in his eyes.

"There's nothing to tell. And all the talk in the world won't change anything in the past." His throat vibrates, and he glances away. A haunted heaviness threads through his voice. "I wish it were that simple."

"Let's start with something easy, then. One truth that no one knows, and we'll go from there."

Rex stills, and for a moment, he doesn't appear to be breathing, but I know he heard me. After a minute or two, he returns his gaze to me.

This time, there's a hardness in them, a glimpse of the damaged Anderson behind the playboy prince the world sees.

"A truth *for* a truth, then. Final offer, *Doctor* Lin."

A truce. He's calling me by my title.

I ignore the red flags in my mind, needing to focus on the white one he's waving. My pulse scatters and hairs rise on my forearms. "Fine. A truth for a truth then."

Why does it feel like a trick? Like I'm giving him far more than I'll receive?

I'm a professional. I can guard my secrets, even if it's the last thing I do.

He stares at me, his eyes unflinching. Then he sits back in his chair and clears his throat.

"I have insomnia. I can't sleep for more than three hours a night." His shoulders slump, like the confession took something out of him.

A chink in his armor.

It makes sense—the dark eye circles, the erratic moods. Chronic insomnia will do that to you.

I collect this scrap and store it away in my treasure chest. As much as the insufferable man drives me up a wall, he's giving me a piece of himself he's never shown others.

"And why do you think that is?"

"I don't want to share that." He cocks his brow as if daring me to berate him.

But I won't. I recognize a breakthrough when I see it.

"That's fair. We don't have to talk about that right now. How long has it been going on?"

"Decades."

He doesn't elaborate. If it's been going on forever, it can't only be insomnia causing his recent spiral then. There has to be something else.

"It must be exhausting to function with so little sleep. How do you deal with it?"

Slowly, Rex sits up, then he leans toward me, inch by inch, the shrinking distance sucking all the oxygen out of the room. I force myself to remain still when the flames I thought were snuffed suddenly reignite and lick up my body.

His gaze drops to my mouth, and his lips hitch into a sensual half-smile. "I *fuck.*"

My clit pulses. I feel those two words like a caress.

He stares at me, his attention unwavering. "I fuck a lot. Until I've wrung out every single orgasm from my partners. Until I'm exhausted."

Strangled breaths reach my ears, and belatedly, I realize they are from me.

His words are barely above a whisper, but I feel them—the tendrils of lust, desperation, agony singeing my skin. My core throbs as I watch his eyes take on a mad haze, his tongue dipping out to wet his lips.

Like he's imagining us in the bedroom.

"Scared yet, Doctor? That's just the tip of the iceberg." His eyes suddenly flare. "Don't do that."

"Do what?"

"Chew on your lip. Waving the red cape in front of a murderous bull."

My breath rushes out of me. I release my bottom lip I didn't know I was mutilating with my teeth.

Straightening my shoulders, I reply, "Bulls are partially colorblind. It's the motion of the cloth that gets them. They don't see red. The color is only for the spectators."

The spell breaks, and he jolts as if I've electrocuted him with a factoid I picked up watching late-night documentaries on the Discovery Channel when I, too, was tormented by the past.

"Does your family know about your insomnia? Have you seen a doctor about it?" I steer the conversation back to safe waters.

"No. I'm not the only one suffering from lack of sleep. They have enough troubles on their plate. No need to worry them." He chuckles, but there's no merriment, only more resignation. "Casey's worried though, but then, he's worried about everything."

"And he is?" I wasn't aware of an Anderson with the name of Casey.

He stares at his hands. "My best friend. My oldest friend. I honestly don't know why he puts up with me." The words are barely audible, but they ring the loudest of everything he's said today.

Shame. He's dealing with shame and doesn't want to burden anyone.

Then, he shifts in his seat and glances at his phone. "Time's up, Doc. But since our conversation has gone so well, I'll throw in a freebie."

Rex reaches into his pocket and pulls out a vial half-filled with white pills. He gives it a shake. "I'm sure you and my family are dying to know, and I can put your worries to rest. These are caffeine pills. I take them because of my insomnia."

With a mock salute, he stands and strides to the door, the earlier laziness in his frame nowhere to be seen.

"Is this why you don't want psychiatric meds?" I ask.

Not that I can prescribe any to him yet. I need to figure out what's going on first. And I don't believe in forcing people to take medication if they aren't ready for it.

He stops mid-stride.

"I don't think meds will work on my problems," he murmurs.

The muscles in his back flex and bunch when he grips the doorknob.

"You owe me a truth, Doc. I'll collect one day." He doesn't turn around as he says, "You can't save me. I need to have something worth saving first."

His pained words echo in the room when the door snicks shut.

My lungs draw in a few frenzied inhales, like I've been running a marathon for the past hour. I pick up my pen and write, my movements barely quick enough to keep up with my thoughts.

Best friend Casey knows him better than his family.

Insists on relying on caffeine pills instead of addressing the root cause of insomnia. Overreliance or addiction? Note to self: research the newest pills on the market and side effects.

Shame is a primary factor in erratic behavior. Appears to be tied to someone he's lost. But why now?

Claims to use sex to fall asleep, but it's a lie.

I don't know how I know it. Perhaps it was the fascinated glint in his irises when he was telling me about his exploits, like my reaction was the high he was chasing.

But the statement rings false.

Rex Anderson is a party animal, a relentless flirt, and supposedly a king in the sack, but I haven't seen him in the news with a woman for almost half a year until Bree, and even then, they both imply their relationship isn't like that. Their interactions are also strangely respectful, not at all how lovebirds or friends with benefits would behave.

Like you would know, Olivia. You had one boyfriend in high school and you had sex three times.

And it was wholly uninspiring, to say the least.

I jot down another question.

Who is Bree to him?

Then I drop back into my chair and close my eyes. I'm equal parts frustrated and invested.

But deep down, I'm afraid I'll never unravel the puzzle that is Rex Cassius Anderson.

And perhaps I'm watching history replay itself, once again experiencing the same emotions.

Desperate. Frustrated.

Useless.

Chapter Twenty

"*Stupid twins. Like they're so special,*" *I mutter, hugging my notebook to my chest.*

A hot feeling burns in my belly. I want to sneak into their rooms and draw on their walls. Rip up their books. Make a mess.

But then I remember what Mom said before.

Tell a story. Make it fun. Maybe I can cook with her later if she isn't busy.

Pain carves into my chest and I flinch. I want to escape, but I can't move my arms and legs.

It's happening again—the nightly torture of horrid memories parading behind my eyelids when I fall asleep.

Darkness suffocates me, and a scream gurgles in my throat.

Nothing comes out—no sound, no movements. I'm locked in.

Stop it, Rex. Stop it before it's too late.

Sweat sticks to my forehead, but the images fire at me like bullets from a machine gun.

The Persian carpet sweeps into my vision again, the clinking of marbles striking against the wall as crisp as if it happened yesterday.

"*You're not a twin. You can't play with us.*" *I mimic Ryland's voice, my tummy clenching.* "*Meanie.*"

A story! Tell a story.

I toss a red marble at the wall, over and over. Sitting on the top step of the big staircase at home, I try to think of a new story. Something fun, something to do with cooking. Mom will like that.

The marble pings then plops on the carpeted floor before rolling down the stairs to the first floor.

Thud. Thud. Thud. Like dominos.

I open my notebook and write with my blue crayon.

There once was a big red dragon who loved to eat little boys...like twins.

I grin, my heart galloping. That's so mean, Rex.

I pull out a new marble, then another, and throw them down the stairs. The colors of the marbles are part of my story, which is about twins being cooked into a stew along with broccoli and beets because those veggies are gross.

A door bangs in the distance. I jump. I hate loud noises. Two voices—a man and a woman. Mom? They sound...mad?

My heart vaults to my throat, my pulse a hurricane in my ears, but I'm still trapped in the straitjacket of my sleep. *Stop them, Rex. Move. Stop playing with your damn marbles.*

I'm in the scene and yet, I'm vaguely aware it isn't reality.

Then the vortex sucks me back in.

My clothes are dripping wet as I run back indoors. It started drizzling the moment I ran outside to get away from the noise, the yelling.

Grinning, I hold the slippery frog in my hands. The twins will get a nice surprise when they go to their bedroom later.

I barely notice the drip, drip, drip of the water from my hair landing on the hardwood floor, or the clumps of mud I'm tracking inside. Morris, our butler, or Agnes, our housekeeper, will shake their heads and say, "Mr. Rex, play indoors when it's raining."

It's the creepy silence I notice first. I hear nothing other than the pit-ter-patter of the rain.

Goosebumps form on my arms, and the little brown frog jumps out of my hands.

"Hey! Come back here!" I chase after it but nearly trip and fall when I see it.

A pair of feet sticking out from the foot of the staircase.

I slowly inch forward.

Then the orange dress with the small penguins Mom loves because Dad got it for her last week for her birthday.

Then her pale arms, her neck, her face, her dark hair.

All twisted in weird angles.

"Mom!" I scream, and run as fast as my short legs can carry me.

Tears wet my face when I finally reach her, because I know something is wrong.

Very, very wrong.

I grab her shoulders and shake her. "Mom! Mommy! You okay?"

But all I see are blank eyes staring at the ceiling.

"Mommy!"

She doesn't answer me.

And around her, red and blue marbles are scattered over the floor and the stairs.

My marbles.

I gasp as I bolt up, finding myself on the floor of the foyer, sweat dripping over my forehead.

Fuck. Again. Another blackout. Something sharp pokes my hand and I look down and choke out an exhale.

A knife. I'm holding a kitchen knife. Why the hell am I in the foyer with a kitchen knife?

I quickly stand, my hand trembling as I set the knife on the nearest table and stumble back into my bedroom.

Mindlessly, I reach for the bottle of Velowake on my nightstand, uncap it, and shove a few pills into my mouth.

I can't let myself fall asleep. I can't do this—the blackouts, the nightmares.

Reliving one of the worst days of my life night after night, remembering in stark clarity her dead eyes, her cold body, the blood pooling on the ground. The split second of elation when I held the frog morphing into utter terror.

And finally, seeing the marbles on the ground. *My* marbles. The ones I didn't put away before I ran outside, notebook tossed aside, angry at the twins, wanting my petty revenge on them.

It's macabre. It's torture even the guards at Guantanamo Bay can't come up with.

For almost thirty years, we thought she had slipped on my marbles and tumbled down the stairs, her neck snapping upon landing. It was the curse of the eldest son when he fell in love with his wife. The woman would die within one year of his confessing his love to her. After all, this had happened for generations.

My family never questioned it. Dad was racked with guilt because he fell in love with Mom, his arranged wife, years after they got married.

Then, a little over two years ago, Maxwell was a mess because he was falling in love with Belle, his wife from a similar arranged marriage. When strange things started happening to her, he spent every ounce of energy trying to defeat said curse. Ultimately, he unraveled everything and caught the culprit behind the generations of deaths.

"It's not your fault, Rex. We never blamed you, but this makes it official," Maxwell told me back then.

I laughed it off, saying I knew that. How could anyone blame a six-year-old who forgot to clean up after himself, the same little kid who found his mother's dead body later on?

But that was a lie. I did blame myself. For years.

It's hard not to when you have a near-photographic memory and relive that night constantly, processing it as an older kid, a teenager, an adult, each time seeing the scene more vividly, each time thinking you can stop it from happening.

A million fruitless attempts at changing the past, the nightmares so real in my mind, I thought I was a little kid again.

I reach for the marble on my nightstand. A reminder of the day that changed my life.

The same day awaits me every night after I go to sleep.

Tossing the glass ball in my palm, I remember the months following Mom's death, how life was sucked out of the Anderson Estate.

Something in the house other than my mother died that day.

Laughter, music, innocence, carefree happiness.

You don't erase that type of guilt from your conscience with the snap of your fingers.

Especially when there's still a part of that day no one knows about, something I've kept inside all this time, unwilling to share.

Because...guilt, and punishment. I don't want anyone to console me. I don't deserve it.

God, Olivia would have a field day with my messed up mind.

Her pretty face appears behind my eyelids—eyes the color of freshly brewed tea, pools I can drown myself in, the elegant slope of her neck, the delicate frame of her body. I grab my phone and swipe to my email to see if the investigator has any updates on the camera search, but there aren't any. He said it may take months to track down.

Then I swipe to my secret album with her images.

The wonder on her face when she pressed her nose against the car window, eagerness rolling off her when we first arrived in Mykonos.

The lonely silhouette of her standing by the cruise ship at the port, camera in her hand, wind rustling her dress. The world moved around her, but she was still. So still, like a sturdy, reassuring lighthouse standing up against a storm.

The devious smirk on her face when she left me speechless on the sun deck, my cock digging out of my pants, because she got in the last word in our little spat.

I smile at the photos, heat spreading through my chest.

For a moment, I forget about the terrible memories, and I can finally breathe.

No. You don't deserve a break, not until you atone for the deaths, if that'll ever happen. Heck, you woke up with a fucking knife in your hand and you don't even know how it got there. You're trying to drag her into hell with you.

Disgusted with myself, I toss my phone on the bed. I bury my face between my knees, my hands shaking, when I smell it—the faint moisture, the damp earth, the brine reminding me so much of that night. Clambering off the bed, I struggle to stay upright before striding to the windows and throwing open the curtains.

Limestone cliffs dotted with muted green loom in the distance. White buildings with terracotta roofs pepper the landscape. A faint mist clings to the shoreline, cloaking the city in a ghostly fog. Thick clouds hang overhead, the dim daylight telling me it's very early in the morning and the rest of the world is still asleep.

Dubrovnik, Croatia. Otherwise known as "The Pearl of the Adriatic."

The historic city calls to me, and I know I need to get off the cruise, away from the crowds, to take a break from everything before Lana and Elias board the ship tonight, after which I won't have a moment of peace.

I need to lose myself in an ancient city that has seen natural disasters and wars, and yet remains standing.

Maybe I'll withstand it all too.

———◆———

Two hours later, after a violent match against a punching bag in the gym, my healing knuckles bloodied again, I take a quick shower and bandage my fresh wounds.

With my navy cap low on my forehead and my eyes hidden behind my aviator sunglasses, I hope I can avoid detection to-day—from Greg Masters, fawning women, everyone and anyone waiting for the Anderson screwup to fail. I straighten the sleeves of my black shirt and smooth my damp palms over my dark jeans.

Unassuming. A stranger. Not Rex-a-Million.

Run away. The voice chants in my head. What if I just ran away from it all? Disappeared off the boat today, never to resurface?

But my family. I can't bring more sadness to them, after I caused so much of it. Heck, that's why I became the jokester. To make them laugh. To give them some joy back.

I scoff. Some jokester I am. They aren't laughing these days.

I shake my head at the nonsense and pull out my phone, needing to do one more thing before I escape.

Rex

Busy today with appointments. You staying on the boat, right?

Elias told her to remain aboard. Can't take any chances with The Association still out there.

Her response comes back a minute later.

Bree

Yep. Don't worry about me. I might do some reading. Do your thing. I'll be fine.

Satisfied with her response—Bree isn't the extroverted, adventurous type to begin with, and we have the best security team on board—I jam my phone back into my pocket and slip out of the stateroom.

My footfalls are quiet, my head dipped low as I pass by passengers staggering out of their rooms, bleary-eyed and clearly in search of strong coffee. Room service staff roll carts filled with silver-dome-covered plates, the smell of poached eggs and bacon wafting through the air.

I hasten my steps, eager to get to deck three to disembark, when a large shadow falls in front of me before I enter the nearest stairwell.

"Excuse me," I mutter, pulling the bill of my cap lower.

The shadow doesn't move.

Fucking asshole. I pivot to the right, not bothering to look up, and the shadow moves with me.

Then I step to the left, and the fucker does the same.

My already thin patience runs empty, and just as I'm about to give the person in front of me a piece of my mind—

"This looks much worse than I thought."

Then comes the sound of the damn lighter.

Fucking Elias Kent.

Chapter Twenty-One

Sorry, the authorities couldn't locate your camera. They said the trail's cold.

My chest caves at the text from the concierge. It's been almost a week since our phone call and the initial shock at the events in Pyrgos Village has passed. People finally stopped finger pointing and whispering whenever I stepped into a room.

Thank God.

From what I've read online, it appears to be a botched robbery.

More importantly, the press, which I'm sure, courtesy of the Anderson family's influence, is quick to point out the autopsy of the motorcyclist showed the bullet killed the man.

Not Rex. And his violence that day was self-defense. No charges.

Relief flooded my body like ice water on a scorching day when I read the articles. I didn't want to care about the devil, one of the worst, most uncooperative patients I've ever had in my career.

But I do.

I still remember his weight on top of mine, his piercing eyes frantic as he checked my body for bullet wounds.

I still hear his furtive rasp when I asked him why he pummeled the assailant to a pulp. To this day, I question my sanity or if he really said those words.

"He hurt you. I'll kill anyone who hurts you."

Disappointed in myself for thinking of him so much, I step into the opulent Bistro La Mer on deck seven, where most of the restaurants and lounges are located. Perhaps a nice strong latte at a table with a sea view will wake me up.

"Welcome back, Dr. Lin. Do you want your usual seat on the patio?" A tall blond I haven't seen before smiles at me.

As I'm about to answer her, my eyes skate over the restaurant, noting the seafoam green walls, the plush pastel pink seating, the overcast skies outside the French doors, before snagging on an occupied table in the corner.

In particular, a stunning brunette sitting by herself, staring morosely out the windows.

Bree.

"Dr. Lin?" The receptionist cocks her head.

"S-Sorry." I force out a chuckle. "Six in the morning, not quite awake yet. But I see my friend."

I thank the hostess and walk toward Bree, not knowing what's gotten into me.

I'm interested in Bree because she knows Rex. She can tell me more about him. She can give me insight into how to get through to him.

Yes. That has to be it.

"Liar, liar," Mia taunts, and I quash her voice away.

Exhaling deeply, I crack the joints in my neck before stopping in front of Bree. She's so lost in thoughts, she doesn't even see me there.

In this proximity, I see what makeup can't hide—dark circles and bags under her eyes, her short brown hair sticking out on the side, like she didn't bother to brush it this morning. She's wearing an oversized gray sweatshirt, but she still looks cold.

And lonely.

Something about her sadness speaks to me. Tells me there's more than meets the eye.

"Is this seat taken?" I ask softly.

She jolts, her eyes flaring in panic before softening when she realizes it's me. "D-Dr. Lin, sorry. I was thinking about things." She grimaces and waves at the empty chair in front of her. "Please have a seat."

I nod and do as she says.

"I hope I'm not interrupting," I say when a waitress stops by and takes my order.

"No, no... Of course not. I...I'd been thinking about reaching out to you, but then I'd run away before I got to your office."

My Spidey sense tingles. She isn't looking at me, but is staring at her nails, and I notice they're clipped very short, no nail polish, the cuticles dry and ragged.

She's fidgety. Nervous.

Something is definitely off.

"I guess it's good I ran into you today, then." A server quietly sets down my latte before slipping away. I take a sip, watching Bree grimace and chew her fingernails. "Something on your mind?"

"How do you deal with grief?" The chewing stops, and her eyes snap up to mine.

I falter, surprised at this random topic.

Then my heart twists at her question. I know the textbook answers—the professional advice I should give her: take it a day at a time, progress is a few steps forward and a step back, grief ebbs and flows and there's no right or wrong way to deal with it—but something holds me back from saying them.

Maybe because she isn't my patient. Maybe because I want to be vulnerable so she can confide in me.

Maybe because I don't really know the answers myself.

"It's death by a thousand cuts, I suppose." I set my cup down. "I don't think anyone truly knows how to deal with it. We just make do and hope the pain lessens over time and, hopefully one day, it'll be a dull ache."

A telltale spasm behind my rib cage flares.

It's been twelve years for me, and the pain is still there.

Laughing softly, I murmur, "I probably shouldn't be saying that as a doctor. Should be more hopeful, right?"

Bree smiles. "No. I appreciate the honesty. It's refreshing."

"Is everything okay? Sorry, I can't help but wonder if your question has anything to do with..." my voice trails off, my mouth seemingly can't form his name.

The man you say you're not involved with and yet are touchy-feely with in public. The man who apparently fucks like a king and drags out orgasms from his partners so he could fall asleep because he has chronic insomnia.

My stomach churns. The contradictions in their behavior. The vibe is off. They're close, but now that I think about it, I've never even seen Rex kiss her on the lips before. I don't think they're intimate like that.

I bite my cheek. *Ugh. Stop it, Olivia. Their sleeping status has nothing to do with you.*

Bree furrows her brows like she's confused, but then her eyes widen. "Rex? Oh, this has nothing to do with him. He's...fine."

Fine? I force myself to remain still. Those Spidey senses are now church bells clanging in my head.

You don't describe Rex Anderson as fine.

He's maddening, hot as sin, smells like sex, has a voice that works better than any vibrator, a sense of humor you want to both strangle and appreciate, a brilliant mind you hope to unravel but have a feeling it's an impossible task, the perfect height for you to climb—

I shake myself. "Sorry. I was assuming...since you're here with him and we're on the world's most luxurious cruise, I just thought he was making you upset."

"No, it's nothing like that." Bree looks around and then dips toward me. She drops her voice to a whisper. "I-I hear you're close with the Andersons. And you're a doctor, so you're bound by...rules."

Cocking my head to the side, I remain silent. Where's she going with this?

"It really isn't what it seems...Rex and me. I know I've mentioned it before, but it's true. He's not my type."

Relief crashes through me and I force myself not to analyze why.

Bree blows out a heavy exhale, like a weight has been lifted off her shoulders. "I don't really know him that well."

My mouth parts and I quickly snap it shut. Then what's going on with their mixed signals? None of this makes sense.

So much for my intention of getting info from her about the infuriating asshole.

"It's about the move..." She sighs, drawing my attention back to her. "I'm relocating. Leaving my life behind. I thought I could do it, but...I guess I'm sad." Tears gather in her eyes.

Unwittingly, I reach out and clasp her hand. She squeezes me tight.

"Do you have to move? If you miss your old home so much?"

She swallows and looks down. "Yes. I made a commitment and I need to honor it. It's the right thing to do."

Her words are cryptic, and while I don't understand what kind of commitment can force someone to leave a place they clearly love, I can understand the sentiment.

I'm on this cruise ship because of a commitment I made too.

"I'm sure this move wasn't a decision you've made lightly. The fact you're here, facing something you're afraid of, tells me what type of person you are."

Her watery eyes meet my gaze.

"You're someone brave." My nose prickles, my heart clenching as I think about my journey on this trip. "You're someone who'll live life no matter what it throws at you. And despite the grief, the fears...you'll survive."

I'll survive.

Tears slide down her cheeks, and she quickly brushes them away. "Th-Thank you." She squeezes my hand before letting go. "Geez, I feel much better already. Just saying it out loud."

"You can always stop by my office if you ever want to chat. It helps to have someone to talk—"

"Surprise!" A soft scent of roses reaches my nose before a curvy brunette dressed in a chic tan sweater dress, hair tied in a ponytail, steps into view.

"Lana? Aren't you arriving tonight?"

A dark scowl crosses her face. "I was supposed to, but the Shadow King said he was coming out here earlier. Then he took it upon himself to rearrange my flight plans and drag me onto the jet with him. The overbearing, mercurial bast—"

My eyes widen. I've never seen the graceful Lana get so worked up before. "Shadow King? Who is Shadow King?"

"You know, Eli—" She stops herself, finally noticing the wide-eyed Bree who's staring at us with rapt interest. "Oh. Sorry. You guys are in the middle of breakfast. I'm clearly interrupting. I've been awake for over twenty-four hours because instead of sleeping last night, I was on the damn jet, and I can't sleep when flying. And—"

Lana blows out a breath and rearranges her lips into a bright smile.

"I'm Lana Anderson." She extends her hand to Bree. "You're Bree, Rex's...friend. I'm the head of PR at Fleur, so I know everything there is to know about anything Anderson-related that might show up in magazines and newspapers."

"Oh. Sorry if I've created more work for you." Bree scrunches her nose.

"You've been an angel, compared to his past...ahem...exploits." She shakes her head. "Ugh. I'm tired and look like crap."

Lana yawns and I snicker. Only she can say she looks like crap and still moonlight as a cover model this very instant.

"I say we all have a girls' day and try out the saltwater float garden. Oh! Or the quartz-crystal cleansing and infrared therapy. That's just in at the spa on deck eight." She grins. "I need some R and R before I hunt down my problematic brother. You gals in?"

"Maybe I'll join you tonight. I'm sightseeing today. Dubrovnik." I wave my phone, my gut pinching when I remember I don't have my Leica anymore. "Work hard, play hard, as someone says. Can't meet a hot man without going out." I give a pointed look at Lana.

She huffs out a dry laugh. "Fine." Then she turns to Bree. "What about you?"

"Uh...I guess so? I'm staying in." Bree's eyes widen, clearly bewildered and pleased at the same time. *I know, girl, I know.* Lana Anderson is a force of nature.

"Wonderful. I can ask you about my brother and why he went all serial killer apeshit in Pyrgos, because I tell you, that's *not* Rex. Bullets come flying, he'd probably duck for cover. You must be the reason he's a hero now. A good influence."

Bree's face pinkens and for a moment, the doubts I have about her relationship with Rex come roaring back. She said he's not her type. Which begs me to ask, why does she seem so close to him? Why does he hold her like he would a lover?

Why do I have more questions and fewer answers now than I had before I sat down this morning?

Chapter Twenty-Two

A CHILLY BREEZE CHAFES my skin and I quicken my pace as I hike toward the western sea-facing walls of Fort Lovrijenac, the distant cry of seagulls keeping me company.

I'm not supposed to be here at a little past seven a.m. because the fort isn't open to the public yet. But earlier, when I was walking over from the Old Town entrance, I saw a guard collapsed in the middle of the road in what appeared to be a seizure. Visions of his body being trampled by cars propelled me forward.

I had to save him—save people in trouble. My calling.

Sprouting the worst Croatian ever—after all, the language glossary in guidebooks weren't meant for these situations—I declared my doctor status to bystanders, whipped into action, moved him carefully away from oncoming traffic, and stayed with him until his colleagues arrived with a medical team.

As a thank you, a stern-looking officer motioned to the towering fort behind him and, in heavily accented English, told me to have a quiet stroll inside before it got overrun by tourists.

In the distance, faint golden rays attempt to break through the clouds, nature clearly not ready for the sun to disrupt this brooding, brisk morning. I stop to take out my phone and snap a picture of a seagull spreading its wings mid-flight, bravely fighting against the frigid gust.

I wish I had my Leica with me. It'd be more meaningful to take photos for Mia with the camera she gave me.

Holding in a sigh, I turn on the panoramic view and sweep the phone from left to right, taking in the sturdy walls of the ancient fort, the limestone arches, the cannon slots, the deep blue sea peeking out in the distance.

And a lonely silhouette of a man wearing a baseball cap, sitting atop a low segment of the walls.

I freeze, then slowly lower my phone.

There's something familiar about him.

I walk toward him, my heart skipping several beats when I take in his corded forearms straining against rolled-up sleeves and his large hands bracing the wall, as if it's taking all his energy to keep himself upright.

He's sitting so still, he almost looks like a statue. If it weren't for the place being empty, I would've missed him.

Another icy gust hits me in my face. My nose tickles. I cover my mouth before I sneeze, but I'm too late.

The sound gives me away.

The man whips his head around and intense gray eyes, framed by deep slashes of dark brows, meet mine.

Rex.

He's the version of him I saw on the sun deck when we first arrived. Raw magnetism. Coiled intensity. Completely opposite of the flirty persona he shows to the public.

Unbidden, I close the distance between us, drawn to him like a magnet finally finding its partner.

He doesn't move a muscle, his face impassive except for the searing heat in his gaze.

I carefully climb onto the wall and sit next to him. Despite the few feet separating us and the icy morning air, I'm not so cold anymore. In fact, I haven't felt this warm in a long time.

We sit there in silence. I don't say hello or good morning to him, and likewise, he doesn't speak to me.

We're just two souls who aren't supposed to be here, staring at the endless azure waves tipped in white, crashing against the rocky cliffs and sand below.

My eyes make the mistake of dipping down, and I shake when I finally notice how far up I am.

One slip and I'm dead.

My mouth dries and teeth chatter. *Carpe diem. Don't be the boring, safe twin. Embrace the rule breaker inside you. Live without fears...for yourself.*

"One hundred twenty feet. Give or take," Rex murmurs, his voice a hoarse rasp.

"C-Come again?" I curl my fingers around the limestone slab.

Look at the horizon. Don't look down. Whatever you do, don't look down.

"That's how far up we are."

"I see."

I close my eyes. No, I don't see. And knowing I'm perched at the edge of a twelve-plus story cliff isn't helping my balance either.

His low chuckles drift to my ears. "You're afraid of heights."

And small, tight spaces, which he probably figured out from the cave fiasco. It's why I admire Alexis, who learned to swim after a near-drowning that left her in an eight-year coma.

It takes guts to face your fears.

"I'm afraid of stupidity and idiocy. Sitting at the edge of a cliff fits both categories."

"Then why are you here? Go stand on the ground like a good rule follower I'm sure you are."

Gritting my teeth, I don't answer him. Resentment builds up inside me. I've been called names all my life and I don't like it, being pigeon-holed. Good follower. Good student. Good doctor.

A part of me clamors to break free. I want to be bewitching. *He called you that on the jet, remember?*

No, that was him trying to annoy me.

Scraping noises reach my ears, and suddenly, a wall of heat appears next to me. "Don't worry. I won't let my good little girl fall to her death."

My blood heats at his words. Good little girl doesn't sound so...obedient right now. She sounds devious, naughty, and decidedly...bad. My pulse kicks up at the thought.

I like it.

He's such a bad influence.

I stiffen, my eyes still squeezed shut. "You're not that much older than me, Rex."

"So it's Rex today? Not Mr. Anderson?"

"We're obviously not in a session."

"Not the session I want anyway," he whispers in my ear, and goosebumps pebble my arms. "Although if we were in one of my sessions, I'd let you call me whatever you want. And I'm seven years older than you... I consider that significant."

His words graze my skin before snaking between my legs, and I shiver.

"I'm cold," I mutter, not knowing why I'm explaining myself.

Definitely not because he's a master in seduction and, apparently, according to Lana, I still need to get laid.

He huffs out a dry laugh. "Keep telling yourself that."

"Do you only have two modes, Rex? Shameless flirt and brooding psycho?" I slap my hand over my mouth, shocked at what I called him.

I, of all people, know psychopathy is a medical condition and not to be used as an insult.

I'm ashamed of myself.

Rex tsks under his breath. "*Doctor* Lin, do I get on your nerves?"

"I wonder what gave that away."

He snorts and moves even closer until his hard body presses up against mine, his thigh acting like an anchor, his arm perched behind me. He's bracing my back and body the way a chair would.

Like he's trying to make me feel safe.

"Open your eyes. I won't let you fall. Trust me."

My heart stutters at his words. *Trust me.* I shiver again, and this time, even I can't pretend it's from the cold.

The next thing I know, something covers my head.

He put his baseball cap on me.

"Trust me, Olivia," he repeats.

I think back to how safe I felt in his arms when I had a panic attack in the caves. How reassuring his weight was on top of me when he saved me from getting shot.

Despite all his red flags and irrational behaviors, I believe him.

I open my eyes, finding him staring at me, his gaze soft. He adjusts the cap on my head and tucks a few stray hairs behind my ears. My skin lights up like fireworks on the Fourth of July.

"There, all snug and warm. A snow bunny."

Rex smiles, a small and genuine one. He grazes my cheek with his finger and my breath hitches. The touch is gentle and sweet—another side of Rex Anderson the world rarely sees.

He murmurs, "Covering your head keeps you warm. Or that's what I'm told."

I hiccup, still mesmerized by the soft smile on his face. At this moment, he looks younger, more lighthearted.

He breaks our stare and turns toward the sea. "Beautiful, isn't it? If you hadn't climbed on top of the wall, you wouldn't have gotten this view. Or the feeling of dangling your feet in the air, the ocean far away yet seemingly at your fingertips."

Heaving a deep breath, I blink and let my vision refocus on the dark waters in the distance.

"If you don't face your fears head-on, you'll never get over them," he murmurs.

Something in his voice—a twinge of melancholy—wrenches my heart, and I look at him, finding his troubled gaze riveted on the horizon.

"Is that what you do?" I whisper. "But you're...fearless."

He lives like no one's watching, making decisions because they serve him, not others.

"I envy you." The words tumble out of me and I gasp, belatedly realizing what I just revealed to myself and to him.

Is my contempt toward him really because of his hedonistic persona, or is it because I wish I could be more like him? Make choices for myself?

His gaze snaps to mine, and for a second, I forget how to breathe, because the pain in his eyes is eviscerating. It's a right hook to my face.

"Things aren't always what they seem. I'm terrified of many things, Olivia. Always have been. I hide it well now, but it's my downfall."

But why? How? He's a daredevil who doesn't care what the world thinks of him.

Is this a facade too?

Questions hang between us, but a strange force stops me from asking.

Because in this moment, with his body pressed up against me, I—the good rule follower who fears everything—am sitting on the edge of a cliff and not afraid. And Rex—the daredevil who runs on adrenaline and caffeine pills—just admitted he is.

It's then I know... He's a man I can't force to give me answers.

The answers are only earned when he feels safe.

Because he's scared of people seeing the real him. Somehow, he believes his true self is unworthy.

And that makes me sad. A different ache ripples under my rib cage.

"And do I make you brave?" The question slips out and I curse myself. *I'm pushing too hard.*

He falters.

The moment breaks. His lips slowly curve into a sensual grin and my pulse leaps.

"Maybe."

Before I can ask what he means, he jumps down to the pavement—quick and graceful, like a panther.

He holds his hand out, a twinkle in his eyes. "But I'm more curious about one thing... Do *you* want to test your bravery with me?"

Chapter Twenty-Three

BEFORE I FULLY CLIMB down from the wall, he grabs my hand and takes off running.

"What the heck? Where are we going?"

Rex doesn't answer and instead quickens his pace into a full-on sprint.

My lungs strain for oxygen. I'm winded and need to exercise more because making trips to the bathroom from my office clearly doesn't count. "Slow down. You're too fast. You're a foot taller than me; your legs are longer. *Eeek!*"

Rex hauls me into his arms in a fireman's carry, and I bat at any part of him I can reach, which is as effective as a fly flapping its wings to put out a fire.

Don't think about his muscles—strong and sturdy. That sexy vein rippling in his neck. I want to lick it.

Don't look, Olivia! Self-control.

He's forbidden. *Verboten. Prohibido.* God, he's drawing out random foreign words I've picked up over the years. He's driving me nuts.

"Put me down, Rex!" I squeal, jostling in his hold, with no recourse but to cling onto him for dear life.

"Live a little, Olive." He looks down and winks, a mad grin on his face. "Trust me! It's good to be surprised sometimes."

My center-of-gravity plummets and a screech tears out of my throat. Stairs, he's flying down stairs. Where did the damn stairs come from?

I don't care anymore. I'm shamelessly gluing myself to him.

Minutes later, he comes to a sudden stop, then he sets me down on a patch of rocks and shrubbery.

My mind still in a daze, my lungs heaving in desperate gulps of air, I glance around, finding the fort far above, and notice the chains and bright yellow signs next to us. I bet the words say, do not trespass in Croatian.

"W-Why are we here? I don't think we're supposed to—" I whip my head toward him, my words freezing in my throat when I take in the sight before me.

Rex Anderson, his dark hair tousled by the wind, a ray of sunlight shining on him like he's some Greek god, is taking off his clothes in front of me, with the cerulean seas as the backdrop.

"Wh-What are you doing?"

His full lips hitch up as he pins me with those mesmerizing eyes. Still not answering me, he continues unbuttoning his black shirt, slowly revealing hard, cut muscles, a body that looks like it's carved by Renaissance artists. Tanned skin glistens with a sheen of sweat, drawing attention to the smattering of hair on his chest, down the ridges of his abs to the happy trail disappearing in his pants.

An image of me trailing my tongue over that ridge flashes into my mind. My mouth waters.

I gulp, unable to look away as my pulse drums in my ears. Rex doesn't speak, but chucks his shirt to the side, then moves on to his jeans.

My eyes bug out and my legs finally wake up because I'm moving toward him, even as my mind screams for me to turn around and run away. Stopping before him, I cover my eyes because seeing him almost naked is crossing my wires and tempting me to make very bad decisions.

"Rex? What on earth are you—"

"You're a good girl, aren't you? Have you seen a half-naked man before? Or am I your first?" He pries my hand from my eyes.

The jeans are off, then the shoes and socks, and seconds later, he's standing before me, clad only in a tight pair of black boxer briefs, which do *nothing* to conceal the deadly weapon nestled between those strong thighs.

"I-I'm a doctor. Of course, I've seen naked men. I've had a boyfriend before too. A-And you aren't anything special."

He arches a brow as if to say, *"Really, that's what you're going with?"*

I bite my lip, stopping myself from saying anything more ridiculous.

Eyes darkening, he leans down—a panther locking in on his prey.

I should flee, back away, or hold my hand out to stop him. But instead, I'm rooted in place. Prickly heat travels down my neck to my breasts, then curls around my legs before settling in my core.

My skin is tight, achy, sensitive, my nerves calibrated only for this virile man before me. I twitch with the need to touch him, but I curl my fingers into my palms, digging my nails into the flesh until it hurts.

Because I'm a goddamn professional.

"My little Olive is all smiles and grace in public. But I've seen them. Your claws. Heard your barbs. You don't back down when challenged, you fight back. I think underneath that neat librarian exterior, the rule-following doctor has a hidden rebellious streak. Bravery waiting to be unleashed," he murmurs.

He reaches out and tugs my lip from between my teeth. I pant out a half moan.

Eyes flaring, he slowly dips his thumb in—not tentative, but dominant. He might as well have touched my clit, which throbs and aches. A pleasurable haze blankets my mind and I suck on his thumb, tasting the addictive saltiness of his skin, watching a flush crawl up his face, making his eyes smolder like burning coals.

"You're a mirage," he rasps. "A temptress and a rule breaker trapped inside, waiting to be let out."

I shake my head. *No, that's not me. You have the wrong twin. That's Mia. Not me.*

But aren't I tired of following the rules? What if he's right?

He must see something in my eyes because he withdraws his thumb. Holding my gaze, he dips the same finger into his mouth, swirling his tongue around it as if to taste me like he did with the cherry at Mystique.

A groan ripples from his throat. "Delicious and sweet."

Wetness slicks my underwear and I can't catch my breath.

Rex skates his eyes over my face, down to my body, my feet, then back up. I resist the urge to tremble under his scrutiny, my erogenous zones on fire.

When he opens his mouth again, his voice has taken on a deep, sexy rasp. He points to the ocean behind him.

"This spot is popular for cliff diving. We aren't supposed to be here, but who cares? Fuck the world."

"You're out of your mind." My heart jackhammers inside my chest.

Rex smirks as he slowly backs away. "Am I? Or am I facing my fears? Join me, Olivia."

Without another word, he spins around and leaps off the cliff.

I gasp and run to the edge, just in time to see him disappear in a splash of white into the Adriatic Sea, which is now a jeweled turquoise under the morning sun.

I wait for him to come up, my mind spinning with what I should do next.

Stay put? Go back to the ship and call this morning a temporary lapse of sanity? Get his clothes and find my way down so he has something to wear when he resurfaces?

But the questions and answers quickly fizzle out when I notice something's wrong.

Terribly wrong.

He doesn't resurface.

Ten seconds. Twenty. Thirty. Did I count seconds or was that milliseconds?

I try again. *One Mississippi, two Mississippi, three Mississippi.*

How long can humans hold their breath underwater? What did I learn in medical school? Ninety seconds? How do people drown? Panic first sets in, followed by fear, then an intense struggle to swim, to breathe, disorientation and not knowing what's up or down.

My mind rattles off factoid after factoid as my heart incinerates like a volcanic eruption.

We're at least seven stories up from sea level. So high up. Why isn't he resurfacing?

Jump in. Save him. You're a good swimmer. Jump in, Olivia.

My body moves before my mind catches up. I quickly strip off my clothes until I'm only clad in my bra and panties.

Without hesitating, I hurl myself off the cliff and pinch my nose as I cannonball into the frigid water. Icy shards stab my body, but I hold my breath as the ocean envelops me.

Holy shit, that's cold.

As soon as I get my bearings straight, I swim toward the light, breaking the surface.

I draw in an inhale and yell, "Rex? Where are you, Rex?"

There are no signs of him.

I dive back underwater, trying to locate the maddening man. Out of nowhere, strong arms wrap around my waist and pull me upward until we come up for air.

His low laughter reaches my ears.

The *devil*.

I grab his forearms and try to spin around to give him a piece of my mind. But he easily overpowers me and cinches me tighter against him.

Against his mostly naked body.

The sensations of his skin against mine throw me straight back to that day in Mykonos when he rescued me inside the caves.

But this time, he isn't the siren, Calliope, or Poseidon, the violent god punishing me for disturbing the peace. He's the most irresistible version of himself.

The charming, sincere, boyish daredevil I've seen snippets of only when he's around his family.

"Worried about me, aren't you, little Olive?"

Between the adrenaline rush, the fear, the relief, and that dastardly sexy rasp in my ear, my body lights up like the Christmas tree in Rockefeller Center. My nipples tighten, goosebumps prickling all over my skin.

"You *asshole*," I seethe, but the words don't hold venom.

Instead, I smile, my chest twitching as I try to hold in laughter.

"Let it out. You know you had fun, you naughty, bewitching rule breaker."

Bewitching. He called me bewitching again, and this time, he means it.

He presses his lips against my ear. "You're afraid of heights and you jumped. I'm so fucking proud of you."

My heart careens out of control.

Bubbles form in my chest and I relive the past few moments.

The rush when I dove off the cliff, the feeling of suspending between life and death, of pushing myself past my limits.

The absolute high.

And I did that—jumped off a freakin' cliff in a foreign country!

I lose my battle. The snort becomes a giggle, which quickly morphs into a full-body laughing fritz.

He joins me. The sound of his happiness, as beautiful as anything I've ever heard, makes my body warm all over.

Hot to the touch.

I turn around and this time, he lets me.

I wipe my tears—tears from laughing too hard. I can't believe this person is me.

This person, standing in the shadows her entire life, has now captured the attention of a sexy, infuriating man.

Who's no longer laughing, his slate-gray eyes hot like molten lava as he stares at me, the smile disappearing on his lips.

The air thrums with awareness and smells like temptation.

He swipes his tongue out, and I do the same, my mouth suddenly parched. His eyes snag on the action, and those dark pupils slowly dilate.

"I'm supposed to stay away because I'm not good for you," he whispers. "But how could I? You make me forget."

Forget what? But I don't ask. I'm held captive by his gaze.

Turbulence swims in his eyes. "I *never* forget, and you...my sweet Olive, *you* make me forget. I...I feel normal around you."

My heart jolts again. I want to throw myself at him and tell him I'll always be here.

I'll make him feel better. I *want* to make him feel better, not just as a doctor, but as...a woman.

My breath hitches when he pulls me flush against him, and I feel a hard bulge prodding my stomach.

He's turned on.

My pussy clenches, needy and empty. What would it be like to kiss him, to be the sole object of his obsession, to have him fill me up and slake his lust inside me?

Clutching his biceps, I look away, afraid he'll see my thoughts.

We're forbidden. This is so, so wrong—a violation of my oath to the profession.

"What are you afraid of, Olive? Why do you walk around looking so sad?" He gently tips my face toward him. "Look at me."

Blinking rapidly, my breath quakes inside my lungs. A familiar ache resurrects in my chest.

No one's ever asked me these questions before. I'm the calm and poised Olivia—loyal friend, dutiful daughter, and successful doctor.

Blending into the background.

"What are you hiding?" He cups my face now, his touch so gentle and reverent, his attention completely focused on me.

I want to cry.

"Olive? Talk to me."

I'm hit with an urge to kiss him, to stop him from asking me more questions I don't have answers for.

To mask our pain under the haze of passion.

But logic stops me. *This is madness. Ludicrous. Not allowed.*

"I'll tell you if you tell me," I murmur, pushing him away.

He yanks me back and clamps his teeth on my shoulder.

Sharp pain ricochets through me and I hiss. "What—"

My words leave me when his tongue snakes out, lapping at the bite marks. The pain morphs into something sensual. Each lick shoots pleasure through my veins.

I tremble, a wispy moan slipping out of me.

Is this his punishment for dodging his question? A reward? A taste of the inferno?

"I've wanted to do this," he murmurs. Another kiss. Another suction.

"What?"

"Your pretty pale skin. I want to mark it up." His voice takes on a dangerous, dark edge.

"You know we shouldn't do this." Using the last of my willpower, I pull away from him.

This time he lets me, and I swim toward the shore.

"Your secret, Olivia. A truth for a truth. You owe me one and I want to collect."

I stop at his words and moisture suddenly pools in my eyes. Keeping my back toward him, my gaze pinned on the shoreline, I reply with one truth.

"I'm a prisoner of grief and guilt. And that's why I'm your doctor today. Because I think, I sense...you're just like me."

Chapter Twenty-Four

IT'S THE SAME SMELL again. Death.

Dewy and thick, the acrid saltiness mixing with damp earth. The stench burned into my nostrils when I found Mom's body all those years ago.

My head throbs, courtesy of the nightmare, this time of Raya with the bullet wound in her chest, asking me to take her daughters to safety. It woke me up two and a half hours into my sleep. I tossed and turned for a long time before finally giving up and reaching for my trusty Velowake.

Four pills this time.

I wonder if I can overdose on caffeine pills.

Then, as my pulse rioted from the side effects, I pulled out my phone and looked at photos of her. Olivia's soft smile. Her kind eyes. The newest one I stole of her when she padded back to the cruise, clothes sticking to her damp skin after the cliff dive two days ago. Those minutes with her felt more real than most of my life. No fake smiles. No jokes. No pretending. No judgment.

She made me forget—about Mom and Raya's deaths, about how screwed up I am with my blackouts, about being lost and half alive. One moment I was staring into the Adriatic, wondering how deep those waters were, and the next moment I was laughing, teasing her, tempting her, making her smile.

I was normal. I was truly *alive.*

I wanted to take a picture of the teeth marks on her shoulder. My mark.

Mine.

No. Not yours. Never yours.

I have to protect her reputation, her career, her heart.

The words aren't sticking. After all, how can they, when in her presence, I can finally breathe?

The chilly wind bites into my skin as I stand on the balcony of my stateroom, waiting for Elias to show up with updates about his investigation into the kidnapping attempt. The man didn't tell me anything when he first boarded the ship. He said I looked like shit and he was close to answers before disappearing like the phantom he was.

The endless ocean stretches in front of me, the rippling waters and muted skies warning me it won't be smooth sailing in the future. I take another whiff, my lungs drawing in the same scent notes from my memories.

There was life before Mom's death and life after. This smell was the demarcation line.

I once read that smell was the strongest sense tied to memories. It was strange how it wasn't the sight or hearing.

What would Olivia say if I asked her in my session later today? Would she give me some biology textbook response or would she prod into my fascination with memories?

Knowing her, I smile, *probably both.*

But then her parting words in Dubrovnik echo in my mind.

"I'm a prisoner of grief and guilt. And that's why I'm your doctor today. Because I think, I sense...you're just like me."

I don't know how she knows, how she can see so clearly through me when no one else can.

But then again, she probably wonders the same thing about me.

There's an invisible rope tying me to her. Whenever I'm around her, I want to push her away so she can't wrench more secrets out of me, or confess my sins and tell her everything—all my secrets and issues.

It'll be cathartic.

My cock stirs when I relive the sensations of her body against mine in the ocean—compact, soft, curves in the right places.

There's a poison corrupting my veins, to possess every part of her as I drag out orgasms upon orgasms, her pleasure making me high.

She'll never be sad again. I'll make it my mission to make her smile.

I think about how she covered her eyes when I stripped down to my underwear on the cliff.

She isn't experienced. Has she been well-fucked before? Is she a quiet squirmer, or does she let out the breathiest moans?

Shit. My cock is hard as granite now.

I groan and bury my face in my hands. I'm a sick bastard.

Then the air around me changes.

The hairs on the back of my neck stand.

"Things are getting chummy between you and the doctor, huh?" Casey murmurs and I jolt.

Am I that obvious now? I shift, angling my body away from him, so he doesn't see the shaft sticking out of my pants.

"You really need to stop with this 'Surprise, I'm at your front door!' thing. Don't you know it's rude? Just because the door is open doesn't mean you can just come in."

I glance over my shoulder, finding his lips flattened, eyes narrowed.

Judgment again. Disappointment, exasperation—what else is new?

"I'll take any opportunity to knock some sense into you."

I scoff. "Please don't act like a martyr. I haven't seen you much these days. Busy partying it up in paradise without me?"

"It's only a party if you're happy. Otherwise, it's just distraction or, in your case..."

He pauses, no doubt to emphasize his next point like a drama queen.

I turn around, and sure enough, Casey arches his brow.

"Spit it out. You have my full attention now."

He smirks. "Addiction. You, my friend, are addicted to things that make you forget. You like to run away from your troubles."

I roll my eyes. "So, what are you? Olivia's apprentice now? Taking a page from her book to psychoanalyze me?"

"Brush me off all you want, but you know it's true." He steps forward, the earlier smugness gone. "Tell me, how many pills did you take this morning?"

I stiffen and look away. "None of your business. And they're caffeine pills. Not hard drugs. So piss off."

"*Prescription* pills, which you got off the black market. You need to sleep. So what if you have nightmares? We all do. Get over yourself."

"Fuck off!"

A muscle twitches in his jaw, and just as he opens his mouth to respond, soft sounds of footsteps reach our ears.

Elias.

My eyes snap to Casey's and he gives me a curt nod before stalking off.

A minute later, the man himself strides through the French doors.

Clad in a slim-fitting black suit and a white dress shirt, unbuttoned at the collar, this is the first time I've seen the mobster not dressed in a three-piece outfit, looking like he's stepped out of a turn of the century British TV drama featuring gentlemen gangsters.

My brow hikes up as I take in the casual tousle of his dark hair, a lock falling over his face, covering that long scar.

"Where's the lighter? Who are you and what did you do with my big, bad crime boss?"

Elias ignores me, but I see the telltale glint of amusement in his green eyes. "I'm on vacation."

"You're wearing a ten-thousand-dollar Armani suit," I deadpan.

He cocks his brow.

"What? I know my clothes. Do you think I look this sexy without effort?"

"I don't even know why I'm entertaining you with an answer, but proper clothes are important. People respond to the way you dress," he murmurs, and for a second, a shadow falls over his face and he glances away.

Before I can ask him about his expression, he takes out his lighter.

This time, he doesn't flick it open. Instead, he stares at the silver-gold surface, an unidentified emotion in his eyes.

"It was The Association. Confirmed now. A John Doe was found in Athens last week. Bullet between the eyes, execution style. My men got hold of the photos and records. It was the other shooter in Santorini. They left a calling card."

He pulls out a thick, black card from his pocket, engraved with the letter A.

My chest seizes, remembering the sheer horror spearing my heart when I saw the man pointing a gun at Olivia. "They're eliminating loose ends and warning us."

Elias nods.

"Bree is a loose end. You never told me what she has on them. Why is she so critical to move to a safe house?"

"The less you know, the better. You're an Anderson. Since they still want your family to join them, they're less likely to touch you. But push hard enough, and they'll act. You don't want to be their next target, do you?"

I scoff and turn back to the sea, watching the clouds in the distance thicken, a heavy weight pressing against the ocean in a declaration of war.

I have a feeling we'll all be victims of it soon.

"It's too late for me."

I don't think I spoke the words aloud, but apparently, I did because Elias frowns.

"Not too late, Rex. You've never seen what 'too late' looks like, trust me." There's a strange urgency in his voice—a warning, a confession, all rolled into one.

"I consider you a friend," he continues, "you and your brothers. There aren't many people in the world I'd say those words to. In my business, sentimentality gets you killed."

He taps his fingers on the railing and stares at his lighter again. This time, he flicks it open and a small orange-blue flame appears. It flickers in the wind for a second before snuffing out.

A lump thickens in my throat. This is the most I've heard the man talk, and I just know he's going to say something I don't want to hear.

I do what I do best—deflect.

"Friend, huh? Wow." Clasping my hand to my chest, I exaggerate a fainting motion. "I'm crying. See my tears?"

I pretend to wipe my eyes when something occurs to me. "Brothers? What about Lana? You've known her as long as you've known us."

Grace and Tay, I won't ask, since they've only been in our lives for the past few years.

Elias snaps his lighter shut, and a muscle pulses in his jaw. "I don't know her well. Nor do I intend to."

But before I can prod into his answer, his expression smooths into one of calmness again. "Don't bother changing the subject. Normally, I'd try to find out what you're hiding because I collect secrets. All the more for people to do my bidding."

I open my mouth to interject, but he holds up his hand.

"If there's one thing I'm good at, it's identifying people with skeletons in their closets. And you reek of them, Rex. Now, I don't know if they're imaginary or real. But with you, I didn't need to extort you to help me. You jumped at the opportunity when I mentioned 'atonement.' Some might say you're fearless or stupid, but I don't think so. It's the damn skeletons baiting you."

He clasps my shoulder. "Take it from me. Don't carry the dead if you don't have to. What happened to Raya wasn't on you. Ditch the skeletons before they make you one of them. Because if you tempt death, he'll come collecting."

A lump forms in my throat. He's worried about me.

Elias's lips twitch into a faint smile. "I have everything under control. There are no more records of Bree on this ship. If they check the system, it'll show she disembarked in Dubrovnik. I've asked her to continue staying on board until Monaco. We just need to make sure your friend, Greg Masters, doesn't post photos of her online. She's a ghost now."

He walks toward the living room. Apparently, the strange, one-sided conversation is over. "Your job, Rex, is to deliver her to the drop-off point in Monaco. Don't draw attention to yourself until then. Don't piss Greg Masters off and get a scandal plastered online. You'll be doing me a big favor."

With a pointed look, he walks off, leaving me in stunned silence.

Chapter Twenty-Five

A CRISP KNOCK SOUNDS at the door just as I finish typing up session notes from my last patient appointment. I look at the clock.

He's on time today.

Rolling my shoulders, I give myself a last-minute pep talk.

I can do this. I just need to be professional.

"Professional my ass, Olive. He marked your skin. You sucked his finger," Mia taunts in my head.

"Shut up," I mutter.

My palms sweat and I rake in a deep breath to calm my rising panic.

It's fine. Everything's fine. Sure, we've crossed some lines, but not the line. I can do this. I can be professional. He needs help. I can help him. I can finish this cruise with my heart intact. I can fulfill my promise to Mia and secure the donation from the Andersons for ADAS.

I can walk away.

My chest spasms. I won't analyze it. It's stress. That's it.

"Come in."

Rex strides in, even worser for wear than his usual self. The circles under his eyes are darker. His light blue shirt is wrinkled on one side, and not the purposeful dishevelment of his usual outfits. The scruff covering his jaw is thicker now, a day away from becoming a beard.

"Olive, you look beautiful today." The same signature smirk, but flat eyes.

I don't respond, because I know he does this when he's vulnerable. And that makes me sad.

It must be isolating to hide his emotions all the time. To believe the world isn't a safe place for him to express them.

The ache deepens in my chest.

"Mr. Anderson, let's have our session here."

I stand from my desk and walk to the open seating area, wanting no furniture between us.

This way, I can see his body language.

Motioning to the cream recliner large enough to fit two people, I say, "Have a seat."

He sprawls into the chair. "Is this where you hypnotize me and steal my secrets?"

"I'm not a hypnotist or a hypnotherapist. And no one is stealing anything. You can rest easy."

Rex snickers and grabs the cup of water I have waiting for him on a side table. He takes out the pill bottle he showed me before and dumps two tablets out before tossing them into his mouth.

His corded throat ripples as he chugs the water. My face heats when I remember how this masculine throat is attached to a muscular body I saw up close and personal in Dubrovnik.

A slow smile twists his lips as he sets the cup down. "What are you thinking of, little Olive?"

I clear my throat. "*Doctor* Lin, and nothing. Just noting how many caffeine pills you took."

His jaw works, but the smirk remains on his face. "Bullshit."

I shrug. "You don't need to believe me since we aren't here to talk about me." Reaching over, I grab my notebook and pen. "Tell me, how many pills do you take each day?"

"You guys and your obsession with my pills."

He doesn't elaborate, and I look up, finding him chewing his lip, his attention on me. I can practically see the gears turning in his head.

"Come on. Do the work. Try. A truth for a truth, right?" I murmur.

I can't help you if you don't talk to me.

His eyes flare and I know he's thinking about what I told him in the ocean, the guilt and sadness I carry that I also see in him.

"You sure this is what you want to use it for?"

"I'm hoping I don't have to use it at all." *That you'll tell me more about yourself without my resorting to bribery.*

Because we understand each other.

Because he's in pain and deserves to feel better.

He deserves to be happy.

He heaves out a sigh and slouches in his chair. "Four on a normal day, sometimes six or seven on the bad ones."

"And how much caffeine is in one of these pills?"

"Two shots of espresso's worth? Something like that." He stares at the ceiling and stifles a yawn. "Doesn't seem to work anymore. Nothing seems to work."

"And how much sleep do you get at night?"

His eyes flutter closed. "I don't know. Three hours, four if I'm lucky."

I stiffen, taking in his weary frame, the way even now, reclining on a comfortable chair in a quiet office, I can still see his eyeballs moving behind his eyelids, like he can't stay still.

It must be exhausting to be on all the time.

"Do you know what chronic sleep deprivation does to someone?" I press a button next to my chair.

The office windows and glass walls turn opaque, then darken. Rex shifts in the recliner, clearly uncomfortable with my question.

Since he's evading me, I answer, "Tremors, headaches, mood changes, poor judgment, psychosis and hallucinations, not to mention increased risk of heart disease, diabetes, high blood pressure, impaired memory—"

He barks out a harsh laugh, his eyes snapping open. "If only."

I flinch. The seething anger in his voice shocks me.

Rex shakes his head, then wipes his eyes with his fingers. "You sound like one of those pharmaceutical commercials." Clearing his throat, he sits up and takes on a professional newscaster tone. "Velowake's side effects may include..."

Velowake? I scribble that in my notebook. Those must be the pills he's taking.

"What crossed your mind just now?"

Snorting, he stifles his laughter and turns to me, bleary-eyed. "What do you mean?"

"You laughed when I mentioned the symptoms of sleep deprivation. Something must have triggered that."

His smile vanishes and in its place is a new mask—flattened lips, clenched jaw, flared nostrils. His knees bounce a restless rhythm.

I used to think his whiplash moods were disorienting, but now they make sense, given how little he sleeps.

His body and brain don't have time to recover.

Glancing away, he murmurs, "I'm feeling generous today. I'll give you another truth. I have HSAM."

I frown, and he adds, "Highly superior autobiographical memory. I don't forget things, even when I want to. That's why I was laughing."

His revelation is a light bulb flickering on in a dark room. HSAM. It's something I've read about in passing in medical school. We don't spend much time studying rare conditions.

But it makes sense.

While he hasn't confided what troubles him, I've always sensed his guilt and self-hatred. It must've been something in the past he thought he did—someone he wronged, a tragedy he caused.

And he can't forget because his mind doesn't let him.

"That's terrible." Without thinking, I place my hand on his knee, stilling it.

He releases a ragged exhale and looks at me. This time, there's no mask—no faked humor, no crude jokes, no shameless flirting.

There's only pain in those storm cloud irises.

"Is that why you can't sleep?" I ask, keeping my voice soft, not wanting to disrupt this rare moment of vulnerability from a man whose entire identity is a lie. "Because something happened in the past and you can't forget it? And you replay it in your mind repeatedly, but it doesn't really matter because the outcome will never change?"

He draws a stiff inhale, and wetness gathers in his eyes. An answering ache twists behind my rib cage.

Yes. That's what his eyes are telling me. *Free me, Olivia. Free me from the past.*

Gripping his knee tighter, I want to transfer his pain to me. "That'll drive anyone crazy...to relive the worst moments of their lives, never escaping them."

His throat works, then wretched gasps saw out of his lips. Tears gather, but they don't fall because he's holding them in.

A new tension ripples through his frame, the muscles in his thighs trembling.

Let it out, Rex. Let it out.

I squeeze his knee, letting him know I'm here.

Perhaps the world doesn't understand his pain, but I do. And it's okay. He'll be okay.

He snatches my hand, crushing my fingers in a vise. I wince, and he lets go. The viciousness of his grip, the stress pulsing inside him—is he even aware of it?

I put my free hand on top of his, gently brushing it over his tense knuckles. *Do you want me to stop asking?*

Rex hisses, then moans, like he's never felt a comforting touch before.

His eyes close, then flutter open, those pupils slowly expanding.

"You aren't alone anymore," I whisper.

A strangled breath snakes past his lips, like I ripped it from him. He blinks, and finally, one lone tear slides down his face.

The sight of it carves my heart in half.

"Will you tell me about a memory that stayed with you?" I slowly wipe his tear away.

He shuts his eyes again and leans back in the recliner. I pull back to give him more space, but he stops me with his hand.

This time, his touch is gentle, and I imagine this is how he'd be in the bedroom—a tempest wreaking havoc on your body, followed by careful worship and soulful kisses.

If you were lucky to see that side of him.

"I found my calling when I was six," he begins, his voice raw.

His thumb traces sensuous circles on the back of my hand and the tingles spark on my skin like fireflies on a warm summer night.

"It was at Mom's funeral..."

CHAPTER TWENTY-SIX

Age Six, Thirty-One Years Ago

I CAN'T STOP FIDGETING.

My dress shirt is rough on my skin as I stare at the big mirror inside the boys' room at the church. I'm waiting while Ryland uses the bathroom and Maxwell washes his hands. Dad has Ethan and baby Lana in the pews. Ethan won't stop crying and Dad won't speak. Lana sleeps all day. Lucky her.

I stare at the mirror again.

I look like a penguin in my black suit and white shirt.

A sad penguin.

I never write about penguins in my stories. They can only waddle around and swim. They are cute and cuddly. They don't scare away monsters like Kazoo the T-Rex does. I hug the fuzzy green dinosaur closer to my chest and sniff it.

It smells like Mom—it's faint, but still there. She hugged it the night before she died.

Mom loved penguins more than T-Rexes. She was supposed to take me to the Central Park Zoo to see them next week.

I hiccup, the itch on my arm worsening. A beach ball sized lump is stuck in my throat.

We won't go to the zoo together ever again.

She won't be able to wear her favorite penguin apron, cook in the kitchen while I stand on the big stool next to her, helping her with tomatoes, carrots, as she cooks her beef ragu pasta and stew.

She'd listen to my stories—dragons who hated spinach, fairies who turned broccoli into big trees so little kids didn't have to eat them.

It's so itchy. My skin is on fire.

Darting a glance at Maxwell, I find him huddled under the window, reading a scrap of paper. He's supposed to give a speech at the funeral. He said it was his duty as the oldest Anderson son.

His lips wobbled when I asked him what duty meant. He said he didn't know and he would've asked Mom, but she wasn't here anymore. Tears slipped down his cheeks, and he quickly swiped them away. *Because he's the oldest,* he told me. *He wasn't supposed to cry.*

It's your fault, Rex. All your fault.

I wiggle my finger under the cuff of my shirt and scratch my arm, but it's no use. If anything, it makes it worse. Looking around, I spot a small pebble, its rough edges shiny under the light streaming in from the stained-glass window.

Setting Kazoo down by the windowsill, I pick up the small rock and stick it under my sleeve. Then, I scratch my forearm again. Tears spring into my eyes when the rock digs into my skin.

But it works. The pain chases away the itch.

I glance at Kazoo. He's sad too.

Scratch. Scratch. Scratch.

No more penguins. No more Mom. No more Mommy and Rex adventures. Her lifeless face floats into my mind and I flinch, the itch growing.

She's gone because of you, Rex.

Why didn't I pick up my marbles that day?

Mom always said I should clean up after myself. Why didn't I do it?

Then there were the voices. The argument. The loud banging door sounded like monsters. I ran outside to escape, even though it was raining.

Why didn't I stay behind? If I stayed behind with Mom, would she still be here with us?

Because you were scared. You were stupid. You were afraid of monsters when everyone told you they didn't exist. Scaredy cat, Rex. And now, Mom's gone forever because of you.

I scratch harder and dig the pebble deeper into my skin.

I look at Kazoo again and whisper, "I miss Mom."

More tears gather in my eyes, but I ignore them.

Crying won't change anything. Crying can't turn back time.

That's when I hear it.

A sniffle, then a choked sob from inside the stall. Then another. And another.

Maxwell walks over and knocks on the door. "Ryland?"

Ryland staggers out and throws his arms around him.

Then, the unthinkable happens. My older brothers, the bravest boys I know, both start crying, their wails echoing against the walls.

My own tears slide down my face, and I run to my brothers and wrap my arms around them, not caring if I'm interrupting another special twin moment.

They draw me in and the three of us huddle, sobbing, snot dripping from our noses, because today, we have to say goodbye to the person who loved us the most.

"I shouldn't be crying," Maxwell whimpers. "I sh-should be strong."

"I st-started it," Ryland cries harder.

It's me. I'm the one who caused all of this. I'm the one you should hate.

I want to tell them the truth. Mom used to say it's important to be honest. I want to tell them what happened that day before I ran outside. How I could've stopped this if I'd just cleaned up my marbles. How I could've saved her. She was angry. Arguing with someone. That was why she didn't see the marbles when she stomped down the stairs. That was why she slipped.

But when I open my mouth to tell the truth, nothing comes out. Because being hugged by my two older brothers, who always say I'm a scaredy cat and no fun to play with, makes me feel loved. For a moment, my arm doesn't itch.

I don't want them to hate me.

I don't want them to cry or be sad. If anyone should be sad, it should be me.

Tell a story, Rex. When you feel sad or angry, cook or tell a story.

"If heaven had moms, they'd better be ready. Mom is going to fix up their kitchen and cook yummy food for all the kids without mommies," I blurt out.

The sniffles stop. The twins stare at me.

"She'll have penguins as helpers." I can't stop the words from spilling out. *Tell a story. Make it bigger. Make it fun.*

"Penguins can't cook." Ryland snorts as he wipes his runny nose with his sleeve.

It's working! They aren't crying anymore. A fire burns inside my belly, and I thump my chest.

"They can in heaven! And Mom will teach reading and art to those kids too. We can't be too selfish and keep Mom all to ourselves. That's what Mom used to say. We can't be selfish."

"Mom is good at art. I miss her painting with me." Maxwell's lips wobble.

No. No. No. Don't cry.

It's all your fault, Rex. You did this. You need to fix it.

"I'll paint with you," I offer.

Nothing will ever fix it.

My arm itches again, and I rub it with my free hand, and the pebble cuts my skin.

Scratch. Scratch. Scratch.

"Your painting sucks."

"Does not!"

"Does too."

"I can cook. Mom taught me. Better than you, Maxwell." I stick out my tongue.

My oldest brother's eyes widen and he straightens, puffing out his chest. He's really good at that—telling me he's older by one whole year without saying anything.

"No one is better than me."

"Who said?" Ryland jabs Maxwell in the ribs. The twins glare at each other.

"Ew...Ryland, you didn't wash your hands. Mom wouldn't let you into her kitchen. Her penguin army will chase you away when you go to sleep." I scrunch my nose.

A snort tumbles out of Maxwell's lips. Then Ryland snickers. And suddenly, all three of us are laughing, tears sliding down our cheeks as we imagine an army of cute little penguins chasing us.

"I don't want your extra flavor in the stew," I quip. We laugh even harder until our noses are runny again.

"You're so gross, Rex." That could be either of them. I'm not sure who.

"Disgusting."

"You mean awesome. Because Rex is awesome." I grin and bat my lashes, and they cackle even harder.

My vision blurs, and I stare at my brothers, who are bowled over, half laughing, half sobbing, twin smiles on their faces.

They're laughing because of me. I made them forget.

I have to fix it.

My arm hurts where I keep scratching. I dig my nails and the pebble in harder.

It stings now. Something warm and wet soaks through my sleeve.

But I don't stop. It really hurts now, but I deserve it.

And the tight feeling in my chest gets a little smaller.

Present

I jolt awake, my eyelids heavy, to her fingers trailing over my face.

My breath snags when I see Olivia leaning over me, her soulful eyes pooling with moisture. A bittersweet smile curves her lips as she brushes her thumb over my cheek.

There's wetness there.

She's wiping away the tears that have somehow escaped. Tears I haven't shed in years because I don't cry. Ever.

Crying is cathartic. It releases the unpleasant emotions—the guilt, the sadness. It helps you move on.

But I don't deserve catharsis. Maybe if this mission succeeds, if I can atone for the past, then I can let go.

Then why are you telling her your secrets, you hypocrite? Isn't that cathartic? Isn't being with Olivia cathartic?

I have no answers. I'm too weak and tired to fight it—this attraction to her.

And she makes me feel safe.

"O-Olive, I-I..."

"Shhh..." She continues her gentle motions. Soft grazes on my right cheek, then my left.

Comforting. Loving. Sensations that should be for someone else, someone better than me.

The ball in my throat grows, every inch of me focusing on how her fingertips scrape over my skin, setting my nerves aflame.

Slowly, I reach into my pocket and pull out the red marble.

"I carry this with me to remind myself of what I did. How Mom died because of me. How Dad lost the love of his life and my siblings lost their mom because of me."

I roll it around in my palm, remembering the sound of it clattering down the stairs.

Thump. Thump. Thump.

Why didn't I clean up after myself?

"You see, I'm not sick, not in the traditional sense. It's guilt. So you can't help me."

Silence falls between us.

"I'm so proud of you for sharing your past with me," she whispers, her voice thick.

She reaches for my marble, but I pull away and stuff it back into my pocket.

I can't let go of it.

Olivia nods like she understands. Then she slides her hand to my left arm and slowly rolls up my sleeve.

When I notice what she's doing, I stop her. "Don't...please."

She pauses, her eyes intent on mine. Her sweet scent of clean cotton wafts to my nostrils and I rake in a desperate inhale.

Life. Love. Second chances. That's what she smells like.

"Please," she repeats. Her tongue dips out.

Heat gathers behind my rib cage and travels south. My cock stiffens when I take in her full lips.

Deep pink. Plump. The perfect curve for me to lick, suck, and bite.

My mouth waters and I slowly drop my grip on her wrist to see what she'll do.

Olivia rolls up my sleeve and flips my arm over. I close my eyes and brace myself.

I know the moment she sees it, because a sharp gasp echoes in the room.

"Rex."

Not Mr. Anderson. Not Rex-a-Million.

Just Rex.

My name sounds beautiful on her lips.

I open my eyes, finding her staring at my forearm.

"It's not your fault." She lifts my arm and slowly, excruciatingly, presses her mouth on my small, raised scars.

Permanent reminders of where I've carved up my skin. For the next eight years after the funeral, I'd find more rocks to continue my pain, to scratch at the invisible itch. I'd wear long sleeves or tell my brothers I banged myself up at school. The scars weren't big enough to sound alarms. It became a calming routine—making those around me laugh during the day, letting out the pain in my room at night.

Until my hormones kicked in and I discovered girls, and later on, alcohol and partying.

"You, my friend, are addicted to things that make you forget. You like to run away from your troubles."

Casey's right, as always, and the old phantom itch strikes again.

My fingers twitch, needing to scratch at the scar or reach for my pills. Or throw myself at Elias's mercy and ask him for more jobs even though I botched the first one he gave me and will probably fuck this one up too.

It doesn't matter. I need a distraction, no matter how dangerous, to make me forget.

Anything but think about the past, or about the temptation the woman before me represents.

My doctor. A gentle, pure soul. Complete acceptance and no judgment.

Forbidden.

But nothing prepares me for what Olivia does next.

She closes her eyes. Her thick black lashes, tipped in wetness, fan across her pale cheeks.

She kisses the scars. Soft caresses. I feel them on my cock. A growl rumbles from my chest and a flush crawls up her neck before invading her face.

What a pretty pink flush.

I want more. I want to see it over her creamy tits, spreading on her stomach. I want to know if the pink is the same color as her pussy or if those folds are a deeper hue—a dusky rose or a shade of coral?

I want to know if her cum tastes as sweet as her moans.

Or how her little mouth looks full of my cock. Can she get it all inside? Every single inch? Will she let me ram it deep down her slender throat until she gags and can't breathe?

My mind spins as I watch her press kiss after kiss on my scars and my dick thickens in my pants, my heavy balls dropping.

Achy. Desperate. In need.

"Yes, little Olive. Kiss it. Suck it. Lick it. Because the next thing you'll kiss will be my lips and my cock."

She gasps, her eyes widening as if she finally realizes what she's doing.

How terribly wrong it is—the lines we're crossing.

How right it feels.

If this goes further, I can protect her. I'm an Anderson. We'll hide this from the world.

The tempting thought takes root.

Olivia springs away and drops my arm like it's a grenade.

But too bad. She doesn't realize that grenades explode when you let go, and it's already too late. She's pulled the pin without realizing it.

I grab her hand, craving her touch. Addicted. She makes me believe I'm worth it.

Like I deserve catharsis.

"Don't go." My voice is guttural and raw. "Stay."

Stay for me.

"I-I can't be doing this, M-Mr.—"

No. Not Mister.

"I'm tired. Stay with me. And Rex...please."

She stills, her eyes roving over my face and whatever she sees there has her sitting back down, her arm slowly relaxing. I twine my fingers with hers, relishing her sharp inhale and pinkening cheeks.

The blush is so beautiful.

She's so riveting. Bewitching.

"Go to sleep...Rex," she murmurs, softly squeezing my fingers.

I skate my thumb over the back of her hand, and by some miracle, my eyelids grow heavy, the sensual heat spreading and morphing into something different.

Peace. Quiet. Surrender.

The last thing I see before I close my eyes is her elfin face—an angel by the bedside of a demon.

CHAPTER TWENTY-SEVEN

THE CRYSTALS ON THE chandelier rattle as the ship pitches to the side. I burrow myself deeper into the comforter on my bed, and hold on to my laptop. Thank God I didn't eat a full meal at dinner tonight.

Lightning splits across the angry skies and booming thunder rattles the floor-to-ceiling window. Rain crashes against the glass as the cruise ship sways again.

The turbulence settles a few seconds later, and I focus on my laptop screen. According to my research, Velowake is a drug used to treat narcolepsy. It's still in trials, so Rex must've gotten them off the black market. And it's not just "caffeine" pills, as he claimed.

The medicine comes with a host of potential side effects, including a heightened risk of heart attacks, strokes, kidney issues, and other mental conditions such as insomnia, anxiety, psychosis, and depression. The maximum recommended dosage is three pills a day. He's taking way more than that.

He's killing himself slowly with his extreme behaviors and unhealthy habits.

It's like he doesn't care.

"You can't save me. I need to have something worth saving first." That's what he told me during our second session.

Then three days ago, he finally gave me a glimpse of his pain, and why his calling was to make his family happy. Because, in some sick, twisted way, he felt responsible for his mom's death. That he took away his dad and siblings' happiness.

That marble I've seen him take out every so often is a sign of his guilt.

So he gave all his joy to others. All the while, he carved ribbons of pain into his skin, hiding his guilt and anguish from the people who loved him most.

He slept for one hour that day in the office. He was restless—groaning and shifting on the recliner, sweat dotting his forehead.

And he wouldn't let go of me. He clutched my hand like it was a lifeline.

The worst part was...

I didn't want to let go.

I wanted to hold him in my arms and tell him he didn't have to hide with me.

He wanted to fuck women so he could exhaust himself enough to go to sleep. And in one horrifying moment, I was tempted.

So very tempted to climb on top of him, to wake him up with my body, and kiss away his pain. I'd suckle the flickering pulse on his neck and worship the ridges of his chiseled muscles. I'd take his hard cock into my mouth and give him pleasure until he's sated. He wouldn't need the pills because I'd be there. He could use me. Any part of me. Over and over again.

Then, I wanted to hold him in my arms while he slept.

It's wrong. It's immoral.

I'm his doctor.

And so, after he left my office that day, I made every attempt to avoid him. I didn't go to the sun deck, knowing he liked it there. When I saw him walk down the hallway, I took a side corridor.

Blowing out a breath, I pull up my email and begin typing.

Dear Mr. Anderson,

I'm stepping back from the therapeutic role of your physician, as it's no longer appropriate or effective.

Regards,

Olivia Lin, MD

My finger hovers over the send button, but I hesitate.

I want to help him. He has no one to talk to.

If I leave him now, what will happen to him?

And my promise to Lana to help him. The funding for ADAS. I'd disappoint so many people.

Sweat beads on my upper lip and I look at the mirrored wall across from the bed. Like everything else on the cruise ship, it's state-of-the-art and high tech.

"Sanctuary, please tell me the weather forecast."

A screen showing the Weather Channel appears on the mirrored panel. "Dr. Lin, for the next two days, a severe weather alert has been issued for the Central Mediterranean Basin. A deepening low-pressure system is bringing turbulent conditions. Mariners should expect winds gusting fifty-to-sixty knots, heavy rains, and rogue waves over twenty-three feet. Passengers are advised to remain inside their staterooms for safety."

Fear sweeps through me. The situation sounds dangerous.

I practice deep breaths and cognitive behavioral therapy techniques.

It's just a storm. We have the best of the best helming this cruise ship. There's nothing to worry about.

I think back to Rex's words that day at Dubrovnik.

"You're a mirage. A temptress and a rule breaker trapped inside, waiting to be let out."

I want to be the siren he's describing. That woman would be fearless. A thought niggles at me.

Good-girl Olivia stays warm and dry inside the stateroom. She eats the almond cookies she hates because that's what she's supposed to do.

But temptress Olivia? She'd embrace the chaos and call it excitement. She'd never force herself to do something she doesn't want.

Huffing a deep breath, I grab the tin of cookies on my nightstand.

Twelve years. I've let the past trap me for twelve years. It's time to let go.

I pad to the balcony door and slide it open. Within seconds, I'm wet—rain coats my face, my hair, soaks through my thin T-shirt and sweats.

My first instinct is to shut the door and yell at myself for being stupid.

But I don't.

Instead, I step onto the balcony—holding onto the doorframe because I'm *not* stupid—and let the weather lash my face.

I dump the cookies into the ocean, then set the tin on the ground. Guilt pricks me.

You're not supposed to litter.

The birds can eat them.

Icy cold water pelts my skin. The wind howls. Lightning splits across the sky, and every inch of me comes alive.

Excitement bubbles in my chest. A laugh rips out of me.

It's messy. It's chaotic. My heart might short-circuit.

But I'm alive. I made a choice for myself.

I feel every single thing, and I love it.

Something is unraveling inside me, just like the storm outside, turning our world upside down.

A shrill alarm suddenly pierces the air, and I jolt, noticing red lights flashing outside the stateroom. Then I hear my phone ring.

Rushing back inside, I quickly pick up and answer the call.

"Dr. Lin speaking."

"We have an emergency on deck three. It's legit all hands on deck. Can you come?" Jessa sounds panicked and I know it's bad when the day shift nurses are working nights.

I change into fresh clothes and grab my windbreaker while Jessa debriefs me. Apparently, a few drunk passengers thought it'd be a good time to reenact a certain scene from *Titanic* and, naturally, they fell overboard when a rogue gust caught them by surprise.

Seriously, Darwin Awards in action.

By the time I get to deck three, it's chaos. Security guards wearing yellow reflective jackets scurry around the deck. Jessa and Fiona usher a shivering man on a stretcher toward the elevators.

Jessa nods when I spot her, just as I hear wet footsteps thudding toward me.

"They called you." Rhys reaches my side, sounding out of breath. "I told them not to. We have it handled."

"How can I help?"

I know the basics, but it's been years since I did a rotation in the emergency room.

"So far, there were two superficial head wounds. The man they wheeled by was trying to jump into the water to rescue the idiots, but he had a heart attack. Dr. MacKintosh is meeting him in the medical bay."

People rush around, bright spotlights sweeping up and down the deck, then over the dark ocean.

Between the roar of the winds and the rain assailing my face, I can barely hear him.

"What about the people who fell overboard?" I holler.

My pulse races when I see personnel huddled by the railing, pointing to the water.

"The two with the head wounds were lucky because we fished them out quickly. There's still one person missing. But with the storm and the frigid temperatures, I doubt she'll make it...if she isn't dead already. I'm heading back to the medical bay, and you should join me—"

I don't hear the rest of his sentence because my entire being focuses on a tall man emerging from the crowd. With his dark Henley soaked and plastered to his body, Rex Anderson is a sight to behold.

Lightning whips over us, rendering his face in stark shadows. Two guards speak to him and he throws his hands in the air, clearly agitated. Then he rakes his fingers through his dark tresses.

He looks up and our gazes lock.

For a moment, with nature inflicting violence upon us—the dark clouds festering with electricity, the deafening gusts nearly obliterating my eardrums—time stops.

Emotions flashing in those iridescent eyes—anger, worry, fear—too many for me to name. He takes a step toward me, his hands curled at his side.

"Go," he mouths. *"It's too dangerous here."*

My feet are rooted to the ground.

How can I go when he's here?

But suddenly, a man calls him, panic in his voice. He points to the ocean, gesturing wildly. Rex stares at the man, then the dark waters, and every hair on my body stands.

No. Don't do it.

He whips his head toward me again, his eyes reflecting the same unhinged glint I saw that day when he threw himself over me in Pyrgos.

The madness within them. The daredevil tempting death.

Don't do it.

I open my mouth to beg him, but it's too late. I watch in horror as he spins toward the ocean and, in two quick strides, vaults off the railing, disappearing from sight.

A scream rips from me, and the next thing I know, I'm hurtling toward the crowd, ignoring Rhys's hollers, ignoring the screams of passersby and cruise personnel.

Rex went after the person overboard.

Without a care for his own life.

He's been tempting the Grim Reaper, and now he's calling his bluff and facing him head-on.

I plaster myself against the railing, trying to find the maddening man, but all I see is the unforgiving sea.

Deep. Dark. Dangerous.

Towering waves crash against the ship, the spray joining the rain, soaking our bodies.

Where is he? Where the fuck is he?

People yell around me—commands, worries, I have no clue. I can't hear them.

Spotlights sweep the waters, the temporary brightness illuminating endless stretches of black.

I don't see him. I don't see him anywhere.

"Rex!" I cry, but it's useless, my voice no match for the surrounding ruckus.

Tears gather in my eyes and acid churns in my gut. I grip the railing for dear life when another rogue wave crashes against us.

Please. Please don't take him.

I sob, a devastating loss stabbing my chest, shocking me with how much I feel toward him, telling me the wretched man has stolen something inside me without me noticing.

And now...now I don't know how I can survive without him.

I can't lose him.

"Rex!" I scream again.

I'd give anything to hear his voice, his ridiculous jokes, and his inappropriate comments. To have him drag me on some adventure I didn't ask for, trade truths with each other. To hear him call me bewitching, little Olive, or good rule follower. I'd give anything to be back in the office with him, to climb onto the recliner and wrap him in my arms.

How did it get this way? How did he sneak inside my heart? What if I've lost him for good?

Agony I've never experienced before rams into my chest, a serrated knife twisting and twisting until I keel over in pain. Images barrel through my mind. His teasing smile, his arrogant smirk. Then I think of Mia, her spark and energy, snuffed out suddenly without warning. Her face, just like mine, colorless the morning I found her.

I can't do this again.

A shrill whistle pierces the air, followed by another. Then more screams—joyous cries.

Heart pounding wildly, I whip my head toward the commotion, and finally notice what's drawing everyone's attention.

Two heads bobbing in the water. Rex has one arm wrapped around an unconscious woman, his free hand gripping a rope thrown at him.

Personnel work together and wrench them up, fighting against the ocean that clearly wants to claim them for good.

Within minutes, they pull them up and over the railing. Rhys hurries over with a few nurses and they load the woman onto a stretcher.

I barely notice the quizzical stare he levels my way because I'm already flying toward the man I have no business thinking about.

The man I shouldn't want to kiss or touch, or know every single facet of his complicated mind.

The man who has reached inside my chest and fisted my heart in his large palm without my permission.

Tears stream down my face and I throw myself at the devil, not caring he's dripping wet.

A deep oomph reaches my ears as Rex's arms automatically wrap around my back, holding me close.

His reassuring heartbeat riots in my ears as tremors rack my body as if I were the one who took a frigid plunge.

I was *this close* to losing him.

He shouldn't have survived it.

His heated breath grazes my ear before I hear his smug, gravelly rasp.

"Just can't keep your hands off me, huh?"

Chapter Twenty-Eight

Olivia stills at my words.

Then I feel it. Her fury.

Her body stiffens, her fists knot, her nostrils flare.

A tickle gathers in my chest and my blood heats. She's going to let me have it. I can't wait to see this.

I grin and my dick jumps in my pants.

"Put me down *now*." Her voice is a seething whisper, but no, I don't underestimate her. She's an atomic bomb seconds from exploding.

"What, Olive? You don't want me?"

I knead her shapely ass and inwardly groan. So supple and soft. I can't wait to spank it and bite it. I'm wide awake now—from the adrenaline, the surrounding chaos, the turbulent storm, the goddess in my arms, or a combination of everything. I don't care what's right or wrong. I'm flying *high*.

"You were the one who leaped into my arms like you'd die without me."

"*Now,* Mr. Anderson. Put me down." Her voice is strangely calm, but I feel it, that enticing little quiver in her thighs. "I won't ask twice."

Chuckling, I set her down just to see what she'll do.

She stares at the floor, her shoulders rigid, chest heaving, then I see her draw in one slow inhale.

Boom.

But Olivia looks up and smiles. Serenely. Fighting chaos with chaos.

I recoil, my pulse sprinting in my ears.

"I'm glad you're okay. Please excuse my unprofessional behavior just now." She spins around and stalks toward the elevators.

Panic sweeps through me—even more than before I dove into the water after the guard spotted the woman. I didn't think about myself then. I only thought of Mom and Raya and how I cradled their dead bodies in my arms. It was an automatic instinct to jump in, to save another family from experiencing the grief I went through.

But now, as I watch Olivia walk away from me, very much done with my nonsense, I finally feel it.

Fear. Panic. *Desperation.* I don't know what the hell I was thinking she'd do. Praise me for a job well done? For nearly killing myself in the process?

Of course she's pissed. She probably thinks I'm beyond saving.

I can't let her get away. *She's done with me. She's giving up.*

She's the only person who's seen me. The only person who can make me forget everything.

Ignoring the camera flashes and people hurling questions at me—Greg Masters and his cronies apparently having caught a whiff of my daring rescue—I chase after the maddening woman.

"Olivia, wait!"

She ignores me. If anything, her strides quicken.

But I'm faster. I reach her in seconds, grab her wrist, and drag her to the nearest door I can find.

I wrench it open, tug her inside, and the metal door bangs shut as darkness falls over us.

"What the hell, Rex? What do you want? To gloat about how you won another woman over? Your doctor, no less?"

I won her over? A thrill shoots up my spine. I quash it. She's pissed. I need to focus on that.

I grapple at the wall until I find a light switch and flick it on.

A dim lightbulb illuminates the tight space we're in—a supply closet, apparently. Olivia crosses her arms over her chest and tilts her chin up, glaring at me.

"Well? If you have nothing to say, I'm going back to my room to get out of these damn wet clothes."

She whirls around and twists the doorknob. The same fear from moments ago jolts my senses.

"Wait! I-I'm sorry." The words tumble out of me.

Don't go. Don't leave me. Hold me in your arms again. Worry about me. Love me. Thoughts swirl inside my mind, more chaotic than the storm outside, but somehow they make sense.

I need her more than I need my next heartbeat.

She stills, her hair half-loosened from her usual bun. Her shoulders rise and fall, and I hear our heavy breathing. She doesn't answer me.

"Look, I know I'm a fucking screwup. I disappointed you again. I joke around all the time and, frankly, have no business leading this cruise. Look what happened. People fell overboard because I couldn't manage shit—"

Olivia spins around, her dark eyes flashing. "You think I'm disappointed in you because idiots fell overboard doing shit they weren't supposed to be doing?"

She steps forward and jabs her finger at my chest. "You think *I think* you're a screwup and that's why I'm angry?"

Another hard jab. Her voice rises in volume.

"I-I was scared *shitless*, Rex. Terrified!" *Jab.* "Y-You just jumped in with complete disregard for your life!"

Renewed heat surges through my chest, spreading to my extremities as I take in this bewitching woman, this siren, making her wrath known.

Jab. Jab. Jab.

"If something happened to you, do you know how your family would feel? How devastated they would be?"

Her eyes flash with anger, her words javelins to my heart. There's anguish, fear, and grief in her voice. Pain from personal experience.

She jabs her finger at my chest again. "Do you know how terrified I was? I thought I lost you. I-If I lost y-you—"

She rakes in a sharp inhale, then freezes, as if realizing she's spiraling out of control.

I grab her hand—the one that was inflicting pain seconds ago but is now limp.

"What would you do?" I rasp. "Why were you terrified, Olive? Don't you hate me? I drive you crazy. I don't listen to you. I make you do things you don't want to do, like leap off a cliff."

Her throat ripples. She trembles and shakes her head. "S-Sorry, Mr. Anderson. It's been an intense night. I-I'm not myself. I need to go."

Blowing out a breath, she tugs her hand loose and turns around.

No.

I don't think, I just react.

I grab her wrist and haul her against me, then I crush my lips against hers.

Nirvana. She tastes like nirvana.

Pleasure explodes as I get my first hit of the woman of my dreams.

That's who she is—somewhere along the way, she's become the light to my darkness, light I don't deserve, but I don't fucking care anymore.

Hauling her up, I grip her thighs and slam her against the door. Fists hit my chest and back as anger and lust roll off her tiny frame in waves. My skin burns, every inch of me on fire, and I kiss her and kiss her, my body taking her punches, her scratches, my mouth swallowing her cries and moans.

"No. You can't do this to me, you can't—" she whimpers and I pull away because I might be halfway to deranged, but I won't force myself on a woman. But she grabs my hair and seals her mouth over mine again.

Lava surges through my veins as we tear at each other. I suck those luscious lips into my mouth, needing to get any part of her inside me.

She cares about me. Too much. That's why she's fleeing. She didn't escape after seeing my scars or glimpsing my monsters.

She sees me and still cares. And she's mad at herself because of it.

I bite her plump bottom lip and she flinches, then returns the favor with a sharp nip of her teeth. Pain scores through me and I taste it.

The warm, salty metallic liquid on my tongue.

Blood. She's drawn blood. My Olive's sharp claws.

I fucking love it.

The thought throws me into a frenzy and I plunder her mouth with my tongue, fighting, dancing, mating with hers as I grind the throbbing shaft between my legs against her pussy.

"Oh my God, yes," she moans, her head dropping back, hitting the door and baring her neck.

Like a monster, I zero in on the fluttering pulse, needing to chase it, to bite it, to mark it as mine.

We're violence and chaos, thunder and lightning. Exhilaration and destruction.

I drag my lips over her cheeks, her nose, her jaw, my teeth scoring the slender column of her neck. Then I reach my target—that rapid fluttering in her throat.

Wrapping my lips over it, I suck. *Hard.*

She cries out, her sensuous body arching back, her curvy tits thrusted at my face.

Our bodies move in unison as I pin her tightly against the door. There are too many clothes between us. Too many layers. It's too hot. Too wet. Too stifling.

I'm on fire.

I grab her heaving breast and pinch her hard nipple poking through her shirt. She trembles, her hips gyrating in a tormenting rhythm, moving that delectable pussy over my aching shaft. I can feel her heat through my pants.

"Fuck yes, Olive. Fuck my cock. Grind that pussy. Feel how hard I am for you." I draw her fluttering pulse into my mouth again, laving, sucking, then I bite it.

Olivia screams, her muscles tensing. I'm so hard I'm leaking all over the place.

"Shit. You like your pleasure with pain, huh? Just like me." I nibble and suck, my wildcat thrashing in my arms. "You need me, don't you? Desperate for my cock. Well, come get it. It's all yours."

She shakes, her hips moving up and down, up and down, each slide hitting my cock perfectly, my leaking tip digging, dipping slightly into her pants-covered, tight, wet notch before dragging up to her clit.

"Yes, oh my God, yes," she cries, her sweet voice hoarse. So that's how she sounds like—she's a screamer, my Olive will be a screamer.

My balls draw up and a scorching burn begins at the base of my spine, ricocheting through my body, the pinpricks of pleasure gathering, sharpening, distilling into a distinct beam. Pleasure moves up my shaft, and blinding light appears behind my eyelids.

"Come on my cock. I want to feel you explode. You're a good girl, right? Be *my good girl.*"

She freezes, her fingernails digging into my back.

Our panting breaths reverberate in the room and suddenly, she goes limp in my arms.

"What am I doing?" she rasps. *Horror.* That's what I'm hearing in her voice.

I set her down, my hands trembling, my fingers clenching and releasing, desperate to touch her silky skin, to pull her against me once more.

To burn us both alive.

She looks up, her face blanching. She shakes her head harder.

"W-We can't do this. I-I can't do this."

Then she opens the door and dashes out.

This time, I don't stop her.

Chapter Twenty-Nine

I miss her.

After tasting her, touching her, it doesn't matter whether I deserve Olivia or catharsis. Whether I'm ruining her by involving her with me, a man whose blackouts are occurring more frequently, a man who can't function without his pills.

I need her. My mind calls out to her. My body craves her.

I've convinced myself I can protect her reputation, that she needs this connection as much as I do. That as long as I behave in public, we can have our moments in private. We'll heal each other. We'll get this out of our systems.

No one else has to know.

But for the past four days since our kiss in the closet, she's been avoiding me like a vampire to sunlight.

I don't see her in the restaurants, on the decks, and when I go to her office, either she's in an appointment with a patient, or she'll tell me she's busy...

Through the closed door.

My chest tightens as I walk toward the elevator bay, not wanting to go to the masquerade ball this evening.

Casey holds open the elevator door and I step in. He's dressed in a sleek black tux, a demi mask in his hand.

It isn't an Orchid cruise without an over-the-top, glamorous ball, which is happening off-site at Casa Rocca Piccola, a 16th century palace in our current stop, Malta.

"What are you supposed to be?" he asks, scanning my outfit—a navy velvet coat with gold buttons, a black waistcoat underneath, a white linen shirt with an old-fashioned cravat fastened at the neck. The attire is finished with fitted black breeches and leather boots.

"An aristocrat. Haven't decided whether I want to be a duke or an earl... Duke of Your Orgasms has a nice ring to it, don't you think?" I smirk.

He rolls his eyes, but his lips twitch. "Why did I even ask?"

"I didn't think you'd be attending," I murmur as the elevator moves.

"Since when do I not go to your parties?"

My lips hitch up. "Drag you to my parties is more like it. I don't need a babysitter anymore. I'm thirty-seven."

Casey dusts the invisible lint off his sleeves. "Trust me, I don't want to babysit you. But until I can trust you enough or pass that job to someone who can manage you, my conscience won't let me leave you alone. And you know I've saved you from making bad choices over the years."

Silence falls in the small space again and I think back to our past decades—the good, the bad, the ugly—he's been by my side through it all. He'd whispered in my ear at high school graduation, telling me to give my keys to someone else because I had three shots and shouldn't be driving. He made me call Lana when I stared into the ocean after Raya's death, wondering if taking a brisk dive in December after ingesting Velowake and vodka would be enough to shock the senses and make me feel something other than grief.

He knew I wouldn't do anything stupid if I was talking to my sister because, as reckless as I was, I'd never do anything to traumatize Lana. And so, that night, as I was sitting on the railing, my body swaying and head dizzy, Lana and I bickered over the phone, her rambling about the douchebags who'd mysteriously ghost her after two dates and I'd make fun of her hopeless romantic self.

To this day, she doesn't know how close I was to jumping into the ocean that night, how if I did, I probably wouldn't have survived.

So yes, Casey has saved my ass a few times.

More than a few. And in a world where I'm often alone, I'm grateful. And I guess that's progress.

"Thank you," I shift on my feet, "for everything. I've been shit to you and you've stuck by me. It means a lot."

He stiffens, his eyes widening at my words. I give him grief and he dishes it right back, but I don't think I've ever properly thanked him for not leaving me, for being the one person I can talk to.

Until Olivia.

The woman whose lips I can't forget, whose kiss reigns supreme as the best sexual encounter I've ever had.

Clearing his throat, he nods. "You should tell the doc the truth. All of it. Maybe I was wrong before...but I think she's good for you."

The truth. She knows more about the events of Mom's death than anyone else in my family. While I still haven't told her everything—how, as I relive that day over the years, I recall the arguments I heard and realize I should've known all along who was behind her and the other deaths in the family.

How I could've stopped Mom from dying that day if I'd stuck around...if I wasn't so afraid of monsters.

Hindsight is twenty-twenty, or so they say. But with HSAM, it's ten times worse.

But I know that's not what Casey's referring to.

Olivia wouldn't judge me for what happened to Mom. I know that now.

But the *other* truth...the one no one knows?

She'll judge me for it. No one in their right mind will stick around, and I'll lose her for good.

"She won't. Have some faith," he murmurs and my head snaps up. *Did I speak my thoughts out loud?*

The elevator doors open, and we step out. Patrons, dressed to the nines in glittering costumes, gather in the main atrium to wait for the limos to take us to Casa Rocca Piccola. A bright flash blinds my eyes, and when my vision returns, I spot Greg Masters slinking away, checking his camera.

When I look back for Casey, he's already gone.

I swallow a gasp as I gape at the surroundings—vaulted ceilings and arched doorways, exposed stonework and iron accents. There's a surprise around every corner.

I've stepped into a piece of history, and now the outfit Lana chose for me makes perfect sense. Shifting on my feet, I tug at the low neckline of my Renaissance-inspired burgundy gown. It's the most beautiful dress I've ever worn. The gold brocade shimmers under the dim lighting, and the flowy slashed sleeves drape over my arms.

But while it's beautiful, half my boobs along with my shoulders are showing. I've never been in anything so revealing before.

"Stop yanking at it." Lana swats my hand away from my dress.

"I feel like I'm one accident away from a wardrobe malfunction. Imagine the headlines, 'Fleur psychiatrist seen flashing her boobs at the masquerade ball.'"

She snorts. "You're wearing a mask...no one will know it's you! And flaunt those girls. They've been stifled for too long. And your *hair*, woman! I didn't know you had such gorgeous, thick hair because you always have it in a bun!"

Heat crawls up my skin as I touch the thick braids hanging down to my mid-back, encrusted with glittering gems.

I don't even know who I am anymore.

Definitely not the woman hiding in the shadows.

It's terrifying and yet, despite my rickety pulse, there's a breathlessness, an exhilaration pumping through me.

I'm reminded of the way Rex's eyes smolder when he sees me and how he calls me bewitching.

How he kisses me like he needs me to breathe.

Bewitching.

Nope. Not thinking about him. Can't think about him.

I've failed far too many times since our tryst in the closet. It was a miracle I stopped us before we took it too far.

If he hadn't called me a good girl, the term triggering my latent resentment over *literally* being the good girl, I would've continued. I would've let him have his way with me.

Of course, when the lust dissipated, I knew his good girl carried a different meaning.

But still, I have a choice to make.

I can end our doctor-patient relationship and be together. Tongues will wag because people aren't stupid. They can put two and two together. My reputation will be ruined. And then what? Rex fucks me until he's tired of me? He's never had a long-term girlfriend before. What makes me so special?

Or I stay the course. Try harder to stay away. Even if my heart is telling me to run toward him because no one has ever made me feel this way before.

Treasured. Loved. Seen.

"Ooh, incoming, Olivia!" Lana whispers excitedly. She nudges me.

"What?" Sweeping my eyes around the room, I take in the crowd in gorgeous costumes before spotting a dark-haired man without a mask heading our way.

Shit. It's Rhys. He asked me yesterday if I had a date to the ball.

I groan and dart into another room, the girls following me.

"What's the rush?" Bree asks.

"I see someone I want to avoid."

"Who? The hottie walking toward us?" Lana grins. "Is he your vacation fling?"

"He's a coworker. And no. Definitely not him. I don't date coworkers." *And yet, you're thinking about dating your patient, you hypocrite!*

"But there's someone, isn't there? Your ears are red."

I ignore her as I come to a stop in another room, which looks completely different from the one we came from.

"Decadent, isn't it?" Lana says as she brushes her hand over her blue sequined gown, which molds to her body like a second skin. She's supposed to be a mermaid tonight.

"You need to give your events director a raise." I marvel at the furnishings in this room, which is nicknamed "The Inferno Hall."

The walls are swathed in crimson silks, the room dark except for flickering candelabras and free-standing candles dripping with red wax. Reverent chants rise and fall from the speakers like I'm at a monastery. Guests dance and mingle, their laughter adding to the ambiance.

We walk to another room. This one is cloistered in black silk with iron lanterns hanging from the ceilings. A ghostly mist hovers above the floor, courtesy of a fog machine. Soft gasps and moans pipe from hidden speakers.

"This is the Purgatory Passage," Lana whispers, glee in her voice. "Spooky and sexy, right? I can't wait to explore them all. There are heaven and hell-themed rooms here." She turns toward Bree. "Aren't you glad I convinced you to come?"

"I was supposed to stay on the cruise ship," Bree grumbles and stares at her feet.

"Why?" Lana cocks her brow. I'm equally curious because Bree is definitely hiding something.

Bree snaps her head up, her voice pitchy. "Uh. No reason. Just a headache. I don't like people and going out. I'm an introvert."

"You need alcohol. That's what you need." Lana grabs her hand and motions at me. "Let's go get a drink, then party it up."

I shake my head. Alcohol and me don't mix. My Asian genes will turn me into a tomato if I so much as take a sip, and I really don't want my face to match the color of my dress. "You guys go, I'll just hang out—"

"Ladies," a gravelly voice murmurs from behind me.

A dark shadow strides up to us.

Black hair, black mask, black tux, startling green eyes, and a menacing air all around.

I think I know who this is.

Lana purses her lips and narrows her eyes. "You aren't welcome here. Go be a Shadow King to someone who wants your overbearing, pompous ass—" She snaps her mouth shut, clearly aware we're gaping at her. Lana Anderson is the poised PR queen of the family, and it's rare to see her in a fit of...well, anything. "Shoo. Go away."

Shadow King. The nickname she mentioned the other day in Dubrovnik finally registers.

Elias Kent. Everyone in New York City and beyond knows who he is. Rumor has it even the mafia is afraid of him. I don't want to find out why that's the case.

Low chuckles rumble from his chest, the mobster clearly unfazed. "Can't. Promised your brother I'd watch over you and your...friend."

He glances at Bree, who blanches and shrinks behind Lana.

I frown. They seem to know each other. But why would Rex's companion know the mobster I've heard so much about? And why would Rex ask Elias to keep an eye out on Bree?

Nothing makes sense.

"Which brother? This is what I get for having four ridiculous, overprotective brothers. It better not be Rex, because if anything, I look out for him. Is it Maxwell? I swear to God—" Lana tosses her hands up in the air then drags a bewildered Bree with her, probably to escape Elias and to grab drinks.

Elias tsks under his breath, his hands knotted behind his back. He takes a step in their direction but suddenly swivels back to me. "Dr. Lin, we haven't officially met before. I'm Elias Kent."

My breath lodges in my throat, the hairs standing on the back of my neck. He really doesn't need to introduce himself.

But how does he know who I am? And how did he even recognize me in costume?

I swallow and give him a curt smile.

He smirks, as if enjoying seeing me squirm.

"Thank you for taking care of him," he murmurs. "If you need anything, I'm at your service."

Then he nods and disappears after my friends.

What the hell? Who is he referring to? And why would I ever need his services?

Questions pinball inside my mind. Why is everyone speaking in code? Bree, Rex, and now, Elias.

But as I stand there, surrounded by dancers and partygoers, I feel it.

A charged current threading the air, heavy and electric.

My breath quickens, my pulse roars in my ears. I turn around, trying to locate the source of my unease.

The shapes of the crowd blur together, dark shadows shifting sinuously, made even more eerie by the white mist swirling in the air.

The hairs stand on my forearms.

And that's when I spot him.

A tall, imposing dark-haired man draped in shadows in the corner, his back against the wall, arms crossed over his chest. His thick hair, which I know is as soft as it looks, is effortlessly tousled, giving off a debonair air of sex and charm. Muscles ripple under his dark coat as he slowly unfurls himself.

The heat in his eyes ratchets up as he catches me staring at him. His face, half hidden in a black mask with gold veins, sparks awareness in me.

I'd recognize him anywhere.

My chest heaves, the corset on my dress feeling too tight, and I inch backward.

Devil. Predator. Monster.

His lips slowly hitch up, then he prowls toward me.

CHAPTER THIRTY

I turn around and flee.

My pulse shoots through the roof as I dash through the crowds. I don't know why I'm running away. Maybe because deep down, I know if I stop, if he catches me, it'll be over.

Or perhaps I sense the inevitable—the two of us burning in the flames of hell as we maul each other to death with lust, kisses, and passion bordering on violence.

The hickey on my neck throbs, a reminder of how easily it burned out of control last time. How I wanted to throw every rule in my rulebook out the window with the last person I should ever fall for.

And so I quicken my steps, weaving around ball goers, ignoring the loud whispers, the quiet moans and shivery whimpers in dark corners.

Away from him. The devil. My temptation.

My panting breaths are loud as I adjust the mask on my face. Every inch of me is attuned to the man hot on my heels.

I plow into someone, nearly toppling them over.

"S-Sorry." I gasp, my pulse frantic now. I dodge into the hallway. How many hallways are inside this castle?

Thud. Thud. Thud.

I hear his heavy footsteps gaining on me, and I sneak a look over my shoulder. His eyes are dark and searing, his attention unwavering as he breaks into a run.

The crowd parts for him.

"Shit." I pick up my skirts and sprint into the throngs of people, hoping I'll disappear into the masses.

I need to find somewhere quiet. Somewhere I can hear myself think.

Somewhere I can slap some cold water onto my face and tell myself to wake the hell up.

Ignoring the open rooms filled with people, I check the closed doors one by one, finding them locked. Eventually, I arrive at a gilded door at the end of the hallway. I pull on the knob, thankful to find it unlocked, before slipping inside and closing the door behind me.

The room is quiet and dark with only the moonlight streaming in from the window on the far wall, the heavy drapes half opened.

I navigate the dark shapes—a settee of some sort, a coffee table, a bookshelf or a cabinet.

My breath still rattles out of me when I reach the window, finding a small courtyard outside. I close my eyes and rest my forehead against the glass, hoping the cool surface will wake me up.

Because every fiber inside me wants to find the maddening man to finish what we started in the closet.

This isn't you, Olivia.

But is that true?

Haven't I been aching to break free of everything? The good daughter syndrome, the forgotten twin, the person who's living life and yet...not really living?

Opposing thoughts clash in my mind and I focus on my breathing.

Calm. Calm yourself.

My insides are so chaotic, I don't even notice anything's wrong until it's too late.

I feel his heat behind me before he tugs me flushed against him, his arms unforgiving.

"Got you," he rasps.

My eyes snap open and I take in our reflections—a masked, dark-haired man with intense eyes slowly dipping his head over a masked woman with raven hair. We look like extras from a historical piece—a rich man with a courtesan, two people sneaking around in dark nooks, as forbidden back then as they are today.

Like Duke Orsino and Viola from Shakespeare's *Twelfth Night*. But does he know this disguise, this seductive siren, isn't me?

Or is it?

Digging his fingers into my waist, he drags his lips up my neck to my ear, a groan scraping out of his throat.

My clit pulses and skin tightens. I feel him everywhere.

"What are we doing?" My whisper turns into a moan when his tongue snakes out and swirls around my hickey. *His hickey.*

"Face your fears to get over them... What are you afraid of?" He bites the mark and I shudder.

"Rules, ethics, responsibilities, I—"

"I will protect you. Always." He places his finger over my lips before sliding his thumb into my mouth.

"Fuck," he rasps when I lick his finger, tasting the saltiness of his skin, imagining it being his cock in my mouth.

Rex growls and hauls me tighter against him, his hard dick pressing into my backside through our clothes. His other hand snakes up my stomach, his fingers dragging trails of fire over my breasts, my collarbone, then wrapping around my neck.

He squeezes and I swallow a gasp.

"I don't know who you are, and you don't know who I am." He tongues my ear before kissing my jaw, then angling my face toward his.

Stormy gray eyes sear into mine—eyes I'd recognize anywhere, even if he were covered head-to-toe in disguise.

"Tonight," he whispers the words onto my lips, "we're two strangers at a masquerade. No names, no titles, no rules. Give me tonight."

I sway, my head dizzy as my senses are inundated with everything that's Rex Anderson—his smell of amber and bergamot, his deep, smooth voice, his fingers firmly digging into my neck.

I want to be his plaything for tonight.

I want to be free.

Barely canting my head into a nod, I watch his eyes flare and darken. He slides his thumb out of my mouth and I whimper my discontent as I try to suck him back in, to hold any part of him inside me.

He groans and presses me against the window, one hand coiled around my neck, the other yanking my low neckline down until my breasts are exposed.

"Fuck," he grunts when he palms my breast.

It feels so small in his hand, but he doesn't seem to care. He kneads it, his fingers tugging at the nipple, sparking pain-laced pleasure in my veins.

I tremble in his arms, my ass rubbing against his front, feeling him elongate and dig out of his pants.

"You're hot for it, aren't you, my whore," he rasps, taking on the role of the nobleman slaking his lust with a fallen woman.

I like it. This degradation. It's freeing.

"Yes," I whimper when he moves to the other breast, slapping it hard before smoothing out the sting with a gentle caress.

"Is that pussy of yours wet for me? Have you been a naughty, filthy girl, waiting in the dark, needing a thick, hard cock to spear you in half?"

My legs turn to jelly, my mind barely processing his words as my blood reaches a boiling point.

Rex fists my skirts, and drags them up, up, and up, baring my leg to the cold air. Then he reaches around and cups me between my legs.

"Soaked. You're fucking soaked for me. You want to be used and degraded, don't you?"

He yanks my underwear to the side and, without warning, thrusts two fingers into my tight channel.

"Ah!" I cry, my head dropping back onto his shoulder as he curls his digits and quickens his rhythm.

Electricity courses through my body as wetness seeps out of me. The brocade chafes my skin, and the dress feels heavy. The corset restricts my lungs from taking a full breath.

He coils his hand around my neck again, and my pulse beats into a turbulent rhythm. He steps back, taking me with him, my pussy stuffed with his fingers, and I'm helpless to fight back.

The slick sounds of him finger fucking me echo in the room, joined by our lewd moans and guttural grunts.

He tightens his hold around my neck and I gasp for breath.

"Look up, my bewitching vixen. Look at our reflections in the window. See how well we fit together. See how horny, desperate you look with your tits hanging out, your nipples hard, begging me to suck on them, to bite them."

"Oh my God," I whimper, my hips gyrating to the hammering of his fingers, my eyes rolling back. The sharp pleasure coalesces into a singular point of ecstasy.

I'm going to break into a million pieces.

Then pain explodes between my legs and his fingers are gone.

He slapped my pussy. The asshole slapped my pussy!

My eyes snap open, and his madness finally infects me. I thrash in his arms, fighting his grasp. His low, deranged chuckles reach my ears.

"That's it. Break free, sweetheart. Now, keep your eyes open and look at our fucking reflection. I won't repeat myself."

Opposing emotions clash inside me—obedience and disobedience, dominance and submission. It's maddening. It clouds my mind and my vision in a haze of red.

I fight, claw, scratch at any part of him I can reach. All the while he grips my tits and twists my nipples, the heady pain joining the fury and oblivion in my veins.

"All you have to do is say stop and I'll stop, vixen," he growls into my ear.

"No. You're not the boss of me," I hiss. Who is this vixen?

His eyes flash before he cinches my throat again and angles my head toward the window. "Really? Are you sure? Because. Look. At. Our. Fucking. Reflections."

He pins me in place, his voice dropping to a low, devilish whisper. "Now, look at us. Look how horny you are in my arms."

My eyes finally refocus as I take in our reflection, my mouth dropping open.

The woman there isn't me—hair wild and tumbling out of her braids, skin reddened, breasts heaving and my core glistening under the moonlight on full display.

Rex chuckles and I watch in fascination as his hand grabs my pussy, then spears three fingers inside me, sending sharp torrents of pleasure and pain through my body once more.

"Fuck. This cunt. You're so tight. You take me so well," he grunts, his fingers pistoning, his eyes smoldering as they meet mine in the mirror. "You are devastation, a natural disaster. You are wildfire and poison."

The sounds grow wetter, my legs already incapable of standing, and I'm completely reliant on him hoisting me up.

My lungs constrict, my nails digging into his hand around my neck, wanting both to break free from the shackle around my throat and to have him tighten his grip.

"Just say no," he reminds me as his fingers quicken to hammering.

My clit throbs and pulses and wetness drips out of me, but I don't care. My lurid cries echo in the quiet room.

My cries. I don't sound like the good doctor, the rule follower.

"Yes, feel your pussy gripping me. Fuck, you make me so hard." He emphasizes his point by whipping his hips against my ass, letting me feel his hard cock against my butt. "Taking me like a good slut, aren't you?"

"Y-Yes, yes, yes..." Our reflection—me gyrating half-naked, moving lewdly against his fully clothed body, my eyes glazed over in passion—brands into my mind.

I don't recognize the woman in the window, and yet I know her. She's been hiding inside me all along.

"Anyone outside can see you. Horny, wet, your soaked pussy aching to come, needing my cock. But I won't give it to you now, won't I? You only get what I give you when I give it to you."

He scissors his fingers inside me, hitting a spot I don't even realize exists.

"Fuck me, fuck me, fuck me," I moan as his hand tightens around my neck, further sharpening my senses to the fire burning between my legs.

Bam!

Someone opens the door.

Rex slaps his other hand over my mouth, muffling my cries.

Logic and fear sweep in as Rex drags me to a nook behind the nearest cabinet.

Muffled conversations reach my ears—the words too soft for me to pick up because of the rioting pulse battering my eardrums.

Just when my mind threatens to awaken, Rex does the unthinkable.

He thrusts three fingers back inside me.

I bite back a cry as he resumes his scissoring motion, the sparks which never faded away growing like a brush fire under one hundred mile per hour winds.

Burns. Everything burns out of control.

"Quiet, or you'll give us away," he rasps, his fingers fucking me.

Harder. Faster.

My muscles lock, then tremble, my teeth chattering, his other hand still covering my mouth. A pulsing I've never felt before begins deep inside my core, then radiates outward, invading every nerve cell.

"Come. Give me your cum, sweetheart, and don't let them hear us."

He nips my earlobe.

The dam breaks. I bite my cheek to silence my scream.

Wetness gushes out of me, making a mess of his hand, my dress, my thighs. I hear droplets hitting the floor before Rex thrusts his thigh between my legs, so my cum drips onto his pants instead.

"Good girl, my fucking good girl. Next time you squirt, I want you to drench my face."

He shushes me, alternating between sweet words and degradation. He strokes my pussy, massaging it, extending the aftershocks.

This time, I melt under his praises, my body not really mine anymore, my mind in a haze.

What on earth was that? Because that wasn't just an orgasm. It felt like so much more.

"A beautiful squirter. I want to see you soak our mattress like the good slut you are." He licks the column of my neck and I shudder.

Squirt. I squirted. My face flames.

Then I hear the door opening, then closing. Whoever was here just left.

Ring.

Rex's ringtone blares like an alarm, and I jolt in his arms.

He kisses my cheek, then slowly steps away from me.

My face is on fire as I squeeze my eyes shut and collapse against the window, the cold glass doing nothing to cool my body.

"What? You've got to be kidding me. I'll be right there," he says into the phone.

I hear his heavy footsteps, then feel his muscular body behind me.

His cock, harder than ever, digs into my back. A ragged sigh throttles out of him. He slides my hair to the side, then presses the softest kiss on the tender point where my neck meets my shoulder.

"Such a good girl. Bewitching. Made for me."

Then he disappears, leaving me half-naked in the room.

Five minutes later, my phone pings with an incoming message.

Rex

We're not done. Not by a long shot.

CHAPTER THIRTY-ONE

REX DISAPPEARED AFTER THE masquerade a week ago. Lana told me there was a brand ambassador emergency in their London office, which he had to personally handle. Something about a high maintenance model who was threatening to pull out of an upcoming hotel launch.

But naturally, her people told Fleur she'd reconsider if she got a meeting with Rex.

Apparently, they dated before—one of the leggy models who'd jet set with him around the globe last year, who clearly had her eyes set on something else...an Anderson last name.

It was a gut punch when Lana told me the news over breakfast, and I feigned a smile and excused myself.

It was a good reminder. The universe's final warning, letting me know who I'm dealing with.

A playboy. Womanizer. Someone who never settles down.

I never answered his text message from that night, and he didn't contact me again either.

What did you expect? The man is half-asshole, half-charmer, and a whole heartbreaker.

Before Rex, I didn't know how much I was missing in my life. How I was marching through my days, eating saltine crackers, drinking water with no ice, not knowing there were other flavors out there, not knowing my taste buds were severely deprived.

But now I know.

And the man who's introduced me to the spices and flavors of life is now in another country, courting another woman, who, no doubt, wants a ride on the party prince, to get another hit of the Rex-a-Million experience.

Dammit, Olivia, why didn't you start off with chicken noodle soup or something? Why did you have to jump headfirst into buffalo hot wings doused in Carolina Reapers pepper sauce?

And to top it off, I've violated my Hippocratic Oath and the American Medical Association's code of ethics by being involved with Rex. There's no use denying it any longer.

"Oh Olive, I didn't know you had it in you. Can't believe you let him finger fuck you in public." Mia's voice snickers in my mind.

I know it's not her. It's grief along with this elusive twin-sense creating a figment of her in my mind. And perhaps, her voice is stronger because we're finally in Valencia at the tail end of the Las Fallas Festival.

The whole purpose of my trip.

"If you're going to talk to me, tell me why. Why did you leave me? What regrets did you have?" I murmur to my reflection in the bathroom mirror before heading offshore.

It's the last day of the annual festival, when *ninots*, sculptures made of wood and paper mâché, are burned to the ground at night.

For the past two days, I wandered aimlessly around Valencia, watching local *falleros* and *falleras* dressed in colorful traditional costumes, dancing and parading on the streets. I watched the *Mascletà* being set off in the town hall square at two p.m., the exciting display of colorful fireworks and firecrackers exhilarating and memorable.

The energy was thrilling, the air vibrating with drumbeats and laughter, with chaos bleeding into joy the closer we approached the last day of the festival.

During this time, Mia's presence lingered by my side—when I tasted the freshness of the seafood paella, or chugged down a citrusy champagne cocktail, the *Agua de Valencia*. She'd be with me when I took photos of the celebrations, awestruck at the towering *ninots* depicting everything from fairytale characters to caricatures of famous people.

Everything was bold, indulgent, exciting—all words I'd use to describe Mia.

For the first time since her funeral, I allowed myself to *feel* everything without guilt—the loss of the other half of me, gratitude for being alive, for being here to enjoy this journey for both of us, anger at myself and my family for never prioritizing me.

When we turned eighteen and my life just began, Mia's life ended. Ever since then, I've been one person trying to fill two people's shoes.

It isn't fair, chasing after a ghost.

It isn't fair, being forgotten by the living for a ghost.

It isn't fair, becoming a ghost myself because I've forgotten to live for *me*.

And now, strolling around the city by myself, experiencing the joy and melancholy in the air, I let myself grieve.

I let myself celebrate *me*.

Who am I?

I'm Olivia Lin, a woman who's spent her life coloring within the lines, afraid of disappointing others. I'm scared of small spaces and heights, but when push comes to shove, will jump off a cliff to save someone.

I'm a woman who apparently likes Carolina Reapers even though they burn the roof of my mouth off. And I hate the taste of almond cookies, no matter how many times I try to get used to it. I'm someone whose blood thrums to life in the presence of a maddening, impulsive man.

I'm the person who looks like she has her life in order when it's taking every ounce of her energy to appear that way.

But it's okay. That's life. It's messy. Chaotic. Beautiful. And I'm learning now.

I've learned some rules are meant to be broken because I'll experience the adrenaline pumping in my veins, the thrill of clandestine kisses, and the icy chill of a storm soaking through my clothes into my skin.

I've learned that being true to myself is more important than pleasing others around me.

I'm learning I don't have the answers. The future is uncertain and I'll fuck things up, but it'll be okay.

As I clutch the envelope full of photos I've printed from my phone, photos I was supposed to take from my Leica, I'm someone who's going to bid farewell to my best friend, my sister, and my past tonight.

Burn away our regrets.

Chapter Thirty-Two

It's late by the time I make it to Valencia. The *cremà*, the final act of Las Fallas, where all the sculptures are burned down in a blaze of glory, is in full swing after my driver picked me up from the jet and dropped me off near the town square.

Adriana, the nuisance of a model, was all smiles and coyness when I met her at our London office. It took some wining, dining, and a few expensive shopping trips to get the petulant woman to sign back onto our campaign.

It took every ounce of control inside me not to lash out at her for pulling me away from the woman who occupied my mind twenty-four seven.

Olivia.

She melted so beautifully in my arms at the masquerade. While my cock leaked inside my pants and I didn't come, seeing her in the throes of passion, her carefully crafted mask shattered on the floor, was the most unforgettable experience of my life. The perfect way she submitted to me, how she absorbed my madness. I'd been as hard as a rock every night, reliving those precious moments in the dark.

I want to push her limits, test her boundaries, and make her come again and again, until she's speechless and sated.

I want to hear her soothing voice asking me questions I've never asked myself, making me face my past.

I want to listen to the sound of her breathing when I lay in bed at night, just to know she exists and wants to spend time with me—the real me under the playboy, jokester persona.

But she never responded to my text.

When I called Lana to give her an update on Adriana, I asked about Olivia.

"It's interesting how you ask about her and not your friend, Bree," Lana hums under her breath, her skepticism loud and clear.

"Bree and I are just friends."

"You've never been friends with a woman before. What gives? And why are you concerned about Olivia if you don't even ask after your 'friend'?"

"None of your business, lil' sis."

"My alarm bells are ringing. You guys are hiding something from me." She gasps, and I hear her chair squeaking. *"You better not be messing with her, Rex! She's one of my best friends and a sweet person with a heart of gold. She can't survive your games with women."*

I stay silent.

"Rex Cassius Wentworth Anderson, I swear to God, unless you plan to put a ring on it, don't mess with Olivia Lin. She's your doctor, she has a reputat—"

I hung up on Lana that night. Everything she said were words I repeated to myself as I fought the impulse to call or text Olivia.

To tell her I miss her.

To tell her she wasn't just a romp in the dark. That if I could, I *would* put a ring on her. The thought shook me to my core. I never thought I'd feel this way about anyone.

But then, what can I give her? I'm a freak—not right in the mind. She doesn't know all my secrets, which, despite what Casey thinks, I'm damn sure she'll have an issue with if she were ever to find out.

Frankly, who wouldn't?

And so, I didn't contact her. I gave us both space.

Instead, whenever I missed her, which felt like every minute of the day, I'd take out my phone and swipe to my secret photo album of her. I'd smile at the moments I stashed away.

The Velowake doesn't keep my nightmares at bay anymore. Alcohol and sex with random women have long lost their appeal.

But Olivia? Tempting her, teasing her, fighting with her, marveling at the contradictions inside her petite frame—vulnerability and strength, control and chaos.

I can't get enough.

The air smells like gunpowder and smoke as I stroll through the crowded streets, watching the flames erupt and consume the sculptures.

Destruction and rebirth.

The dark sky glows orange from the fires as the crowd chants, with the sound of crackling flames as the backdrop.

Something stirs inside me—a restlessness I can't explain. My heart pulses, my hands twitch, my muscles ache. It's different from the surge of energy I get from the Velowake.

I need to do something. Anything. It's why, instead of resting in my stateroom after a tiring trip, I'm wandering aimlessly through nooks and crannies.

Pausing at a street corner, I take out my phone and snap a photo of the beautiful destruction. On an impulse, I open my text messages and reply to Ava, who I still have as "unknown number" in my contacts. I guess this is a step in the right direction—not avoiding my past.

Rex

I'm in Valencia for Las Fallas. Let the past burn. Focus on the future. Take care of yourselves.

She replies a minute later with an attachment of her own.

Unknown number

You're so close by. Thanks for the pic. Here's a card I made for your birthday. Forgot to text it to you last time.

I open it, finding a simple watercolor painting—two girls' silhouettes against a beautiful sunset with a happy birthday written in script.

After thanking her, I make a right into a small courtyard, away from the larger crowds heading toward the burning of the main *falla* in the town hall square, the last event to bring the festival to a close.

My feet come to a stop and my heart pulses.

I see her, my Olive, standing next to a small sculpture already engulfed in flames. Happiness sweeps through me. I missed her this past week.

I miss her so damn much.

Without thinking, I hold up my phone and take a photo of her to add to my secret stash—a phoenix rising from the ashes.

But as I zoom in on my photo, I notice her expression.

Tears are streaming down her face.

My lungs constrict, her grief robbing me of my breath.

I want to know who did this to her, who made her cry.

I want to kill that person.

She sobs into her hand as she tosses small scraps of paper into the inferno, her lips moving like she's whispering to the fire.

My feet move of their own accord.

I want—no, need—to make her feel better. This is my life's purpose at this very second. My heart will give up on me if I can't make her smile.

Make her smile, Rex. Make her laugh. Be the Anderson jokester. That's what you're good at.

But I can't bring myself to speak, to intrude on the outpouring of emotions on her face. And with the time I've spent with her on this trip, I know one thing.

Olivia holds everything inside her. In some ways, we're the same—I act out, but she restrains herself.

But both of us are hiding. And sometimes, we just need to let it out. To cry. Jokes won't be appropriate.

I stop a few steps from her, and she must've sensed me because she looks up, her mouth parting, clearly in shock.

Her black hair is undone and flowing down her back. Wetness streaked over her ivory cheeks, her dark lashes clumped from moisture.

She's so beautiful. So bewitching. So broken.

Just like me.

Without speaking, I walk up to her and cup her face, my heart twisting as I dry her tears with my fingers.

Olivia hiccups. Suddenly, she trembles, like something has knocked her off her feet.

She sways, and being the bastard with no impulse control, I haul her to me and crush her in my arms.

And she sobs.

I don't know how many minutes pass by. I don't care how passersby might look at us, wondering why we're crying during a celebration to bid farewell to the winter and to welcome the fresh hope of spring.

If there were anything I could do to take away an ounce of her pain—jump off a building, walk through the literal flames before me—I would, no questions asked.

It's madness. It's illogical. It's righteous.

Maybe *this* is my purpose, my calling. Maybe all the pain I've been through has led me to this very moment, to be the man to hold her when she cries.

"There is no closure," she whispers into my shirt, already soaked through with her tears.

I stay silent, hoping she'll let me in.

"I was an identical twin."

I startle, wondering how none of us knew this about her. I've never heard her or my siblings mention anything about Olivia other than her family is on the West Coast. She's kept her past hidden from everyone.

"Her name was Mia."

Was. A boulder sits on top of my lungs. She's lost someone close to her, just like I have. I pull her tighter against me, wanting to give her my warmth.

"She was the rebel, the extrovert, the sun. You couldn't help but be drawn to her energy. She had this gift," I hear a smile in her voice now, "even if she pissed you off, you couldn't stay mad at her. And she'd piss me off so often, always getting us into situations we weren't supposed to be in. Breaking rules. There was one time she pulled the fire alarm before sixth period because she found out there was a pop quiz in calculus and she didn't study for it. She made us run in opposite directions, because if they suspected us, but they couldn't tell which one of us did it, they couldn't punish us, you know?"

I chuckle, imagining the rule-following Olivia scared shitless as she sprinted down the hallways of her school. "She sounds like a riot."

It sounds like shit I'd pull.

"She was. She always said, '*carpe diem*,' like it's an excuse to do shit because you only get one life to live. God, I was so mad at her. If she'd studied weekly like I did, she would've been prepared. A bad grade wasn't worth a potential suspension. I didn't speak to her for a week."

Olivia looks up, her beautiful brown eyes soft, and she gives me a sad smile. "But Mia would weasel her way into my good graces again. She'd give me her slab of barbecue pork when Mom made ramen for dinner. She'd save the purple Skittles, my favorite flavor, into a bag and give them to me. She'd sneak 'I'm sorry' notes into my pencil case so I'd see them when I opened it. I couldn't stay mad at her."

I brush her hair out of her face, relishing the soft silkiness I never got to enjoy before. Olivia's eyes flutter shut.

"She was the sun. I was the shadow she cast on the ground. I let her shine because I was more comfortable being in the dark, in the background. No one knew she was depressed. She partied hard, worked hard. She was beautiful and brilliant. She had the world in her hands."

Her eyes fill with moisture again. "I had to work twice as hard to accomplish what she could easily do. If anything, I should be the one to be depressed, right? It'd be easy—I was the forgotten twin, the second fiddle. None of us ever expected her to be sad. She had everything."

Olivia pulls away from me and steps toward the fire. "We were supposed to start college together. It was prom. She had a hot date with the student body president. I was going with my first and only boyfriend. He booked a hotel room for our first time." A flush creeps up her face and I try to tamp down the burn rising in my chest at the idea of her with another man. "We were going to talk about our experiences the next morning."

She tosses another scrap of paper into the fire. From this distance, I see they are photos—this one of the cave excursion in Mykonos. "When I went home the next morning, wanting to tell her sex was overrated, I knew something was wrong. You see, twins would have a connection. When she was scared, I felt it. When she was happy, I sensed it."

Olivia shakes and I walk over and pull her against me as a foreboding weight sinks deeper into my gut.

I smell the damp earth tinged with metal from the night that changed my life. Visions of my mom's twisted body appear before me.

"It was the nothingness I felt when I stepped inside the house that morning. Dead silence. An eerie hollowness. It was wrong, terribly wrong. I remember sweating when I made my way up the stairs. I remember holding my breath when I turned the doorknob of her bedroom door."

She pulls in a sharp inhale, then the rest of her story flows out in a strange monotone. "I knew she was dead before I saw her up close. She swallowed a bottle of sleeping pills and tucked herself into bed, the comforter up to her shoulders like she was going to sleep."

Olivia shook her head. "She didn't do the work, Rex. This is why I always say you have to do the work. No one can help you unless you want to help yourself. I thought something was bothering her before. I told her she could talk to me. I even took her to the bookstore so we could get self-help books. I thought it was stress—graduation, moving across the country, something run-of-the-mill. But she never confided in me. She laughed and told me I should get books for my overactive imagination."

I close my eyes, remembering the small boy who found his mom, his marbles scattered around her. Then the maids screaming and my siblings bawling when they heard my cries.

And my dad, the great Linus Anderson, who was strong, brave, and everything I wanted to be when I grew up...

He collapsed.

"I'm so sorry, Olive," I rasp, knowing exactly the pain she went through and how one event could change the rest of your life.

"She asked me to come to Las Fallas when I turned thirty. I thought nothing of it then, how she made it seem like I'd be making the trip alone, but it was her last wish for me. 'To burn our regrets,' she said. But she didn't leave a note. She didn't leave a reason. She didn't tell me what regrets she had. I don't even know why she wanted me here at thirty, not twenty-five, not any other age."

Olivia knots her hands into tight fists at her side.

"I missed the red flags. I didn't realize she was severely depressed. I was her person, and I had no idea."

Let go, Olivia. You don't have to be strong anymore. I'm here.

I squeeze her shoulder. "Scream. Yell at her. It isn't your fault. None of this is your fucking fault."

Why can't you tell yourself that? How many times did your family, did Casey tell you this?

"Why are you so selfish, Mia? Didn't you think about what would happen to me after you left? Why didn't you talk to us and get help?" she cries into the roaring flames. "*Carpe* fucking *diem*! You could've had a whole long life to do crazy stuff. Did you know how many people would've wanted that time? How could you? How could you leave me?"

The courtyard is empty now. Only me, her, and the small burning fire.

"Let it out, Olive. Let it all out. It isn't fair. What happened to you isn't fair at all."

Tears eke out of her eyes and I see the tendons flexing in her neck.

"You didn't give me closure! Do you know our parents miss you every day? That I can never replace you? How can a shadow replace the sun? They don't even know my favorite food," she sobs. "I know I shouldn't blame you, that it was a mental illness. You were miserable and sick and you didn't want this either, but I'm so angry. I wish I could hate you, but I miss you too damn much!"

She shakes like a leaf and my heart shreds into pieces, grieving for her, for me, for every lonely soul who's left behind after the death of a loved one.

A corrosive burn, one I've quashed down repeatedly when I wake up at night, bathed in sweat after reliving the past, makes its way up my esophagus, my throat, then before I know it, I'm yelling at the flames.

"I'm sorry, Mom! I heard you arguing that day. I knew you were upset, but I ran away because I was scared shitless about loud noises. If I'd gone to you, if I hadn't left my marbles all over the place, you wouldn't have died. I heard him, you know. I should've known you were in danger. He said, 'They'll never believe you, Joanna. You won't be here to tell them anything.'"

My confession spills out of me.

I hear Olivia's sharp gasp, and I know I've surprised her. But I can't help it. This poison has been bottled up inside me for too long.

I shove my hand into my pocket and clench the marble, a reminder of what I did to my family.

This is why I couldn't forgive myself as a kid or as an adult. When I was younger, I didn't understand what I'd heard. I thought my memory was playing tricks on me, because the voice was muffled and I didn't recognize it. I couldn't parse the statement—it made no sense. Mom had no enemies. But I knew Mom had slipped on my marbles, fallen down the stairs, and broken her neck.

Even as a six-year-old, I knew it was my fault. If I'd cleaned up after myself, Mom would still be here.

But when we caught the culprit a few years ago, *everything* made sense.

Those words I heard—they weren't from a scared kid with endless imagination.

They were threats from her murderer moments before she died. Mom must have figured out the culprit behind the mysterious deaths of the Anderson wives of first sons. She must have confronted the murderer.

And instead of going to her, I ran away.

That's why I couldn't forgive myself when Maxwell unearthed the killer, when he told me it wasn't my fault.

None of them knew.

It was my fault.

I had opportunities to stop it from happening. Instead, I caved to my fears and ran away.

Useless. A scaredy cat.

I robbed my mom of her life and my family of happiness.

No matter how many jokes I crack, how many smiles I put on their faces, how much of a daredevil I am now, I'll never be able to heal those wounds.

"I'm sorry!" I yell into the fire. "I'm sorry for what I did. I'm sorry for being a fuckup now. I'm so fucking sorry!"

My words echo as the flames crackle and my vision blurs.

Ragged gasps etch out of my lips—ugly, horrible sobs—the poison inside me finally overflowing, leaking out of my pores in streaks of black.

Then, I feel it.

Her hand on my arm. She slowly steps into my vision and I see her.

My angel. My siren. My salvation.

Tears stream down her face, no doubt matching mine.

"It's not your fault," she whispers urgently, her fingers shaking as she brings them up to my cheek. "Just like how it isn't my fault."

Her words are a balm to my soul, an antidote to the poison.

I grip her hand, my breathing heavy, needing to tell her my thoughts as much as I need my next breath. "And you're wrong. You aren't a shadow. You're glorious—a shooting star at night. You don't need the sun because you burn brightly all by yourself. People worship at your feet. People trust you with their wishes. You, Olivia Lin, are bewitching, breathtaking, fucking incomparable, and I see *you*."

Her lips part, her eyes widening. A gasp slips out.

Then she pulls my head down and kisses me.

For the first time in my life, I feel it.

Peace.

Chapter Thirty-Three

Our kiss spins out of control. We're oil and water, gasoline and a match. We aren't supposed to be together, and yet, nothing else makes sense. An inferno scorches through me as I hoist her in my arms, my mouth plundering hers, needing to taste her, to stave off the poison inside me with her antidote.

I'll protect her. The words bang around inside my head because I know we're taking a risk, that she's putting her career on the line by kissing me in public.

I'll protect this woman with my life. Anyone so much as looks at her in the wrong way will suffer the wrath of The Andersons.

"Rex," she moans when we break apart for air.

"My Olive. My sweet, sweet Olive."

Groaning, I crush my lips to hers again. This time, I invade her mouth with my tongue, and she fights back, teeth nipping my tongue, my lips, anywhere she can reach.

My body thrums, the heat going straight to my head, and my cock throbs against the waistband of my pants.

"Fuck," I exhale, "you fucking undo me."

I need her. Over me, under me, any part of me inside any part of her.

I want to drown in Olivia Lin and never resurface.

Wordlessly, I set her down, taking in her flushed face, her swollen lips, the way her perfect tits heave as she drags in breath after breath, her dark, hard nipples showing through her shirt.

My dick twitches and I growl, taking her hand in mine as I haul us out of the courtyard.

With my mind mad with need, lust, and other turbulent emotions I have no business naming, I drag her down the streets. I'm probably walking too fast for her, but I can't slow down.

She follows me, no questions asked, like I can lead her to hell and she won't object.

She submits so beautifully.

Wetness seeps out of my rock-hard dick. If I don't get inside her now, I'll blow inside my pants like an untried teenager.

I spot a motel ahead and make a break for it because I can't last that long. I can't wait until we get back on the cruise ship.

After handing the attendant more money than he's probably ever seen behind the counter, I grab the room key and dash up the stairs.

Our labored breaths are loud in the narrow hallway, but I barely notice as I slide the key into the lock, my hand shaking.

A second later, the door opens, and we're on each other.

"Olive, Olive, Olive, my bewitching Olive." I fist her tits as I grind on her against the closed door.

She lets out a mewl when I scrape my teeth over her neck, zeroing in on her throbbing pulse.

"Rex," she cries out when I bite down.

She loves it when I bite her there. The pain, the agony, the pleasure. I make a note of that to add to my thick file of everything Olivia in my head. I want to catalog a hundred ways of making her scream with pleasure. Then, I want to invent more. Thousands. Millions. I want to make her cry, shriek, and shatter from ecstasy.

That's my calling. My new calling I want to dedicate the rest of my life to.

This will fill the emptiness inside me.

My pulse soars at the thoughts, a low whisper inside me saying, *"You're out of your mind, Rex. She'll leave you when she finds out the extent of your madness."*

But I shove it away and instead, with one yank, whip her shirt off her, and snap off her bra.

She whimpers, her tits heaving, but those whiskey eyes of hers only grow darker, drunk with lust.

Olivia claws my head and clamps her lips on mine.

We fight again.

With our teeth, our hands, our fingers scratching, pinching, and twisting. She fists my shirt, trying to tug it off me, and I set her down with a growl. With one hand, I pull it over my head, hearing the buttons ping against the walls and the floor.

I shred the rest of my clothes at breakneck speed, watching her eyes widen when she sees my cock for the first time, the hard inches curled up against my stomach, my pre-cum already dripping from the tip. I tug it...once, twice...and it pulses in my grip.

Then, I'm all over her again. I need her pussy, her hot body writhing on me. I need everything she can give.

Take. Take. Take.

Rational thinking vanishes, and what remains is frantic need.

I tear off her leggings, not caring if I've ruined them.

"Rex, my cl-clothes," she whimpers when I bite her neck again, on that spot she loves.

She melts, her body going limp. I pick her up and wrap her legs around my back.

"I'll buy you dozens more—dresses, pants, shirts—whatever you fucking need." Anything she wants to make her stay and put up with my darkness.

My vision blackens when I thrust my cock against her pussy, feeling her bare against me for the first time.

Blind with lust, I stumble with her toward the bed, but it's too far away.

I can't wait.

Judging from the way she's riding my cock, her hot, wet pussy rubbing it from my base to tip, up and down, up and down, I know she feels the same way.

And so I drop us onto the carpet, my hand snaking between us, angling my cock into position, my mind screaming at me to spear her in half.

But I pause, hovering over her, our breaths colliding, our gazes snaring at each other.

Maybe I still have a shred of decency inside me. I know once I cross this last line, we'll never be able to go back. I'm asking her to forsake her morals, her ethics, every rule she's probably followed, for me.

And I don't even know what I can give her. It's not forever, that's for sure.

But I'll give her everything I'm capable of.

"Yes," she whispers, seeing my thoughts, hearing my questions, understanding me once again without me having to say anything.

"I'm clear...haven't been with anyone since my high school boyfriend. And I'm on the pill."

My balls clench and draw up, loving the idea of being the only man inside her, because let's face it, a no-name kid in high school is probably a one-pump chuck.

A spurt of cum seeps out of me. My eyes roll back and a groan rattles in my throat. My arms shake with restraint, with the need to slam myself deep inside her and never resurface.

"I haven't been with anyone for half a year and I've tested and am cleared."

She nods.

"Are you sure? We can't go back." *Fucking decent Anderson behavior here.* I surprise myself.

"Yes."

My mind shuts down, and I power my hips forward, thrusting inside her in one full stroke.

And I see stars. Literally.

"Shit, shit, shit." My hips move of their own accord, driving inside her wet heat. "You're so fucking tight, my good girl, my filthy slut, my perfect angel."

"Oh my God, fuck." She claws at my back, her sharp nails digging in, and the pain only drives me forward.

I throw her legs over my shoulders, needing to be deeper than anyone's ever reached before. Her pussy grips my dick so tightly, I can barely breathe.

"Feel that, Olive? You were made to take my cock. Look at you, taking all my fucking inches in that tiny, pretty cunt. I didn't think we'd fit, you know. How can a tiny thing like you take on all of me?"

I ride her hard.

Electricity courses through my veins, frying my senses. Every part of me is aware of everything that is her. Her sweet smell, her soft skin, her breathy moans in my ears.

Slam. Slam. Slam.

"Olive. My Olive," I chant. "I'm obsessed. With this wet pussy, with your tight body, with your perfect tits. But most of all, I'm obsessed with this." I lick my way down her neck, between her breasts, to where her heart pounds rapidly. "Your heart. Your pure, beautiful heart."

"Rex, I-I feel, I feel so much," she gasps, her back arching up as I plunder her from below.

Unable to help myself, I bite down on her perfect nipple, sucking it until it becomes a perfect eraser bud. Then I flick it with my tongue.

She's shaking now, and I know she's close.

"Will you let me corrupt you?" My dick lengthens as a telltale pressure radiates from the base of my spine, going up, up, up, spreading to my balls, running up my shaft. "Even though I don't deserve you? Will you burn in hell with me?"

I don't know what I'm saying. The words tumble out of me without a filter. My cock throbs and the first gush of cum streams out, but I'm holding on.

I need her answer.

Hips snapping, the wet sounds of our bodies colliding loud in the room, I stare at her, watching as her eyes flutter open, glazed over in passion, her lips parting.

I want to take a photo of her like this—perched on the edge of an orgasm.

"Always, Rex. Always," she whispers.

And I'm done.

A roar bellows out of me and I thrust in as deep as I can—once, twice, three times—and she screams. Wetness drips out of her, her tight cunt fisting my cock almost to the point of pain.

But I persist, jamming it in again and again, sealing my lips over hers as I topple off the edge into nirvana.

Unending cum flows out of me, my heart exploding in my chest, my lungs constricting. Our bodies pulse in rhythm, her pussy drawing more and more out of me, my balls emptying everything I have to give inside her.

I suckle her neck and massage her tits as my cock tunnels in and out of her, my rhythm slowing to gentle gyrations.

Her legs won't stop trembling, her body twitching underneath mine.

So fucking perfect.

So perfectly mine.

Sex before her was a means to an end, a flash of pleasure to make me forget.

But sex with her...no words can describe it.

Transcendent.

Catharsis.

More. Much more.

"Mine," I rasp into her ear, and she stills under me. I've shocked her and myself.

"You're mine, Olive. And I'm never letting you go." *Not until I have to.*

I take her, over and over, cleaning her up only to dirty her up again. Loving her with my body, until we both fall, exhausted and spent, into bed.

And when I pull her into my arms, the mattress squeaking underneath us, she sighs in contentment and snuggles into my hold.

For the first time in a very long time, I fall into a deep, quiet sleep.

The nightmares don't come.

CHAPTER THIRTY-FOUR

I WAKE UP TO a cool breeze grazing my skin.

Then I feel him.

Rex's muscular arm drapes across my waist, one hand resting over my breast, his leg tucked over mine.

He's a cuddler.

I don't know why, but the thought makes me smile.

Soft, even breaths puff against my head, the intoxicating smell of sex and his cologne in the air. Then I remember the events of last night.

I had sex with Rex Anderson. Not once, not twice, but three times. After he took me against the carpet, he carried me to the shower, where he then fucked me against the tiled wall. My cries—sounds I didn't know I could make—and his grunts reverberated in the small space. Then when he slid into the small full-sized bed with me. He spooned me from the back, but not before inserting his hard cock inside me and making slow, sweet love to me.

"One more orgasm so you'll have good dreams," he said right before ecstasy washed over my body in tremors.

He whispered, "Mine," repeatedly before he groaned long and low, his cock throbbing as he unloaded his hot cum inside me.

I broke all my rules. Trampled my ethics like castles built of sand.

He's high profile, a public figure, a known womanizer, and has the press breathing down his neck.

We were in public—anyone could've seen us making out by the fire last night, or they could've seen him holding my hand, dragging me into a nondescript motel. It wouldn't take a genius to figure out what we were up to.

Holy shit.

My pulse races, a knot forming inside my chest, even as a smile tugs on my lips. It's strange, having this collision of emotions—fear of being discovered mixing with guilt after making a bad choice—the worst choice, really.

But also happiness and excitement. Despite everything, it feels...right.

Butterflies swarm inside my stomach, and my heart skips several beats.

Then I slowly deflate.

While I'm discovering the new me, I do know one thing—I'm not a temporary plaything. My heart is already too tangled up, and if I continue, I'll only get hurt in the end.

"I can hear you thinking," Rex murmurs and pulls me tighter against him.

I wince, my core aching when I shift on the bed.

"Was I too rough?"

"A little, but I loved it." I love it a lot—being used, degraded, worshipped, my mind completely blank as pleasure consumes me. It was freeing, embracing the degradation, being the imperfect, bad girl.

He slides his hand between my legs and cups my pussy.

A moan slips out of me when he massages it, his hips moving slowly behind me, his cock hardening and digging into my ass cheeks.

"I'm insatiable for you. Last night was the best night of my life." He tugs my earlobe into his mouth.

Sparks renew inside me and I'm getting wet again. My core aches, both from our rough sex, but also from an emptiness only he can fill. I want to lose myself in his arms.

An insidious voice—my own—whispers, *"He's the prince of plea-sure. Rex-A-Million. This is probably a normal night for him. Don't think too much of it."*

"You probably say this to all your women." I pull his hand away from my core.

He stills, and without warning, he flips me over and cages me below him.

Eyes flashing, he leans down and grazes his nose with mine. "Never. I never say this to anyone. You're the first."

My heart skips another beat. *Really? Is this more than a tempo-rary fling?*

Then a thought occurs to me—something I've always wanted to confirm with him.

"What's your relationship with Bree? You guys mentioned you weren't together, but then in public..."

My voice trails off and I brace myself. While my gut tells me they aren't intimate, I should've verified before I slept with him. But things got out of hand.

A muscle twitches in his jaw and my heart sinks. *Please don't tell me I'm wrong.*

Obviously guessing my thoughts, he cradles my face and says, "Bree and I are friends. That's it. Nothing more. I wouldn't have slept with you if I had something with her."

I frown. But what about the intimacy between them? The way they act like a couple sometimes?

"Please trust me. I can't tell you everything now, but maybe someday I can." He sweeps his thumb over my cheek. "What hap-pened last night has never happened to me before. Sex was a means to an end to numb myself...but with you," his eyes glitter and he kisses me, "I could finally breathe. Like I was reborn."

My gaze roves over him, trying to identify any tells, any signs he's lying. But all I see are honesty and vulnerability.

Then indignation churns inside me. *If I'm so special, why can't he tell me everything? What is he still hiding?*

It doesn't matter, anyway. There are so many other problems.

"But, Rex. I'm your doctor. There are rules about it. It's forbidden—"

"You're fired."

I shake my head, knowing it isn't so simple. Good reputation, once ruined, is hard to get back. "Even if that's the case, people will figure it out. You were once in my care and..."

I'm going to be brave and honest. This new me embraces uncertainty. I'm no longer standing in the shadows or hiding indoors when it rains.

"I know myself. I can't be a temporary fling. I can't have sex without strings. I'm looking to settle down, for a relationship, for the potential of forever. Unless you can give me that, I need to protect myself."

His body stills, his eyes scanning my face, his nostrils flaring. I hold my breath and wait for his response, wishing, hoping he'd say something that would dissolve the knot inside me.

Say you want the potential of forever with me too. Say I'm worth the risk.

I want him to choose me because I've never been chosen before.

But then he swallows and looks down, and that infinitesimal gesture tells me what I need to know.

A sharp pain pierces my chest.

If it feels like this after one night, he could destroy me if we let this continue.

His eyes are sad when he says, "If I were a better man, if things were different—"

"It's okay. You don't need to say anything."

I roll out from under him and silently get dressed.

"Olive, fuck. Please. I need you. Let me think."

Turning around, I give him a sad smile. "It shouldn't be a hard decision."

No. I deserve someone who'd jump at the first opportunity to be with me.

Chapter Thirty-Five

For the past two days, I cloistered myself in my stateroom, working and teleconferencing with my team back home since our summer marketing campaign was about to kick off. My investigator sent me an update, saying he had some leads on the camera, but it was a cash trail, so it'd take some time to run down.

The cruise is coming to an end. Only Monte Carlo left after our current stop in Tuscany.

Olivia, from what Lana told me, had her schedule full of appointments with passengers after some argument broke out on the Rose floor decks.

Olivia's words from that morning rolled around in my mind whenever I resurfaced from work.

I want to give her the potential for forever.

But there's so much shit going on.

Heck, I had two more blackouts—once waking up slumped over a workout bench, freaking out the housekeeper assigned to my stateroom. Another time, I was in the kitchen again, a pot burning on the stove, its contents charred. One of these days, I'm going to hurt myself or someone else.

I called up another neurologist, doctor number twelve, if you count Olivia. I booked an appointment for when I get back to the city.

"I have to say, your symptoms are odd. You said you've done MRIs and CTs already and they found nothing? Any changes to your medical history? Anything you left off? Have you done a full psychiatric workup?"

I didn't answer him. I didn't want to mention the Velowake or my horrible experience with my last psychiatrist before Olivia. I was ashamed. But now I wonder if I should give psychiatry another chance.

Just tell Olivia the truth. What if Casey's right? What if she doesn't leave you? What if she helps you instead?

My ribs tighten and I can't breathe.

What if she *does* leave me? *But she's going to leave you anyway if you can't promise her the potential of a forever.*

I can't think straight.

"You didn't have to do this."

Bree's voice draws my attention back to the room. We're gathered inside the central demonstration kitchen aboard the cruise.

Staff hustle around the brightly lit space, preparing for the cooking class about to start.

"Of course we do!" Lana drapes her hand over Bree's shoulder. "I'm sorry you have a headache and don't want to go out. But we leave no man or, in this case, no woman, behind."

Bree frowns, the orange glow from the sunset outside the windows highlighting the guilt in her eyes. I couldn't get any more information out of her, and she's grown more withdrawn the closer we get to Monaco. Elias, the asshole, has been dodging me as well. To say it's frustrating to have no answers would be an understatement.

But at least Bree's been following instructions with The Association still out there. Other than the masquerade she cleared with me beforehand, she's rarely ventured outside her stateroom, much to Lana's disappointment.

That's why Lana announced we're staying on board for the cooking class today. She thought that would be easier on Bree, who clearly didn't want to go on the offshore excursions. And we can't say no without rousing more suspicion from my sister, whom we've kept in the dark about the mission. No use in worrying her when she can't do anything.

Bree grumbles, "But we're in Tuscany. Shouldn't you guys visit vineyards, drink wine or something?"

"Nah. I've been to Tuscany many times, but I haven't gotten a private lesson from Chef Giacomo Valenti. Trust me, I'm staying for him. Hot and knows how to cook? Sign me up."

I groan. "Don't even try anything funny, Lana."

Lana strides up and jabs her finger at my side. I bat her away. "Don't you dare go all protective older brother with me. You and your parade of women. Me cleaning up your PR messes in the past. I'm single and ready to mingle, and Giacomo Valenti is a looker."

Her eyes suddenly narrow.

Someone clears his throat, and I turn around, spotting a flash of black hair and a man in a navy suit disappearing around the corner. Then I hear the familiar click of a lighter.

Fucking Elias, hovering around like a ghost.

"Am I late? Is Chef Valenti here yet?" Olivia bursts into the room.

My head snaps up, my gaze colliding with hers, and she skids to a halt, her face flushing.

My blood heats as our eyes lock. I can't look away.

A strange silence falls over the kitchen.

"Dr. Lin," I murmur.

"Mr. Anderson."

My little Olive blushes and scurries away to the corner where Bree is, and I grip the marble counter in front of me to restrain myself from chasing after her.

"Seriously?" Lana's gaze pinballs between us, then she glares at me. "Really, Rex?" she whispers.

"Calm down. Don't get your panties in a twist."

"You and I are talking. Tonight. After class," she growls under her breath.

Then something catches her attention. Her eyes widen, and she blinks.

"*Signori e signore... Buonasera!*" A dirty-blond man with curly hair and brown eyes strides into the kitchen. He's dressed in chef whites, a red bandanna around his neck, his lips cocked in a flirtatious smile.

I look at Olivia, then at Lana, finding their eyes riveted on the handsome man.

Motherfucker. This must be Chef Valenti.

"Close your mouth. You're drooling," I mutter to my sister, who elbows me again, but I barely notice.

Because the modern day Casanova is going around the room, saying hello to the guests. He winks at the women, pats the men on the back, gives Bree one of those European cheek kisses, and I swear, she practically expires in front of him.

And when he smiles at Olivia and winks at her?

I see red.

My jaw tightens, and I grind my molars.

He's saying some shit to her, in Italian no less, and I watch as she beams at him, starry-eyed.

Then the asshole touches her.

He puts his meaty paw on her hand and lifts it to his lips.

I bite my cheek, tasting blood, and grab the wine glass next to me. I imagine snapping the stem in half and stabbing the man with it. Then *I'll* teach Olivia how to cook while he bleeds out on the floor.

The bastard is touching what's mine.

Mine.

No, she's not yours, you imbecile. You can't give her forever until—no, if—you can even figure your shit out. That's what she wants, remember?

She wants the white picket fence, the doting husband.

She doesn't want someone mentally ill, riddled with guilt, and definitely unstable.

She doesn't want someone who relies on caffeine pills to function.

I toss back the wine, barely tasting it. It could be cat piss for all I care.

But then, a thought occurs to me.

What if we delay the decision? What if we give ourselves this trip—this paradise on earth? We'll take all the precautions—meet in private areas out of sight from other passengers so her reputation remains intact. I'll keep a low profile with her. We can be with each other even if it's only for the rest of the cruise. Then once we're back in New York, if I could figure things out, maybe things would be different.

The idea takes root and a low current sizzles through me.

I watch as the bastard Valenti moves to Lana, who practically prances in front of him, excitement vibrating from her. She grins shyly and extends her hand, and just as he reaches for it, someone clears his throat again.

Our attention snags on the shadow lurking by the kitchen entrance. Elias knocks his lighter against the wall, his gaze cold and face impassive.

He cocks one eyebrow.

I shiver—the damn man can menace without trying.

Valenti stiffens, his hand dropping to his side.

He murmurs to Lana, "Thank you for your invitation, Ms. Anderson. I'm honored to teach a group of distinguished people today."

Then he returns to the center of the room.

Lana frowns and mouths, *What the hell?*

I look at the entrance, but there's no one there, the mobster vanishing like an apparition.

"Today, we're learning the art of handcrafted pasta. You'll roll and cut *tagliatelle* by hand, then we will create the perfect *Ragù Toscano*," Valenti explains. He strains a grin.

Ragù Toscano. Mom's favorite. I smile, thinking about the wonderful memories of her and me cooking the same dish a long time ago.

Valenti walks us through the steps, then directs us to the flatscreen hanging on the wall, which also shows the instructions of the simple, yet flavorful pasta dish that's a cousin to the spaghetti bolognese.

"First, get into groups of two." The Chef claps his hands and the room scurries into action.

Lana beelines for Bree, who looks like she'd much rather be in her room, tapping away at her laptop than cooking. The other folks pair up one by one—most of them with friends or partners.

And then there's my Olive, looking like a deer in the headlights, standing frozen on the far side of the large marble island.

"*Signora*, no partner for the beautiful lady?" Valenti asks, the charming smile back on his face.

The bastard has a fucking dimple. Women love dimples. Maybe that's where my scar should go. A dimple would beat a dangerous scar on the cheek.

I think about the ridiculous conversation I had with Elias in the hangar before the trip.

I really need to lay off the Velowake and get some sleep.

Maybe it can happen again—no nightmares, just resting. It happened in Valencia at Las Fallas, didn't it? Six blissful hours of darkness—no light, no sound, no images.

But it was with Olivia. Something about holding her in my arms that night gave me bone-deep peace.

It didn't happen again.

Olivia told me she thought she was a shadow compared to her twin.

But she doesn't know shadows can't chase away darkness—shadows amplify the dark.

She chased away my nightmares, my memories. She gave me peace.

She burns brightest in my eyes.

My earlier idea echoes in my mind. *Yes. That's the answer.* Enjoy this trip with her. Delay the decision about the future. I don't have to give her up right now.

Maybe after the mission, I'd feel better. I'd stop having blackouts, I could sleep again, and I'd finally move on.

I'll tell her everything then—all my secrets.

Then we can decide.

Lots of maybes, but fuck that for now.

She's *mine.*

"First, you take the flour and you do this," Valenti murmurs as he stands next to Olivia, clearly ready to be her partner.

Not on my watch.

I stalk toward her.

Chapter Thirty-Six

"I GOT THIS," I snarl, pretty damn proud I'm not strangling Valenti with the red bandanna around his neck.

Because he's flirting with *my* woman.

Only for the rest of the trip.

The warning doesn't stick, and I shove it away. God, if Casey were here, he'd have a field day.

Valenti's eyes widen before bouncing between Olivia and me.

"Mr. Anderson, go be an overbearing caveman somewhere else. Find your own partner," Olivia hisses under her breath, her head dipped down, hands punching the dough.

Smack. Smack. Smack.

A different thrill sweeps through me. My Olive's fiery temper.

Fuck, that makes my cock hard.

I shift and hide my stiffening lower half behind the counter.

Then I lean down and rasp, "I. Just. Did."

My gaze snaps to the offending man. *Back off.* He shakes his head and walks away.

"Seriously, did you have to do that? We aren't anything. Stop it." Olivia mixes the ingredients together and throws the dough hard onto the counter.

Smack.

"You know you're making me hard, right? I love my women feisty."

She's now poking the dough like it's her worst enemy. "I'm not your woman."

Chuckling, I slowly get behind her and step close until our bodies are a hairsbreadth apart. Reaching around, I cover her hands with mine.

Her breath hitches. "Wh-What are you doing?"

"Teaching you how to knead dough. You're doing it all wrong."

"And what makes you the expert, mister I have a personal chef my entire life?"

"You're making it worse," I murmur as I press her hands down, using the heel of our palms to work the gluten.

"What's worse?" Her voice is breathier now.

"This."

I look around the room, noting everyone focused on their cooking. Under the guise of teaching her, I press my hips forward, letting her feel the raging hard-on threatening to dig its way out of my pants. Thank God the island is tall enough and perfectly hides our hips away from prying eyes.

Sharp frissons tremor through me the moment her curvy ass cradles my shaft. I want to succumb to my urges, toss her over my shoulders, and carry her back to my stateroom to show her all the ways we're perfect together, even if I can't give her everything she's asking for.

Yet.

The smallest moan slips out of her and she shakes—she fucking shakes in my arms.

Scratch that. I'll just toss her onto the counter and have my way with her.

But then everyone would see her come around my cock, and no one gets to see her orgasm face except me.

Fucking shit. Now I'm most definitely indecent now.

"So damn sensitive, little Olive," I rasp. "Are you just this sensitive to me?"

I punctuate the sentence with a small forward cant of my hips—one tortuous grind of my cock against her legging-clad ass.

I want to take her there. I wonder if she's experienced it inside her little rosebud yet?

Someone giggles and I jolt, suddenly aware we're in a room with other people.

Shit. Get yourself together, Rex.

Thankfully, everyone seems to be busy with their tasks and Valenti is currently hovering over Bree and Lana's disaster that's more water than flour. No way I'm going to taste test that shit.

Clearing my throat, I take a small step back. *She has a reputation to uphold,* I remind myself. I can't jeopardize her career because I'm selfish.

I guess the Anderson manners were drilled into me—Maxwell would be proud.

Biting back a bitter grin, I curve her hands in mine, showing her the proper way of preparing the dough.

"Feel this?" I ask as I fold the dough in half and then push it away with the heel of my hand. Then, I turn it ninety degrees and repeat. "You want it smooth and elastic. Fold. Push. Turn. Easy rhythm. The texture should be just right—springy but not sticky."

She whips her head around. "How do you know this?"

Smiling, I wink. "Rex-a-Million is not only good in the sheets."

Olivia stiffens. "You're doing it again."

"What?"

"Putting yourself down. You have a lot to offer...much more than your prowess in bed."

Warmth floods me at her compliment and a pretty pink flush appears on her cheeks. She turns to the dough and repeats the motions I taught her.

"*Good girl.* That's right. It's not just about the strength, but the motion." The flush brightens, and I groan. "You make it so *hard* for me to behave."

"I don't think you ever want to behave, so don't pin this on me."

I bark out a laugh, and heads swivel toward us. Quickly, I step away from the tempting doctor and stand at her side. I take out another chopping board and dice the tomatoes for the meat sauce.

My knife snaps in a quick, staccato rhythm as I work the vegetables, the motions as effortless as breathing. And after a few seconds, I notice Olivia's stopped moving.

Frowning, I find her gaping at my hands.

"I'm dreaming. I must be dreaming. I had too many orgasms and now can't tell dream from reality."

I snort. "You're most definitely not dreaming. Because if you were," I dip my mouth next to her ear, "you'd be wearing nothing other than a tiny apron and my cock would be buried deep inside you while you work the dough. I'll show you how it's all about the rhythm, not the strength. The fucking rhythm."

That seems to do the trick because she takes a wide step to the left. "You're impossible."

"Always. There's no standard too low for me. I aim to please."

"Ugh," she grumbles, clearly exasperated, but I see her lips twitch. She knows I'm joking. "How do you know so much about cooking? And your knife skills...you clearly know what you're doing."

Turning my attention back to the task, I smile. "My mom. We had a chef, but Mom still loved spending time in the kitchen. She used to say it was her way of nurturing us with her love."

I think about the time the four of us, Ethan included, huddled around a low table she set up there because we were too short for the high counters. She'd put out plates of chocolate chip cookies, fresh from the oven, with a sprinkle of cinnamon and nutmeg. We stuffed ourselves, then laughed at the chocolate sauce all over our faces.

Maxwell would grumble when it got on his art. Ryland cackled as he whacked his twin with a picture book. Ethan babbled his happiness. I'd sit there, happy to be included, while Mom would wipe the crumbs from my lips.

"If you asked Maxwell, he'd say I was making shit up. But when we were kids, I was afraid of everything. It's hard to believe that since I'm the Anderson daredevil now, but it's true. And while we're a close bunch now, back then, we didn't get along. I was ostracized...the twins attached at the hip, Ethan and Lana were too young, and I didn't know better. Girls had cooties, you know."

She smiles as she cuts the pasta into strips.

"So it was just me, the middle child. You're a psychiatrist, so I'm sure you've read about the middle child syndrome—rebellious yet people-pleasing, feeling like an outsider, the works. Mom loved to cook, and I'd spend time with her in the kitchen. She taught me how to be creative—make up stories, try new recipes, create fun for myself. It became an outlet over the years."

I put the tomatoes to the side and work on the carrots. "She'd be so disappointed now, seeing what a clusterfuck I'd become. But then again, I also had a hand in her death, so..." I shrug.

Her hands stop moving. "It isn't your fault. I'll tell you that until you believe it. And you aren't messed up."

"You don't have to lie."

"I'm not." She touches my forearm, stilling my knife. "You have the same amount of mess we all have. You just hide it better and for longer."

Something in my chest twitches and a heaviness sits atop my lungs. She squeezes my arm, her thumb circling the small scars she saw up close before.

"Look at me, Rex."

"Rex, huh? What happened to Mr. Anderson?" I drag my gaze to hers and my breath throttles.

Such beautiful, soft eyes. So gentle, so kind.

"Trash festers when we don't deal with it. Do the work and deep clean. And once you're done, you'll be okay again. I know you will."

The heaviness morphs into a weighted blanket, settling over me, and I swallow.

She smiles, the whites of her teeth showing.

Her glorious hair, fastened into her usual low bun, is different this time. She let a few strands escape, and they frame her face perfectly.

Maybe she's breaking free from the shadows.

Her eyes rove over my face as she murmurs, *"Carpe diem."*

I cock my brow, knowing that's what Mia used to say to her. But I thought there was resentment in that statement.

She shakes her head, like she knows what I'm thinking. "I'm mad at Mia, but I actually like her motto. Life is too short to live in misery, to surround yourself with trash. Clean it out. Do the hard thing. Try the scary thing. You only live once."

Flour dusts her hair and her cheeks, getting onto her shirt.

She goddamn takes my breath away.

"And what about you?" I murmur, holding her gaze as the room fades away. "When will you deep clean?" *And can I be there to help you?*

Her pulse feathers her neck—the same lovely spot I still see a faded bruise she tried to cover with makeup.

My mark.

Heated blood pumps inside me, and I curl my hands around the knife and the cutting board, stopping myself from pulling her into my arms.

"They don't even remember my favorite dish," she replies, her eyes glistening with moisture. "You know, in my family, we don't say 'I love you.' They ask me if I've eaten. *Ni chi fan le ma?*"

She rolls her lips inward. "But when they ask me that question, they always talk about Mia's favorite food."

I remember the outpouring of grief at Las Fallas. How she's been trying, but failing, to be both Mia and Olivia. How her family doesn't see her.

But I do.

"What is it, Olive? What's your favorite dish?"

I'll remember it, Olivia. Because I see you.

She doles out a wobbly smile. "*Pappardelle al Cinghiale.*"

"Wild boar ragu," I murmur. "Can be gamey and earthy. Bold flavor."

Bold—just like her.

"I ordered it one time we were out to celebrate a friend's birthday. Mia grumbled because she wasn't a big fan of Italian. I picked a dish

I couldn't pronounce just to do something interesting. I loved it. Mia thought I was nuts because she said it was gamey." Olivia scrunches her nose.

Then she looks at me and gives me an impish smile. "I'd get it every time we had Italian if it was on the menu. It was *my* favorite dish. Just mine."

My heart flips. My little Olive trying to break free. I wish I were there to see it.

Slowly, I bring my fingers to her face, then I flick the flour off her cheeks.

She draws a sharp inhale and leans forward infinitesimally.

Sharp current ripples up my fingers from the tiny point of contact.

My eyes dip to her plush lips, drawn to them like a sailor spotting a lighthouse during a violent storm.

Click. Then a bright flash.

We spring apart as the room comes rushing back.

I look up, my heart sinking when I see Greg Masters lowering his camera, a smug smile twisting his thin lips.

"Payday," he mouths.

CHAPTER THIRTY-SEVEN

AFTER EATING OUR PASTA creations for dinner, during which Olivia polished everything on her plate, including the sauce, Lana dragged me to her stateroom as the dessert wine was brought out. She suspiciously disappeared in a huff half an hour into class, only to resurface, her face grim, five minutes ago.

She told the group we had a conference call.

"What's so urgent?" I mutter, sprawling onto the ivory sofa.

Then alarm sweeps through me.

Is it Greg Masters? I didn't see him after he snapped the photo of Olivia and me. But it's only been hours, and it wasn't like we were doing anything inappropriate.

Lana fiddles with a remote. "You'll see."

A screen on the wall flickers on and I groan.

Because Maxwell is on camera and is clearly displeased.

"Shit." I sit up, watching my older brother, dressed in a three-piece suit, his hair perfectly coiffed, glare at me.

I glance at the time on the screen and do some mental calculations. "Seriously, it's four in the morning for you. Why are you already up and dressed for work?"

"You tell me," he says cryptically.

"Stop with this cloak and dagger shit. Clearly, I screwed up and am about to get it. Go on. Tell me what I did."

"I've got some photos for you to look at. They came through during class," Lana says, drawing my attention back to her. She sits down next to me and gives me a sympathetic smile. "And Greg Masters reached out to me."

Shit. The damn bastard.

"Look, whatever he's insinuating, it's bullshit—"

She shakes her head and presses another button. Black-and-white photos pop up on the screen.

My argument stalls in my throat.

They're pictures of me and Olivia. Me kissing her in the small courtyard during Las Fallas. A grainy one of us entering the motel together. Boarding the cruise early morning after our night together.

Fuck. We—no—*I* wasn't careful enough.

Cold sweat gathers on my forehead, and nausea makes an appearance. This was what Olivia was worried about. How many times had she tried to push me away because we were breaking the rules? And who took these photos? Greg Masters? I didn't even see him tailing me. How could I have missed him?

"I'm going to fire her and have her escorted off the cruise." Maxwell's words are soft, but I hear the strain in his voice—his anger.

My eyes snap back up to him and I see a telltale tic in his jaw.

He's pissed. Betrayed. Furious.

No. Panic rears its ugly head inside me.

He can't take my Olive from me. I want the rest of this trip with her.

"You got it all wrong," I begin. "It's not what you think—"

"You think I'm stupid? You guys were kissing. Going to a motel and spending the night. She's your doctor! I trusted her to treat you. What would you do if Lana were sick? If she went to a doctor and he took advantage of her?"

Maxwell's words echo in the room, and I bury my face in my hands. It looks bad. If it were Lana, I'd strangle the doctor myself for preying on my sister.

"You're mentally unwell. That's why we got you help. But I've obviously misplaced my trust in her. In you. This behavior is unacceptable. She was supposed to help you, not sleep with you. She was supposed to—"

"She did!" My voice comes out sharp and desperate.

I stand up and stride to the hidden camera, needing to get in his face somehow. Fury surges up my spine. They can't twist this into something dark and sordid. It's anything but that. I need them to understand.

"She's the only one who's been able to help me! The only one who saw me. I-I could breathe around her. I felt hope for the first time in a fucking long time. She...She's *everything*."

Silence falls in the room. Maxwell looks shocked, his mouth dropping open. I glance at Lana, finding her forehead pinched, a wet sheen misting her eyes.

"Rex," she whispers. "I had no idea you felt this way."

I shake my head. "No. It's not your fault. You guys are right. I-I've been struggling. Splitting at the seams. But don't blame Olivia for this...for us. She saw past my masks. My defenses."

A labored exhale escapes my lips. "She made me feel things I never thought I could feel. Like life is worth living. I pursued her." I glance at my siblings. "She tried to draw the line. To be professional. To keep her distance. But I'm a relentless bastard. It's me. If you need to punish someone, punish me. It's not her fault. It's all on me. Please. Don't fire her."

Suddenly exhausted, I walk back to the sofa and sit down. The seconds tick by, the silence heavy in the room.

"But she should've known better. She's the professional," Maxwell murmurs, but the anger isn't in his voice anymore. "I like her. She's good at what she does, but this isn't right."

"You're her patient too. You've known her for years. Does she strike you as a person who'd jump into inappropriate relationships? She helped you, Taylor, Ethan. Trust me, she fought it for as long as she could."

Maxwell rubs the scruff on his face, resignation clear in his eyes. "If I didn't see the photos, I wouldn't have believed it. Olivia's damn excellent at her job."

"She is. You see? It's all me. Please don't fire her. Don't make this a thing. She's a good doctor." I glance at Maxwell, then Lana, knowing they can turn the life of the woman who's given me a taste of forever into a living hell.

I need to protect her. They have to understand this isn't some fling.

Is it though, Rex? You're only spending the rest of this trip with her. For now. Until I fix myself. If I can fix myself.

"She's a good person. One of my best friends," Lana murmurs, her lips tilting into a sad smile. "On paper, a doctor-patient relationship looks bad, but...but I can understand. I just wish you guys told us."

"So, are you two in a relationship now? Or is this one of your flings?" Maxwell asks.

I grit my teeth, unable to answer him. I want to be in a place where I can be in a relationship with her.

"Fuck. Figure it out before you take her down with you. I need some time to process this." He sighs and rubs his temple.

"That's fair." More than fair. He's being logical. Too bad the heart isn't rational.

I stare at the photos on the screen. "Did these come from Greg Masters?"

"No. I had an inkling about you guys for a while and asked security to pull footage using facial recognition," Lana says as she squeezes my shoulder.

A relieved sigh escapes me. Thank God it's not from the paps.

"The Las Fallas ones came from ATM and storefront cameras. I only pulled them after a passenger showed me pictures from the festival. In one of them, there were two people in the background. Grainy pic, but they looked like you two. So I dug deeper. The footage came in during class. Let's just say I did a full dirty delete. Took a lot of money and a few threats. Buying out debts, applying pressure. I'm not proud of it, but I can't let that footage stay on record."

"You what?" My sister is good at her job, but this is the first time I've seen her use coercion to get rid of evidence.

She shrugs. "Gotta protect my family. Lucky for us, the passenger took a bajillion pics and didn't notice one missing. And those stores were more than happy to delete after I wired over 'donations.' But all this meant I had to pull Maxwell in to move the cash. And we needed to get the truth from you."

Guilt settles inside me and I look at them, finding their gazes concerned.

I'm so damn lucky to have my family on my side.

Swallowing the lump in my throat, I remember something she said earlier. "But why did Greg Masters contact you?"

She snorts. "He has a photo of you guys standing too close together making pasta. I have him handled. Don't worry."

Then her voice turns solemn. "Maxwell and I will process this new...development and monitor if anything was leaked to the press. But Rex, figure out what you're doing with Olivia. We don't want to see you guys get hurt."

I close my eyes, a heaviness sitting atop my chest.

The last thing I want to do is hurt Olivia.

But I don't...I can't stay away.

CHAPTER THIRTY-EIGHT

"I GOT THIS. I'M a freakin' adult with self-control," I mutter under my breath as I pace inside my office, practically wearing down the carpet.

I've never felt this out of sorts in my entire career. Heck, I treat people with impulse control issues. If this were a colleague coming to me for advice, the answer would be straightforward and simple.

Recuse yourself. Stay away. *Far away.*

I've already obliterated the oath I made to the medical profession by sleeping with Rex—something I still think about nightly as I lie in bed while missing his caresses and kisses.

And now the press is on to us.

Lana told me this morning that Greg Masters approached her with a photo he took of Rex and me during our Tuscan cooking lesson the day before yesterday. He wanted a payout. She got him to back off by promising an exclusive after the cruise plus a fifty thousand dollar bonus.

She told him Rex was a flirt and had amazing chemistry with all women. That was why the photos looked intimate. And because Lana could be ruthless when she wanted to, she told him if he didn't back off, she'd release photos of Rex being friendly with other women to make his picture worthless.

I asked if she had any photos of Rex with other women. She shrugged and told me it could be arranged.

But Lana wasn't dumb. She was suspicious, like she knew something.

She peppered me with more questions, but I pretended to be late to a patient appointment and ran away before she could poke through my lies.

Something happened in the test kitchen. There was a different energy from Rex. A fierce spark, not the resignation I saw in his eyes the morning after we had sex.

It was hard to resist him.

How can something so wrong feels so right?

How do I feel so alive with someone obviously not for me?

"I'm going to quit. Official paperwork, not just the damn email. We're almost to Monaco anyway. I've done a few sessions and have tried my best." I pace faster and blow out a breath. "Yes, that's it. I'll refer him to someone else—"

A low laugh reaches my ears and I stop, whipping my head toward the office door.

The man himself is leaning against the doorframe, his arms crossed over his chest, his fingers toying with his marble. He's in a crisp white shirt and gray slacks, carrying the same lazy air I saw when he straggled in for our first appointment.

But this time, there's amusement, warmth, and heat in those gray eyes—eyes I know glint gold next to a burning fire and smolder in passion.

"What's troubling you, little Olive?" He unfurls himself and walks toward me, closing the door behind him. "Thinking about me? About how good we are together?"

My pulse scatters. I hold my hand up to stop him. "We talked about this. I'm serious. I can't be your doctor anymore, Rex."

"Good. I don't want you to be." A shadow crosses his face, but it disappears almost instantly.

"I can't be your fuck toy, either."

I back up, my shoes dragging on the carpet as he advances on me, all casualness vanishing from his frame.

"I would *never* ask that of you."

His muscles bunch in his shoulders, a small furrow appearing between his brows. Those beautiful eyes of his are now sharp.

Determined.

My core pulses.

Oh shit. I fist my hands and repeat the affirmations. *I'm a professional. I have excellent impulse control. I'm staying away.*

The backs of my legs hit the recliner.

Then he's standing less than a foot away from me.

My gaze darts to the glass walls, which I didn't turn opaque because I didn't want to make it easy for me to fall for his tactics. He must be thinking the same thing because he reaches over and presses a button.

The room plunges into darkness.

Rex taps another button and the small desk lamp turns on.

"H-How—"

"This is my cruise, remember? I've seen all the specs." He taps his temple with his finger. "And I never forget."

Then he pulls me flush against him, and my nerves come alive.

"What do you want with me, then? I won't change my mind about what I need." I whimper as he dips his nose to the spot on my neck.

His spot.

"I want you. Every part of you." He flicks his talented tongue against the spot. "I want you to wear my marks on your skin so everyone knows you're mine."

"I'm not your fuck—"

"Listen, and you listen carefully." Pulling apart, he bends down and holds my gaze. "A fuck toy is someone I don't care about. We both want to get off and that's it. It's a transaction. You'll *never* be that to me."

My heart thuds against my ribs. What is he saying? I'm so damn confused.

"I'll always care for you. Even if I can't be yours forever. Because," he murmurs to my skin, "I'm not right in the head and I still have enough of my mind to recognize that. I can't provide *anyone* the happiness they deserve. But you, Olive..."

With a gentle caress, his thumb sweeps over my cheek. "You're the closest to forever for me. The closest I've ever been to happiness. With you, I almost feel normal. You already hold in your hand what's left of my rotten heart. Give me the rest of this cruise, please. A few more days of paradise."

The pain in his voice steals my breath and carves into my chest. It hurts.

Because he's already stolen my heart too.

I freeze. *I love him.* I love Rex Anderson.

Why does it hurt so much?

My vision blurs and his breath hitches. "I'm a bastard for doing this to you, but...I-I can't help it. You're a high I can't get enough of. Will you pity me? Give me a few more days? We'll stay under the radar. It'll be our secret."

My heart rams against my rib cage, my eyes roving over his face, seeing his desperation, his earnestness.

He isn't lying. It's not lip service.

If it could be anyone, he would choose me.

And it kills me he doesn't think he deserves the happily ever after his siblings have.

I still want to fix him. To heal him. To love him because he doesn't love himself.

With one swift motion, he grips my chin and seals his lips over mine.

His madness, our madness, incinerates us whole. Every atom inside me thrums with awareness as I melt into his kiss, his passion, the truth in his words burrowing deep inside me.

In my profession, they say it's foolish to attempt changing someone who doesn't want to change themselves. It's a Sisyphean task. I'll be pushing that boulder uphill for eternity and eventually, because reality isn't Greek mythology, it'll roll down and squash me.

He's trying to save me from the tragic ending. I recognize that now.

Rex pulls away, his lips tilting in a heartbreaking smile as he taps his temple again. "I'll relive these memories over and over. This will be my forever."

"I'll get you help! Even if it's not me. This doesn't have to end—"

Shaking his head, he presses a finger to my lips. "You don't know the whole truth. Maybe someday I'll be brave enough to tell you, but I can't. I'm not ready yet. Let me worship you. Let me be your spotlight. Please...just let me have this version of forever."

I see the resolution in his eyes. The earlier pain burrows deeper inside me.

I should say no. I should push him away.

But for the first time in my life, I want to be in the spotlight.

His spotlight.

Even if it's only for a few more days. Because I love him.

"Until the end of the cruise," I whisper.

A groan ripples from his throat and he hoists me up and tosses me onto the recliner.

Then he falls upon me.

CHAPTER THIRTY-NINE

Rex kisses me like he needs me to live. Our lips tangle with each other. He sucks on my tongue, groaning like it's the best thing he's tasted.

"You're the only addiction I want. You drive me crazy," he rasps, his hands tugging up my shirt until my breasts are bared.

"These beautiful tits," he yanks down the cups of my bra, then swats one side, "redden so beautifully."

"Rex." I hiss when he bites my nipple. The pain soon disperses when he lashes the hard tip with his tongue. The pinch and pleasure combination drags a moan from my throat.

"Shhh... Sweetheart, these walls aren't thick. Be quiet or I won't continue. Okay?"

The maddening man stops his torture, clearly waiting for my response.

Damn him.

I heave out a shaky exhale. "Okay."

Satisfaction glints in his eyes, a sly smile on his lips. "My good fucking girl."

Wetness drips out of my core and my clit throbs at his words. Unlike the time in the supplies closet, I no longer rebel against that sentiment.

Because it's an endearment from him—naughtiness, goodness all rolled into one. It's no longer a pat on the back for a job well done because I colored within the lines.

He suckles my other breast, molding the curve with his hands, groaning like he's in heaven. Then he draws up my skirt, drags down my panties, and tosses them onto the ground.

I shiver, the AC hitting my wet pussy, sharpening the sensations.

"Now, be quiet and keep your hands above your head. Don't move or you won't get to come."

I do as he says, and he stands up, his eyes darkening as he yanks down his zipper, the sound loud in the room.

His cock—long, thick, and hard—is dripping, wetness coating the sexy veins on the side. He fists it and thrusts, a small spurt of wetness shooting from the tip, and he groans his pleasure into his other fist.

Every part of me throbs, my skin incinerating under his heated gaze. He looks like a Greek god, his eyes half-lidded in ecstasy.

I need him. Inside me. Dominating me. Owning me.

Wordlessly, I slide my hand between my legs to play with myself, watching his eyes flare. I don't know who this vixen writhing on the recliner is, or maybe I do, because she's been waiting to break free.

Light strokes. Hard flicks. Quick pinches.

I rub my clit to the rhythm of him tugging his cock. Our panting breaths join the sound of my heartbeat in my ears.

"God, you drive me out of my mind," he says. "I want to dirty you up. I want to love and destroy you. I want to put you on a fucking pedestal and worship you. I can't control myself around you."

His words are caresses to my core and the pressure gathers, coalesces where my fingers are circling. Harder. Faster. More.

"Yes baby, you want to come? Do you see this? How hard my cock is? How I'm leaking before I even touch you?"

Moans escape me, and I bite my tongue to keep from crying out. My legs shake, and I'm perched on the precipice, ready to leap.

"Don't. You. Dare."

Without warning, he yanks my legs apart and grabs my hand so I can't touch myself.

Rex's voice is guttural. "Let me tell you what you're going to do. You're going to spread those legs, yes, just like that, and let me see that beautiful wet pussy."

He grunts when he swipes his fingers through my essence, then dips inside my hole.

"Shit, please, Rex. Please." I arch my hips up, needing more pressure, more everything. I'm going to explode.

"It's so wet. All for me, huh?" Without waiting for my answer, he dives in, his tongue swiping my clit before licking from top to bottom. Then, it's a flurry of flicks, lashes, sucking like he's getting himself off by bringing me straight back to the edge.

I cry out his name, and he slaps his hand over my mouth.

"Bad, *bad* girl."

Rex lifts his head, his tongue licking at the wetness on his lips, a lethal gleam in his eyes. "Now you have to wait longer to come because you just made a noise."

"No. Please. Please, Rex."

"Yes, Olive, only good girls get orgasms. Now tell me, are you a good girl?" He sucks my clit again and thrusts two fingers inside me.

I thrash on the recliner, sparks gathering deep where he's tunneling in and out of me, my moans trapped inside my mouth because I want to be a good girl for him.

"That's right, sweetheart. Tell me you like this as much as I love eating you out. Do you like my tongue on you? Kissing your clit, sucking that swollen nub like it's the best thing I've ever tasted?"

Mindless with pleasure, my eyes open but not really seeing, I bob my head.

"Fuck. You're cum drunk and you haven't even come yet. You should see yourself. Go on, fuck my face. Feel your pussy throbbing? Work it over my lips and tongue. Get yourself to the edge again."

I do as he says, riding his face as he slurps and groans, savoring everything I'm giving him. It's almost an out-of-body experience, suspended between heaven and hell as the tide rises rapidly inside me, slowly turning off all my senses until only the sense of touch remains.

Yes. I'm almost there. *Yes.*

Then he stops.

"No!" I pant, my muscles tensing and shaking, burning like I've run a marathon.

My eyes snap open and slowly refocus, finding him staring at me with his molten gaze, the same unhinged spark I saw that day at Mystique, except tenfold more potent.

"You don't get to come until I'm inside you. I own your orgasms now."

He climbs over me and notches his hard cock at my opening. Then he punches it inside, just the tip. I tremble.

"Are you aching, Olive? Do you need my hard cock filling your little hole? Are you desperate to come?"

My voice doesn't work, but I claw his back and nod.

"Please," I beg. "Please."

He chuckles. Then he slams home.

I clap my hand over my mouth, a shriek ripping out of my throat when he plunges his dick deep inside me like a battering ram.

A match ignites. Firework sparks. My lips part in a silent scream as I arch my back, the inferno gathering strength, ready to detonate.

But it doesn't come.

It's endless torture, waiting for the right person to punch in those nuclear codes.

"Oh sweetheart, look at you. My good doctor isn't so good, huh? She's a filthy slut underneath that prim and proper exterior. Fuck, do you know how good you look? Your tits red, nipples so fucking hard. Your legs spread and tight cunt leaking. Come, Olive. Come for me."

I explode, his permission the last push I need.

Pleasure obliterates my senses, my body pulsing uncontrollably. I grab his arm and bite down on his wrist as he roars his satisfaction.

"Fuuuck."

He pistons harder and deeper while unloading himself inside me. I feel every twitch, every throb, his cum acting like lighter fluid to a blazing fire, my orgasm unabating. I can only clutch him tightly as I shake beneath him, letting him use me, lose himself inside me.

Soon, the sparks rise again and I bite down harder as my body quakes. It's too much. I can't breathe.

Then I taste blood.

Rex hisses as a smidge of wetness coats my lips.

"Yes, fuck yes! Another one, Olive." His cock tunnels inside my pussy, slamming home again and again. The sounds of our bodies colliding are an erotic soundtrack in the room.

"I can't stop corrupting you, Olive. I can't stop myself. I'm going to be so fucking selfish and imprint myself on you so you'll feel my cock even after this trip. So you can think about this at night in your apartment, about me, my cock, about how I make you come so hard, you see stars."

A dam breaks and I burst, wetness spurting out as my vision darkens. I'm barely aware of my surroundings, my nerves short-circuited, my body twitching, throbbing. I'm a marionette under him.

Then I feel another spurt, another load from his cock as he slams his lips on mine, kissing me, sucking the soul out of me, stealing my breath away.

Knock. Knock.

I don't register the sound initially, but then I feel it.

Rex freezing.

Knock. Knock.

"Dr. Lin? You in there? I thought I heard noises and wanted to check on you. You okay?"

Rhys.

My eyes widen, catching Rex's. He huffs out labored breaths, sweat dripping down his forehead, his face flushed and eyes wild.

He snaps into action and leaps off me. Tucking himself in with one hand, he fixes my shirt and my dress, then pulls me up.

I sway on my feet, my legs not quite working, my mind barely online. "Dr. Lin? Olivia?"

"One second," I yell, thankful my voice has returned. "On a call."

Rex steps to the side, away from the door, and I wipe my face and smooth my hair.

Who am I kidding? I'm sure I look like a mess.

I'm sure I look like someone who's been fucked out of her mind.

Looking around the room, I spot my jacket draped over my chair. I quickly put it on and zip it all the way up my neck, pretending it's freezing cold.

Legs trembling, I walk toward the door. "Sorry! Coming now."

Without warning, Rex grabs my wrist and tugs me to him. Dark eyes flash in my vision before he presses a deep, soulful kiss into my mouth, once again rendering my thoughts haywire.

Then he pushes me toward the door.

Blowing out a breath, I twist the doorknob and yank it open. "S-Sorry. I was on a call with a patient. A migraine slammed into me out of nowhere. I actually feel really sick right now."

Rhys frowns, his eyes darting from my face to the dark room, then back again.

He's suspicious. He steps across the threshold and I quickly grab his arm.

"C-Can you help me? I'm dizzy."

Concern flashes across his features. He nods and curls his hand over my shoulder, tucking me to his side. "Of course. Let's get you to a patient room. I hate migraines..."

I follow him, my pulse racing, a freshly carved hole throbbing inside my chest.

Because Rex Anderson didn't only have my heart in his grip, he also yanked it out and made off with it.

And I can't bring myself to regret it.

Later that night, I take a deep breath and close my eyes before pressing send on the email I drafted during the storm.

The end is near, but until then, I'll enjoy every moment with him.

CHAPTER FORTY

CLOSING MY EYES, I take off my hair tie and shake out my hair, letting it billow against the crisp evening wind as I make my way to the sun deck, where I'm supposed to meet Lana.

There's a reckoning coming. She's after the truth about Rex and me. There's only so much dodging I can do on a ship—even one of this size.

Even though I'm running late because of a call with my parents gone long, I take a quick minute to admire the melting sunset on the horizon, the skies a veritable display of gemstones—sparkling stars making its existence known against a watercolor of oranges, purples, and blues.

I think back to the conversation I had with my mom a few minutes ago, when I promised her I was booking a trip to LA.

For my thirtieth birthday at the end of April.

It's time to stop fleeing my past. Perhaps going on this cruise was what I needed to finally recognize the path I was on wasn't sustainable.

I don't want to live life to please others, to follow each rule to a T and not allow myself the grace to try new things, to make my own mistakes and learn from them.

I want the world to see me for me, like how Rex sees me.

Maybe my time with him is limited because, for whatever reason, he doesn't want to be with me, and I won't force him because I deserve more.

My forever will choose me. He'll pick me over and over again.

And in the meantime, I'll treat this trip as a break—have fun, make mistakes with a sexy man who can't be my forever. The old me would never have done it—broke rules, set myself up for heartbreak.

But the new me?

She's scared of pain, but isn't afraid of heartbreak. She's still afraid of heights and small spaces, but won't stop challenging herself. Because I would've lived. I would've done something worth risking everything over.

That's got to count for something, right?

And so, when Mom rambled about braised pork belly again, asking me, *"Ni chi fan le ma?"* if I'd eaten yet, because she's still incapable of saying "I love you," I stopped her.

The thick pause, the way my heart seized when I told her one of the many truths I'd held inside me all these years.

"Ma, I'm Olivia, not Mia. I'll never be Mia. I never liked braised pork belly. Mia did. My favorite dish is not even Chinese. It's Italian. Wild boar ragu. I hate almond cookies, but tolerated them because you and Mia loved them. I'm not outgoing, don't need to try out a new restaurant every week because I'm happy eating the same ten dishes on rotation. I love you and don't blame you. I just want to let you know I'm not Mia, and I'll never be her. And I need you to be okay with it."

I hung up without waiting for her response.

It's rude. Filial piety—respecting, taking care of, and obeying your parents and elderly relatives without question—is something that has been drilled into me since I was young. It's my cultural heritage, but I guess that's the issue with being second generation—I'm not Asian enough for my parents, nor have I forgotten my culture.

I'm a blend.

That's me. Unapologetically me.

Harried whispers reach my ears as I approach the lounge chairs by the infinity pool where I'm meeting Lana. My feet come to a halt at the scene before me.

Bree is standing next to Elias. She's gesturing wildly, her face scrunched up. She's clearly stressed about something. The mobster, dressed in his usual suit, leans casually against the railing, but the tense clasp of his hands tells me he's anything but relaxed. He murmurs a few words, which seem to calm Bree down, and she stalks off.

What is Bree doing with Elias? The puzzle pieces float around in my mind—the strange interactions between Rex and Bree, the vagueness when I ask about their relationship. The sadness in Bree's eyes when she talks about moving. And now, her interacting with a dangerous man everyone in New York City fears.

Something is brewing.

Elias huffs out a sigh before he unfurls himself from the railing. He reaches into his jacket pocket and pulls out a metallic object—a lighter I've seen him carry around.

Then he turns around and walks toward the aft of the ship, pausing when he reaches a figure lying on a lounge chair, clearly asleep.

Lana.

My breath catches. Something tells me to stay put to see what he'll do.

The man steps forward and shrugs off his jacket, then he drapes it over my slumbering friend. He reaches down, his lips curving up slightly into a rare smile. His hand almost grazes her face, but he pulls back before they touch. For a moment he freezes, so still he almost doesn't even seem human.

Then he stands up, his head whipping toward me, his piercing eyes intense. He lifts his index finger to his lips as if to tell me to be quiet, which would be silly since I'm not making any noise.

He's telling me not to tell her what he did.

Strange indeed.

When I nod, he returns the gesture, then walks away.

Frowning at the bizarre sequence of events I just witnessed, I walk over to Lana, biting back a smile when I see her normally sleek brown hair windblown and covering her face, her nose scrunching, her mouth slightly parted. Any second now and she'll probably start drooling. Her fingers are loosely clasping a small black box.

The graceful Anderson has a decidedly normal side.

"Earth to Lana. I'm here for you to dissect," I singsong and poke her arm.

She jolts up, her head whipping around, and yanks out a strand of hair that has slipped into her mouth.

"Shit! You scared me."

"Had to wake you up. You were snoring. Scared everyone away."

"No way! I don't snore. Lana Anderson never snores. I wasn't even sleeping. I just closed my eyes a bit to rest."

I snort. "If you say so. Although I have to admire you for that. I can never fall asleep in public."

Lana stretches her arms above her, the black box tumbling out of her grasp, and she quickly snatches it before it falls off the chair.

"Whew, that was a close one." She blows out a breath, her eyes as big as dinner plates.

"What's that?" I motion to the box.

She shrugs. "A puzzle box. I love them and usually have one or two with me to fiddle with whenever I'm bored. There's supposed to be a secret hidden inside if only I could open it—"

Lana pauses and stares at the gray suit jacket that has fallen onto her lap. "What's this?"

For a moment I want to tell her about Elias, but something about the mobster's expression—a flash of vulnerability when he lifted his finger to his lips—gives me pause.

Plus, I don't think I want my friend to be wondering about a man who blackmails and kills people for a living.

So instead, I smack my lips and give her my best Lana Anderson imitation—big eyes, wide smile, a slight batting of my eyelashes. Reverse interrogation, take that!

"I don't know. You tell me. I thought you were just 'resting your eyes.' Do you have a secret admirer?"

"What?" A strange flush creeps up her face. She clutches the black box tighter in her hand. "That's impossible. No way."

"Really now?" I plop down on the chair next to her and soften my tone, using the most calming voice I've perfected for my profession. "You seem agitated, Lana. What were you just thinking about?"

"I'm perplexed. I mean, there's no way I'd have—" She frowns, eyes narrowing. "Oh, don't you dare, Olivia. Don't use that doctor voice on me. We're here for you and I'm wide awake now. Spill. Tell me what the heck is going on with you and my brother, and don't even bother denying it. You, Ms. I can't lie for shit, are throwing all sorts of guilty signals, yes—just like that."

I groan and bury my heated face in my hands.

"Come to mama. I want to hear the truth from you." She pulls me into her arms and the scent of roses hits my nose.

Warmth unfurls inside me even as amusement joins the party. She pats my back like I'm a little child, even though she's only two years older than me.

"You aren't giving up, are you?" I mumble into her shoulder.

"Nope. I grew up with four older brothers who tried everything to stop me from butting into their business. Never giving up is my middle name. I can compete in the Olympics with my mad skills."

I snicker and pull away.

Staring at my friend, noting her familiar gray eyes pinched in concern, I force out a smile, a lump suddenly forming in my throat.

"I...I may have made a bad decision, and the worst thing is, I don't regret it."

She stays silent, clearly waiting for me to continue.

What will she think about you if she knows? She hired you to be on the cruise as a doctor. She trusted you to be professional. You've broken the cardinal rule. What will she—

My lungs tighten in a vise and my palms grow clammy.

Aren't I embracing my new self? Raw honesty and truth. No more hiding? Be brave enough to make mistakes, fall down, and get back up?

"Olivia... You can tell me. I won't judge you, I swear."

Something in her voice makes me look at her. Lana smiles—a soft, sad smile—and an answering ache blooms in my chest.

She knows already.

I take a deep breath and gather my courage.

"I...I love Rex. I know I'm not supposed to. He's my patient. There are rules. Boundaries. Ethics. But he makes me feel so much and I...I—"

"Oh, sweetie." She pulls me into a hug as tears slide down my cheeks.

Everything catches up to me—the events of the last few weeks, my call with Mom earlier, the things I've learned about myself, how deprived I was of acceptance, and how deep I've buried my feelings. Then there's the grief from losing Mia, from losing my identity to my parents and the world. Finally, the ecstasy and heartbreak I simultaneously feel with Rex, knowing our time is limited because he's unwilling to fix whatever's plaguing him.

It's overwhelming.

The tears become sobs as I shake in her arms.

"I'm going to kill him. I'll find Rex and rip him a new one. I told him not to mess with you, that you aren't a plaything—"

Shaking my head, I whisper, "He treats me like I'm precious."

It might be easier if he treated me like the other women, a good time he didn't care about.

"Then what's wrong?"

My lips tremble and I tell her everything—well, as much as I can without violating confidences from my sessions with Rex. Lana is quiet as she listens, and true to her promise, she doesn't pull away or appear to judge me. She nods when I tell her about Mia and her suicide, about my family, about feeling invisible because I've been trying to live for my lost twin, to not cause pain for my parents, who'll always grieve for their dead child. I tell her about Rex—how he, for the first time, made me see colors I was blind to, made me believe Olivia Lin was bewitching just as herself.

And when everything is said and done, I lean against her shoulder and stare at the dark skies, now navy blue, the sunset long having disappeared.

"You know, I knew you guys were together. I just wanted to hear your side."

I freeze, then look up. *My* side? She's talked to Rex?

Lana nods. "Maxwell and I got the truth out of him back in Tuscany."

I gasp. Maxwell? Oh no. I'm going to lose my job, my reputation. This is bad. Well, it was bad all along, but this is *bad*.

Lana must see my panic because she pats my hand and says, "You guys weren't exactly inconspicuous. Then Greg Masters threatened with the photo. It wasn't hard to put two and two together. Rex fessed up when we asked him. I won't lie and tell you we weren't upset initially. A doctor being involved with her patient doesn't look good, you know?"

"I'm sorry," I look down, "for keeping this from you guys. But not for loving your brother. He's a special man. He has so much love to give. A generous soul. It's impossible not to love him." It's true. I have regrets, but none of them include loving Rex Anderson.

"Well, if there's one thing I know by watching my siblings fall in love in impossible situations, sometimes life puts the right person in front of you at what seemingly is the wrong time or wrong place. But things have a way of working themselves out, as long as you follow your heart and live with no regrets. That's all that matters, isn't it?"

A soft breeze carries away her words, but they've burrowed deeply inside me already. "I must've disappointed you, Lana. I'm a board-certified doctor. I should know better. I'm—"

She squeezes my hand. "If emotions were easy to turn on and off, I think you'd be out of a job."

We chuckle at that.

"Why are you single? I never asked before." I nudge her side.

It's nice to finally open up to someone. The world didn't collapse.

She sighs, leans back, and stares at the stars in the sky. "Maybe I'm waiting for someone from a long time ago. It's silly. They all leave... I just wish one would stay."

Her answer is cryptic, and I wait for her to continue, but she doesn't.

"And no, I'm not disappointed in you. Do I prefer my best friend not to risk her career with my heartbreaker of a brother? Yes, I do, because I don't want you to get hurt. Do I love you and Rex? Yes, I do. Do I wish Rex could settle down, and if he did, would I be happy with him being with someone I'd love to call a sister? Yes, I do."

Sister. My eyes prickle and my nose burns. I hold everyone at arm's length, but Lana has never held that against me.

I'd love to have her as a sister too.

"Th-Thank you," I whisper, my voice hoarse.

Then, she turns toward me and smiles—a gentle, kind smile I know from her.

"I envy you, to be honest. Even if the person who has you in knots is Rex, who drives me nuts on the best days, to feel so much you'll risk everything for? That's something, you know? Not everyone has that. You're one of my best friends and I love you just as you are, Olivia—shy, quiet, loyal, the best *Twelfth Night* actress I've ever seen."

A half snort, half giggle tumbles out of my lips.

She winks. "I don't have your answers. I know you don't expect them from me. Just remember, I'm always here for you, and I'll never leave."

I burst into tears again and throw my arms around her shoulders.

I'll never leave.

That's it, isn't it? The people I love have left or are going to leave me. My twin, my parents, and now...Rex.

"I love him so much, Lana. But he has issues—I can't fix him. We only have this trip left before life catches up to us."

Lana heaves out a sad sigh. "Then, in that case, make the best of the time you have left. Live with no regrets."

Carpe diem.

Mia's words rattle inside my mind, but this time, the cadence is different—it's softer, quieter.

My voice.

Carpe diem. Live for myself.

CHAPTER FORTY-ONE

"Jacques will meet Bree at the side entrance an hour into the gala tomorrow. We have her costume ready. It should be easy for her to blend in as waitstaff on site." Elias's gravelly voice, along with some background noises, comes through the line.

The man disappeared soon after we docked at Port Hercules in Monte Carlo, Monaco, this morning.

And now, with the sun sitting low on the horizon, washing the coastline in gold, I'm standing at the pier, leaning against my custom vintage motorbike, as I get my instructions for Bree's extraction. Dread and anticipation pulse inside me. The moment I've been waiting for. Will I finally get the atonement I was seeking? Will I finally be able to let the past go?

Elias murmurs, "Your job is to keep the crowd's attention on you so Bree can get to the meetup point."

To this day, the mobster still won't tell me the extent of her involvement with The Association.

He adds, "I won't be attending the gala—too many eyes on me—but I'll be nearby. Does everything make sense?"

"Yes." I wince as an ache throbs in my head. Damn headaches join the blackouts now. "Are you ever going to tell me what's going on? I have so many damn questions."

He chuckles. "I know you do, and I suppose I owe you answers." A heavy exhale comes across the line. "Bree has something I need to get to a ledger."

"A ledger even the Elias Kent is interested in? I thought you held the biggest black book out there."

"This one has The Association contacts in it. I want it."

"That's it? You want a ledger, and that's why we're all risking our lives right now?"

A few beats of silence.

He murmurs, "It's personal, and if everything works out, it'll save many people and take down The Association. That's what we want, right? No more rapes or assaults. No more trafficking. No more innocent sixteen-year-olds being traumatized for life."

My blood freezes, and I grip the throttle. I think about Taylor, about what The Association did to her when she was sixteen, her future bright in front of her.

How we almost lost her, and then later, Ethan and Alexis, who almost drowned in the Hudson because of them.

So yes, whatever Elias's personal reasons are withstanding, I want that—revenge, take out some bad people causing harm to innocents. My life and health are shit. And with the way things are spiraling and I still have no answers, no relief, who knows how much time I have left on this earth before I end up mad or dead?

Perhaps this is a way I can contribute to society.

By taking out the trash.

"And Bree will help you do all of this."

"Yes. It has to be her. No one else can do what she does. If she gets hurt or killed, we're back at square one. That's all I'm going to tell you. Do you understand what needs to happen tomorrow?"

I grind my teeth, knowing this is the most I'm going to get out of him. Images of Mom and Raya's bodies appear behind my eyelids and I shove them away.

"Yes. I understand."

I'm saving Bree. This is my way of atonement. The Association, an organization I hate with my guts, might go down because of this.

I don't have all the answers, but I have enough. And when the dust settles...maybe I'll be able to sleep. Or a miracle will occur and I'll be at peace and the strange symptoms I'm experiencing will...disappear.

And I can be with her. Olivia.

"Good. Will be in touch."

He hangs up as a fresh wave of dizziness hits me, followed by the same nagging headache. It's my body reminding me of my fucked-up symptoms—how someone as screwed up as me can never be with someone as perfect as her.

I pop a few Velowakes into my mouth. My sleep has dwindled to two hours a night now, and I know why.

My trip is ending.

A seagull cries in the distance before taking flight, soaring over the yachts and sailboats docked nearby. A few tourists amble along the coast, taking photos, laughing and chatting.

This is the last stop on the cruise, and in three days, we'll be chauffeured to our jets to resume normal life in the real world.

Three more days until my temporary forever with Olivia ends.

It's a strange phrase, but it's true. While I have the curse or, in this case, the blessing of remembering every moment with her, for Olivia, these memories are temporary.

One day, her memories of me will fade like they do for most folks. Maybe she'll be on her honeymoon in Greece, holding the hand of a respectable man—a surgeon or a lawyer—and she'd think about the wild month she had a long time ago with a playboy who knew how to fuck but couldn't give her anything more than that.

Maybe she'd remember how she dove off a cliff for him and she'd smile because it wasn't something she was keen to do, but at least she did it once.

Maybe she might think of me or search my name online to see what I was up to.

If I were still around then.

It's debatable, given that my blackouts are happening more often now. This morning, I woke up in the main auditorium when a staff member shook me.

I'm going crazy. After all, that's the only explanation, right? I've seen so many doctors—everything coming back normal.

While I have another appointment with the neurologist next week, I'm not hopeful.

Perhaps one day, I'll be so out of my mind, I won't remember her.

Huffing a soft laugh under my breath, I shake my head.

That'll never happen. I think if I were to forget everything else, I'd still remember her.

The closest to forever. My forever.

"Good luck tomorrow," a voice murmurs behind me.

I turn around, finding Casey standing a foot away, his hand resting on top of his suitcase.

"You're leaving." My chest tightens, and for a moment, I can't breathe.

"Yes."

"Why? You never leave early." *Don't leave me. I can't be with Olivia. I can't lose you too.*

His lips hitch up on one side and he shrugs. The wind ruffles his dark hair. "I don't know if I can stay any longer. I don't want to be here for the next part."

"So, you're just going to chicken out when things get dangerous? Aren't you the one who called me a coward?"

He shakes his head, clearly not falling for my bait to rile him up. "I trust you'll make the right decisions this time. You don't need me here anymore. It's not like I made a difference in your choices before."

I think back to the times he's saved me—the nagging, the laughs, the arguments—he *has* made a difference.

"And," he slides on his aviators, "you have someone better now. Someone who really understands you, someone who can anchor you.

You've changed on this trip—in ways I never thought possible. I know I had nothing to do with it."

"I can never be with her. You know my issues."

"I know what you *think* are your issues. If there's anything I say that I want you to carry with you always...things aren't as bad as they seem. Or as hopeless." Casey turns away and takes a few steps toward the street.

He looks back and says, "You don't need me anymore, Rex. You can make the right choices. Starting with that bottle in your hand." He motions to my Velowake. "Let her in. Let her give you peace."

Lifting his hand in a wave, he strolls away, leaving me behind, conflicting thoughts rioting inside me.

My chest is heavy. I can't breathe.

But then, I feel everything.

A phantom ache like I'd lost a limb. A heaviness in my chest at his parting words—the faith laced in them even after all the years I've disappointed him. My old friend—fear—trying to say hello, whispering in my ear that I'll always be a disappointment. That Casey and Olivia's faith in me isn't misplaced.

And maybe, just maybe, a twinge of pride. He thinks I'm ready. He thinks I don't need him to babysit me anymore.

"Why do you look so sad?"

The sweet scent of cotton and honey wafts to my nose.

I smile. My sweet, darling Olivia. The woman I've spent most of my waking hours with since we decided to pursue our temporary forever.

She taps my shoulder, her eyes brimming with concern.

I look at where Casey was, finding him long gone, then turn toward my bewitching vixen.

"Nothing. You ready for a day you'll never forget?"

Chapter Forty-Two

THE SMILE ON HIS face doesn't quite reach his eyes, but the warmth is there.

That's the thing with Rex Anderson. He's like one of those classic movies—*Forrest Gump* or *The Shining*—entertaining to watch for the story and the acting. But when you rewatch it each time, you'll pick up on something different—a hidden meaning about the human condition, symbolism, or other messages with deeper themes.

And this smile tells me he's battling both joy and sadness at the same time.

Looking around, I scan for any paparazzi or coworkers. Rhys believed my migraine story, but I think he's still suspicious, so I need to be extra careful.

We're standing in a relatively secluded spot, and few people are loitering about since there's a big party happening on the ship right now.

When I don't see anyone I recognize, I place my hand on Rex's cheek, his perfectly groomed scruff scraping my fingers.

He lets out a sigh—a soft one, but I hear it, nonetheless.

"Do you know what's one of the most common emotions I see in my practice?"

Rex shakes his head, his brow lifting.

"Guilt. Over the past, over what a person should do but isn't doing. Over not feeling one hundred percent one way, like when you're happy but also sad, when you're grateful but also resentful." I stroke his cheek, watching his breaths quicken, a flush crawling up his face.

Sliding my hand to his neck, I rest my fingers there to feel his pulse. It's fluttering rapidly. I've hit the mark.

"It's okay to feel that way. Life isn't black and white or two-dimensional, and neither are we," I whisper.

The Adam's apple bobs in his throat as he swallows, and he stares at me.

I want to spend forever staring into those gray, mesmerizing pools. I want to know what secrets and hidden meanings they hold.

I want to watch his movie again and again.

A slow smile curves up his lips, and he lifts my hand away from his cheek, turns it over, and presses a soft kiss on the backs of my fingers like a gentleman.

My blood heats from the intimate gesture—the small touch holding so much emotion in it.

In this moment, I'm his forever, the forever he thinks he can't have, the one I want to give to him.

Why Rex, why are you sabotaging yourself? Why are you rejecting us?

I'm sad and angry. I don't understand, and I will never understand. I want to shake him and walk away because I deserve someone who will fight for me. But I also love him and want to enjoy the last few days with him in our small slice of paradise. It's messed up and toxic. It's beautiful and bittersweet.

And that's okay.

"Come on," he murmurs, his voice hoarse. "Let's go create some chaos."

Without warning, he picks me up and deposits me on the back of a motorcycle, chuckling when I shriek and swat at him for scaring the shit out of me.

"You are nuts if you think I'm going with you on...this. Do you even know how to ride this?"

He plucks the pins from my hair, and my bun unravels.

"Hey!" More swatting and chuckling.

"Your bun is in the way and your hair is gorgeous." He smiles when he fastens a helmet on my head before tightening it.

My heart skips a beat, warmth gathering in my chest. Being this close to him is like I'm staring straight into the sun. But instead of being a shadow cast on the ground, he's shining his light on me, showing me off to the world.

"I'm a great rider. You think only Maxwell owns the bragging rights to anything with wheels?" His straitlaced brother loves street racing. In fact, that's how he and Belle met.

Rex climbs onto the bike and slides my hands around his waist. "Well, there was one time when I crashed Ryland's car in high school, but that was four wheels. Fuck, he was so pissed."

"Is *that* supposed to make me feel better? You crashed something with four wheels and somehow two wheels make this safer?"

"Well, I guess you'll just have to trust me and be brave, huh? What is it you like to say? *Carpe diem.*"

Without waiting for my response, he twists the throttle and we're off.

Squealing, I squeeze my eyes shut and clutch his waist in a death grip. I'm sure my nails will leave marks on his stomach.

I try to speak, but he doesn't hear me, and it's then I realize the roar of the engine, the rustling of the wind, and the honking and beeping of other vehicles speeding by are eclipsing my words.

I just have to trust him.

And I do.

He laces one hand with mine, giving it a squeeze like he knows I'm terrified, then he pats it as if to say everything will be okay. Slowly, I open my eyes, my pulse racing, my breathing sawing in and out of my lungs.

Rex tugs at my fingers, motioning to the surrounding scenery.

Be brave, Olivia. Be the new you. Embrace new things. Carpe diem.

Blowing out a few quick exhales, I slowly look to the side.

And my breath crystallizes in my throat.

We're soaring down a winding cliffside road, and the views of Côte d'Azur, the French Riviera, are breathtaking. With the sun dipping on the horizon, spreading warm embers into the crisp blue of the skies, the ocean glitters like stars far below. Boats and yachts ebb and flow in the calm waters, small waves gently grazing the golden shores.

I marvel at the lemon trees in bloom, the ancient stone walls twisting around the path, the distinct fuchsia flowers, bougainvillea, draping over wrought iron balconies of estates half hidden by trees.

It's stunning.

The faint scents of crushed wild thyme and salt are carried by the breeze, mixing with the intoxicating blend of Rex's cologne, gasoline, and the aged leather on the bike.

My hair flutters to the wind, and in this moment, I want to do something the old me will think is dangerous and nuts.

Thighs clamped tightly around the bike, I let go of Rex and lift my arms, the breeze grazing my fingers.

My heart thunders in my ears, and my stomach swirls. I've never felt so alive as right now, at this moment, on the back of a speeding motorcycle in a foreign country with a man I have no business being with.

I laugh, though I can barely hear the sound above the ruckus.

"Wohooo!" I yell when the bike jostles from a bump on the road. Then more laughter spills out of me.

When was the last time I laughed like this, not caring if I looked like a freak to others, my mind not swirling with a never-ending list of things I should do?

I'm free.

Rex reaches back and pats my leg, and I swing my arms back around him again. Then he suddenly swerves and parks at a scenic overlook.

Before I can ask him why we're stopping, he tugs off our helmets. With one hand gripping the nape of my neck, he smashes his lips with mine.

My heart somersaults, the earlier adrenaline now spiking with lust, love, and exhilaration. I fist his hair, kissing him back, telling him with my lips, teeth, and tongue everything I'm not saying, how I'm finally at home in my skin, how I'm looking at the world with my blindfold off.

It's all because of him.

"This moment is my forever," he murmurs against my lips, and my lungs squeeze at the anguish in his voice.

I pull back and trace the planes of his face with my fingertips, and his eyes flutter shut. The masculine brows, the tall, sharp nose, the hollows under his eyes I wish could go away, the masculine angle of his jaw.

I want to memorize him. The way he feels, the husky rasp of his voice, the spice of his scent and the safety it evokes in me even as we do things that are decidedly dangerous.

"Rex..." I swallow, watching as those startling irises look at me. "Thank you. Thank you for seeing me."

His gaze roves over my face and for a moment, I can only hear cars speeding by or the distant squawking of the seagulls. Rex smiles, his soft lips curving so the wrinkles appear at the corners of his eyes.

A genuine smile.

"I've always seen you, Olive. Even when I shouldn't."

Then, he puts our helmets back on and whisks us off to God knows where, taking me on a road trip around the city.

He stops at the Formula 1 Grand Prix Circuit where he finagles us a modified F1x2 two-seater race car and tests my ability to let out ear-splitting screams as he swerves on the asphalt, the car nearly kissing the guardrails. Needless to say, he's a much better driver than he was in his younger days, but my legs are jelly when I climb out.

He rides by the Casino de Monte Carlo, the grand and iconic coral-colored building, which looks as beautiful in person as in Bond films, with luxury cars parked out front. The charity gala tomorrow will be next door at one of Fleur's umbrella establishments, the iconic Hotel de France.

For the next few hours, Rex shows me a side of the city I don't see in movies or guidebooks. The small nooks and crannies, the private gardens bursting with succulents, off the beaten path neighborhoods where locals lounge in lawn chairs, kids kick soccer balls down the streets, enjoying life after school.

Then finally, he comes to a stop in a nondescript building tucked away in the Condamine district per the signage I saw moments ago. Blue Old-World shutters frame the windows, and laundry hangs from iron balconies.

"What are we doing here?" I ask when he laces his fingers in mine and tugs me toward a partially open door.

Inside, I hear the soft buzzing sound of a needle, smell the distinct scent of antiseptic agents and leather, and see a few chairs and stations in a brightly lit space.

Rex has taken us to a tattoo parlor.

Wide-eyed, I look at him, and he winks before turning to a bald, burly man with two beautiful sleeves of ink. They speak in rapid French because, of course, Rex would know French too.

Then, he pulls me with him as the man leads us to a station in the back.

"Wh-What are you doing?" I watch in bewilderment as Rex sits down. He's getting a tattoo? Now?

"I should think that's obvious." He smirks and rolls up his sleeve, exposing the arm with the scars from his childhood.

The old ache flares again as I imagine a young boy doing this to himself because he holds so much pain inside him, but has no outlet because he thinks his role is to bring happiness to others.

A familiar burning appears behind my eyes, and I smooth my finger over the small marks.

Then I frown, because I notice new black marks over the scars. It's shaped like a bite mark.

Is that what I think it is? My mind flashes to our romp in my office a week ago, when I bit his wrist in the throes of orgasm, tasting blood. It was feral, messy, and so hot.

My eyes snap to his, finding a smug smile on his lips.

"Just to prove to you what I told you is true, I'm getting my first ever tattoo on this pristine, glorious body for you. You should be honored."

I swallow, my mouth running dry. "What?"

He shrugs, not elaborating further as the artist comes back and preps Rex's arm. Then the man begins his work.

An hour passes by as I admire the intricate artwork appearing on his wrist—the bite mark linking with the small scars like vines, followed by one single, lifelike olive. I'm in awe.

Underneath the olive are two words written in script.

My Forever.

My throat prickles as I stare at the image of me inked on his skin.

Me.

Unable to help myself, I press a quick, but thorough kiss on his lips when the artist steps away.

"Rex, I love you," I whisper.

He freezes, his breath hitching.

"I don't need you to say it back." I kiss him again. "This is the new me. Honest and brave. I don't expect anything. I just want to let you know."

Rex's throat works, and he remains silent. I try not to let it get to me, even though that's impossible. But I'm a person who believes in actions over words, and for this man—someone who never settles down, who goes from fling to fling without a care—to put something so permanent on his body, I mean something to him.

Wordlessly, he frames my face with his hands again and presses a searing kiss onto my lips. I lose myself in the pleasure and warmth only he can give me.

This is enough. This has to be enough.

CHAPTER FORTY-THREE

SHE LOVES ME.

She's seen the most of me—the fucked up, the crazy, the unhinged—and she still loves me. I wanted to say the words back to her then, but I'm afraid if I can't fix myself, if I can't be with her after this trip, then those three words will only hurt her more.

The thoughts play inside my mind a few hours later, a favorite song set on repeat, as I usher her through a side entrance in Absinthe, a club on the Rose decks of the ship.

I'm careful, timing our entrance to the cleaning schedule, so no one will see us together. I would've taken her to my stateroom, but the staff always hovered nearby, and I couldn't dismiss them without rousing suspicion.

If there's anything I wish for, I wish to hold her hand in broad daylight in front of my friends and family, because I want everyone to know she's mine.

That I, Rex Anderson, have fallen hopelessly in love with a woman who makes me feel something so elusive I've been searching for all my life.

Peace and acceptance.

My worries and nightmares don't matter when I'm with her. She's my sun and my stars and I orbit around her, living to tease out one more smile, one more laugh, one more orgasm, one more everything from a woman who's spent her life being invisible.

Like she's saving herself for me.

But I know what will happen if we get together, if she finds out how messed up my mind is, how I lose segments of time, not knowing how I end up being where I am.

Unless I find a cure—either from the doctors or because this mission will somehow fix me—it's only a matter of time before I do something irreparable and hurt someone.

I can't risk that for her. I can't pull her into my hellish orbit. It's selfish.

Olivia is silent as I whisk her into a private room I reserved in advance. Her mouth parts when she looks around, taking in the pink neon lighting lining the ceiling, the four-poster bed in the center with hookups for straps, chains, and other equipment.

There's a cabinet with more toys and machines for those who are curious and a one-sided window for the adventurous sort who want to watch or be watched.

But tonight, I don't want any of it. None of the extreme things I've partaken in the past.

I only want to worship her and tell her with my body the three words I can't say out loud.

Silently, I walk up to her and link our hands together before bringing them up to my lips.

I press kisses on each fingertip, marveling at how dainty her hands are compared to mine, how fragile she appears to be, but I know she's one of the strongest women I've ever met.

We don't speak as I kiss my way up her arm, then to her neck, my mouth zeroing in on the special place I know will make her wild.

A whimper escapes her lips as I slowly remove her clothes, and soon she's gloriously naked before me. Olivia's face is flushed as she climbs onto the bed and scoots back, her luminous eyes dark when she takes in the skin I'm revealing when I take off my shirt, then my pants, then my boxer briefs.

My cock is dripping, as always, with her. I climb over her and brush my hand on her cheeks. She releases a satisfied sigh, like she needs the touch to breathe.

Like she needs me.

Heart hiccupping in my chest, I bear down on her as I kiss those pouty lips and taste her sweetness. It doesn't matter how many times I kiss her, how many times I touch her, I can't seem to get enough.

I mainline her honeyed taste into my mouth as I swallow her moans and sighs. My hands slide up her body, gripping her breasts, the perfect little handfuls, before thumbing those sensitive nipples.

"Rex," she moans when I pinch the tip—just the tip—because I know it'll drive her wild.

"Yes, Olive, my sweetheart. You need this, don't you? You need more?"

She arches up in answer, her legs automatically coiling around my backside, heels digging in.

"Fuuuck," I groan when my throbbing cock glides over her slick folds.

"Yes, yes, yes," she chants, gyrating her body in a tortuous rhythm so the tip of my cock digs into her clit, once, twice, three times, each motion overloading my senses, frying my nerves.

It's never been like this before, being so out of control with just the slightest touch.

Only with her.

I need to taste her. I need to taste her juices at the source. My mouth salivates at the thought of it.

Groaning, I move my way down her body, trailing open-mouthed kisses over her stomach, then her legs, licking the sensitive area between her thigh and her pussy.

"Please, Rex. Please, I need you."

"Yes, Olive, I'll give you everything." Everything I have to give.

Olivia cries out when I draw her swollen nub into my mouth and my eyes roll back from pleasure as her sweet taste hits my tongue. She thrashes underneath me, her feet half fighting to kick me away, half fighting to pull me closer. I hold her tighter and bury my face in her cunt.

I suck, lick, and tongue her pussy, then I gently pull apart her folds to get deeper.

"You're my obsession, Olive," I whisper between licks, letting her flavor wash over me as my blood heats and mind blanks. "So fucking delicious, so fucking mine."

She trembles, her nails digging into my neck and back, her hips canting and moving, clearly needing more friction, but I don't give it to her yet. I hiss and instead, thrust my cock into the sheets.

I can't wait today.

I need to be inside her, to bury myself deep within her so she'll feel me with her always.

Unable to stop my maddening thoughts, I climb over her and stare into her whiskey eyes, her bee-stung lips, and those beautiful rosy cheeks.

"I'm yours, Olive. All of me, whatever's left of me...all yours." The words pour out of me without filter, and I watch as a small furrow appears between her brows, her gaze skating over my face.

She's thinking, trying to parse out the meaning, everything I'm not saying.

Doling out a shaky smile, I brush away the hair sticking to her face.

Before her, sex was surface-level pleasure, a way to numb my mind. It was quick, rough, and sometimes intense.

But tonight, it's so much more.

I nip her bottom lip, biting until she hisses out a sharp breath, then I lave it with my tongue. It's plumper and redder now.

So beautiful.

She wears all my marks so beautifully.

"You're everything, my temporary forever. All of it is yours," I rasp. Then, I slam home.

My ears ring as white-hot pleasure sears me, her tight pussy, warm and wet, gripping my cock so perfectly. My balls draw up, ready to unload, to mark her up from the inside.

"Rex, I love you," she moans and wraps her arms around my back.

But she's much smaller than me, her hands only able to claw at my sides, unable to fully wrap around me.

She's mine.

In this moment, I'm all she sees, hears, feels, smells. I am her everything.

The thought fans the obsession licking up my spine. My blood churns hot in my veins, my skin on fire. Madness creeps into my mind, not unlike the disorientation after my blackouts when I don't remember where I am or how I got there.

But right now, I know.

All my nerve endings, the atoms vibrating inside my body, all live for this woman underneath me. This petite woman who owns me. I'll live, breathe, and die for her, no questions asked.

"You bewitch me, Olive. And I never want to wake up."

My thrusts are harder now, my dick elongating and growing with each piston. A sharp pleasure begins deep inside my abdomen, spreading out. My balls constrict, the pressure tightening and relentless.

"Yes, please, fuck me, please." Olivia meets me thrust for thrust, her tight body shaking, trembling underneath me, needing release.

I'm going to give it to her. Make her see stars. Make her come like she has never come before.

"I'll fuck you. I'll make love to you. I'll goddamn put my cum so deep inside you, it'll never come out. And when it does, when you see it dripping out, I want you to use your finger and put it back in, to keep all that sticky goodness inside you."

She grows wetter, and I groan. Her walls spasm against me. My little Olive is close.

My hips snap in a firm rhythm, the wet sounds of our fucking joining her little whimpers and mewls.

"Yes, sweetheart. Your cunt strangling my hard dick. God, I'm going to give you so much cum, fill you right up. Give you that sweet cream pie you've been waiting for."

Reaching in between us, I flick her clit and she cries out, her pussy tightening to the point of pain around my cock.

My vision whitens, and every nerve ending focuses on that point of connection.

Mindlessly, I grapple around the bed until I find her hands. Then I link our fingers together tightly, needing this soul-sucking connection, this sex that is more than making love.

It's a communion of souls.

"I want to make love to you, to be the reason for all your smiles, all your laughter. My heart beats for you. My lungs draw in oxygen because of you. Every part of me exists for you, Olive. Don't you forget that. Whenever you're sad, whenever you're in the shadows, remember me. Remember there's someone out there who thinks you're his world, that you burn brightest. Remember that...fuck!"

I explode, the pleasure spearing out of me as my cock throbs and gushes out streams of cum inside her.

"Rex!" She spasms underneath me, her body shaking like she's been shocked with a live wire.

A torrent of wetness spurts out of her.

"My beautiful Olive. My prim and proper doctor. My filthy, lusty squirter."

The words inflame her, and her shaking becomes full body quakes, the walls of her pussy constricting and releasing in strong tugs, further milking my cock.

Mine.

Pleasure I've never felt before blinds my senses. My mouth parts in an open gasp, my words, my voice leaving me as I move harder, faster over her, hitting her deep inside, angling so I can graze her clit on the way out. The sounds of our skin smacking against skin echo in the room as my orgasm throbs and continues, unending.

She shrieks. "I-I'm coming again."

I slam my mouth over hers, swallowing her cries as she thrashes underneath me. Her perfect pussy pulls out all my cum, all my pleasure, all of me, and as I slow down our movements, my soul soaring high in the skies, I'm consumed with so much love, so much peace, I never ever want to wake up.

I kiss her again and again. Until I don't even know if she's kissing me or if I'm kissing her. Until I don't know where she begins and I end. I press my thoughts and sentiments onto her lips, words I can't say but are bursting out of my chest.

I love you so fucking much, Olivia Lin. You're my forever, even if I have to let you go.

Because I love you. I love you. I love you.

Chapter Forty-Four

My stomach roils and my skin is clammy, all sensations I don't expect to feel in the middle of a luxurious charity gala inside one of the most iconic buildings in Monte Carlo. It's like ants are crawling all over me, and I don't know why.

It's unsettling. If I believe in signs, this feels like an omen.

It's all in my head. Omens aren't real.

I brush my damp palms over my purple silk gown, which Lana claimed was perfect for my complexion, then pat my classy low chignon, making sure strands aren't escaping.

Taking deep breaths, I focus on my surroundings, a tactic which can help stop an anxiety spiral.

Salon Paris is gorgeous—one of the primary spaces in the hotel and casino. The vaulted ceilings are adorned with intricate frescoes, gold filigree wrapped around an oval stained-glass skylight of sea foam and amber hues. Tall Corinthian columns bracket the space, and multi-layered crystal chandeliers illuminate the room in a warm glow.

It's beautiful. I should focus on this once-in-a-lifetime experience. Buttery aroma of the hors d'oeuvres lingers in the air. I hear the soft clinking of champagne flutes and laughter from crowds gathered around the blackjack tables throughout the space.

I shiver, hairs standing on my forearms. The unsettling pit in my stomach won't go away.

I blow out another deep breath. *Calm yourself.*

"We're not in Kansas anymore," Lana says from my right and I flinch.

"Shit! You scared me."

"Whoa, you don't look so good. You okay?" She steps in front of me and frowns. Then she puts her palm on my forehead. "No fever. But you're a bit pale."

I shake myself. This is ridiculous. Maybe I caught a bug, or I didn't sleep well last night.

I think about how I woke up this morning in the Absinthe suite alone when housekeeping knocked on the door, carrying a tray of assorted pastries, fruits, and coffee.

Then there was his note.

Olive,

You shine the brightest in my eyes.

Remember that.

And don't believe everything you see. Trust me.

Rex

My heart tightened then, as it's doing now. The note is bittersweet and ominous. What is he hiding, and why can't he tell me?

I haven't seen the man all day—it's like he's vanished from the ship.

My stomach churns again, the same foreboding weight settling over me.

"Have you seen Rex?" I ask Lana.

"I haven't. I swear, I'm going to kill the man when I see him. This is the last big event before the cruise ends, and he's pulled a Houdini on me." Lana tosses her hands into the air, drawing attention to her figure-hugging gold gown.

I gnaw my lip. "Maybe something came up? This cruise is important to him. I doubt he'd ditch you unless it was urgent."

If you asked me a month ago if I thought Rex Anderson had a serious bone in his body, I'd tell you no. But now, I know much of that is a facade, an act he's putting on for others because he thought that was expected of him.

I wish I could make him see himself—his selfless heart, his sensitive soul, how he cares about the people he loves, like his family, with his whole being.

"I would've heard about it. I get morning briefings on everything happening on the cruise, and it's all run-of-the-mill, nothing unusual. Although now that you mentioned it, there is something weird."

"What?"

Lana deepens the furrow between her brows and scans the sizable crowd around us. "Yeah, definitely weird. I didn't put two and two together before, but..."

"Stop talking in riddles. What's going on?"

She turns to me, a sharpness in her eyes. "Bree said she wasn't going offshore today, which isn't strange, considering she rarely leaves the ship. But earlier, I saw a waitress who looked just like her, but when I called her name, she scurried away. I thought I must've been seeing things. And now Rex isn't here, and he and Bree are good friends. The Shadow King isn't here either, and that man is everywhere."

The Shadow King? Oh, Elias.

The image of him talking to Bree on the sky deck the other day flashes into my mind. All these seemingly random puzzle pieces floating in the air—perhaps they form the same image all along.

I stiffen. "Lana, I saw something the other day on the sky deck."

I tell her about what I saw, the heated discussion and panic on Bree's face, how Elias calmed her down. I left out the part about the man giving Lana his jacket. That didn't seem relevant here.

"Something has to be going on with the three of them." I tick my fingers. "Rex isn't with Bree, and he's close to Elias. Elias has connections to Bree. And now, they're missing. They must be planning something."

As soon as the words leave my mouth, the orchestra suddenly stops playing. A clamor rises in the crowd as rapid staccato flashes bathe the room in bright light.

The devil himself strides in, a model on each arm. He lifts their hands in the air, and the ladies spin as the press gathers around them. Then he kisses their cheeks.

I can't stop the sharp hiss from escaping my lips, and Lana looks at me.

I turn away, not wanting her pity.

I know this is bound to happen—the playboy prince will resume his normal life because I'm not his forever, despite what he says, despite that fresh tattoo he claimed he got for me.

But these actions, him flirting, holding, kissing other women, speak louder than his pretty words and that beautiful tattoo.

I just didn't expect to see the fallout before the cruise is over.

His words from the note appear in my mind. *Don't believe what I see. Trust him.*

Is this what he meant? But how can he ask me to trust him when he doesn't trust me with whatever he's planning? And he hasn't really promised me anything beyond this trip.

His temporary forever. Maybe we've come to an end.

I take a deep breath, the raw pain radiating from my heart, the organ pulverized from a mere moment.

"I'm going to kill him," Lana seethes. She takes a step toward her man whore of a brother.

I grab her arm to stop her. "Don't make a scene. This is your family's cruise. The press is here. And i-it's not like we were anything to e-each other. Just a vacation...*fling.*"

The last word tastes bitter on my tongue. I drag my gaze away from the happy trio, trying to stop my eyes from tearing up.

Because it isn't worth it to cry over this maddening man.

Because any man lucky enough to have me will know my worth and treat me well.

Because a true spotlight isn't only for a moment, but should be enduring.

"Always the beautiful ladies around you, Mr. Anderson," someone hollers, and the crowd laughs.

"I never disappoint. Then again, with a face and body like mine, can we expect less? It'd be a shame not to share it with the world."

More guffaws and flashes, the crowd growing larger, clearly drawn to him like kids to an ice cream truck.

"What about your doctor friend, Rex? She's looking awfully lonely over there."

A chill sweeps through the room and shoots straight into my veins. Several hundred pairs of eyes bore holes into me. Lana steps in front of me, an angry grizzly mother bear, and I want to hug her for it.

"Ladies and gentlemen," she begins, her voice taking on her gracious PR persona.

I'm thrown back to our *Twelfth Night* reenactment, the discomfort when the scene ended and I felt everyone's gazes on me. The thought that crossed my mind—how I was meant to be in the shadows.

The same sensation is back tenfold, but there's also something new in the mix.

A fire licks up my spine, a surging heat scorching my body—anger, indignation, frustration, whatever other emotions colliding into a force to be reckoned with.

Straightening up, I tap Lana's shoulder. She stops talking and glances at me, clearly concerned.

Staring at the crowd, the reporters in their tuxes with their phones thrusted my direction, the blinding flashes searing my eyes, I focus on the one man who asked the question.

Greg Masters, a sleazy smile on his face, no doubt peeved we've ruined his attempt for an immediate payday after the test kitchen incident.

"How can I be lonely at the world's most exclusive gala surrounded by my friends," I wink at Lana, "and all these wonderful guests?"

My pulse skedaddles, and I continue, "But I have to say, there are two types of folks who are worried about other people's loneliness. They're either kind and empathetic, or they have unmet needs and issues they aren't dealing with. Let's guess which of those categories you fall into."

The asshole's face reddens as a colleague elbows him. Chuckles sweep through the crowd.

I arch my brow, barely containing my disdain. "I take pro bono cases sometimes. You can find me if you ever want to talk, sir."

Cheers and applause spear through the audience as I turn away from the sniveling man.

And then I see *him* staring at me.

Rex's lips are hiked up to the side, his hands clapping like the rest of his entourage. His dark eyes shine with pride and mirth, and for a moment, my traitorous heart skips several beats, my body heating from the intensity of his attention.

Then I see the socialites next to him, grabbing his arm, patting his chest, and the heat swiftly vanishes from my body.

Gritting my teeth, I ignore him, the twinge in my chest flaring again.

Back to the real world, Olivia. This man isn't for you.

CHAPTER FORTY-FIVE

She looks glorious.

I froze in my tracks when I saw her the moment I walked into the ballroom. She was the beacon of the lighthouse on a stormy night. It was impossible to look anywhere else.

The purple dress clings to her figure, held together by two tiny spaghetti straps. I could chew them off and watch the top slide to her waist, baring her exquisite tits. Then there's the thigh-high slit showing a sliver of leg, which I remember digging into my back as I fucked her senseless.

It was almost impossible to leave her in bed this morning. She looked so content, a happy, sleepy kitten curled up next to me, her body marred with marks from our lovemaking last night. When I pulled away, she whimpered. It took Herculean effort to put distance between us because there were more things at stake.

Dangerous things.

I didn't want to drag her into the mission in case everything went sideways. And so, I put the shackles over my heart, telling myself this vacation, this slice of paradise, was over.

I thought I was setting her free.

But sirens don't just let you walk away. Even when they try, their song lingers.

Calliope tried to save her lover and still lost him.

And Olivia—the way she lit into Greg Masters? It almost dragged me straight back to her.

I wanted to kill the man when he singled her out, when I saw the panic in her eyes.

I wanted to bash him over the head with his precious camera, then I'd slowly strangle him with the strap.

But then she spoke up, loud and clear, in a way the past Olivia couldn't.

She stood tall and confident, her brow elegantly arched, the perfect amount of haughtiness in her voice.

A different impulse rushed through me then. My dick twitched, quickly forming a half-semi, and if it weren't for Gracie or Charlene—or whatever their names were—clinging to me like deadweight, I would've rushed over, pulled Olivia into my arms, and kiss the daylights out of her.

Give the crowd a show they'd never forget.

"Rex, is it true you've once fucked five women at once?" the redhead next to me asks. She's a top influencer model in the region, one of the reasons I chose her to be part of my distraction tactic today.

"I heard it was ten," the raven-haired beauty murmurs before blowing kisses to the reporters who are still snapping photos.

"A gentleman never kisses and tells." I lead them to the center of the room as the orchestra strikes up a tune and we dance.

"Will you show us later?" The redhead slides her hand inside my tux jacket, blatantly feeling me up.

Acid rushes up my esophagus, and my hackles rise. I want to yank her hand out and push her away.

But I don't. Because this is the plan Elias came up with. This is the perfect distraction, the perfect cover.

The world is watching us, leaving Bree to follow the plan—meet Elias's contact at the back side entrance.

So, I throw my head back and laugh, drawing more attention to us. Incessant camera flashes blind my eyes, the shutter sounds a riot in my ears, but I pull the ladies closer to me, ignoring the clench of my heart, the way it's tearing at the pain I saw in Olivia's face just now before she put her mask on.

She doesn't know I'm doing this to protect her.

Doubt niggles inside me. This morning, I thought it was best to keep her in the dark.

I was keeping her safe.

But now, I can't help but wonder if I've made a big mistake.

The ladies giggle as I twirl them one by one, dipping them outrageously low toward the floor, making sure to throw in a few flirtatious winks to the reporters and other women in the crowd.

Rex-a-Million is back in service.

The world spins around me, a swirl of rainbow colors washed in gold, but I search for that deep purple, that petite figure poured into silk.

I don't see her.

She's gone. She's finally given up on me.

My lungs heave in ragged breaths, my body almost caving from the sudden liver punch as the revelation hammers into my mind like a freshly handed death sentence for a convict.

This is what you wanted, Rex. It's for the best. The memories will live forever in your mind.

The healing tattoo itches, reminding me that my Olive is permanently inked to my skin.

Someday, if I'm lucky, if I can be normal again, I'll find her.

I'll beg her to take me back.

Cheers erupt in the crowd as I execute a few complicated dance moves, my hips and body working the floor on autopilot.

But I'm not here. Not really.

In my mind, I'm dancing with a certain raven-haired doctor, tornadoes and hurricanes raging around me, but I don't care.

She'd stare at me with those trusting, soulful eyes, her lips curving before the cutest laughter escapes from them. At that moment, I'd be the motherfucking king of the world because I made her laugh.

In my mind, I'm in my forever—where I'm just Rex and she's just my Olive.

And we're happy.

The imaginary moment is so perfect, it almost feels fragile.

Then the room plunges into darkness.

Sharp sounds crack through the air. My body reacts before my mind does.

Gunshots.

Olive.

People slam into me, bloodcurdling screams rippling through the room.

"Gunmen. Run!" someone yells.

The women on my arms flee for the exit. But I stay rooted, scanning the chaos.

Where is she? Fuck. Please let her be okay.

It's too dark. Too many shapes moving, shifting, crashing into one another.

Utter chaos. Madness.

My eyes sweep the room again. I don't see Olivia or Lana anywhere. Or Bree.

Fuck. The mission. The Association must be here for Bree.

Bang!

More gunshots. More screams.

Icy panic floods my veins as I push through the crowds in the dark, guided only by the pulsing red emergency lights.

The side exit. The meeting spot.

"Olivia! Bree!" I holler, the sound of my voice swallowed by terror.

Dread rises like a tsunami inside me.

Bang!

More cries. People trample over each other, running for the exits.

I brace myself against a game table, my head jerking, eyes scanning.

That distinct shade of purple. The waitstaff uniform. Anything.

I'll die if anything happens to Olivia. I can't let anything happen to her. I also can't let anything happen to Bree. Raya's tragic ending can't repeat itself tonight.

Then, just as panic pulls me under—

I see her.

Olivia in the far corner. Alarm on her elfin features.

Someone's dragging her through a door.

A waitstaff uniform.

Bree.

I break into a run.

And then a stampede barrels into my path.

CHAPTER FORTY-SIX

"Follow me! I know another way out." Bree pulls me behind her, her grip surprisingly strong.

Before the shots rang out, I was trying to escape the gala because I couldn't stand it.

I couldn't be in the same space as Rex as he flirted with other women.

The old me would've stayed because I didn't want to disappoint my friends, but the new me needed to protect my heart first.

But then chaos broke out.

I spun around to look for Rex and Lana when I spotted Bree. The utter terror on her face. She was wearing a uniform and a blond wig. I almost didn't recognize her.

Her eyes widened when they met mine. She rushed over and grabbed my hand before making a break for it.

"But Rex and Lana!" I struggle to pull free from Bree's death grip.

She's fucking strong.

"No time! I saw Lana running out the front door and Rex could take care of himself. We have a plan for this."

A plan?

"What the hell's going on?"

More gunshots ring through the air, and we duck.

People fall down. Trampling on each other. My feet almost slip on something wet.

I look down and see the crimson liquid.

Blood.

Then I spot two men on the ground, their eyes vacant. They're dead.

My pulse ricochets in my ears, fear in my veins.

Shit. What did Rex get himself into?

Bree pulls me through another set of doors before leading me into a dark, dank alleyway.

More gunshots bellow inside the ballroom as the door slams shut.

We plaster ourselves against the wall, my lungs heaving in frantic gulps of air.

"Fuck. Where is he? He said he was going to be here! He was going to take me to the safe house," Bree whispers urgently.

I whip my head toward her, finding her scanning our vicinity, her eyes wide with terror.

"Who? What? Fill me in, Bree." She better tell me what's going on.

"I should've known it wouldn't be easy. I should've known..." she rambles, her body shaking, sweat dotting her forehead.

My years of medical training snap in on autopilot. I stand in front of her and tilt her head down so our eyes meet.

"Bree, breathe. You're panicking right now, which won't do us any good. I need you to focus on my voice and breathe. Deep breaths in. Deeper breaths out."

She follows my lead, her eyes still unfocused.

"Good. There's no one on this street right now. We're safe." I have no idea what I'm saying. "Again. Let's do this again. Then you can tell me what's going on and we'll figure it out."

Bree nods and does as I say. Her wig slides off her head and, with a frustrated growl, she grabs and hurls it onto the ground.

Eventually, her breathing evens.

Leaning closer to me, she whispers, "Bree isn't my real name. I'm not really moving. I'm on the run. Elias and Rex are helping me escape some dangerous people."

The puzzle pieces finally slide into place. The strange interactions between them. The secretive discussions. The sadness and fear in her eyes whenever she brings up her "move." How she rarely left her stateroom after Pyrgos Village in Santorini.

The near kidnapping.

My eyes widen, my pulse soaring off the charts. "Santorini?"

She nods, her lips trembling. "It was for me. The Association. They want me dead."

Shit. I've been around the Andersons long enough and have seen the newspaper headlines to know about The Association and how dangerous they are.

I survey the dark alleyway.

"We should leave then, if you're the target. We can't stay here. We're sitting ducks," I whisper.

Screams emanate from behind the closed door.

Bree vehemently shakes her head. "Elias told me to stay put. Whatever happens, to stay here. His contact is coming. W-We just have to be patient and trust him. He must have a plan."

I press my hand over my chest, trying to stem my chaotic heartbeats.

Trust Elias. The Andersons trust him—the mobster has helped them time and time again.

And what can I do by myself? Run where? And I won't leave Bree behind.

"Okay. We'll stay. But if we hear or see anyone other than your contact, we run, okay? I don't care what Elias or Rex says."

Bree nods.

Swallowing the bile rising in my throat, I grip the wall behind me, trying to find purchase. My breath throttles out of my lungs, and then the shakes start.

Shock. I can't go into shock.

"Distract me. Tell me why The Association is after you."

Box breathing, inhale—hold—exhale, four seconds each, repeat. I circle through the various exercises drilled into us in medical school. *We'll get out of this alive.* I look around for a weapon, spotting a crowbar on top of some boxes. I quickly grab it.

"The Carusos. Have you heard of them?" Bree says.

They sound familiar. Old money, secretive. I don't really follow these circles, so I don't know.

She continues, "They're the controlling interest of The Association. Few people know that because they keep a low profile."

Something in her words gives me pause, and I swivel toward her. "But how do you know this? *Who* are you?"

Bree's eyes dip down, her face crumbling in an expression I know as shame.

"My real name is Gabriella Caruso," she says, her voice so soft, I can barely hear her.

"You're part of The Association?" My feet inch back, and I shake my head.

No way. She can't be—I've been calling a monster a friend?

I remember the headlines—the mysterious organization rumored to infiltrate governments and companies to control the world. I remember how Taylor, one of my strongest, no-nonsense friends, broke down when she told us how she was brutalized at an initiation ceremony.

Apparently, the price of entry to this organization is to commit a felony of their choice. Leverage for blackmail. No one gets out once they're in.

Then there was Ethan, Alexis, and others who were impacted by these assholes.

I shake my head and stare at the quiet girl. She's part of them? The cold-blooded bastards?

"I know. I deserve to die just because I'm associated with them. But I swear, I didn't know until recently. My family kept me from it. I'm only a second cousin, a distant relative. I swear I never knew."

"B-But why would they be after you if you don't know everything?"

"I'm a hacker. When I was poking around my family's servers, I stumbled upon a firewall I wasn't supposed to spot. I started digging, making connections. Then I realized there were files, documents, org charts I didn't have access to. But Elias must have flagged something because he contacted me out of the blue and asked me to help him."

"And you said yes."

I knock my head on the back of the wall, finally understanding the picture I wasn't seeing before. I had heard from my friends that Elias has a vendetta against The Association, but no one knows why.

He must need something from Bree.

But I still have unanswered questions.

Why is Rex involved? Why is Elias so interested in this personally? Why didn't they pick a middle of the night, disappearing people method to get Bree to safety?

Being with Rex has to be high profile and risky.

Bree nods. "The more I learned from Elias about what my family did to innocent people like the Andersons, the more I couldn't let this fly. I had to do something. So I said I'd help him. And it turned out only I could help him because of my blood."

"What? What's so special about your blood?"

"I have an ultra-rare HLA type. Apparently, we're one of the few families to still have this in our DNA. Because of this, The Association hid a lot of their info on drives with a biometric lock that scans for this. But the antigen disintegrates upon death."

HLA, human leukocyte antigen, part of the immune system's fingerprint that is unique to individuals but is also heritable. It's already used in medical authentication and tissue matching for organ donations. Rare haplotypes, if I recall correctly, are nearly impossible to fake or replicate.

"You're a walking key," I exhale.

Oh shit. This is why she's so valuable. This is why Elias is risking it all by being on this cruise, by escorting her in person. "But won't your family suspect you? Hanging out with Rex on this cruise?"

She shakes her head. "The rich mingling with the rich isn't strange. And it's Rex. Everyone knows he's a party animal. No one would suspect him. I'm safe by association. At least, I thought I was. My hacker name is an alias, but I guess they must've figured it out."

And Rex, I don't know his reasons for doing this, but the man has been on the edge for a long time, tempting fate, tempting death. He blames himself for his mom's death, for the sadness his family endured for years. He thinks he has nothing to offer other than fake happiness and charm. Maybe this is his way of giving back to the world by doing something meaningful with his life.

The man has a death wish.

I'm rocked by a sudden burst of anger. I clench the crowbar so tightly my arms shake.

He knows I care about him, that I love him. I've told him to take care of himself, and he's promised me. I've tried knocking some sense into him. That he shouldn't let the past haunt his present, and what happened to his mom was a tragedy nobody wanted.

I can't save him. I can't fix him. I should've known this.

You can't change someone who doesn't put in the work.

Suddenly, quick footsteps reach our ears. We huddle behind the tall boxes, my crowbar lifted and ready.

A silhouette of a tall, muscular man in a baseball cap comes into view, his boots clomping on the wet puddles in the alley. He's holding a gun.

I don't recognize him.

Thud. Thud. Thud.

I hold my breath, readjusting my grip on the crowbar.

I can aim for his balls. Then a swift jab into his eyes before stomping on his wrists. I'll kick the weapon away and crush the windpipe. The side benefit of being a doctor is knowing the human anatomy very well. Never piss off a doctor.

"Bree? This is Jacques. Elias sent me," the man says.

Bree moves, but I grab her wrist. How do we know he's telling the truth?

She swivels her head my way, her eyes widening when she no doubt thinks the same thing.

"Cottontail," the man murmurs.

Bree's shoulders relax. She mouths, *"That's the code word. He's legit."*

Blowing out an exhale, I nod.

She steps out of the shadows, and the man scans her before approaching. His steps falter when he sees me behind her.

"She's my friend. Got caught in the crossfire," Bree says.

Jacques nods. "Not surprising. These things rarely go according to plan. But we can deal with this. Let's go. No time to waste. The Association sent assassins into the gala."

He lowers his gun and beckons us to follow him. We walk at a rapid clip, my sweaty hands losing grip on the crowbar. But something tells me the night isn't over yet, so I clutch it to my side as we hurry through the darkness.

Before we turn a corner, another shadow comes into view. Someone shorter. More slender.

"I'll take her from you," the shadow murmurs.

A woman steps into view, pointing a gun at us. Bree gasps, and I freeze.

She's young, early twenties. Clad in all black. If it weren't for her blond hair and pale skin, she'd blend into the night.

Leveling her weapon at Jacques, she motions to Bree. "Hand Gabriella over to me now before I put a bullet in your head."

Without warning, Jacques pulls Bree in front of him, like she's a human shield.

"You'll have to go through her first," he rasps.

My jaw drops. What? Isn't Jacques on our side? Isn't he supposed to protect Bree?

"I knew Elias had a snake on his team," the woman says. "If Gabriella dies, you die."

"If she dies, you get nothing. The Association always gets what it wants. And they'd take care of my family." Jacques presses the barrel of his gun against Bree's head. She whimpers and trembles in his grasp.

Shit. My mind spins a mile a minute, trying to catch up on what's happening in front of me.

Jacques is a mole. We've walked right into The Association's trap.

The woman laughs, her eyes taking on a maniacal glint. "You're funny. You think The Association will take care of your family? Like how they took care of me and Cora after they killed our mom? Our dad worked for your bosses. He was a lieutenant. And how did they repay us? They killed my mom and hunted me and my sister for years. You think your family will be spared? *Please.*"

She suddenly stops laughing, the change in demeanor unsettling. She cocks her gun. "Maybe I'll just have to take a risk. If she dies, then it's one less Caruso in this world."

"No!" I scream. "Bree's innocent. She's on your side. Don't do this!"

The woman flinches, like she's finally noticing me there.

Jacques uses the distraction to his advantage. He pushes Bree toward the woman and makes a break for it. The woman snaps to attention and fires off a few shots in rapid succession. She misses. Jacques retaliates and fires off a shot, but it's too wide.

And Bree is standing in the bullet's path.

"Bree, watch out!" I cry, pushing her away, putting myself in harm's way.

I brace myself for the pain, but out of nowhere, a large mass plows into me as the sound of a bullet entering skin and muscles reaches my ears.

Someone blocked the shot for me.

The mystery man who saved me then turns around and aims his gun at Jacques.

The man fires off a single shot, and Jacques collapses on the ground.

Bree screams, and my ears ring from the gunshot.

The mystery man groans and falls to the ground.

I quickly spring into action, first running to Jacques. Traitor or not, the doctor in me always sees to the injured first.

But it's too late.

Headshot between the eyes. Jacques is dead.

Then I dash to the mystery man's side to see where he was shot.

My heart stops when I see his face.

Because I recognize the thick hair, the beautiful gray eyes now clouded in pain.

Rex.

He threw himself over me just like he did in Pyrgos Village, and this time he wasn't so lucky.

"Rex!" I cry out, seeing his white shirt coated in red. My hands move on autopilot, unbuttoning his tux, checking to see where the blood is coming from.

Where's the wound? Is it a through and through?

He groans as ragged breaths saw out of his lungs.

"Olive," he whispers. "Thank God you're o-okay."

"I'm here. I'm a doctor. I'll save you. Don't you worry about a thing."

Tears blur my vision as I pat him down. *Please tell me it didn't hit any vital areas, please.*

A relieved sob wrenches out of me when I find the bullet wound.

A through and through hitting his shoulder, inches away from his heart.

"You're okay. Shoulder wound. Through and through. You're okay." I swipe my blurry eyes with my arm and quickly reach inside my dress to yank off my strapless bra.

I press it on his wound, keeping a firm pressure. It's the most sanitary thing I have around, considering my dress is dirty and ruined.

Blood gushes out, more blood than I'd expect from a shoulder wound.

Shit. Did the bullet nick an artery?

Fuck. Fuck. Fuck.

My pulse races, but I force myself to calm down. Focus on the patient. Stem the bleeding. Get help. Blood loss is my most pressing concern right now.

"Bree, reach into his pocket, grab his phone, and call the police." My voice is clear and I'm thankful for that, even as I'm dying inside.

Bree leaps into action.

Amid the chaos, a pair of black boots suddenly fills my vision. I glance up, finding the blond woman who nearly got us killed gaping in shock. She drops to her knees, her face crumbling when she sees Rex on the ground.

"*Casey?* Oh my God, what have I done?" she whispers.

My fingers falter, and for a moment, my world stops spinning. A low buzz rings in my ears as her words echo like the sound of a gong.

Casey? Why is she calling Rex, Casey?

Casey is Rex's best friend.

What the fuck?

CHAPTER FORTY-SEVEN

OLIVIA'S EYES SNAP TOWARD mine, her hands still on my shoulder. A myriad of emotions appear in her eyes—shock, confusion, disbelief, understanding, anger, and finally...betrayal.

"What?" she rasps. "What did she just call you?"

My eyes flutter shut and I focus on the pain in my shoulder and chest, because the alternative is unbearable.

If my Olive didn't decide to give up on me before, she sure as hell did just now.

"Casey, I'm so sorry," Ava wails, her blond hair falling over her eyes, as she grips my arm. "I-I just knew something was going on. When I saw the news of you almost getting shot and an attempted kidnapping in Greece, I knew shit was up. I pulled up all the videos of the incident. I'm not an idiot. It looked like a hit. And then, you didn't go back home and instead stayed on this cruise. It made no sense. Shit was going on. I had a feeling."

Oh, Ava. I try to pat her hand to console her. I don't blame her. Raya was brutally murdered by The Association. As her daughter, of course she would be livid.

I only blame myself for not knowing she was spiraling.

Her lips tremble, her watery eyes imploring me to believe her. "I planted a bug on your phone with my text message—"

I shudder, my fingers turning into ice. "The damn birthday card," I rasp. "I should've known."

Ava nods. "I picked up bits and pieces of what you were planning. And when I saw the photo of the woman," she glances at Bree, "I sent it to someone I knew back at home. Someone I trusted. They said she was a Caruso. Gabriella Caruso. A-And I just went nuts."

She looks up, her face wet with tears. "It's been so hard. The Association is always onto us. Cora would get scared at the most random noises. She'd jump when someone knocked on the door. We've had people tail us, take photos of us. We can never get out. It's like they want us to know they're watching, that we'll never be safe."

"It's okay, Ava. I don't blame you." Sweat drips down my forehead as I slowly sit up and lean against the wall.

Bree kneels next to me, her lips trembling. "I'm sorry, Rex. You were shot saving me."

A weak chuckle snakes past my lips. I cough.

"No. *You* saved me," I whisper.

I stare at her face, the image splitting.

Atonement. That was the whole purpose of this mission, right? Bree survived. The Association's mole is dead. I don't hear anymore gunshots, so I assume the assassins sent in earlier are either dead or apprehended.

We just need to hold out for Elias's people. I'm sure he's sending over reinforcements.

But the victory is hollow.

A chill settles in my body and I'm woozy.

Olivia doesn't need to tell me, but I know. I'm losing too much blood.

I look at the woman I love. She's quiet. Too quiet. Her gaze is focused on my wound, but I see a vein pulsing in her temple, a new tension bracketing her mouth.

She's worried, scared, and...furious.

Ava murmurs, "I just thought if I could just kill one of the bastards, maybe I'd feel better and I wouldn't miss Mom so much. I would have avenged her death. And these bastards wouldn't mess with us. It's stupid, I know. I wasn't thinking."

She buries her face in my lap, and I gently sweep my fingers through her hair.

Does any of it matter anymore? Why she did what she did? How I got hurt and how I might bleed out tonight?

How the truth...my most shameful truth I've hidden from everyone, has finally come to light?

Olivia knows now. The ugly truth. The extent of my madness.

"Olive." Her nickname comes out in a shaky exhale. "P-Please, I want to explain everything. I-I—"

"No." She shakes her head and this time, when I look down and gaze upon her face, I see tears pooling under her eyes, her nostrils flaring. "I need to focus. Need to stop the blood. Dammit, where's the ambulance?"

Quickly, she swipes away her tears with her arm. But then, her eyes fill again and she mutters to herself, "Fuck. Stop it. Stop it, Olivia."

Agony twists inside my chest, far more painful than the bullet wound. Seeing her cry for me, at me, her anger at herself for not reining in her emotions, something she was very good at before being with me, I want to bash my head against the wall or dig my fingers into my bleeding wound to show remorse.

She's innocent. I dragged her into this because I couldn't stop my selfishness, because I wanted a taste of her starlight, because I wanted the peace only she could give me.

I told myself I'd protect her.

Delusions. They were delusions of a drugged-up, sleep-deprived man.

"Olive." I shiver. Fuck, it's cold. My fingers tremble as I clutch her nape and pull her head down so our foreheads touch. "I'm sorry for not telling you. Lying by omission. P-Please, listen to me. If I don't make it—"

"Stop!" She shakes when I caress her face. "Save your energy. Survive this, then we'll talk. I-I'm so fucking mad at you—"

The wail of sirens echoes against the walls, followed by flashing lights.

Then, I see the vans, then the crowds.

Reporters, cameramen, more chaos.

Tick-tock.

Time's up.

CHAPTER FORTY-EIGHT

MY PHONE PINGS NONSTOP as I stride down the hospital hallway two hours later, after a long and exhausting interview with the police. My pulse riots, my stomach churning as I follow the nurse's instructions to get to Rex's room.

He's fine. He has to be. He wouldn't be resting in a room if he weren't.

I look at my phone, my chest tightening when I see text messages from the girls. Then there were urgent emails from the New York State Office of Professional Medical Conduct, otherwise known as OPMC.

Alexis

OMG, are you guys okay?

Belle

Maxwell just called. He told me Rex is stable. Bullet didn't hit any vital organs, but nicked an artery. He lost a lot of blood, so they did a transfusion and will keep him there for a few days for monitoring.

Alexis

Thank God you were there, Olivia!

Belle

> Maxwell said the same thing. If Olivia didn't slow the blood loss, Rex might not have made it.

I release an exhale, relief washing over me. *Stable. He's okay.* The cops wouldn't give me an update at the station.

I'm still angry. I feel stupid, but during this entire ordeal, the dominant emotion circling through me was fear. If anything happened to him, I don't know what I'd do, or how my heart could survive it.

Grace

> But are YOU okay? I mean, we saw the photos.

Taylor

> I'm going to cut his balls off when he gets back. I'll avenge you, Olivia!

I look at the photos they sent over—all taken from articles posted online.

Rex at the gala with the two models. Dancing with them. Kissing their cheeks.

Me holding Rex in my arms after he was shot, cradling him like he's precious.

Him looking desperately at me before pressing his forehead against mine.

Then there are images taken by strangers wanting their two minutes of fame. Folks must've spotted us in their pictures when we were touring the city, riding the motorcycle, strolling down the alleys hand in hand, looking very much like a couple in love. One of them even shows us kissing.

I don't think Lana shared with the girls what I told her about Rex. They must think he's toying with me, treating me like one of his flings.

The press is having a field day.

Crap. This must be why the OPMC is contacting me. They must've seen the articles and photos.

Nausea roils in my gut when I remember the chaos in the alley earlier. How the reporters hurled questions at us, the cameras flashing incessantly when they loaded Rex into an ambulance and whisked him off to the hospital.

The cops asked us to stay behind for questioning.

Greg Masters hurled questions. "Who are you to Rex? Why did you guys look so intimate just now?"

Then the vultures dove in to join the chaos.

"There were rumors of amorous noises from your office during your sessions with Mr. Anderson. What were you doing in there? Are you guys in an inappropriate relationship?"

I froze as the lights battered my senses, my blood curdling when I realized not only my heart was broken, but my career was probably over too.

The questions got more and more disruptive before the cops took us back to the station to conduct their interview in peace.

Thankfully, Lana found us and brought with her an army of lawyers, one of whom was hired by Elias. They quickly settled the rest of the inquiries, and Elias's man whisked Bree and Ava away.

Lana said we were lucky, how everything could've ended differently.

She's right.

Physically, we are fine, but mentally?

I don't know how I'm going to recover.

You will, Olivia. You treat veterans with war traumas. This too shall pass.

But deep down, what bothers me isn't the danger I escaped or the women he was dancing with. It's clear now that was a smokescreen to draw attention to himself while Bree escaped.

What bothers me the most is how Rex never told me the truth about Casey.

He says I'm his temporary forever. That he'll remember me always. That if he could be with me, he would.

But was it true? Did he really try everything?

He had plenty of chances to tell me. I asked about Casey before—more than once. I wanted to meet the person who knew Rex the best. And every time, Rex chose to lie. He said his best friend had social anxiety. Gave excuses for why I couldn't meet him. It was odd, but I thought he needed more time before letting me completely into his life.

I wouldn't have judged if he told me the truth. I would've understood, given my profession and how I sometimes heard Mia in my head.

I could've helped him because Casey was just another symptom.

A psychological one. A key one.

But I missed it.

The Velowake. The insomnia. The dissociation. I didn't connect the dots.

Just like last time.

Memories of that morning sweep into my vision as I round the corner. Rex's room is just ahead.

I remember how happy Mia was on prom night. She had on a bright red dress with tiny skulls sewn on the bodice. Mom shook her head, saying nice girls didn't dress like that, but Mia only laughed. She seemed extra relaxed that day, like a weight was lifted off her shoulders. I thought it was because of our upcoming graduation.

My dress was a simple blue gown with capped sleeves—nothing too revealing but did the job. Mia rolled her eyes when I bought it, saying it was boring. But I liked it because it was unlike hers. My neckline was high, while hers was low. My hem length was long, while hers was short.

The Lin twins looked different.

I remember thinking how awesome it'd be if I weren't walking around with someone else's face, body, and voice, differentiated only by hairstyles, clothes, or personality. If I weren't a twin, would I need to try as hard to be unique? Would I need to make myself smaller or more invisible?

And when I found her the next morning—silent and lifeless, a permanent punctuation mark in her short life—I realized I got my wish.

I was the only person with my face, body, and voice in the world now. I lost my twin, someone I should know better than anyone else.

I should've seen the signs, noticed the red flags—how she never spoke about her future, how she gave me her precious jewelry box the night before, saying she didn't want "that shit" in college, how she suddenly stopped caring about her grades.

I should've known then, just as I should've known now.

Love and emotions clouded my judgment with Mia, and I swore to myself I'd never be their victim again.

But here I am, missing *everything* with Rex.

Again.

Twisting the doorknob, I quietly open the door and enter his room. When his bed comes into view, I notice him sitting up, his eyes closed, his breathing even, like he's sleeping.

With my heart heavy, I make my way toward him.

This beautiful, complicated man.

His movie—full of twists and turns, drama and upheaval—is laden with meaning. I still want to watch it, but realize I shouldn't.

It's not good for me. *He's* not good for me. And I haven't really done anything for him.

In our month together, he didn't get better.

He didn't stop his Velowake, he didn't give himself grace for his mom's death, he hadn't stopped his reckless nature.

He almost died.

I missed the truth about Casey. It was obvious, suspicious from the get-go. But I took what Rex said at face value because I loved him and, against all common sense, trusted him. If I were apathetic, if he were just another patient, I would've spotted the red flags, the glaring anomalies.

"I'm sorry, Olive," he rasps, his eyes closed as I take a seat by his bed.

"How did you know it was me?"

His lips curve into a sad smile. "Your footsteps. The cadence of your breathing. Your smell—clean cotton and honey. Everything tells me you're here, and I don't need to open my eyes to know."

His words fist around my broken heart and twist it. Tears spring into my eyes.

I wish things were different.

"Why didn't you tell me?" I stare at my lap.

"I didn't want you to think I was crazy."

"I wouldn't."

Rex shakes his head. "*I* think I'm crazy. What normal, grown-ass adult has an imaginary friend he talks to and treats as a real person? I actually see and hear him, you know. They should lock me up in a psych ward."

Derision and scorn pulse from his voice, and it's then I notice the judgment, the same self-hatred I've heard from him before.

Deep down, *this* is the crux of his shame. He thinks he's abnormal and broken. He thinks people will leave him if they find out.

"Tell me, when did it start?"

His eyes flicker open. They're haunted and hollow.

"I told you I had a great imagination ever since I was a kid. It makes me good at what I do now...marketing. But back then, when I was scared, Mom taught me to use my imagination to beat the monster in my head—fear. She had a toy bunny called Alice, who was her friend. I had my T-Rex stuffie. His name was Kazoo." Rex chuckles, his eyes taking on a faraway look, and I can't help but smile at the image of little Rex, innocent, afraid, running to his mom because his older brothers wouldn't play with him.

"I couldn't say my middle name, Cassius, back then. So, Kazoo was born. He went everywhere with me. In my backpack when I went to school. In my bed to keep me company at night. I'd tell him everything. Whenever the twins did their thing and excluded me, I'd complain to Kazoo. When there was a storm and it got too loud, I'd hug him." Rex sighs, his jaw working, like he's gearing himself up for the next part.

"After Mom died, and I found her body with my marbles on the floor, I held Kazoo when I spoke to the police. He listened to me when I told him it was my fault. Mom's dead because I didn't clean up my toys.

He didn't judge me. Kazoo was with me at her funeral. He was there when I made the twins laugh in the bathroom. He knew I had the pebble scratching my skin, and he knew all my secrets. He never judged me."

"Oh Rex," I whisper, my eyes clouding up for a different reason.

My brave, brave Rex, the selfish hedonist was the most selfless all along. He didn't want to burden his family with his pain.

He bites his lip, his eyes shining with moisture. "One day, I lost him. We went to Coney Island, and I remember every moment of that day—Dad didn't work, which was rare. We had ice cream, and I got chocolate chip and yogurt sprinkles. All of us had so much fun, even Lana, who just turned four. But I didn't remember when I lost Kazoo. Someone must've taken him because I searched, searched, and searched, and he was nowhere to be found. I was devastated—he was my best friend. He made me brave. He helped me face the world."

Rex squeezes my hand, his thumb trailing circles over my wrist. I squeeze him back, urging him to continue.

"I was alone again. By then, the twins were cooler, and I could join their games. But it wasn't the same. I always thought I had to be on my best behavior. Had to make them laugh...to serve my purpose, you know? I was lost. Then one day, when I was looking through cookbooks, crying because I missed Mom, a little boy appeared in my room."

His eyes are steady as he asks, "Guess who he was?"

CHAPTER FORTY-NINE

"Casey," I answer. "Kazoo came back for you."

Casey. Kazoo. Cassius. The answers have been staring at me all along, and I missed them all.

It makes sense—grief and trauma do strange things to the brain. I hear Mia's voice in my head years after she passed. A little boy inventing an imaginary friend is definitely normal.

"He did. I thought he'd leave because I wasn't nuts. I knew he wasn't real. But as I grew up, he stuck around, growing up with me. He'd judge me, try to get me off the ledge. Later on, I thought he was a guardian angel sent by Mom to protect me." Rex barks out an incredulous laugh, the harsh sound seeming out of place in this sentimental moment.

Slowly, he untangles his hand from mine and looks away.

"I talk to him just like he's a real person. He looks real, sounds real. You must think I'm crazy. *I* think I'm crazy. And that's why I couldn't tell you, because why would I subject you to this? If Lana dated a man who talked to his imaginary friend at thirty-seven years old, I'd give him a piece of my mind. Stay the fuck away from my sister because that shit isn't normal. I don't sleep. I'm unstable. I can't function without caffeine pills. I'm a clusterfuck."

He scoffs and shakes his head. "Two years ago, I helped Elias with Raya, another woman hurt by The Association. I was guilt ridden when we finally caught Mom's killer. When I finally had context to the conversation I heard all those years ago. Elias took pity on me. He needed help and thought that'd give me purpose."

Shame clouds his eyes as he says, "I thought since it was an undercover mission, I should use a different name. You know, to get into the scene. I picked Casey because I'd remember it easily, because Casey's me. That's why Ava called me that. She was Raya's oldest daughter. But unfortunately, Raya died because I couldn't follow instructions. I wasn't supposed to let her out of my sight that night. But I left the hotel room for thirty minutes. I had a clingy woman situation. I thought Raya was safe. We didn't see anyone trailing us. It was simple. I was supposed to stay with her until Elias's contact met us to take her off my hands. But I was too careless, and she died."

"What would you have done if you were there? They might have killed you too."

He shakes his head. "I doubt it. I'm an Anderson. The Association wants us to join them, not to make an enemy out of us."

I release a heavy breath. That guilt—that's why he became more unstable in the last few years. It wasn't only because of his mom's death. It was because he thought he had caused another woman's death. A mom with kids. His past trauma all over again. That was the final trigger for his spiral.

Rex's gray eyes burn with desperation. "Don't you see, Olive? Why I can't be your forever? I'm a selfish bastard. If I didn't have a shred of decency inside me, I'd have taken you, swallowed you whole, savored every inch of you because being around you is...magical. It's addictive. I feel everything I thought I couldn't feel with you."

My pulse throttles, my breathing uneven. I want to throw myself at him. My heart hurts—viscerally in pain—for this wonderful man in front of me.

And I still love him, imaginary friends and all.

Yes, there are flags. Heck, I can sell red flags at this point.

But the heart wants what it wants.

Carpe diem.

Aren't certain risks worth taking? After all, how often will I meet someone who makes me feel everything?

"But Rex, I wouldn't have judged you," I begin, and he opens his mouth, no doubt to argue with me. But I stop him. "Listen, are there issues we need to address? Serious problems? Yes, definitely. But I'm a doctor. I'll be with you every step of the way. We'll find you the best team to figure out what's wrong with you. We'll put together the best treatment plan for you. We can do it together—"

"That's not all, Olivia. Far from it." A tear trails down his cheek, and he quickly wipes it away. "I've seen so many doctors over the years. Endocrinologists, neurologists, all the 'ologists,' even a shrink, who, I swear, started ranting about unresolved mommy issues."

I gnash my teeth together. I know those types of doctors—very old, barely read current literature, holds on to Sigmund Freud theories like the Bible, and well connected with a bunch of awards from back in the day.

No wonder Rex was so resistant to therapy.

Rex leans toward me, his eyes soft when he cradles my face. A thousand tiny shocks light up my skin.

This feeling with him, I don't think will ever go away.

"I *lose* time, Olivia. It started two years ago after Raya's death. I'd black out, usually at night, and wake up in another place. I'd be holding a knife or leaving a fire burning in the stove. Dangerous situations. Doctors have ruled out the usual suspects—sleepwalking and things like that. I've gotten tested for every fucking thing under the sun. They can't figure out what's wrong."

His nostrils flare, his voice urgent. "Don't you see, Olive? It's not one or two things. It's a landslide of crazy shit. I'm *literally* going out of my mind. How can I ask you to be with me? How can I do that to the woman I love?"

I gasp. My heart jolts.

Love.

"You love me?" I can't help but ask.

He hangs his head, his shoulders shaking, and delirious chuckles rip out of him. "Of course I'd fuck this up too. I shouldn't have said that. It only makes this much harder. But yes."

Rex pulls in a ragged inhale and slowly lifts his head. His dark eyes snare mine as he rasps, "I love you, Olive. So damn much. And it's because I love you, I have to save you and let you go. I can't fail another woman again."

The elation from seconds ago morphs into anger, a cannonball tearing through my chest.

I recognize the resignation in his eyes, the acceptance. He isn't even willing to work through this with me, even after I tell him I'd be with him every step of the way. How can a team function if one player gives up?

You can't change someone who doesn't put in the work.

And I won't force him to change, to love me, to choose me despite whatever hardships he's going through.

He needs to make the choice himself.

I deserve that and more.

A heavy weight presses on my chest as tears pool under my eyes. Gradually, I stand up, my breathing uneven. I lean down and dip my forehead against his.

"Thank you for trusting me with the truth. Life isn't hopeless, even if you think it is. Sometimes, we need hardships to grow. In my culture, the phoenix is a lucky animal. Beautiful, powerful, good. And if you remember, it grew out of the ashes."

I press a soft kiss on his forehead, then walk away. But before I leave the room, I pause at the door.

"Hope is there, Rex. Even if you don't see it. Get help, even if it isn't with me."

CHAPTER FIFTY

"THERE'S ONLY SO MUCH we can do. The OPMC is scrutinizing every move with this case. High profile, splashed all over the news. But I'll try my best to pull some strings," Dr. Xavier Cross, a renowned cardiologist and the only doctor I can call a friend outside of Olivia, says over the phone. He has inroads into the New York State Office of Professional Medical Conduct.

"I don't care. Dr. Lin is innocent in all of this."

"The headlines don't look good. And the photos, man," Xav murmurs.

It's been a week since Monaco, and I'm seething as I scroll through the headlines on my laptop inside The Orchid's gentlemen's club.

"Prominent NYC psychiatrist under investigation for inappropriate relationship with patient."

"Who is Dr. Olivia Lin? The woman in the center of a doctor-patient scandal with the party prince."

"How many more victims? How to protect yourself from predator doctors when seeking treatment."

"Shit!" I slam my laptop shut and stride to the floor-to-ceiling window overlooking Central Park in the private room permanently reserved for my family.

Calm the fuck down. Treat this like any other marketing crisis.

But it isn't.

"Is there anything I can do? The photos aren't that risqué." I blow out a breath.

"You were caught kissing, and she's your doctor. I honestly don't know how you can spin it. Have you talked to her?"

I close my eyes, imagining her delicate face—her soft eyes, full lips. Her smile. Her voice.

I miss her so damn much, it hurts to breathe without her.

"No," I rasp. "I haven't seen her."

Regret lanced through me the moment she walked out of that hospital room. I wanted to chase after her, to throw myself at her feet and beg for forgiveness. But I'd hurt her too much already.

Two days after the accident, I discharged myself and flew straight back to the city. Lana and Olivia also came back early. Elias told me Bree and Ava, along with her sister, Cora, were safely moved to an undisclosed location. The mobster is currently on a warpath to figure out how The Association infiltrated his team.

But Olivia and I haven't talked since the hospital. Lana mentioned Olivia was doing okay, but how could she be fine? I messed up her life.

"It's probably best you don't see her for now. The press will go nuts. I'll be in touch. Got to prep for surgery." Xav hangs up.

Desperation whips through me, and I smack my fist on the window.

I did this. I taunted her, tempted her, pulled her into my dark, chaotic web, even though I knew we were breaking the rules. Casey and Lana both warned me. I can survive scandals—I'm the king of scandals. But it won't be the same for her.

And now her career is at risk. She doesn't need to tell me, but knowing what happened to Mia, I'm sure she became a psychiatrist to save people like her sister. It's her way of atoning for missing the signs.

Just like my twisted shit with the mission.

My Olive and I are the same—both wrestling with grief and guilt. But she went about it to make the world a better place. I only wreaked more havoc.

But I need to save her career. It's the least I can do for the woman who means the world to me.

Deep in my thoughts, I don't notice the door opening until I hear someone clear his throat.

"I've never seen you like this before. Why did you let her go? Why didn't you come to us sooner?"

Startled, I look up, seeing the reflection of my quietest brother, Ethan, staring at me with sympathy in his eyes.

Lana and Maxwell already filled them in on everything.

Dad called, saying he was coming straight back to the city after finishing a volunteering session in Southeast Asia.

My siblings have been great at giving me space, but I'm guessing that ends now.

I snort and shake my head at Ethan. "You're the one to talk. You didn't let us in either—all those years secretly in love with Lexy, waiting for her to wake up."

Unbeknownst to us, Ethan was about to propose to Charles and Liam's younger sister, Alexis, after secretly dating her for a few years behind his best friend Liam's back. But when she got into a coma for eight years, Ethan silently suffered and waited, not telling a single soul about his lost love.

"Lexy was in a coma, then. There was nothing anyone could do. I didn't want Liam to feel betrayed when he was already devastated about her condition." Ethan clasps my shoulder. "You, on the other hand...you could change the situation. I couldn't control *if* she'd wake up."

Ethan clears his throat again, and when I turn around, I see a haunted glint in his eyes.

I can't imagine the torture he went through.

"She's fine now. Healthy. And married to the most boring asshole on the planet." I nudge him.

He chuckles, the fear on his face vanishing. "We don't give you enough credit. Lexy told me she thought you were a lot more sensitive than you let on."

"Is that a compliment? But seriously, imagine the devastation if I unleash that into the world. Hot as fuck. Knows how to bring on the party and fuck like a porn star. And sensitive on top of that?" Humorless chuckles escape my lips.

"Don't do that. Minimize yourself," Ethan says.

For a split second, I'm thrown back to my sessions with Olivia, when she called me out on my self-hatred. She's the first person to truly see me.

And she never judged me, never made me feel less than. She made me feel worthwhile.

Worth saving.

"I need to save her career," I murmur.

Ethan scans my face, not bothering to ask me who, because we all know. "Do you love her, Rex?"

Love.

My heart pulses at the word. It's a sentiment I once thought was impossible for me.

"More than anything."

The words are quiet, but a small weight lifts off my chest.

The truth's out there—at least I'm honest with myself this time.

It's progress. She'd say that if she were here.

God, I wish she were here.

Is what she said true? She really wouldn't judge me? She would still be with me even after everything?

No. I can't be that selfish. It'd kill her eventually to see the man she loves waste away.

"You should go to her. If there's something I learned from my experiences, life is short and unpredictable." A muscle twitches in Ethan's jaw. "Don't waste the moments you have with your loved ones, because the clock keeps ticking. You aren't guaranteed more time."

"Work with her, Rex. You deserve happiness too. I know I was hard on you when I first found out about you and Olivia. But we all can tell you've changed for the better because of her. You're opening up. That's a start." A new voice chimes in, and we look at the door, finding Maxwell standing there, his face pensive. "I had my problems with Belle. I acted in what I thought was best for her, and it hurt her. In the end, we were stronger together."

That's true. Maxwell pushed his wife away when he thought the Anderson curse was real, especially when strange accidents happened to Belle. But later, he realized he needed to fight their problems *with* her. And now they're happy together, with a cute toddler in tow.

He arches his brow as if he knows he's getting through to me. "It pains me to say this, but don't be stupid like me."

My lips twitch. "Did you just insinuate I'm smarter than you?"

"Don't push it, C."

"I'm having your words inscribed and tattooed on my skin." I waggle my brows, and he rolls his eyes.

Charles strides into the room, his blond hair shining under the overhead lights. "You know, you Anderson men are idiots when it comes to women. That's all I have to say. Complete idiots."

"Like you're a paragon of success." Another voice, and I groan.

Ryland. He even brought his laptop and what appears to be an enormous stack of papers to grade. The man looks like he's planning to camp out here for a few hours.

This must be another intervention. I'm so fucking slow today.

"He actually is, if you think about it. Once he and Tay got through the 'I hate you' phase, he pretty much sicced himself on her like a rabid dog and never let go," Steven quips as he enters the room too.

"You guys planned this, didn't you? How the hell did you know I'm here?" I grumble.

Then I hear it.

Click. Clack.

Fuck. The damn lighter.

Elias saunters in like he owns the building, his eyes roving impassively over us before landing on me. He flicks his beloved lighter in his hand—a motion which, to this day, seems random to me, and I'm pretty observant.

"The last I checked, you're not an Anderson or soon-to-be married to an Anderson." I walk back to the living room and plop down on the sofa.

The mobster smiles—or maybe it's an amused grimace, if we can call it that—and he strides to the wet bar and pours himself a drink. "Your lot can't survive without me."

"Our *lot*? What are you? Living in the eighteen hundreds?" My head hurts, and I close my eyes.

"I'm well read. What can I say? And half of you still owe me favors."

Elias Kent has a system—a favor for a favor. It's no doubt why he's powerful—lending a helping hand and collecting favors from powerful people, cashing them out to his advantage. From what I remember, Steven, Ryland, and Maxwell all owe the man favors. Charles and Ethan, I think, got freebies from him.

I can't keep track.

"Cut to the chase then. Why are you all here?" The headache quickly morphs into migraine territory.

At least I haven't had a blackout today. That's progress.

"To talk some sense into you and to tell you not to give up on yourself because we haven't given up on you," Maxwell says. "But I think you know what to do with Olivia, right, Rex?"

He walks up to me and kneels down, so we're at eye-level.

Our gazes meet, and for a moment, I'm the six-year-old idolizing my oldest brother again, wanting him to include me in his games.

His eyes soften. "People underestimate you, Rex. I know I do. But I realize that now. We Andersons carry burdens that aren't ours to carry. I think you know that. And somehow, I think you're the smartest one of us."

My breath hitches, my pulse clamoring. The tightness in my chest—a sensation I thought was normal before—suddenly releases.

The smartest Anderson. *Recognition.*

Not a party prince. Not Rex-a-Million. Not the comedian only good for making people happy.

"You really think so?" I ask, my voice rough like sandpaper.

Maxwell's lips curves in a ghost of a smile. "Tell me, what were you doing before we got here?"

"Trying to pull strings with the OPMC. Save her career."

"And why would you do that?"

My brows twitch. "Because I love her so damn much. Because this is her calling, and I need to protect it."

"And?"

The seconds pass by, the silence heavy in the room.

The throbbing pain pulses in my head, the headache unrelenting, but I mull over Maxwell's words.

Aside from saving Olivia's career, what was I hoping for?

It starts small.

My heart skips a beat, then two. A jolt of energy sweeps through my veins.

Then my chest seizes.

I need to talk to her.

I don't know how, or if, I can even fix myself, but I need to talk to her and treat her as an equal.

Despite everything, I want her to stay by my side.

"Good." Maxwell smiles, a full teeth-baring one this time.

He stands up. "Get down to business then."

Dazed, I look around the room, finding the guys nodding and smiling encouragingly at me.

My team. My family.

"You guys." My voice cracks.

Elias tosses back his drink and sets his tumbler down. "You handle getting your woman back. Let's chat about the press. We need to be creative..."

CHAPTER FIFTY-ONE

I STARE AT THE cursor blinking on my screen, then scroll through the twelve-page document I drafted last night.

CONFIDENTIAL PSYCHIATRIC OBSERVATION REPORT

Patient: Rex Cassius Wentworth Anderson

Prepared by: Olivia Lin, MD, Psychiatrist

Purpose: Observation summary, initial diagnostic impressions, and treatment recommendations for transfer of care.

Note: This report is compiled based on observation and informal clinical dialog. It is intended as a transition document for future formal care.

I. OBSERVED PRESENTING SYMPTOMS

The following symptoms were observed or reported:

- **Dissociative episodes:** Includes moments of blackouts or "lost time," particularly under emotional stress or after ingesting large doses of stimulants (e.g., Velowake). The subject had completed a sleep study in the past, and the blackout moments did not qualify under the clinical definition of sleepwalking. However, the symptoms mimicked sleepwalking and may be other forms of dissociation.

- **Internalized hallucinations:** Subject reports recurrent, life-like conversations with a persona named "Casey." The subject acknowledges this voice is not real but often experiences him as emotionally and viscerally present. Casey typically appears after the subject ingests Velowake.

- **Emotional dysregulation:** Extreme guilt, shame, and persistent low self-worth, often masked by risk-taking behavior and performative charisma. Emotional outbursts and mood swings are often noticed by the practitioner.

- **Chronic insomnia** and **stimulant overuse** (Velowake, up to 800mg caffeine daily) potentially exacerbate symptoms. Velowake is a drug currently under trials to treat narcolepsy symptoms.

- **Hypervigilance, emotional numbing, and avoidance** when discussing early trauma or recent emotional intimacy. The subject would attempt to deflect the topic of discussion using various tactics, ranging from flirtation to belligerent threats.

II. PROVISIONAL DIAGNOSTIC IMPRESSIONS

- **Complex PTSD (C-PTSD)** with **dissociative features**, stemming from:

- Early childhood trauma related to maternal loss.

- Chronic public scrutiny and unresolved survivor's guilt.

- Repressed grief around recent traumatic exposure.

- Chronic sleep deprivation, adrenal overload. Severe sleep deprivation can cause hallucination-like experiences.

- **To Rule Out: Stimulant-Induced Psychotic Symptoms**

- Velowake overuse may contribute to hallucination-like experiences and sleep deprivation-related confusion.

- Subject appears to be heavily reliant on Velowake. Recommend evaluation for drug addiction and rehabilitation protocols.

- **To Rule Out: Persistent Depressive Disorder**

- Given a baseline of low self-worth, functional impairment, and recent anhedonia.

The report goes on and on, a compilation of my notes from my past month. Casey's identity is the final clue, tying everything I've observed together.

But still, I should've seen the answers, the diagnoses, sooner. They were in front of me all along.

Jessa and Rhys from the cruise texted me after the scandal broke out. I sent them polite replies, thanking them for their concern, and told them I was fine, but really, I wasn't.

My life was upside down.

The OPMC suspended my license pending investigation after the photos and stories splashed all over the internet. They should. I deserve it. But at least, as promised, Fleur wired their donation to ADAS. They even issued a press release to announce their partnership with the organization.

Many people with mental health conditions will benefit from the funding and the attention. So at least there's that.

Frankly, I wonder if I'm cut out for this. If my motives for becoming a psychiatrist were selfish instead of selfless.

But the sad thing is, despite everything, the price I'm paying...

I can't bring myself to regret my time with Rex.

With him, I was alive. I felt seen.

I was loved for being me.

The screen blurs in front of me, my heart aching.

Then the doorbell rings.

"Coming!" Quickly wiping my tears away, I hurry out of my bedroom, brush past the small luggage I packed for my trip to LA, and open the door.

My breath freezes when I see who's standing on the other side.

Rex looks wrecked—unkempt in a way I've never seen him before.

He's unshaved, deep circles under his eyes, his hair sticking out in all directions. His plain white T-shirt stretches over his tall frame, but it's wrinkled, like he grabbed the first thing in his hamper and threw it on.

"Olive," he whispers, his familiar gaze, full of love and concern, twists the bleeding organ behind my rib cage. His gaze skates behind me to the luggage. "You're leaving?"

Swallowing the lump in my throat, I reply, "Yes. It's time for me to go home. My parents are worried sick about me."

"I see."

Ask me to stay, asshole.

He glances at his feet, his shoulders slanting. Then he looks up again.

"I regret everything."

I can't help the sharp gasp from escaping my lips. The damn tears are back again.

How can you regret us when I'm paying the price and I regret nothing?

I shake my head and step back into my apartment, hurt and anger boiling inside me.

"Fuck you." I slam the door closed.

But he holds it open.

He steps inside, his eyes widening, no doubt realizing how his words came out.

Rex tugs me against him, and I flinch before fighting back, crying, screaming, scratching his neck, his shirt, anywhere I can reach.

"Damn you, Rex Anderson. Damn you to hell!"

He tightens his hold on me, pressing my face against his chest. I hear the rapid thudding of his heart. His masculine perfume wraps me in a tender embrace, and for a second, I want to stay still, to feel safe in his arms again.

But then I remember how he pushed me away, how he said he regretted us.

"Let go of me, you asshole!" I stomp on his foot.

He hisses. "No." His hold tightens.

"You don't get to do this to me! You don't get to regret us. Regret me! You have no right!"

More fists to the back, followed by kicks to his shins.

Pained grunts reach my ears, but he doesn't let go. Instead, he presses kisses to my hair, my temples. Tears slide down my face.

Everything I've been holding onto comes crashing down.

I'm a mess. Not the perfect Olivia Lin. Just a normal girl with her heart broken and her career in the pits.

"That's not what I meant," he murmurs, his voice hoarse. "But I deserve it. Your anger. I should've protected you better. Casey warned me.

My sister warned me. Everyone fucking warned me this would happen, but I was too weak."

He drops to his knees and hugs my thighs. He looks up. "Don't you see? I couldn't stay away from you. I wanted you for myself. You made me feel alive. Loved. Accepted. You were the one addiction I never wanted to get rid of. So I stole you from your safe little nest. I made you take risks you should never have taken. Because I love you, and I'm so damn lucky you love me back."

My lips tremble as I clutch his face, finding his eyes gathering moisture.

Rex rasps, "I love you, Olivia. I'm sorry for hurting you, for pushing you away. I should've known. My Olive would stay and fight with me. We're better as a team. I shouldn't have taken the choice away from you, and I regretted it the second you walked out of the hospital room. Can you forgive me? Can you—"

He stutters and gasps, like his lungs can't draw in enough air. I hold my breath too, because I know whatever he's going to say will be monumental.

"C-Can you stay? With me? Be with me? I don't know how we'll get out of this shithole. I don't know how to fix myself...if I can even be fixed. I don't know if I'll lose my mind and push you away again. But can you stay with me? I can't live without you."

His words echo in the small foyer, heavy and ladened with meaning. My heart beats so rapidly, I think it'll tunnel out of my chest.

I know what I want to say, an impulse stronger than breathing.

But the last few weeks have exhausted me. Mentally and physically.

I deserve more. I deserve more. I deserve more.

I deserve a man who not only loves me, but will do everything he can to protect himself and our future.

The man at my feet isn't him.

If we're both broken, clinging onto each other with multiple holes in our raft, we'll sink and drown.

Releasing a ragged exhale, I step back.

"Stand up. And wait," I murmur.

I return to my room and print out the report, then I bring it back and hand it to him.

Rex's eyes widen when he sees the title page. His eyes snap to mine. "What's this?"

"Things I should've noticed. Concluded a long time ago. But, like you, I was haunted by the past and my feelings for you. I missed the signs. Rex," I step up to him and cup his jaw. His eyes flutter shut.

"You aren't broken. I think you have an addiction and you've been misled by the medical practice, which, unfortunately, happens often. Most doctors don't receive training to identify C-PTSD and dissociation. It's fairly recent when it's gotten more attention, and even then, it still isn't in DSM-5, the US diagnostic manual. It's only in the international standards."

His throat works and nostrils flare. He opens his eyes and whispers, "What are you saying?"

I give him a sad smile. "I don't think you're going crazy. I think you need the right help. It's been long overdue."

Then I step back again, my fingers tingling from the warmth of his face. A strong urge pistons through me—to run back into his arms and bask in his warmth and need for me.

It'll be easy.

But it isn't the right path.

And the new Olivia Lin isn't afraid to do scary and hard things anymore.

That includes standing up for me.

"I deserve a man who'll actively fix himself. I deserve someone who not only will put me first, but will make sure he's taking care of himself so we have the best shot at a happy forever. You need to do the work, Rex. Velowake is easy, but it isn't good for you. Indulging yourself in pleasure and alcohol will numb your pain, but it doesn't change you. Words are cheap, action is hard. You need to put in the work, then we'll talk."

My chest aches, but I know it's the right thing to do. I need to put in the work for myself too.

For the next few minutes, there's nothing but the quiet sounds of our breathing. His deep gaze roves over my face, as if he's reading my mind, my thoughts, as if he's memorizing every inch of me.

And I do the same to him. His beautiful, expressive eyes. His soft lips. The thick, rough scruff hiding his jawline.

Rex rolls his lips inward, then straightens, a new determined glint in his eyes. My report crinkles in his tight grip.

He dips his head in a curt nod. "Understood."

Then he steps out of my apartment, but before he turns away, he gives me a vow.

"You won't be disappointed."

CHAPTER FIFTY-TWO

I PULL THE BILL of my baseball cap low on my forehead as I slide my phone back into my pocket, satisfied at the email I just read from the private investigator I'd hired during the cruise.

Subject: Mission Accomplished (Almost)

Rex,

The item you asked me to track down has been located. Finally.

I'm confirming the details and ensuring the seller's not trying to pull a fast one, but so far, everything checks out.

Do I have your green light to move forward with the transaction?

Let me know. Preferably before they change their minds or vanish into the ether.

Regards,

Emerson

I, of course, told him he has carte blanche. Anything he needs to get the item to me.

Emerson Clarke is one of the best in the business, known to be snarky, discreet, but professional when needed. He helped Grace and Taylor unravel some sensitive issues a few years ago that could've derailed their lives.

A cool spring breeze drifts across my skin as I stop in front of the building housing Eataly in the Flatiron District. A faint whiff of basil and garlic wafts from the vents. Moisture clings to the air after the light showers this morning.

End of April in the city is beautiful.

At the recommendation of my new psychiatrist, Dr. Evan Sturgeon, who specializes in post-traumatic stress disorders, therapy isn't only about talking and medication. It's also about getting in touch with yourself and doing things that bring joy. Even if the joy is tinged with pain.

Considering how much I've improved in the last three weeks, the doctor knows his shit.

This is why I'm about to walk into a cooking class taught by none other than Giacomo Valenti.

Olivia was right. I've been officially diagnosed with PTSD since, as Olivia said, C-PTSD isn't officially recognized in the States yet because it isn't in the diagnostic manual. But Dr. Sturgeon said practitioners up to date with the newest science and the international standards will agree that's what I have—C-PTSD with dissociative features.

Disassociation because of trauma, sleep deprivation, and the fucking Velowake. Apparently, I had unresolved PTSD from Mom's death, which triggered hallucinations in the form of Casey. Things took a turn for the worse after Raya's death. My mind then played tricks on me with the blackouts. The doctor said my consistent lack of sleep and heavy reliance on the Velowake I got from the black market deteriorated my condition, since both could cause these symptoms.

Who'd have thought it was that simple?

It's a travesty no one made the connections until now, but then I wasn't completely honest with my doctors before. I didn't want to shed my mask or talk about my past. I was ashamed of my Velowake usage too—a grown-ass adult who needed pills to function.

It'll be a long journey to undo the damage I've done to my mental and physical health, but we have a plan. I'm currently knee-deep in the first and second phases of a three-phase treatment plan.

Phase one is to wean me off Velowake—a gradual tapering off to avoid relapses. Dr. Sturgeon prescribed bupropion to help with the withdrawal process and to stabilize my mood, then melatonin for nighttime to help with my sleep.

Phase two happens concurrently with phase one and is trauma therapy focused—EMDR, cognitive and dialectical behavioral therapies, including reframing and positive self-talk strategies to deal with my recurring nightmares of Mom and Raya's deaths. This includes journaling, rewriting my nightmares into something less distressing, like talking back to the little kid inside me who never forgot, telling him he's okay because I'm okay.

Then there are the affirmations.

I'll never forget, but I'll learn to live with the memories instead of inside them.

They'll remind me how precious life is and how I should make the best of it.

Eventually, we'll move to phase three, which is forward looking—going to support groups if I'm ready, finding a passion outside of marketing I can devote my time to, something meaningful, things of that nature.

A few minutes later, a small group of us hovers over our stations in the kitchen.

Valenti, the smug bastard, strolls in, all smiles and charm. He falters when he sees me and looks at his clipboard, clearly confused because my name isn't there.

He frowns. "Mr. Anders—"

"Casey. Casey Wentworth."

He blinks a few times. I return with a wink of my own. "Just call me Casey."

Valenti cocks his brow, then shrugs. "Welcome to the class, Casey."

Whispers sweep through the room. I know people recognize me. A baseball cap and a plain T-shirt won't hide my identity, but it's obvious enough I'm pretending *not* to be Rex Anderson today.

It's my way of honoring the version of me I've always hid—raw, vulnerable, and truthful.

My conscience.

Casey has appeared a few times in the past month, usually to give me his usual snarky opinions about how I fucked it up with Olivia. But just as my brilliant Olive predicted, and Dr. Sturgeon later confirmed, Casey's appearances, along with the blackouts, have decreased ever since I started sleeping more and cutting back on my Velowake use.

Lana told me Olivia is still in LA, staying away from NYC until the scandal dies down.

We haven't spoken.

She's right—talk is cheap, actions are much more valuable, and I want to reach out to her when I've put in the work and made good strides. To show her I'm serious about my health, about her, and our future.

But I miss her every day.

Every night before I go to sleep, I fight a battle to stop myself from calling her just to hear her voice. Or, if she doesn't speak, the reassuring sounds of her breathing and the idea we're connected somehow.

I've started dreaming about her—how she argued with me on the sun deck, the way she screeched when I drove too fast on the F1 racetrack. I'd wake up with my heart clenching, but also more determined to get better.

Technically, Dr. Sturgeon recommended I avoid new relationships during the first year of my treatment. But he conceded upon evaluating my history and symptoms that my case appeared to be more aligned with a misuse of and dependence on Velowake, not a full-blown clinical addiction, which is more of a compulsion and a craving. He said that if I reach out to Olivia, I should take things slowly and be cognizant of my mental health.

I promised him I would take his advice seriously.

And deep down, I don't consider Olivia and me to be a "new" relationship. We took a pause in our existing one.

"*Buongiorno*, class. Welcome to the only Italian pasta class you'll ever need to take." Valenti claps and the small group cheers.

I smirk. The damn cheeky bastard.

"Today, we'll make a four-course meal. The starter will be *bruschetta al pomodoro,* where you'll learn how to perfectly grill the bread for the tomatoes, garlic, and basil toppings. Then, we'll have the pasta course of tagliatelle served with *ragù alla bolognese.* Next will be the main course of *pollo alla cacciatora,* and finally, dessert, which is my special boysenberry panna cotta with light cream."

Assistants hand us the ingredients, and we follow his instructions to make the starter. I have to admit, because I was thoroughly distracted in Tuscany and pissed off at his flirting with my woman, I wasn't paying much attention then.

But the asshole is actually a good teacher. He interlaces humor into his demonstration, goes through the steps slowly, giving tips borne from his experience that I file away for later, because they're damn useful.

Peace I haven't felt in a while settles over me as I slice and dice the ingredients, my hand moving in tune with the knife. I'm thrown back to the happy moments I treasure—cooking with Mom, then later on cooking by myself when I miss her. The act gives me joy.

I chuckle at his horrid jokes when we finish the starter and prep for the pasta course.

He saunters over, a rolling pin in hand, and stops next to me. "Casey, eh?"

Smirking, I don't answer him. But I do have a question—a favor. Something I hope will help win Olivia back.

"I'd like to change the pasta course for me, if possible."

Valenti arches his brow again. "Oh? What's your proposal?"

"Teach me the *pappardelle al cinghiale* and I'll get you in the door to teach classes at The Orchid."

His eyes widen, his mouth gaping. I bite my cheek to keep from smiling. It doesn't take a genius to figure out what he's thinking. The Orchid is invitation-only. No money or connections can buy entrance. Only the elite of the elite walk through those doors. It's a place where deals are made and power is exchanged.

And I just gave him a way in.

Valenti shakes himself and clears his throat. "Is this for your beautiful friend? The lady doctor?"

Scanning his face, I notice only curiosity, not malice. Not like some folks who want a sound bite from me to sell to the gossip rags.

I nod. "Yes. It's her favorite dish."

"Hm." He rocks on his heels and taps his chin. "I think we have all the ingredients we need for that dish here. Do you want to do it the easy way or make from scratch?"

"The latter." I think back to what Mom said about infusing love into her dishes, hoping the people who eat it later would feel it. There's no shortcut to this.

"It'll be done in two parts. Today, we marinate the boar, and then we wait overnight. And just for you, I'll clear my schedule tomorrow so we can finish."

"Lucky me." I'm sure getting into The Orchid has nothing to do with it.

The bastard winks. "They say the way to a man's heart is through his stomach. I call bullshit. The way to *everyone's* heart is through their stomachs. With delicious Italian food—*my* Italian food. With my help, you'll win your woman over. No problem."

Chapter Fifty-Three

Dear Mia,

Happy 30th birthday. I've written this letter in my head a thousand times. They say, practice what you preach, but they don't tell you how hard it is.

Grief is strange.

For some people, it's an explosion—fast, chaotic, over in a flash.

For others, it's a slow simmer—gradual, escalating torture of being slowly burned alive.

That's me. The latter.

For the last month, I've been seeing a therapist. Her name is Marybeth Connors. She's a mentor and someone I trust. I told her everything. About you. About the silence in our house since you left. About our parents still processing their grief but not saying it aloud, because that would make it real. About how I tried to live my life for both of us, to be the perfect daughter because they had already lost you. About how I buried myself in work because I didn't want to miss the signs again.

About how I wanted to save everyone.

THE BACKS OF MY eyes burn as I sit at my parents' dining room table and scribble a letter to my dead twin, something Marybeth recommended in our last session. Some people are better at saying their thoughts out loud. Others are better at writing them down.

I told her the truth I hadn't admitted to anyone until the cruise.

Deep down, I was unhappy. I wasn't truly living. I was *performing* a life I thought others needed me to live.

In the past, Olivia Lin didn't really exist. She was your twin. She was our parents' dutiful daughter. She was a rising-star psychiatrist who had it all together. She played it safe. Always.

But that stops now.

Rex taught me that. With him, I felt like I could breathe for the first time.

I felt worthy of being me.

Marybeth didn't judge me, and I didn't expect her to. I've sat across from patients and listened to their darkest confessions before, knowing life is rarely black and white. Sometimes, good people make the wrong choices.

The condemnation came from within me. I broke my own rules.

I should've recused myself the moment my emotions changed flavor, when they became more than professional concern. But I didn't.

I should've protected Rex by finding him the proper care so he could get the diagnosis and treatment sooner. I was blinded by my emotions.

Loving someone doesn't mean fixing them. Healing through pain doesn't happen through control.

But that's life. We all make mistakes. And that's okay.

I don't regret loving him though, and I think if you're up there looking down at me, you are probably cheering him on because he's a daredevil, just like you.

I wouldn't be surprised if you sent him to me.

A chuckle escapes my lips as my tears dot the paper. I imagine Mia laughing when Rex scared the shit out of me after I leaped off the cliff in Dubrovnik. Or how she'd snicker when she saw me white-faced, stumbling out of the racecar after Rex cosplayed as an F1 driver.

The last two months have been painful, but necessary. I'm finally letting myself feel everything I used to bury.

Anger—because you left me behind without telling me why. Not even a note, Mia? Really? You didn't think I would be a mess with you gone? You were my best friend.

Guilt—because we were always together before. I should've known something was wrong. But as twins, you were probably as good at hiding as I was. I wish you would've talked to me.

Grief—because of all the milestones you'll miss. The tattoo I'll be getting someday. Joining Lexy to swim with sharks in Hawaii for her bucket list. Falling in love. Getting married. Having kids. And later, grandkids.

Acceptance—because I know I'll miss you forever, but I don't need to carry your absence like a punishment.

I have to let go and just...be.

You'll always be a part of me, but I need to live the part you couldn't.

So, this isn't just goodbye.

This is me choosing to keep going.

Choosing to be me.

I'll miss you and love you forever, but it's time.

It's time for Olivia Lin to shine.

Always your dearest sister,

Olive

Sometimes, there is no why in life, or if there is, the answers are hidden. Sometimes, grief and acceptance are best friends, sitting quietly side by side, and your only choice is to survive and thrive.

Sniffling, I wipe away my tears and stuff the letter into a plain envelope, which I'll take to the cemetery later. The ache deep inside my chest lessens a little.

My phone buzzes on the table, and then it rings.

Snatching it up, I glance at the caller ID. A video call from Lana.

"Happy birthday!" she screams into the receiver when I pick up. "Thirty years old. Welcome to the cool club!"

I snicker, my earlier melancholy vanishing. "You look like you're going to a New Year's Eve party."

The woman even has on a gold cone party hat and a noisemaker.

"I would be flying over and taking you to party in person if it weren't for—ouch!"

Five more heads pop onto the screen, all of them wearing the same identical party hats. They look like they're gathered at the Anderson Estate.

"Lana! Seriously, zip it." Taylor playfully smacks her on the head.

"So violent, sorry, Lana. Tay is only graceful in the ballet studio." Grace grins at the now scowling Lana.

"What's going on?" My brows furrow. "I'm confused."

The girls swivel their attention toward me, their eyes comically huge.

"Nothing. Absolutely nothing." Alexis blinks as if a stray lash fell into her eye.

Suspicious. They're up to no good.

"We want to say happy birthday and tell you we're thinking about you today," Belle says. "We miss you on our girls' nights."

"You just want to party it up without little Levi." Millie snorts and plops a gummy bear into her mouth. She loves those things, and Ryland buys them in bulk for her.

Belle grabs a fistful of gummy bears and chucks a few at her. Millie squeals.

"What are your plans for today? Hope you're doing something nice for yourself," Lana says.

"Going to visit Mia at the cemetery, then spend my day at a bookstore. I might even try to squeeze in a facial."

"You coming back soon?" Grace asks. "Any updates from OPMC?"

A bowling ball settles on top of my chest. The last update was this morning via email, a simple *"Dr. Lin, we have concluded our investigation and will rule on your case soon."*

It's nerve racking, not knowing if I even have a career to return to.

I shake my head. "No. Not yet. I think I need to find a Plan B. Go into academia like you, Millie. But who would want a disgraced faculty on their roster?"

"Things will work out. If I believe it, who's to say it isn't true?" Alexis quips.

I smile. This is one of her many positive mottos and I love her for it.

"You're right."

"Keep your chin up," Lana says. "I have a feeling *everything* will work out just fine."

The mysterious, secretive smile is back, and once again, my hackles rise.

"What are you hiding, Lana?"

She jolts, her face flushing, and the girls groan.

Taylor grabs the phone from her.

"Oh look, uh, we're late for an appointment," she stammers. "Gotta go. Love you. Happy birthday, girl."

Then the line goes dead.

What the hell?

Befuddled, I stare at the black screen when I hear footsteps behind me.

Ma and Ba idle in the doorway, smiling at me. Ma, her salt-and-pepper hair tied back in a low ponytail, holds a small steaming bowl in one hand and a plate in the other. Ba, standing tall and dignified as always, clutches a red envelope.

"Happy birthday, sweetheart," Ma says, and sets the bowl and the plate onto the table.

I look at the bowl first.

Noodles. In particular, *rou zao mian*, otherwise known as minced pork noodles.

My eyes mist with tears because I understand. I hear what they aren't telling me.

"You have to eat on time," Ma whispers, her eyes tearing up, "and it's not a birthday without noodles, right?"

In our culture, eating noodles on your birthday means longevity. But this isn't just noodles, she fixed me minced pork noodles.

"I don't know how to make that fancy Italian dish you like, but I looked it up online. Boar ragu is like our minced pork, or at least, it looks like it."

"Ma." My voice shakes as I stare at the small bowl. Dammit, why am I so emotional?

She squeezes my shoulders and slowly enfolds me in a hug. "I'm sorry, sweetheart. Your ba and I love you so, so much, and we miss your sister a lot. But we never realized how much we've hurt you by not recognizing you as you. We're lucky to have you, our wonderful daughter."

"But aren't you disappointed? The scandal? I might not be a doctor anymore."

Ba harrumphs, and I glance at him through my blurry vision. He takes off his glasses and wipes his eyes. "Doctors are a dime a dozen. My Olivia can do anything she wants."

A teary smile curves my lips, and I blot my tears with a tissue. "That's not what you said when I graduated from Harvard."

"I was young then. I didn't know any better."

I arch my brow.

"Fine. Not young, young. But we never stop learning, Olivia, you hear me? We make mistakes, fall down, and we get back up. Your ma and I will never stop believing in you. We are your mountain. We will block the winds and storms. You are always welcome here."

He shoves the red envelope into my hands. "We didn't know what to get you for your birthday. Use the money to do something nice for yourself. Something you like."

"Thank you." I stand and throw my arms around them.

From their gasps, I know I've surprised them. Physical affection isn't their thing, but I know they love just as hard.

Ma murmurs, "I fixed you some cookies too. Not almond. You tell me which ones you like the most, and I'll make more."

I glance back at the table. The steaming noodles and the plate, which I now see, holds an assortment of cookies, from chocolate chip to gingerbread.

With my heart full, I say, "The noodles look delicious. And the cookies look perfect. I have a feeling I'm about to find some new favorites."

— ◆ —

Three hours later, I walk down the quiet paths inside Mountain View Cemetery, holding a large paper bag carrying the things I need for later.

The weather is balmy. I'm thankful the skies are overcast, so I won't be subjected to the wonderful but hot Southern California sunshine. The soft breeze caresses my skin and I brush my hand through the knots in my hair before giving up. Letting my hair down means it'll get messy, and I accept it because it feels good. Birds chirp overhead, and a squirrel dashes up a tree when he sees me approaching.

A few minutes later, I'm in front of Mia's grave, a place I can count on one hand how many times I've visited in the last twelve years. I read the words inscribed on her marker.

Mia Shuwen Lin

Beloved Daughter, Sister, and Friend

Carpe Diem, Live Every Day Like It's Your Last

I wasn't ready before...not like I am now.

Slowly, I set down my bag and pull out a checkered picnic blanket. Then I take out a glass container and open the lid, revealing a small slice of vanilla cake with rainbow sprinkles. Her favorite. I prefer chocolate but today isn't about me. It's about us; the end of one journey and the beginning of another.

A sad, bittersweet smile tilts my lips as I take out a small metal can and place my letter inside.

Grabbing a lighter, my pulse ratchets up as I look around, because what I'm about to do is probably illegal. Wildfires are a real threat in California.

But sometimes, it's okay to break the rules.

Not recklessly. Not carelessly.

But because some moments in life are meant to be felt fully.

Because sometimes, living fully means bending the edges.

Suddenly, I hear the crunching sounds of twigs snapping behind me. The distinct, familiar footsteps. The heated presence and scorching intensity.

I freeze, goosebumps forming on my arms.

"My naughty Olive, what will Smokey Bear say when he sees you starting fires in the wild?" a deep voice says.

I smile.

CHAPTER FIFTY-FOUR

My heart jolts to life like it's been hit with a defibrillator when Olivia turns around and smiles at me.

Smiles. A sweet, beautiful smile.

She's bewitching, standing there, a breeze rustling her sleek black hair and her simple purple sundress.

I'm hit with an urge to kneel at her feet, because what did I ever do to deserve her?

What did I do to deserve her precious smile, her kindness, and her love?

I thought she might tell me off or give me the silent treatment. Both are the least of what I deserve for hurting her, for not trusting her enough with my secrets.

But instead, she's giving me grace and understanding.

"Olive," I rasp, my hands behind my back, the thick straps of the paper bags I'm holding digging into my flesh. "Happy birthday."

"How did you know I'm here?"

"A little bird may have told me." Five little birds, to be exact. I think back to my sisters slash sisters-in-law's faces when they video called me earlier. All of them clamored to give me advice on how to win Olivia back.

"Buy her books. Lots of them!" Grace says.

"The smutty ones." That's Millie.

"What's smut?" I ask, and the girls cackle.

"Men. I swear, if we didn't need you to procreate, you'd be extinct," *Taylor mutters. "Just trust them. You'll benefit from the smut."*

"I'm sure your presence is the best present." Alexis beams. Damn it, I hate to admit it, but Ethan has good taste. His wife is a good cookie, unlike the rest of these...hyenas.

"You have a present for her, right? You better not show up empty-handed, or else." Lana scowls at the camera.

Olivia's eyes widen, then she grins. "The girls. They knew you were coming."

"Maybe. I needed to get info somehow."

"But how did you know I would be *here*?"

I shrug and kick the grass, my skin heating. "They told me you were going to the cemetery but didn't know which one. I may have gone to your childhood home and had a chat with your parents. Where I told them the PG version of what happened, apologized for torpedoing your career, and then declared my undying love for you. I think it worked since they gave me the address. But I honestly couldn't tell. They have really good poker faces."

When she doesn't respond, I look up.

Her shoulders shake, and she covers her mouth with her hand.

My chest seizes. I'm second-guessing everything. *Is she mad? Did I do this all wrong?*

But then I see the laughter in her eyes.

My beautiful, whiskey-colored eyes.

"You're really going to make me say it, aren't you?" I mutter, my lips twitching.

Olivia takes a deep breath and folds her hands in front of her like she's interviewing to be an etiquette teacher. Her face is wiped clean of whatever amusement I glimpsed just now.

She cocks her brow as if to say, *what are you here for?*

My stomach turns and my palms sweat. I hand her one of my bags, and she stares at me quizzically.

"I've been seeing a psychiatrist—taking meds, going to therapy, doing all the work, as you like to say. It'll be a long journey. Lots of therapy. But in one week, I'll be completely off Velowake. We're tapering off slowly, and while it was hard initially, things are better now. I sleep five hours most nights."

She clutches my bag to her chest, her eyes widening. Olivia has seen me at my lowest. She's seen my monsters and how deeply their talons are embedded in my skin.

She knows it hasn't been an easy path.

"I still have nightmares. I still think about Mom and the what-ifs. I still regret not having done everything I could for Raya. I still reach for my half-empty bottle of Velowake, thinking if I just take one pill, I can stay awake and not live through the nightmares. But I don't. I stop myself, and you know why?"

An urgency fills me—the need to be closer to her, to touch her, to feel her warmth against my body. I take a step toward her, and another, the pull between us unbearable.

Her chest rises and falls, but she remains quiet and still.

Slowly, I take her hand, closing my eyes as our skin touches. Euphoria washes over me from the simple contact, my nerves lighting up one by one.

"Because," I slowly open my eyes and stare at her, "I want us to have a future together. I want, no *need*, you in my life, Olive. You're my star, my sun, my gravity. You're the spotlight I want to stare at for the rest of my life. I love you so, so much, more than I'd ever imagined possible."

Her slender throat works, and she rolls her lips inward, clearly becoming emotional.

I push through. "I want to be healthy for you and also for me, so we can have a long, long life together. So I can enjoy the ride with you—all the ups and downs, all the laughter, all the fights. I'll remember them all, and while there'll be some moments I'll rather forget, I'll treasure every second, because you're with me. Because with you, everything is worth it. Every moment is precious."

I pull out a package from the bag I'm still holding and hand it to her. She sets down her bag and takes it. She cocks her brow.

"Open it," I murmur.

She tears the wrapping paper and gasps when she sees the album.

A photo album, to be exact.

"You once told me you thought you were a shadow. That you blended into the background and no one saw you. But you were wrong. You shine the brightest, and I've always seen you."

"Rex," she whispers as she flips through the book, which contains all the photos from my secret stash.

There are photos of her gazing at the caves in Mykonos, her staring into the ocean on the sky deck, a snippet of her on the phone in her office when she wasn't looking. Hundreds of little moments I stole from her, thinking I wouldn't get to experience the joy of having a lifetime with her.

I'm so glad I was wrong.

"Will you take me back, my bewitching, beautiful Olive?" I ask, a clamoring rising in my chest.

"But you shouldn't be in a new relationship now, right? At least for a year. I don't want to derail your progress," she whispers.

I shake my head. "You make me stronger, Olive. And we aren't new, are we? We love each other. We've gone through things no couple should ever experience. But we'll take it slow. I just want you by my side again...if you'll still have me."

Her breath hitches and her small frame trembles. This time, it's not from laughter.

Please take me back, Olive. We're stronger together.

She runs and throws her arms around me.

Her nose digs into my neck as I wrap my arms around her, relief flooding my insides.

I'm probably holding her too tightly, but I don't care. This feeling—her warm weight, her sweet cotton scent, the way her face fits perfectly in the crook of my neck.

I never want to lose it.

"I love you, Olive. I love you more than anything in my life. I love you so, so much."

"I love you too, Rex. I'm so proud of you," she whispers and pulls back to look at me. "And I'll be by your side. This journey you're on...you aren't alone."

Her fingers trail over my hair, which I know is due for a cut, then to my freshly shaven face—I didn't want to look too shabby in front of her parents.

She doles out a watery smile, and I grin. Damn butterflies are flapping their wings inside me.

"Will you do something with me?" she asks.

"Anything."

Olivia nods. She picks up a lighter, sparks a flame, and lights up the edge of the envelope before putting it back into the metal canister.

My chest pinches when I see the quiet grief on her face as she stands. "For Mia?" I ask.

"Yes. It's a letter—a farewell to a chapter. It's long overdue."

It's time for me to let go too.

I pull the marble out of my pocket and toss it in the canister too.

Her eyes widen and I say, "It's time for me to let the past stay in the past too. The marble won't melt, but the sentiment is the same."

We stare at the flames together, watching the letter burn to ashes, tendrils of dark smoke wafting into the air.

"I never explained to you why I was burning photos for Mia in Las Fallas, did I?"

"No. But I have an inkling."

I did some research a while back, and it turns out in her heritage, the living can give the dead gifts by burning them. Those gifts are usually made of paper, but tradition dictates once they are burned, the dead will receive them like real objects to use in the afterlife.

"I think it's a beautiful sentiment." I link our fingers together, and she leans against me. "I bet your sister appreciates it."

"I hope so. I'll always miss her, but I won't live in the past anymore."

Pride sweeps through me as I press a kiss on her hair. "She wouldn't want you to."

Then a thought snaps into me. "Shit. I just gave her my marble, didn't I?"

Olivia laughs, the sound bright and beautiful, and I chuckle too.

"I'm sure she appreciates it. She'll probably find your mom and gossip about you." She snickers.

Facing the grave marker, a new weight settles on my chest.

But this is a good weight—a responsibility, a promise.

A vow.

"Mia, I'm Rex, the man who loves your sister very much."

Olivia's breath hitches, but I continue, "I'm far from perfect, but I'm damn lucky your sister loves me back. I'll treasure her, protect her, love her for all my remaining time on this earth. We'll have adventures, big and small, and we'll have a fulfilling life. If you're up there, looking down on us, don't worry about Olive anymore. I got this from now on."

"Rex," Olivia whispers, her eyes glistening.

Gently, I wipe the moisture from her eyes and motion to the bag at her feet. "Another small present."

She blinks a few times, like she's noticing the bag on the ground for the first time.

Grinning, she looks inside and fishes out a gift-wrapped box. Like a little kid on Christmas, she gleefully opens it, and I can't help but laugh.

Her eyes snap up to mine. "Rex? Is this what I think it is?"

I nod. "Your sister's camera. I found it. A collector bought it off the black market. Your film is still inside."

Her lips tremble as she stares at the camera, her fingers grazing the body. "Th-Thank you. You have no idea how much this means to me."

"There's more. Keep looking."

She arches a quizzical brow, then pulls out an envelope from the bag.

Her eyes widen when she sees the return address. Her hand flies to her lips.

"It's okay. Everything will be fine. Just open it."

With shaky fingers, she carefully opens the envelope and pulls out a single sheet of paper.

I know what's inside since Xav gave me a heads-up earlier. He told me I owe him a big one for giving me the letter instead of mailing it directly to Olivia.

It's the ruling for her case from the OPMC. They've cleared her and reinstated her license. She's free to practice again.

"How?" she whispers, her eyes roving over the text like she can't believe it.

"A technicality. You sent me an email to end our doctor-patient relationship. While it isn't as binding as an agreement, it shows a digital timestamp of the end of our professional arrangement. And the email was dated before the photos in Monaco."

"B-But, we still had s-sessions?"

"I wouldn't volunteer that info if I were you. Your friend Rhys and I had a chat, and while we don't see eye-to-eye on things, he says he won't say anything because you're a damn good doctor. Then the fucker said if I make you cry again, he'd go to the committee and say I extorted you or some shit."

She slowly looks up. "Th-That's it? I get to practice again?"

I nod.

"Thank you!" She jumps up and down. I grin and pull her into my arms.

"You're the best doctor I've ever met. As long as you don't fall for another patient again, I think we're good."

"Shut up."

"But I don't think you'll ever meet another patient as sexy and irresistible as me." Leaning down, I whisper in her ear, "Rex-a-Million, a million orgasms for the only woman I love."

She shivers in my hold and heat courses through my body. I cup her face, my thumbs grazing her cheeks, needing to taste her lips again.

I've been deprived, and I intend to claim.

But then, I remember my last surprise for her.

Using all my remaining willpower, I disentangle from her and pick up the last bag a few feet away.

"One last present for you."

"What? Really? I'm already the happiest woman on earth right now," she says as she takes the bag from me and looks inside.

The smile freezes on her lips and her head whips up.

"*Ni chi fan le ma?* Have you eaten yet, dear Olive?"

Her lips part as recognition sparks inside them. She told me her family used to say this instead of I love you, and I want to take part in the tradition.

I want to be part of everything that is her.

"*Pappardelle al Cinghiale*, your favorite dish. Took me ten tries to get it right. Damn Valenti was so smug when I called him after the fifth failed batch. Who knew boar was so difficult to marinate?"

Olivia presses her hand to her chest.

"I'm sure it's the best pasta in the world," she murmurs, her voice thick, as I close the distance between us.

"Damn right it is. Even better than Valenti's, and you know why?"

She cocks her head, and I smile.

"Because it has my love in it."

Olivia grins, then her eyes take on a saucy light. "But what if I tell you pasta's no longer my thing and my new favorite food is the meat lover's pizza?"

I freeze, then throw my head back and laugh when I think about how she bluffed me on the cruise.

"Just kidding," she says. "I still love the *pappardelle*."

"And you'll only get your meat from me now." I growl and pull her against me.

Then I finally kiss her. Kiss the woman who's taught me to be brave and to choose love not because it's safe, but because it's worth the risk. The woman who's shown me healing is messy, and it's okay. The woman who's accepted me, flaws and all, and made me face my fears.

The woman who's taught me the meaning of true love.

As she melts into my embrace, our lips tangling, our kiss quickly spinning out of control, a scorching heat flows through my body, searing into my muscles and bones.

Love. So much love.

And I'm finally home.

EPILOGUE PART ONE—OLIVIA

Six Months Later

"Olive, you're so good at this. Fuck yes!"

Pleasure rolls through me as Rex fists my ponytail and rams his dick into my mouth. My mind is mush and I relax my throat, taking him in deeper, feeling every thick inch of him sliding in and out of me. When he thrusts harder, I gag and tears spring into my eyes.

"Look at me, sweetheart."

I'm in a strange space—like an out-of-body experience. I barely remember how I got here. How one moment, I was stressed about the last-minute preparations for the culinary therapy center opening ceremony in a few hours, and the next thing I know, Rex has me completely naked on my knees inside our shared apartment on the Upper West Side.

Dazed, I blink at the man I love and take in his appearance—his brown hair perfectly styled with just the right amount of rakish dishevelment, his scruff perfectly groomed, and that hot body clad in a bespoke navy suit.

Sex. God.

A muscle pulses in his forehead as he twists his lips into a smirk.

"There you are, Olive," he rasps as he tunnels his cock faster into my mouth.

I swirl my tongue against him with each glide, tasting his addictive saltiness, and his eyes roll back.

"Fuck, that's good. Shit." He grips my hair tighter, and I moan. "Deep throating my cock like a good girl."

Then I do something that used to give me pause but now sends a thrill through my veins.

I bite him. Slightly, just enough to earn me a pained hiss.

I don't want to be a good girl today. I want to be his naughty, filthy girl.

Rex growls, his stare burning into my skin. He pulls himself out in one swift motion and tosses me face first onto the bed.

"Ass up. So that's how it's going to be, huh? My filthy slut needs to be punished?"

Whimpering, I wiggle my ass in the air. I'm leaking all over the place, his dirty talk sending me into the stratosphere.

"Shit. Fuck me. Look at that pretty ass."

Slap!

I cry out at the initial pain, which softens into unending pleasure as he massages my backside.

He slaps me again, each stroke ending with him sliding a finger inside my dripping pussy.

"Rex, please," I beg, delirious with want.

Arching my ass up higher, I flinch when he grabs my face and turns it to the side.

I love it when he manhandles me.

"Look at you, Olive. My good doctor is horny, depraved. Look at you all naked on the bed on all fours, your face drunk with pleasure. You need my cock inside you like a good slut, huh? Fuck, you drive me wild."

Moans tumble out of me when I see our reflection.

Me completely naked under his fully clothed.

The possessive way he has my throat in his hand.

The unhinged, feral gleam in his eyes.

But this time, I know that glint is from the pleasures of sex, not from Velowake or his C-PTSD. He's been doing so well for the past six months. The hollows under his eyes have disappeared.

"Give me that cock, Rex. I need it." I twist my nipple, my legs spasming with the need to come. "Stuff it in my tight cunt, ram it in."

"Shit!" he roars and slams inside me in one hard thrust.

A cry rips out of me as pain and pleasure twist into something more intense. Rex gives me no break, no mercy. He rams inside me at breakneck speed.

"Y-Yes. Yes. Yes," I chant with each thrust, the pleasure electrifying me in pulsing waves. He brings me to the edge in seconds, his dick grazing a spot that makes me see stars.

My muscles seize; my lungs struggle to breathe. I fist the comforter, trying to hold off the orgasm approaching as quickly as a rocket barreling toward space.

Then I hear him spit, and he inserts a finger into my tight rosebud. My mouth drops open in a silent cry. The foreign sensations only add to the burgeoning pleasure.

"I'm going to take you here, Olive. We've worked hard at it for the last few weeks, haven't we? Make that pretty asshole ready for my big cock."

His dick throbs inside my pussy, and he groans.

"Just thinking about fucking your ass makes me want to come." Rex grips my throat again and nips my earlobe.

"But I won't," he rasps, "because I want to unload inside your ass this time."

Without warning, he withdraws.

"No," I mumble, collapsing on the bed, my legs twitching, my pussy pulsing with unmet need. "Come back. I need you."

Dark chuckles reach my ears and a few seconds later, he's back, and I feel something hard and thick sliding into my pussy. He clicks something, and it vibrates.

He put a self-thrusting dildo inside me.

I moan as the sensation kicks up, the dildo doing a decent job but not the same as his thick shaft inside me moments ago.

Nevertheless, my hips gyrate of their own accord, my body needing the friction, needing to come because I can't stand it anymore.

Rex groans. "You have no idea how hot you look right now. Horny, my beautiful whore, just for me."

I hear him uncapping something. He grunts, and I look in the mirror, seeing him dribbling lube over his turgid length.

A muscle bulges in his neck as he grits his teeth and tugs his cock a few times. Seeing him get himself off has me racing toward the edge again.

He snaps his eyes to mine and holds our gaze in the mirror.

A sinister smile twists his lips. "Not so fast, little Olive."

Reaching down, he shackles my throat with his hand, drawing me off the bed. Then he slaps my tits with his other hand, his eyes darkening when he sees them jiggle.

"Ready Olive? Ready to be fucked in the ass?"

My eyes widen, and I nod.

Then I feel it, his hard tip notched at my back hole and slowly sliding in.

My breath leaves my lungs as discomfort and pain sweep through me.

"Shhh…" He massages my throat. "Breathe and relax."

"It's too big." I whimper when he slides another inch in. All the while, the dildo is tunneling in and out of my pussy.

"Your ass is made to take my cock. Your whole body is made for me." Rex presses kisses all over my face, my throat, my hair, all the while murmuring gentle praises as I melt under him. His ability to switch from rough to gentle is one of the best things I love about him.

"That's it, Olive. Oh fuck, shit…yes, good girl," he groans as he bottoms out, his panting breaths loud in my ears. "I'm about to burst. You have no idea how good your ass feels. So tight. So perfect. I can feel the dildo pulsing in your pussy."

My mind numbs again as sparks gather in my pussy and ass and quickly burgeon into a fire. I've never felt anything like this before, like all my nerve endings are lit up, ready to explode.

I fall against his chest, him holding me up with his arms.

"So fucking mine," he growls.

Then he moves. His cock tunnels in and out of my ass in tandem with the dildo in my pussy. My entire body shakes and trembles, and dots appear in my vision.

"Oh my God, I'm so full. I feel you everywhere." I'm stuffed to the brim and I can barely see, hear, or feel anything other than Rex and what he's doing to my body.

Claiming it. Owning it. Mastering it.

Getting me off like it's his life's purpose.

Mindlessly, I grab his arm, his neck, anywhere I can reach with him behind me.

My legs give out, but he holds me tightly against him as he pistons quick and hard, his movements brutal.

"Open your eyes. Keep them open or I won't let you come."

My eyes flutter open, and I take in the lewd image of us in the mirror. His fully clothed body cradles my naked one, sweat glistening on every inch of my skin. My tits are red and bouncing as he slams his cock into my ass while the dildo fills my pussy.

I look filthy. Depraved. Naughty.

And so perfect.

His lips curve into a feral smile. "That's my perfect slut. My perfect ass and cunt. You were born to be used by me, to be double penetrated like a champ. You've been a good and naughty girl, and you deserve a reward."

He reaches between my legs and pinches my clit. "Now come."

I cry out, my body convulsing in his arms as pleasure explodes in a kaleidoscope of colors. Exhilaration and euphoria shoot through my body, seeping into every cell, every particle. I've never experienced anything like this before. Wetness spurts out of me and for a few seconds I can't see, my vision blinded from the orgasm.

Rex huffs out a few grunts, then his cock thickens and throbs before he lets out a raw, guttural groan. "Yes, fuck yes!"

His cum unloads inside my ass, the warmth prolonging my orgasm as my body continues to shake in his arms.

I don't know how much time has passed before my mind flickers back on.

But the next thing I know, we're both on the bed, him cradling me, his lips trailing tender kisses on my face and neck.

"Still stressed, Olive?" he asks, amusement in his voice.

I grumble something unintelligible.

"I'll take that as a no." He chuckles. "I love you so damn much, and I want to spend more time cuddling with you, but now I need to change into a new suit."

Another gentle kiss later, he releases me and slides out of bed. But before he reaches the bathroom, he turns around, bows, and winks. "Rex-a-Million at your service. Do give me a five-star rating."

Using the last of my strength, I grab a pillow and hurl it at him. He dodges and laughs before disappearing inside the bathroom.

And I smile.

EPILOGUE PART TWO—REX

A SCREECH PIERCES THE air and I wince from the microphone feedback. Stepping to the side of the stage where a small fire pit has been set up, I let the staff fix the audio.

I'm about to make a speech—a speech where I'm just Rex, someone dealing with mental health issues, someone choosing to wake up each day to fight.

After the equipment is fixed, I walk back to the podium and the crowd quiets.

"Thank you for coming to celebrate the opening of the Anderson Culinary Arts Therapy Center."

The audience cheers and I spot Maxwell smiling, his arm wrapped around Belle. Levi sits on her lap, clapping like he understands what's going on. Ryland grins and gives me a thumbs-up as he tugs a smiling Millie against him. Charles laughs at Taylor, who's wolf-whistling like a pro, and Steven and Grace cheer loudly. Alexis is jumping and clapping with a smiling Ethan next to her. Lana sits next to Dad, who's smirking, his ankle crossed over his knee, every inch the proud Anderson patriarch.

I glance to my right and spot her, my Olive, standing behind the curtain in a white turtleneck dress because our lovemaking gave her a few fresh marks on her neck.

Sorry, but not sorry.

She blows me a kiss and motions for me to continue.

Turning back to the audience, I say, "As some of you may know, I suffer from a host of mental health issues—C-PTSD, substance dependence, and related disorders. The Rex-a-Million persona was a mask I crafted to hide my problems from the world."

My hands shake and my pulse skyrockets as I bare parts of me I've held under lock and key until recently.

Olivia helped me see the light.

"It wasn't healthy. It prolonged problems and impacted people I care about. What I should've done was seek help earlier and let others in. I know how hard that can be, how sometimes even the smallest step can feel like a Herculean effort. Luckily, I had help. I had the support of my family and the woman I love. And one day, on this journey to recovery, I took a cooking class."

My eyes sweep over the audience and land on Giacomo Valenti, who's waggling his brows because the fucker knows it's his class I'm referring to. Begrudgingly, I admit he's a decent guy underneath all that suave charm.

"Through the process of learning to cook, I felt relief. It has been a passion of mine, something my mother loved and I enjoyed doing with her when she was alive. It has always grounded me. It sparked an idea I later discussed with Dr. Olivia Lin." The crowd cheers as Olivia steps into the spotlight and waves to the crowd.

I grin, noticing how tall she's standing, how she's no longer flustered by the attention.

Because she knows she deserves her own spotlight, one I can't look away from.

"Studies have shown that cooking can elevate moods and help patients suffering from eating disorders, depression, anxiety, and other mental illnesses. Cooking and eating healthy foods can improve our gut biome, which then improves mental health as well. And so, Dr. Lin and I decided to combine therapy with the culinary arts, resulting in the Anderson Culinary Arts Therapy Center. Here, we will offer mindfulness-based cooking classes, individual and group therapy, and psychiatric help for free to anyone who needs it."

Lighting up a match, I hold it over the makeshift fire pit before dropping it in. The flames flicker and grow, bathing the space in a warm glow.

"This flame will be transferred back into the kitchen and be used to cook the first meal for all of you as a thank you for supporting this important cause."

A knot loosens in my chest when I look into the audience again. This is my phase three—looking forward and finding meaning in my life, which to me is helping others in need.

"Because," I swallow, "mental health is crucial, and access to help should be available for all. Thank you."

The auditorium erupts into a standing ovation, and I bite my lip, my face heating. I feel out of sorts, suddenly unused to the cheers, whistles, and clapping from an adoring crowd, not because of some deviant behavior, but because I was unflinchingly honest and vulnerable.

Because of something good I'm doing for the community.

When I step down from the podium, Olivia is there to greet me, a wide, beaming smile on her face.

"I'm so proud of you, Rex. So proud of you," she whispers before pulling me into a kiss.

Warmth ripples through my body. And as our kiss deepens, my roaring heartbeats eclipse the applause still booming in the room.

Quietly, I pull back and brush her hair from her face.

I dip my forehead to hers and murmur, "I love you, my Olive. Thank you for loving me."

Later that evening, we're gathered on the rooftop bar at The Orchid. Even Olivia's parents have flown out to join us. The night sky is exceptionally clear, with stars winking at us amid a swath of dark navy.

My phone buzzes, and I see a text from an unknown number.

Ava.

Unknown number

> *Sends a photo of a beach with palm trees and the silhouettes of three women in swimsuits.*

Unknown number

> The ABCs are enjoying life in paradise. Don't worry about us.

Unknown number

> And don't worry, no funny business with the photo this time. *smiley face*

ABCs? I frown, and then I huff out a laugh.

Ava. Bree. Cora. Ava must've gotten over Bree's connections to the Caruso family.

They're safe now.

Laughter reaches my ears and I slide my phone back into my pocket.

Dad, Ethan, and Charles are smiling as they walk over from the bar, holding trays of champagne and then hand them out to us. Everyone accepts a flute except Grace, who suddenly turns beet red in the face.

Taylor narrows her eyes. "Sis, you aren't drinking."

Grace shakes her head, her eyes downcast. I snap my gaze to Steven, finding the man biting back a smile before tipping the flute to his lips.

Olivia gasps, then squeals follow as excitement bubbles from the girls.

Lana elbows her way to stand in front of Grace and stares at her belly, then at her face. "Are you? Am I going to be an aunt again?"

Grace nods. "Yes! We're three months along."

"Oh my God, yay!" Lana hugs Grace, and everyone offers their congratulations.

I ask Steven, who looks completely smitten. "Boy or girl?"

He shrugs. "We don't know. It doesn't matter. He or she will be perfect."

"All my grandchildren will be perfect," Dad agrees.

"There's a baby inside Auntie Grace?" Levi exclaims as he pokes Grace's belly, and everyone laughs.

"Yes, sweetheart. You need to take care of him or her when he or she comes out, okay? You're the oldest cousin." Belle ruffles his hair and Levi puffs his little chest out, clearly eager to take on the role.

"And while we're at it, good news and all, Tay and I have something to share too," Charles murmurs as he tucks Taylor against him.

My goth ballerina half sister flushes, and it's then I notice her nose piercing—a symbol of her mood as she says—is a red heart today.

"You tell them or me?" Charles bops her nose, and she mock scowls before grinning.

Huffing out a sigh, she faces us and holds up her left hand. "Fuckers, I'm now Mrs. Vaughn."

More shrieks and whistles erupt as they tell us how they did away with all the pomp and circumstance and eloped at city hall last week.

"Congratulations." Ryland clasps Charles's shoulder. "You're doing a reception, right?"

"Maybe. Depends on what Tay wants."

"Still debating. I might make you all go to a punk rock concert with me." Tay grins and we groan.

RIP to my eardrums.

Then I notice a flash of orange next to me. Alexis is rocking on her feet, clearly excited about something.

She whispers to Millie, "Can I tell them? Please? Please?"

Millie rolls her eyes and nods. "Yes. You're clearly dying to."

Alexis giggles and says, "Millie and Ryland have *finally* set a date for their wedding. She's asked me to help plan it because one of my bucket list items is to plan a big party."

"This bucket list of yours keeps changing," Ethan mutters, affection obvious in his voice.

"Oh shut up. It keeps things exciting. You just tag along for the ride." Alexis pecks him on the lips.

We laugh and heckle Ryland because the damn asshole took long enough to seal the deal with his girl.

"It's not my fault! I asked so many times, but Millie wants to wait until she gets her PhD," Ryland grumbles.

"I like following a specific order," Millie quips.

"Which means I'll be getting more grandkids soon, right?" Dad murmurs, and Millie turns red.

"Maybe. But after the wedding ceremony...because, order."

Ryland snakes his hand behind his fiancée's nape, pulls her to him, and kisses her.

"Damn. Someone wants to skip to the baby making already." Taylor snickers.

"We're married first. Don't let them cut in line," Charles whispers not so quietly.

Taylor's eyes snap to Charles, and the two have an entire conversation without words.

"So, when is it your turn, Rex? The last single Anderson male other than little Levi." Steven nudges me.

Arching my brow, I smile and turn to Olivia, who's still laughing with the girls, happiness brimming on her face.

"Funny you should ask, because something is weighing down my pocket," I murmur and tug Olivia's hand.

My palms grow sweaty and my pulse batters my ears.

She swivels her head toward me, her eyes comically large when she sees me dropping a knee to the floor.

"My sweet darling Olive, the reformer of bad boys, the healer of hearts. I love you so much." Pulling the black velvet ring box out of my pocket, I snap it open and turn it to face her.

Five carats. Flawless color, cut, and clarity. A central princess-cut diamond framed by a halo of smaller stones.

For my lover, my princess, my life.

"Will you be my forever and let me love you for eternity? Will you make me the happiest man on earth and marry me?"

Someone shrieks in joy—Lana, I think—before the sound is abruptly cut off.

I spot Elias lurking in the background, his hand covering Lana's mouth and muttering, "Calm yourself, woman. She hasn't answered him yet."

Biting back a smile, I wait with bated breath as Olivia stares at the ring, then at me.

I nod to her parents standing behind her. "I've gotten permission from your parents. I think I won them over because I'm learning Mandarin and can cook a mean stir-fry. Doesn't hurt to know I can run a dishwasher and I definitely want kids." I wink, even though my heart is careening out of control.

The room breaks out in laughter, and her parents beam at us.

Olivia blinks, her lips curving into a watery smile.

Moisture gathers in her eyes.

Then she nods.

"Yes. Yes, oh my God, yes!"

The space bursts with cheers and clinking of glasses. People murmur congratulations to us, but I barely notice, because all I can do is stop my hand from shaking when I slide the ring onto her finger, still not believing she said yes.

This beautiful, bewitching angel and seductress wants me—monsters, scars, and all.

She's seen my darkness and not only hasn't shied away from it, but has embraced it.

"You're worth everything," Olivia murmurs and slides her arms around my neck, pulling my head toward her. "You're one beautiful man, Rex Anderson, and I'm so honored to spend my life with you."

Elation spears my heart, and if I die right now, I'll leave this world the happiest man alive.

Crushing her to me, I seal my lips with hers just as the fireworks I've arranged weeks ago erupt in the sky. The popping sounds and bright lights are a fitting ending, or a wonderful beginning for the rest of our lives together.

When we pull apart minutes later, I twine our fingers together and pull her in front of me, cradling her in my arms as we watch the beautiful firepower display stealing the breath from everyone here.

With my heart full of love, I glance around the bar, taking in the faces of my loved ones.

Maxwell grinning, little Levi perched on his shoulders, clapping as more fireworks bathe the dark skies in light. Belle is trying to adjust the toddler soundproof headset over his ears, no doubt to protect his eardrums.

Dad, smiling contentedly, points out something in the sky to Levi.

Ryland kisses Millie, then murmurs in her ear. Her skin turns pink.

Steven is kneeling on the floor, kissing Grace's belly as she stares lovingly at him.

Charles dips Taylor in a dance move to music only they can hear.

Alexis whispers excitedly to Ethan, who smiles fondly at his wife. I hear something about adding another item to their bucket list, which Ethan will never say no to because he indulges her.

Olivia's dad is taking a photo of his wife with the fireworks as a backdrop.

Then there's Lana scowling at an icy Elias, who has his arms crossed over his chest. She spins away in a huff, and that's when I notice it—the soft smile curving his lips as the mobster stares at my sister with something that almost seems like affection. He sneaks a glance at me and falters when he notices my attention on him.

I narrow my eyes, then arch my brow.

He gives me the middle finger, then pulls out his damn lighter, flicking it on and off again.

Shaking my head in amusement, I turn to Olivia, finding her staring awestruck at the colorful fireworks in the sky.

"I never thought I could be so happy, Olive. Never thought it would happen to me."

Smiling, she turns to me and lifts her left hand—my beautiful ring sparkling on her finger—to my face.

I sigh with contentment. Her touch always grounds me.

"You've always been deserving, Rex. Always."

Drawing her into my arms, I whisper in her ear, "Olive, let's go back to Valencia next year. Not for the past, but for us. The future."

She looks up at me, her eyes bright with excitement. "Burn more stuff?"

I smirk. My little secret deviant. "Burn anything you want. But I'm thinking more about creating our own sculptures. Sending our wishes to the universe. Shit like that."

"You're a secret softie, Rex Anderson." She rises on her tiptoes.

"Shhh, don't let the others hear you. It'll ruin my image." I wink.

Olivia laughs and kisses me.

And in this moment, I finally believe my life can end one way.

Happily ever after.

Oh, we aren't done yet. You thought we were, didn't you? Like all good stories, this one doesn't truly end here.

Where there's light, there are shadows.

Turn the page to see what waits on the other side of happily ever after...

AFTERWARD

ELIAS

Tête de Chien, France—Dusk, the Evening After the Gala Disaster in Monaco

THE WIND CLAWS AT my coat as I stare down from the edge of the limestone cliff. The lights of Monaco blink through the mist as dusk drags in the unwilling night, the last vestiges of the sunset swallowed up by the dark sky.

Those people down there are living life like normal, totally unaware of the dangers around them.

The sheer evil in this world.

The weathered stones crunch beneath my boots as I check my watch.

Ren is late. Which can mean he's careful or something's wrong.

Judging from what happened last night at the gala, how Bree barely escaped with her life, it could be either.

A twig snaps behind me. I draw my gun and cock it in a matter of seconds.

Whipping around, I aim at the intruder. My pulse pounds in my ears.

Ren, the bastard, stands before me, dressed in all black, his black hair draping over the black mask he has on.

The man rarely shows his face.

"You're losing your touch," I murmur as the wind kicks up. "I heard you coming."

His lips, one of the two features showing on his face, curl into a slight smile. He signs with his hands because besides not liking to show his face, the man also doesn't speak.

"What made you think I was trying to hide? Maybe the sound was to alert you to my presence and to let you know you're losing your touch."

"Asshole," I mutter, putting my gun back into my holster.

He's been with me since the beginning and is part of our team of equals, united by one purpose.

To end The Association.

"Is she safe?"

He cocks his brow, and I don't explain because he doesn't need to know. But Ren is smart. He knows I'm not talking about Bree, who he personally delivered to a safe house last night.

He knows I'm talking about her.

Lana.

Dark brown hair. Mischievous smile. Gray eyes blazing with hatred when they meet mine.

She didn't use to look at me that way.

Too bad she doesn't know who you really are. And she'll never know.

Ren signs, *"Rattled but safe. I trailed her back to the cruise after the gala."*

I nod. "Make sure the paparazzi don't bother her. If they come a foot near her, cut off their hands."

The damn bastard arches his brow again and I get annoyed.

"Seriously, if you want to wear a mask, get one that covers your entire damn face. I don't need your judgment. Any more of it and I'll personally carve your brows off."

The grin makes a reappearance, and madness reflects in his eyes—the same madness I have inside me.

This is what years of killing will do to you—make you laugh at the most morbid jokes.

Exhaling sharply, I clench my fists and finally ask the question I've been waiting to ask my entire life.

"Do you have it?"

He nods and pulls a laptop from his messenger bag. He powers it up, and the blue light slices through the darkness like a knife.

Then he hands it to me.

My hands tremble. I bite my tongue to distract myself with the pain and the metallic taste of blood.

Years—fifteen fucking years.

I've waited for this moment for that long.

Bree's blood unlocked a drive to a ledger holding the next clue to my search for the identity of the man who killed my parents and little Beatrice. The man who made my sister Sofia and me orphans.

The man who destroyed our lives.

The name burns into my memory, and violence teems in my blood.

But I don't let it out. Not yet.

A bitter smile curves my lips as I snap the laptop shut.

"Let's go wreak some havoc, shall we, Ren?"

They will all die a painful death.

Vengeance will be mine.

———◆———

Thank you for reading WHEN HEARTS UNRAVEL. Hope you enjoyed Rex and Olivia's story.

Elias and Lana's Story: A vow for vengeance. A marriage of enemies. A love that could ruin them both. **SWORN IN DECEIT** is book one of my new series, **THE ANTIHERO SYNDICATE**. Read their story here: https://geni.us/swornindeceit

Three Bonus Epilogue Chapters: Don't want The Orchid series to end? Want to know how Rex and Olivia's honeymoon went? The who gang is there. It's hot and there are surprises. Grab your **THREE BONUS EPILOGUE CHAPTERS** here: https://www.victorialum.com/bonus

THANK YOU

WHEN HEARTS UNRAVEL MARKS the end of *The Orchid* series—and my tenth published book. It's bittersweet to say farewell to this glittering world and its unforgettable cast of characters, but that's what I love about the Victoriaverse: everything is connected, and it's never truly goodbye.

The idea for Rex and Olivia's story actually came from an article I stumbled across about a real-life, adults-only cruise. I thought, *What better setting for our playboy bad boy, Rex Anderson?* Of course, it became much more than just a spicy cruise. It grew into a story about grief, guilt, healing, and love. I hope you enjoyed traveling to these beautiful destinations with me.

Since the very first book of *The Orchid* series, *When Hearts Ignite*, one side character—who only appeared for a handful of pages—stole the show. I received countless emails and messages asking about him. *Will he get his own book? What's the story behind his scar and the lighter he always carries? Why is he so darn sexy and mysterious?*

You already know who I'm talking about: Elias Kent. Our enigmatic mobster. Dealer of secrets. Feared by many. At last, his story is here. Elias will kick off my next series, *The Antihero Syndicate*, with his romance with the beautiful Lana Anderson in *Sworn in Deceit*. It's a twisty enemies-to-lovers arranged marriage, with mafia wars and a secret society at its core. I hope you'll join me on this next adventure.

As always, thank you to everyone who has supported me:

- **My family**: To my husband and children—without you, this career wouldn't be possible.

- **My editors**: Theresa Leigh and Amy Briggs, thank you for your edits, your coaching, and for making me a better writer with every book.

- **Proofreader**: Virginia Tesi Carey, thank you for your eagle eye in catching what slips past the rest of us.

- **My PA**: Nikki Johnson, thank you for always being on top of everything.

- **Cover designer**: The talented LK Farlow of Y'All That Graphic—thank you for bringing my vision to life with such stunning covers.

- **Beta readers**: Malia, Jenn, Jess, Denny, Alicia, and Erin—your insights mean the world. And Alicia, without you, the Rex-a-Million nickname wouldn't exist. Love you all so, so much.

- **My ilLUMinati girls, street team, and ARC team**: You keep me going. I'm the luckiest author to have you on my side. Thank you for being here for the ride.

- **Fellow authors**: Your talent and kindness inspire me daily. I'm eternally grateful for your friendship.

- **PR Firm**: The Author Agency, thank you for helping me share these stories with the world.

- **My readers**: Thank you. Thank you. Thank you. I'm honored every time you choose my books. Here's to many more stories to come.

With love,
Victoria

Also by Victoria Lum

Catch up on Victoria's backlist! Don't miss these swoony, romantic stories with all the sizzling spice and angst. All stories are standalones and can be read out of order.

LA Hearts:
The Sweetest Agony (James and Jess)
The Coldest Passion (Parker and Liz)
The Harshest Hope (Adrian and Emily)
The Brightest Spark (Jack and Sarah)

The Orchid:
When Hearts Ignite (Steven and Grace)
When Hearts Collide (Ryland and Millie)
When Hearts Surrender (Maxwell and Belle)
When Hearts Awaken (Charles and Taylor)
When Hearts Remember (Ethan and Alexis)
When Hearts Unravel (Rex and Olivia)

The Antihero Syndicate:
Sworn in Deceit (Elias and Lana)

About the Author

Victoria Lum writes angsty, emotional romances that dive deep into the complexities of love and the human heart. She's the author of *The Antihero Syndicate, The Orchid,* and the *LA Hearts* series, which follow characters through love's twists and turns, secrets, and second chances. A true romantic at heart, Victoria loves crafting stories that resonate with readers who crave a mix of passion, tension, and genuine connection. When she's not writing, you can find her curled up with a caramel latte and a good book or spending time with her family in sunny California.

Keep in touch!
Sign up for her newsletter below:
Newsletter
Follow Victoria on social media:
Victoria Lum's Luminaries Facebook Group
Facebook Page
Instagram
Tiktok
Bookbub
Amazon
Goodreads
Scan the QR code below for all the links!

www.ingramcontent.com/pod-product-compliance
Lightning Source LLC
Chambersburg PA
CBHW020328010826
48973CB00005B/1169